HIGH
DERYNI

HIGH
DERYNI

KATHERINE
KURTZ

ACE BOOKS, NEW YORK

THE BERKLEY PUBLISHING GROUP
Published by the Penguin Group
Penguin Group (USA) Inc.
375 Hudson Street, New York, New York 10014, USA
Penguin Group (Canada), 90 Eglinton Avenue East, Suite 700, Toronto, Ontario M4P 2Y3, Canada
(a division of Pearson Penguin Canada Inc.)
Penguin Books Ltd., 80 Strand, London WC2R 0RL, England
Penguin Group Ireland, 25 St. Stephen's Green, Dublin 2, Ireland (a division of Penguin Books Ltd.)
Penguin Group (Australia), 250 Camberwell Road, Camberwell, Victoria 3124, Australia
(a division of Pearson Australia Group Pty. Ltd.)
Penguin Books India Pvt. Ltd., 11 Community Centre, Panchsheel Park, New Delhi—110 017, India
Penguin Group (NZ), 67 Apollo Drive, Rosedale, North Shore 0632, New Zealand
(a division of Pearson New Zealand Ltd.)
Penguin Books (South Africa) (Pty.) Ltd., 24 Sturdee Avenue, Rosebank, Johannesburg 2196, South
Africa

Penguin Books Ltd., Registered Offices: 80 Strand, London WC2R 0RL, England

First revised edition: December 2007
Originally published in 1973 by Ballantine Books.

Library of Congress Cataloging-in-Publication Data

Kurtz, Katherine.
  High Deryni / Katherine Kurtz.—1st ed.
     p. cm.
  ISBN 978-0-441-01526-9
  1. Deryni (Fictitious characters)—Fiction.   2. Gwynedd (Imaginary place)—Fiction.   I. Title.

PS3561.U69H54   2007
813'.54—dc22
2007021621

PRINTED IN THE UNITED STATES OF AMERICA

10 9 8 7 6 5 4 3 2 1

For Margaret Frances Carter,
because every mother
with an offspring who writes
should have a book from her Author-Child.

And with special thanks to
Tania Ryan,
for scanning both *Deryni Checkmate*
and *High Deryni* from the original
paperback editions.

The Eleven Kingdoms

Northern Sea

Atalantic Ocean

Gulf of Northarch

Khetoish Mts
Rhemuth
Stavenham

Claibourne
(Old Khelbour)

Rhendall

Rhemuth Mts

Tolan

Tigre

Rheljan Mts.

Eastmarch

Ionaire Plain

Llyndruth Plain

Llyndruth Meadows

Coamer Mount

Truvorsk

TORENTH

Beldour R.

Sasovia

The Fertile Crescent

Kuman

Gulf of Khelbour
Kilshane

Kierney

Eransha

Cassan

Kiladen
Bay of Kiladen

Cudi
Cuilet Highlands

Ratharkin

Rathark Mts

Cloome Mts

Lough Cloome

Lxas Bay

Meara

Culleine

The Purple March

GWYNEO

Carbury

Valoret

Ramos

Eirian R.

Carcashale

GWYNEO

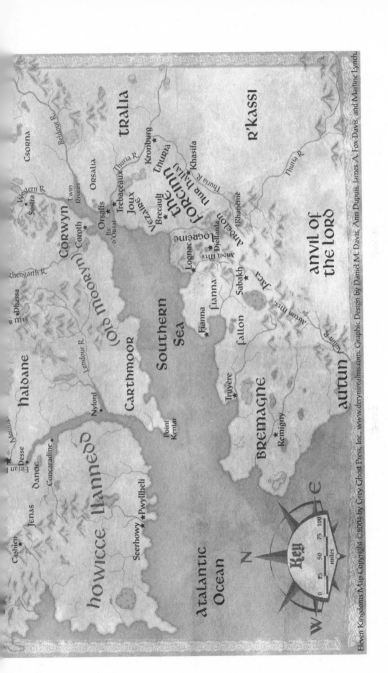

HIGH
DERYNI

INTERLUDE

THE first spring following the coronation of Kelson King of Gwynedd should have been a time of eager anticipation, as the land lay a-greening along with his newly begun reign. Sadly, he knew full well how precariously lay the crown upon his young head. Only fourteen when his father, King Brion, was slain by magic, the boy-king had immediately taken counsel of the controversial Duke Alaric Morgan, his late father's close friend and confidant, along with Morgan's cousin, Father Duncan McLain, who was also chaplain to the royal household. Both were now known to be Deryni, wielders of the same sort of magic that had killed King Brion—and all magic was forbidden by Gwynedd's powerful Church. Its presiding bishop had suspended Duncan McLain from his priestly function, and the hastily summoned Curia of that same Church had now excommunicated both men.

Not that Gwynedd's individual bishops presented a united front. While all of those present at the Curia convened in Dhassa had consented to the excommunication of the pair (albeit with varying degrees of enthusiasm), they remained sharply divided on whether further sanctions should be imposed on Morgan's Duchy of Corwyn; so divided that Gwynedd's presiding bishop, supported by a slender majority of the other bishops present, had declared the six dissenting bishops to be schismatic and threatened disciplinary action against them. The Six, in turn, had declared for the king and expelled Archbishop Loris and his adherents from the city. Rumor had it that the archbishop and his followers had fled southward and were taking refuge with the anti-Deryni rebel Warin de Grey while they sought support from bishops who had not been present at Dhassa. At least a few of Loris's supporters had taken their master's anger seriously enough to attempt more direct disciplinary action against the dissident Six.

"Someone attacked *Wolfram?*" Bishop Siward blurted, when a trembling and shaken household chaplain had repeated his disturbing news to several of the Six huddled in Bishop Cardiel's private withdrawing room.

"*Several* 'someones,' apparently," Bishop Tolliver replied, taking off his own cloak to lay it around the shoulders of their informant. He had been present when the young priest had burst into the stable yard, gasping for breath, and had been first to hear the news. "Father Jodoc tells me that they were in the service of Archbishop Loris."

"They *were*, my lords!" the priest agreed. "One of the men even wore the archbishop's badge under his cloak!"

"Dear God, has it come to this?" Cardiel whispered.

"At least we are fortunate in that Wolfram was not harmed," Bishop Arilan said coolly. "What of the attackers, Father?"

"All dead, my lord," Jodoc said promptly, nodding his thanks as a priest called Father Hugh, now secretary to the dissident bishops, pressed a cup of mulled wine into his hand. He indulged in a deep gulp before he continued. "One was killed outright, and another died of his wounds before he could be questioned. They say that a third was pulled to pieces by the crowd." He looked away briefly before adding softly, "It must have been dreadful."

Bishop Istelyn had gone white at the account, and Richard of Nyford shuddered and crossed himself, shaking his head. The pair had joined the original six dissenting bishops at Dhassa several days after the departure of Loris and his adherents, first Istelyn and then Richard, bringing their number to eight. Together, they believed and hoped that Loris had gained no additional support, without which his decree of Interdict for Corwyn still did not technically have the force of law.

"I must go to the king," Istelyn said quietly. "He should know of this latest development."

"True enough," Bishop Arilan replied. "He will not take it kindly that one of his bishops tried to kill another."

"Indeed, he will not," Cardiel agreed. "And he should have one of us in his household to give him heart when Loris continues to make demands. Nor should he be without spiritual counsel when he must eventually face Wencit of Torenth."

SOMEWHAT farther north and east of Dhassa, hard on Gwynedd's border with Torenth, that same Wencit of Torenth was receiving a report of other occurrences in Kelson's kingdom. Though it had not been he who had threatened Kelson's crown at the coronation just past, he was of the same dynastic line as the woman whose challenge had failed, and he now counted himself as next in that line of succession. He had long coveted the lands of his neighbor to the west, and but awaited the coming thaws to take advantage of Kelson's youth and press an invasion plan well advanced even before the assassination of the boy's father.

"No one seems to be certain who worked the magic to slay the pair, or whether it was even wholly intended," Wencit's informant told him, though his gaze was unfocused, his voice a monotone, for it was not he who spoke to the Torenthi king but a skilled and powerful agent far away, using more reliable magic to convey the information. "Nonetheless, it will have hurt Alaric Morgan to lose his only sister. In addition, the death of the Earl of Kierney leaves Jared Duke of Cassan with only a priest as his heir—though, as you know, Father Duncan McLain does seem to have Deryni powers. Certainly, Gwynedd's bishops believe that to be true—and have excommunicated both him and Morgan. They even threaten Interdict for Corwyn."

"That little concerns me," the Torenthi sorcerer-king replied with a negligent flick of one beringed hand.

Shortly after the coronation of his new rival the previous autumn, as soon as the first snows closed the Cardosa Pass from the west, Wencit had begun assembling his army for the next year's campaign and laid siege to the disputed mountain city of Cardosa, lurking through the winter at the Royal Abbey of Sankt Nikolas with his general staff and a unit of crack cavalry to prevent possible relief efforts to the city. He had occupied Cardosa early in June, immediately after the spring thaws allowed an approach from the east. By then the city had been very hungry. The apartment where he now made his headquarters—and where he had received the messenger seated before him—had belonged to the former royal governor, who now languished in a sparse but decent cell deep in the bowels of the fortress known as Esgair Ddu. The darker man with the scarred face, standing at the king's elbow, had helped him take the city.

"Interdict for Corwyn," the man murmured. "Now, that *is* an intriguing notion."

"But will it make a difference?" Wencit countered.

"Perhaps." The dark man jutted his chin toward their ensorcelled informant and raised an eyebrow in query as the Torenthi king glanced in his direction. "If I may, Sire, I should like to explore an earlier point," he murmured.

At Wencit's nod of agreement, the man eased a trifle closer.

"I would hear more about this attempt on Bishop Wolfram," he said softly. "Were the assassins truly in the service of Archbishop Loris?"

The messenger's expression did not change save for a flicker of comprehension behind the blank eyes. "It may be that they were . . . encouraged to take such action," he stated baldly.

Wencit's lips curled in a sardonic smile beneath the fox-colored moustache. "My dear cousin, I sometimes think you are altogether too devious, even for one of our kind. Have you no shame?"

The reply came in the same monotone as before, but still managed to convey a hint of smug satisfaction. "I was under the impression that my lord held little regard for Gwynedd's religious authorities."

"Not for Edmund Loris," Wencit's companion murmured almost inaudibly.

Wencit clucked his tongue in an indication of mild chastisement. "Now, now, Rhydon. You are a son of Gwynedd. A man should have *some* faith."

"He serves your purpose, I suppose, my lord," Rhydon allowed, returning his gaze to the face of their intermediary. "My Lord Volmer, do you know whether the Six at Dhassa have gained any further support?"

"Only the two I have already reported, my lord," came the uninflected reply. "However, there is word from elsewhere that the Haldane's troops are on the move. The Dukes of Cassan and Claibourne have been sent to secure the northern borders, and the Earl of Eastmarch occupies the plain below the city, where the king will bring his royal armies. Nigel Haldane is said to be probing into Corwyn."

"And the Duke of Corwyn?" Wencit asked, allowing himself a tiny, satisfied smile.

This time, their intermediary's tone suggested that he shared the opinion of the man whose voice he provided.

"Apparently on the run, my lord, along with the discredited McLain."

"Excellent," Wencit said softly. "Then it appears that we may proceed exactly as the Haldane has been fearing. How fortunate for us that the thaws come so late to Gwynedd's side of the mountains."

"And how unfortunate for Kelson of Gwynedd," his informant replied, a trace of smugness coming through the uninflected tone.

CHAPTER ONE

"Abroad the sword bereaveth, at home there is death."

LAMENTATIONS 1:20

THE name they had given the boy was Royston—Royston Richardson, after his father—and the dagger he clutched so fearfully in the deepening twilight was not his own. Around him in the fields of Jennan Vale, the bodies of the dead lay stiffening among the rows of newly ripening grain. Night birds hooted in the deathly silence, and wolves yipped in the hills away and to the north. Far across the fields, torches were being lit along the streets of the town, beckoning the living toward what slim comfort numbers might afford. Too many dead of both sides lay cold at Jennan Vale tonight. The battle had been brutal and bloody, even by peasant standards.

It had begun at midday. The riders of Prince Nigel Haldane, uncle to the boy-king Kelson, had approached the outskirts of the village just past noon, royal lion banners billowing crimson and gold in the noonday sun, the horses sweating lightly in the early summer heat. It was only an advance guard, the prince had said. He and his troop of thirty were merely to scout a route for the royal army's march toward Coroth to the east—no more.

For the city of Coroth, seat of local government for the rebellious Duchy of Corwyn, was in the hands of the insurgent archbishops, Loris and Corrigan. And the archbishops, aided and supported by the zealot rebel leader Warin and his followers, were urging a new persecution of the Deryni: a race of powerful sorcerers who had once ruled all the Eleven Kingdoms; the Deryni: long feared, long suppressed, and now personified by Corwyn's half-Deryni Duke Alaric Morgan, whom the archbishops had excommunicated for his Deryni heresy but three months before.

Prince Nigel had tried to reassure the folk of Jennan Vale. He had reminded them that the king's men did not plunder and pillage in their own lands; young Kelson forbade it, as had his father and Nigel's brother, the late King Brion. Nor was Duke Alaric a threat to the peace of the Eleven Kingdoms—even if the archbishops *had* ruled otherwise. The belief that the Deryni as a race were evil was superstitious nonsense! Brion himself, though not Deryni, had trusted Morgan with his life, time and again, and had so esteemed the Deryni lord that he had created him King's Champion, over the objections of his Royal Council. There was no shred of evidence that Morgan had ever betrayed that trust, then or now.

But the Vale-folk would not listen. The revelation of Kelson's own half-Deryni ancestry at his coronation the previous fall, though unknown even to Kelson before that day, had opened the door of distrust for the royal Haldane line—a distrust that had not been eased by the young king's dogged support of the heretic Duke Alaric and his priest-cousin, Duncan McLain, now revealed as Deryni himself.

Even now it was rumored that the king still protected Duke Alaric and McLain; that the king himself had been excommunicated as a result; that he and the hated duke and a host of other Deryni planned to march on Coroth and break the back of the anti-Deryni movement by destroying Loris and Corrigan and the beloved Warin. Why, Warin himself had predicted it.

So the local partisans had led Prince Nigel's troops the long way around Jennan Vale, luring them with the promise of ample water and grazing for the royal armies that would follow. In the fields green with half-ripe wheat and oats, the rebels had fallen on the troops in ambush, cutting a swath of death and destruction through the surprised royalist ranks. By the time the king's men could disengage and retreat with their wounded, more than a score of knights, rebels, and warhorses lay dead or dying, the lion banners stained and trampled amidst the ripening grain.

Royston froze with his hand on the hilt of his dagger for just an instant, then scuttled past a still body and continued along the narrow cartway toward home. He was only ten, and small for his age at that, but this fact had not prevented him from doing his share of the afternoon's plundering. The leather satchel slung over his shoulder bulged with food and bits of harness and such other light accoutrements as he had been able to harvest from the fallen enemy. Even the finely etched dagger and sheath thrust through his rude rope belt had been taken from the saddle of a dead warhorse.

Nor was he squeamish about picking over dead bodies— at least not in daylight. Scavenging was a way of life for peasant folk in time of war; and now that the peasants were in revolt against their duke—indeed, against even their king—it was an urgent necessity as well. The peasants' weapons were few and crude: mostly pikes and scythes and clubs, or an occasional dagger or sword gleaned from just such an activity as Royston now pursued. Fallen soldiers of the enemy could provide more sophisticated weaponry: fighting harness, helmets, even gold and silver coinage on occasion. The possibilities were unlimited. And here, where the retreating enemy had picked up their wounded and the rebels had cared for their own, there were only dead men to worry about. Even so young a boy as Royston was not afraid of dead men.

Still, Royston kept a watchful eye as he walked, quickening his pace to make a wide detour around another stiffening corpse. He was not timid in the least; such was not the way of the country-bred folk of Corwyn. But there was always the very real possibility that he might come upon a dead enemy who was not really dead—and *that* he did not like to think about.

As though in response to his growing mood, a wolf howled, much closer than before, and Royston shivered as he headed for the center of the cartway again, beginning to fancy he could see furtive movement in every bush, every ghostly tree stump. Even if he need not fear the dead, there would be more dangerous, four-legged predators prowling the fields once night fell. These he had no desire to meet.

Suddenly a movement caught his eye ahead and to the left of the path. Hand tightening on his weapon, he dropped to a crouch and let his other hand fumble among the rocks in the roadway until it could close on a fist-sized stone. He had held his breath as he hunched closer to the ground, and his voice came out hoarse and quavering as he craned his neck to peer into the bushes.

"Who's there?" he croaked. "Say who ye be, or I'll come nae closer!"

There was a second rustling in the bushes, a moan, and then a weak voice: "Water . . . please, someone . . ."

Royston eased his satchel farther around his back and straightened warily, easing his dagger from its sheath. There was always a chance that the caller was a rebel soldier, and therefore a friend—one *could* have been missed all afternoon. But what if he were a royalist?

Inching his way closer, Royston approached until he was even with the bushes that had moved, rock and dagger poised, nerves taut. It was difficult to make out definite shapes in the failing light, but suddenly he knew that it was a rebel soldier lying in the brush. Yes, there was no mistaking the falcon badge sewn to the shoulder of the steel-gray cloak.

The eyes were closed beneath the plain steel helm; the hands were still. But as Royston leaned closer to look at the man's bearded face, he could not control a gasp. He knew the man! It was Malcolm Donalson, his brother's closest friend.

"Mal!" The boy crashed into the brush to drop frantically by the man's side. "God ha' mercy, Mal, what's happened to ye? Are ye hurt bad?"

The man called Mal opened his eyes and managed to bring the boy's face into focus, then let his mouth contort in a strained smile. He closed his eyes tightly for several seconds, as though against excruciating pain, then coughed weakly and tried to look up again.

"Well, me boyo, it's about time ye found me. I feared one o' them cutthroat rascals would get to me first an' finish me off t' get me sword."

He patted a fold of his cloak beside him, and young Royston managed to make out the hard outline of a cross-hilted broadsword under the bloodstained cloth. His eyes went round as the shape registered, and then he lifted the edge of the cloak to run his fingers admiringly along the length of bloody blade.

"Ah, Mal, 'tis a bonny sword. Did ye get it off one o' the king's men?"

"Aye, the king's mark is on th' blade, lad. But one o' his kinsmen left a piece o' steel in m'leg, curse him. Take a look an' see if it's stopped bleedin' yet, will ye?" He raised himself up on his elbows as the boy bent to look. "I managed t' wrap me belt around it 'fore I passed out th' first time, but—*aiiiie!* Careful, lad! Ye'll start me bleedin' again!"

The cloak draped across Mal's legs was stiff with dried blood, and as the boy lifted it away to look at the wound it was all he could do to keep from fainting. Mal had taken a deep sword-thrust to his right thigh, beginning just above the knee and extending upward for nearly six inches. Somehow he had managed to improvise a bandage before applying the tourniquet, which had saved his life thus far, but the bandage had long outlived its usefulness and now glistened a brilliant red. Royston could not be sure in the failing light, but the ground beneath Mal's leg looked damp, stained a deeper, redder hue. Whatever its source, Mal had lost a great deal of blood; there was no doubt about that. Nor could he afford to lose much more. Royston's vision began to blur as he looked up at his friend again, and he swallowed with difficulty.

"Well, lad?"

"It—it's still bleedin', Mal. I don't think it's goin' tae stop by itself. Ye've got to have help."

Mal lay back and sighed. "Ah, 'tis nae good, laddie. I cannae travel like this, and I dinnae think ye can get anyone t' come out here, wi' night fallin'. It's that bit o' steel that's causing the trouble, it is. Mayhap ye can get it out yerself."

"Me?" Royston's eyes went round and he trembled at the thought. "Aie, Mal, I cannot! If I even loosen the tie, ye'll start bleedin' all over again. I cannae let ye spill out yer life because I dinnae know what I'm doin'."

"Now, don't argue, lad. There's nae one el—"

Mal broke off in mid-sentence, his jaw dropping in amazement as he stared over Royston's shoulder, and the boy whirled on his haunches to see two riders silhouetted against the sunset not twenty feet away. He rose cautiously as the two men dismounted, gripping his dagger just a bit more tightly. Who were the men? And where in the world had they come from?

He could make out little detail as the two approached, for the setting sun was directly behind them, turning their steel helms to red-gold. They were young, though. As they drew closer and bared their heads, Royston could see that they were scarcely older than Mal—certainly no older than thirty or so—and one was dark and the other fair. Steel-gray falcon cloaks swung from the shoulders of both men, and each wore a longsword at his hip in a worn leather scabbard. The fairer of the two tucked his helmet in the crook of his left arm as he stopped a few yards away and held his empty hands away from his weapons. The darker man stood back a pace, but there was a kindly and concerned smile on his face

as he watched the boy's reaction. Royston almost forgot to
be afraid.

"It's all right, son. We won't hurt you. Is there anything
we can do to help?"

Royston studied the men carefully for an instant, noting
the gray cloaks, the several weeks' growth of beard on both
men, their apparent friendliness, and decided he liked them.
He glanced at Mal for reassurance and found the wounded
man nodding weakly. At Mal's signal he stepped back to let
the two men stoop down across from him. After a second's
hesitation, he, too, knelt at the side of the wounded man,
his eyes dark with worry as he wondered what the two
strangers could do.

"Ye be Warin's men," Mal observed, managing a trace of
a smile as the darker of the two men put down his helmet
and began stripping off his riding gloves. "I thank ye for
stopping, what with th' darkness sae near an' all. I'm Mal
Donalson, and the boy is Royston. That steel's goin' t' have
to come out, ain't it?"

The darker man probed gently at Mal's wound, then got
to his feet and returned to his horse.

"There's steel in there, all right," he said, pulling a
leather pouch from his saddlebag. "The sooner we get it out,
the better. Royston, can you borrow a horse?"

"We have nae horse," Royston whispered. He watched
wide-eyed as the man slung a water skin over his shoulder
and returned. "Could—could we nae carry him home on
one o' yours? It's nae far tae me mother's house, I promise."

He glanced anxiously at both men as the darker one
knelt across from him again, but this time it was the blond
man who spoke.

"I'm sorry, but we haven't time. Can you get a donkey? A
mule? A cart would be even better."

Royston's eyes lit up. "Aye, a donkey. Smalf the Miller
has one he'd let me borrow. I can be back before it's full
dark."

He scrambled to his feet and started to move off, then

paused and turned to peer down at the two men once more, his eyes sweeping over the falcon cloaks with admiration.

"Ye be the Lord Warin's men," he said softly. "I'll bet yer on a special mission for the Lord himself, and that's why ye cannae tarry long. Have I guessed rightly?"

The two men exchanged glances, the darker one stiffening slightly, but then the blond man smiled and reached up to slap Royston's arm conspiratorially.

"Yes, I'm afraid you *have* guessed rightly," he said in a low voice. "But don't tell anyone. Just go and get that donkey, and we'll take care of your friend."

"Mal?"

"Go, lad. I'll be all right. These men be brothers. They be on the Lord Warin's business. Now, scat."

"Aye, Mal."

As the boy hurried out of sight down the road, the darker man opened his leather pouch and began removing bandages and instruments. Mal tried to raise his head slightly to see what he was doing, but the blond man pushed his head gently back to the ground and supported it there before he could get a good look. He felt a cool, wet sensation as the other man began washing away the caked blood on his leg, and then a faint ache as the tourniquet was tightened ever so slightly. The blond man shifted on his haunches and glanced at the sky.

"Do you want more light? I can make a torch."

"Do," the second man said with a nod. "And then I'll need your assistance. It's going to take both of us to keep him from bleeding to death."

"I'll see what I can do."

The blond man nodded at Mal reassuringly, then got to his feet and began rummaging in the bushes near Mal's head. Mal twisted around and watched in silence for several seconds, wondering how the man planned to get a torch burning out here, then glanced back at the man who was working on his leg. He winced as the man prodded the wound and accidentally jarred the steel, then coughed weakly and tried to clear his throat.

"By yer speech, ye be strangers here," he began tentatively, trying to take his mind off what the man was doing and was about to do. "Have ye come from far tae aid the Lord Warin?"

"Not from too far," the darker man replied, bending closer over the wounded leg. "We've been on a special assignment for the past few weeks. We're on our way to Coroth."

"Coroth?" Mal began. He saw that the blond man had found a length of branch which suited him, and was now wrapping the end with dry grass. He wondered again how the man planned to light it.

"Then, ye'll be goin' directly to th' Lord Warin himself—*aiie!*"

As Mal cried out, the darker man murmured, "Sorry," and shook his head as he continued working. Light flared behind Mal's head as the torch caught, but by the time he could twist around to look again, the torch was already burning brightly. The blond man steadied it where he had jammed it into the ground beside Mal's leg, then knelt down and began removing his gloves. Mal's face contorted in bewilderment, his eyes watering from the smoke of the torch.

"How did ye do that? I saw nae flint an' steel."

"Then you missed it, my friend." The man smiled and patted a pouch at his belt. "What other way is there? Do you think I'm Deryni, that I can call down fire from heaven simply to light a torch?"

The man flashed him a disarming smile, and Mal had to grin, too. Of course the man couldn't be Deryni. No one who served the Lord Warin could be a member of that accursed race. Not when Warin was sworn to destroy all those who trafficked with sorcery. He must be delirious. Of course the man had used flint and steel.

As the blond man turned his attention to what his colleague was doing, Mal chided himself for his foolishness and turned his head to look up at the sky. A strange lethargy was stealing over him as the men worked, an inexplicable, floating feeling, as though his very soul were hovering a little way outside his body. He could feel them probing in his leg, and it hurt a little, but the pain was a thing apart, a warm, disjointed sensation that was somehow alien. He wondered idly if he was dying.

"I'm sorry if we hurt you," said the blond man. The low voice cut through Mal's meanderings like the steel in his leg, and he was suddenly back in the moment. "Why don't you try to tell us what happened? It might help to take your mind off what we're doing."

Mal sighed and tried to blink the pain away. "Aye, I'll try. Let's see. Aye, ye be on a mission for th' Lord Warin, so ye could nae know what happened here." He winced as the blond man shook his head.

"Well, we won for today." He laid his head back and stared up at the darkening sky. "We routed thirty o' the king's men led by Prince Nigel himself. Killed nigh a score, an' wounded the prince, too. But it will nae last. Th' king will just send more men, an' we'll be punished for risin' against him. It's all the fault o' Duke Alaric, cursed be his name!"

"Oh?" The blond man's face, bearded though it was, was handsome and calm, and not at all threatening. Still, Mal felt a cold shiver in the pit of his stomach as he met the slate-gray eyes. He looked away uneasily, unable to decide just why he felt so uncomfortable talking about his liege lord this way to a total stranger, but he found his gaze returning to the man's face. What was there about the man's eyes that seemed so—compelling?

"Does everyone hate him as much as you do?" the man asked softly.

"Weel, t' be perfectly frank, none o' us here at Jennan Vale really wanted to rise against th' duke," Mal found himself saying. "He was a good enough sort before he started dabblin' in that accursed Deryni magic. There were even churchmen who called theyselves his friend." He paused for an instant, then slapped his palm against the ground for emphasis.

"But th' archbishops say he's o'erstepped the bounds even a duke may go. He an' that Deryni cousin o' his desecrated th' Shrine o' Saint Torin last winter." He snorted contemptuously. "Now *there's* one who'll pay in th' Hereafter—that McLain: a priest o' God, an' Deryni a' the while.

"Anyway, when they would nae surrender theyselves to the judgment o' the Curia for their sins, an' some o' the Corwyner folk said they'd stand by the duke an' his kinsman even if they *was* excommunicated, th' archbishops put th' Interdict on all o' Corwyn. Warin says the only way we can get it lifted is to capture th' duke and turn him over to th' archbishops in Coroth—an' help Warin rid the land o' every other Deryni, too. That's the only way to—*aiiie!* Careful o' me leg, man!"

Mal sank back, half-fainting, against the ground, dimly aware through the haze of pain that both men were now bent intently over his leg. He could feel hot blood streaming down his thigh, the pressure of the bandage one man applied, the surge of new blood as that bandage soaked through and had to be replaced by a fresh one.

Consciousness was fading with the ebbing blood when he felt a cool hand on his forehead and heard a low voice say, "Just relax, Mal. You're going to be fine, but we'll have to help you along a little. Relax and go to sleep . . . and forget all of this."

As awareness slipped away, Malcolm Donalson heard the second man murmuring words he could not understand, felt a warmth creeping into his wound, a soothing calmness pervading every sense. Then he was opening his eyes, a bloodied sliver of metal clutched in his hand, and the two men were packing up their belongings in the brown leather pouch. The blond man smiled reassuringly as he saw Mal's eyes open, and raised the wounded man's head to put a water flask to his lips. Mal swallowed automatically, his mind whirling as he tried to remember what had happened. The strange gray eyes of the blond man were only inches away.

"I—I'm still alive," he whispered dazedly. "I thought I'd died, I really did." He glanced at the sliver of metal in his hand. "It—it's almost like a miracle."

"Nonsense. You fainted; that's all. Do you think you can sit up? Your ride is here."

As the man eased Mal's head back and stoppered the flask, Mal became aware of others standing nearby: the boy Royston holding the tattered lead of a scruffy donkey; a thin, fragile-looking woman with a rough-woven shawl over her head who could only be the boy's mother. Abruptly he was aware of the sliver of metal still clutched in his fist, and he glanced up at the blond man again, avoiding the gray eyes.

"I—I dinnae know how to thank ye," he stammered. "Ye saved—"

"There's no need," the man replied with a smile. He held out a hand and assisted Mal to his feet. "Leave the bandages in place for at least a week before you try to change them, and then be careful to keep the wound clean until it's healed. You're lucky that it wasn't as bad as it looked."

"Aye," Mal whispered, moving dazedly toward the donkey and limping heavily.

As Mal reached the side of the donkey, Royston threw his arms around his friend in a brief hug, then held the animal's head while their two benefactors assisted Mal to mount. The woman stood back fearfully, not understanding what had happened, yet eyeing the falcon cloaks on the pair with awe and respect. Mal steadied himself against their shoulders until he could ease his leg to a comfortable position, then sat more erect and held precariously to the animal's wispy mane. As the two men stepped back, Mal glanced in their direction and nodded, then raised his hand in farewell. The sliver of metal still glittered in his clenched fist.

"I thank ye again, good sirs."

"Think you can make it now?" the darker man asked.

"Aye, if the beast does nae go mad an' dump me in a ditch. Godspeed ye, friends. An' tell th' Lord Warin we stand ready to do his biddin', next time ye see him."

"I will that," the blond man replied.

"That I certainly will," he repeated under his breath as man and donkey, boy and woman, headed back down the road and into the night.

When they were out of sight and hearing, the blond man crossed back into the brush where they had been working and retrieved the torch. He held it aloft until his companion could recover the two dusty warhorses, then snuffed it out against the damp clay of the roadway and tossed it aside. The gray eyes were again grim.

"Well, would you say I 'o'erstepped the bounds even a duke may go,' by healing that man, Duncan?" he asked, pulling on his gloves in an impatient gesture.

Duncan shrugged as he handed over a pair of reins. "Who can say? We took a chance—but that's nothing new. He shouldn't be able to remember anything he oughtn't. But then, you can never tell with these country folk. Or need I bother telling you that? After all, they're your people, Alaric."

Alaric Anthony Morgan, Duke of Corwyn, King's Champion, and now excommunicate Deryni sorcerer, smiled and gathered up his reins, swinging up on his tall warhorse as Duncan did the same.

"My people. Yes, I suppose they are, God bless 'em. Tell me, Cousin. Is all of this really my fault? I never thought so before, but I've heard it so often in the past few weeks, I'm almost beginning to believe it."

Duncan shook his head, touching steel-shod heels to his horse's flanks and beginning to move off down the road. "It isn't your fault. It isn't any one person's fault. We're simply a convenient excuse for the archbishops to do what they've been wanting to do for years. This situation has been building for generations."

"You're right, of course," Morgan said. He urged his horse to a trot and fell in beside his kinsman. "But that isn't going to make it any easier to explain to Kelson."

"He understands," Duncan replied. "What will be more interesting will be his reaction to the information we've been gathering for the past week or so. I don't think he's realized the extent of unrest in this part of the kingdom."

Morgan snorted. "Neither had I. When do you reckon we'll reach Dol Shaia?"

"Soon after noon," Duncan stated. "I'd stake money on it."

"Would you?" Morgan gave a sly grin. "Done! Now, let's ride."

And so the two continued along the road from Jennan Vale, pushing on ever faster as the moon rose to light their way. They need not have worried about revealing their identities, these two young Deryni lords. For even had they been told, Malcolm Donalson and the boy Royston simply would not have believed that they had been in the presence of the infamous pair. Dukes and monsignori, Deryni or not, did not ride in the guise of rebel soldiers in the service of Lord Warin, with falcon cloaks and badges and three weeks' growth of beard. It was unimaginable.

Nor would two heretic Deryni have stopped to help a wounded rebel soldier—especially one who, only hours before, had brought death and injury to a number of royalist knights. This, too, was unheard of.

So the two rode on, ever faster, ever closer, to rendezvous next day at Dol Shaia with their young Deryni king.

CHAPTER TWO

"Thy princes are rebellious, and companions of thieves."

ISAIAH 1:23

THE young man with the night-black hair sat at ease on a low camp stool, a kite-shaped shield balanced face-down across his knees and on the edge of the velvet-draped bed. His slender fingers worked slowly, painstakingly, as they wove a new strip of rawhide round and round the hand-grip. His gray eyes were hooded beneath long, dark lashes.

However, the young man's mind was not on the repairs he made. Nor was he concerned just now that the device on the reverse of the shield was rich and finely crafted, the royal lion of Gwynedd gleaming gold on red beneath its canvas cover. He was equally oblivious to the priceless Kheldish carpet beneath his dusty boots, the jewel-hilted broadsword hanging within easy reach in its plain leather scabbard.

For the young man who worked alone in his tent at Dol Shaia was Kelson Haldane, son of the late King Brion of Gwynedd. And this same Kelson Haldane, but a few months past his fourteenth birthday, was now himself King of Gwynedd and ruler in his own right of a score of lesser duchies and baronies. At this moment, he was also a worried young man.

Kelson glanced at the doorway of the tent and scowled. The flap was pulled over the entrance for privacy, but there was enough light seeping beneath the flap to tell him that the afternoon was fast slipping away. Outside he could hear the measured tread of sentries patrolling beside his tent, the rustle of silk pennons snapping in the breeze, the stamping and snorting of the great warhorses as they tugged at their picket ropes beneath the trees not far away. He returned resignedly to his task, working on in silence for some minutes, then looked up expectantly as the tent flap was drawn aside and a mailed and blue-cloaked young man entered. The king's eyes lit with pleasure.

"Derry!"

Sean Lord Derry paused to sketch a casual bow as Kelson spoke his name, then came to perch uneasily on the edge of the state bed. He was not much older than Kelson—in his mid-twenties, perhaps—but his blue eyes were grim beneath the shock of curly brown hair. A narrow length of leather dangled from his calloused fingertips, and he laid it on the shield with a slight nod as he glanced at Kelson's handiwork.

"I could have done that for you, Sire. Mending armor is not a king's work."

Kelson shrugged and pulled the last of the rawhide lacing taut, then began trimming at the ends of the leather with a silver-chased dagger.

"I had nothing better to do this afternoon. If I were doing what a king *should* be doing, I'd be long into Corwyn by now, putting down Warin's revolt and forcing the archbishops to resolve their petty quarrel."

He ran his fingers along the shield grip and sheathed his dagger with a sigh. "But Alaric tells me I must not do that—at least not yet. And so I wait, and bide my time, and try to cultivate the patience I know he would want me to display." He shoved the shield back onto the bed and rested his hands lightly on his knees. "I also try to refrain from asking the questions I know you are reluctant to answer. Except that now the time has come when I must ask. What was the price of Jennan Vale?"

The price had been high. Of the thirty who had ridden out with Nigel two days before, less than a score had returned. The remnants of his patrol had limped into Dol Shaia at midmorning, angry and footsore; and several of those who returned did not live past noon. In addition to the loss of life, Jennan Vale had taken a heavy toll in morale. As Kelson listened to Derry's report, his fourteen years weighed heavily upon him.

"This is even worse than I feared," Kelson finally murmured, when the last grim details of the rout had been told. "First the archbishops and their hatred of the Deryni, then this fanatic Warin de Grey. . . . And the people support him, Derry! Even if I *can* stop Warin, reconcile with the archbishops, I can't defeat the entire duchy."

Derry shook his head emphatically. "I think you misjudge Warin's influence, Sire. His appeal is powerful when he is nearby, and after a few miracles the people flock to his side. But the tradition of loyalty to kings is older and, I believe, stronger than the lure of a new prophet—especially one who proposes holy war. Once Warin is removed, and the peasants leaderless, their impetus will be gone. His fatal mistake was to take up residence in Coroth with the archbishops. Now he's practically counted as one of the archbishops' followers."

"There's still the matter of the Interdict," Kelson said doubtfully. "Will the common folk forget that so quickly?"

Derry flashed him a reassuring smile. "Our reports indicate that the rebels in the outlying areas are poorly armed and only loosely organized, Sire. When they have to face the reality of a royal army marching through their midst, they'll scatter like mice!"

"I didn't hear of them scattering like mice at Jennan Vale," Kelson said with a snort. "In fact, I still fail to understand how poorly armed peasants were able to take an entire patrol by surprise. Where is my uncle? I should like to hear *his* explanation of what happened yesterday."

"Try not to be too hard on him, Sire," Derry murmured, lowering his eyes uncomfortably. "He has been with the surgeons and his wounded since he rode in this morning. It was only an hour ago that I was able to persuade him to let the surgeons see to his own injuries."

"He's hurt?" The king's eyes were suddenly concerned. "How badly? Why didn't you tell me?"

"He ordered me not to, Sire. It isn't serious. His left shoulder is badly wrenched, and he has a few superficial cuts and bruises. But he would rather have died than lose those men."

Kelson's mouth twitched in sympathy and he forced a wan smile. "I know that. The fault is not his."

"Be sure to remind him of that, then," Derry said quietly. "He feels he has personally failed you."

"Not Nigel. Never *him*."

The young king stood wearily and flexed his shoulders in his white linen tunic, stretching his neck backward to gaze at the ceiling of the tent a few feet above his head. His straight black hair, cropped close above his ears for battle, was disheveled, and he ran a tanned hand through it once again as he turned back to Derry.

"What further news from the three armies in the north?"

Derry stood attentively. "Little you haven't already heard. The Duke of Claibourne reports that he should be able to hold the Arranal Canyon approach indefinitely, so long as he isn't attacked from the south simultaneously. His Grace estimates that Wencit will make his main drive farther south, probably at the Cardosa Pass. There's only a token force readied at Arranal."

Kelson nodded slowly and brushed bits of leather scrap from his tunic as he moved toward a campaign table spread with maps. "No word from Duke Jared or Bran Coris?"

"None, Sire."

Kelson picked up a pair of calipers and sighed, chewing on one end of the instrument reflectively. "You don't suppose something has gone wrong, do you? Suppose the spring thaws finish earlier than we predicted—suppose they've already finished? For all we know, Wencit could already be on his way into Eastmarch."

"We would have heard, Sire. At least one courier would have gotten through."

"Would he? I wonder."

The king studied the map before him for several minutes, gray eyes narrowing as he considered his possible strategies for at least the hundredth time. He spread the calipers and measured off several distances, mentally recalculating his original figures, then stood back to weigh the possibilities again. He only reconfirmed what he already knew.

"Derry," he gestured to the young lord to join him as he bent again over the maps, "tell me again what Lord Perris said about this road." He used one arm of the calipers to trace out a thin, wiggly line that meandered across the western slopes of the mountain chain dividing Gwynedd from Torenth. "If this road were passable even a week sooner, we could—"

Further discussion was curtailed at the sound of a galloping horse being brought sharply to rein outside the tent, followed by the precipitate entrance of a red-cloaked sentry. Derry moved slightly closer, ready to protect the king if necessary, but the man sketched a hasty salute as Kelson spun in query.

"Sire, General Morgan and Father McLain are on their way in. They've just passed the eastern guard post."

With a wordless cry of delight, Kelson flung down his calipers and bolted for the exit, nearly bowling over the surprised sentry. As he burst into the sunlight, closely followed by Derry, a pair of leather-clad riders drew rein before the royal pavilion in a cloud of dust and dismounted, only wide grins and scruffy beards visible beneath their plain steel helms. The gray cloaks and falcon insignia of the day before were long gone. But as the two pulled off dusty helmets, there was no mistaking the pale gold head of Alaric Morgan or the darker one of Duncan McLain.

"Morgan! Father Duncan! Where have you been?" Kelson drew back in faint distaste as the two slapped the worst of the dust from their riding leathers.

"Sorry, my prince," Morgan said with a chuckle. He blew dust from his helmet and shook dust from his bright hair. "Holy Michael and all the saints, it's dry around here! Whatever made us pick Dol Shaia for a campsite?"

Kelson folded his arms across his chest and tried unsuccessfully to control a smile. "As I recall, it was one Alaric Morgan who said we should camp close to the border, as near as possible without being seen. Dol Shaia was the logical spot. Now, do you want to tell me what took you so long? Nigel and the last stragglers got back earlier this morning."

Morgan cast a resigned look at Duncan, then threw an arm around Kelson's shoulders in a comradely gesture and began walking him back into the tent.

"Suppose we talk about it over some food, my prince?" He signaled Derry to see to it. "And if someone could call Nigel and his captains, I'll brief everyone at the same time. I have neither the time nor the desire to tell this tale more than once."

Inside, Morgan collapsed into a camp chair beside the campaign table and swung his boots up on a footstool with a grunt, letting his helmet slide to the ground beside him. Duncan, a bit more mindful of social amenities, waited until Kelson had seated himself opposite before sinking into another camp chair beside Morgan, laying his helmet at his feet.

"You look terrible," Kelson finally said, surveying them critically. "Both of you. I don't think I've ever seen either of you with beards before, either."

Duncan smiled and leaned back in his chair, lacing his

fingers behind his head as he stretched. "Quite likely not, my prince. But you must admit, we fooled the rebels. Even Alaric, with his brazen manner and outrageous yellow hair, was able to pass as a simple soldier when he put on his act. And riding for the past two weeks in rebel uniforms was nothing short of inspired."

"And dangerous," Nigel said, slipping into a chair at Kelson's left and motioning three red-cloaked captains to positions around the table. "I hope you made it worth the risk. Our venture certainly wasn't."

Morgan sobered instantly and took his feet down from the stool, all levity gone now that the complement was complete. Nigel's left arm was supported by a black silk sling, a dark bruise purpling his right cheekbone. Other than that, he was almost the image of the dead Brion. Morgan had to make a conscious effort to force that image out of his head.

"Nigel, I *am* sorry. I heard what happened. In fact, we saw the aftermath at Jennan Vale. We couldn't have been more than a few hours behind you."

Nigel grunted noncommittally and lowered his eyes, and Morgan realized that he would have to do something to lighten the mood.

"It has been an instructive few weeks in other respects, however," he continued brightly. "Some of the information we picked up in talking to rebel soldiers was very enlightening, even if useless strategically. It's amazing the number of rumors and semi-legendary notions the common folk seem to have concocted about us."

He folded his hands across his waist and sat back in his chair, smiling faintly. "Did you know, for example, that I am rumored to have cloven hooves?" He stretched out his booted feet before him and glanced at them wistfully as the eyes of all present followed his gaze.

"Of course, few people have ever seen my feet without shoes of some sort—especially peasants. Do you suppose it could be true?"

Kelson grinned in spite of himself, and the three captains exchanged uneasy glances.

"You're joking, surely," Kelson said. "Who could believe a thing like that?"

"Have *you* ever seen Alaric without shoes, Sire?" Duncan inquired slyly.

At that moment Derry intruded with a platter of meat, cheese, and bread and extended it with a grin.

"I've seen his feet, Sire," he said, as Morgan speared a gobbet of cold beef on his dagger and took a chunk of bread. "And regardless of what they say, I can assure you that he has no cloven hooves—not even an extra toe."

Morgan saluted Derry with the skewered meat and took a bite, then cast an inquiring look at Kelson and Nigel. The royal duke was himself again, sitting back in his chair and smiling faintly, well aware of what Morgan had been trying to do, and that it had succeeded. Kelson, somewhat taken aback at the exchange, glanced from one to the other of them several times before he finally concluded that they were sporting with him. At length, he shook his head and broke into a grin, making a shooing motion toward the three captains, who were only too happy to absent themselves.

"Cloven hooves, indeed!" He snorted. "Morgan, for a moment you almost had me believing you."

"One cannot labor under tension *all* the time, Sire," Morgan said with a shrug and a faint smile. "Now, what news since we left? What has been happening to put you in this agitated frame of mind?"

Kelson shook his head. "There's nothing new, really. That may be why I'm so uneasy. I am still trying to decide the best way to end this internal contention, and that brings us back to the basic question of how best to honorably reconcile ourselves with my clergy and my rebellious subjects."

Duncan washed down the last of his meat with a swallow of wine and nodded in Kelson's direction. "We have also given that matter considerable thought in the past few days, my prince. And we've about reached the conclusion that the most reasonable approach is first to attempt a reconciliation with the six rebel bishops in Dhassa. They *want* to help you; their quarrel is with Alaric and me only. You are not involved."

"That's true," Kelson agreed, considering. "If you could be formally reinstated and cleared of the charges that the Curia brought against you, I could accept their aid without worrying about compromising their honor. I have been reluctant until now to even communicate with them because of just that factor. If they have been loyal to me so far, it's because I am the king—and maybe a little because they know and trust me personally. At least Bishop Arilan does."

Morgan wiped the blade of his dagger against the side of his boot and returned it to its sheath. "That is certainly a factor, my prince. It is one reason we considered this proposition so carefully, before even discussing it with you. Whatever we do, we would not wish to endanger that trust which the Six in Dhassa still hold for you."

"Yet you propose to go to Dhassa and attempt a reconciliation," the king said. "Suppose you don't succeed? Suppose the Six cannot be persuaded?"

"I believe I can put your mind at ease on that matter, Sire," Duncan said. "If you'll recall, I was on Bishop Arilan's staff for some time. I know him fairly well. I believe he will deal fairly with us, and in doing so, will persuade his colleagues to do likewise."

"I wish I could be as sure."

Kelson drummed his fingers lightly on the arm of his chair, then folded them together in his lap. "So you would throw yourselves on the mercy of the bishops, on the strength of your trust in one man." His grimace of distaste showed reluctance as well. "Yet, the fact is that both of you *are* guilty of the charges for which you were excommunicated. There is no denying the events at Saint Torin's. To be sure, there were extenuating circumstances—and hopefully, canon law will support your defense, at least in the major issues. But if you should fail, if the excommunication should stand, what then? Do you think the Six will let you walk out of there?"

There were the sounds of low voices outside the tent, a verbal altercation of some sort going on, and Kelson paused to glance in the direction of the doorway. As he did, a sentry withdrew the flap and stepped inside.

"Sire, Bishop Istelyn wishes to see you. He insists it cannot wait."

Kelson frowned. "Admit him."

As the guard stepped back into the dusk, Kelson glanced quickly at the faces of his companions, especially Morgan and Duncan. Istelyn was one of Gwynedd's twelve itinerant bishops with no fixed see, one of those who had not been in Dhassa when the Curia had split last winter.

But Istelyn, on hearing of the events in Dhassa, had declared himself to be on the side of Arilan and Cardiel and the rest of the Six, and several weeks ago had attached himself to Kelson's army here at the Corwyn border. He was regarded as a sober, even-tempered prelate, not given to flexing his ecclesiastical power. For him to force himself on a royal meeting as he was about to do was quite out of character unless something were drastically wrong. Kelson's face almost betrayed his anxiety as the bishop stepped through the tent opening, a sheaf of parchment in his hand and a very solemn expression on his face.

"Your Majesty," Istelyn said with a grave bow.

"My Lord Bishop," Kelson replied, standing slowly at his place as the rest followed suit.

Istelyn glanced around the tent and nodded acknowledgement, and Kelson motioned the rest of his menie to be seated.

"I surmise that your news is not good, my lord," the king murmured, not taking his eyes from Istelyn's.

"You surmise correctly, Sire." The bishop moved closer to the king and extended the sheaf of parchments. "I—regret being the bearer of these, but I felt you should have them."

As Kelson took the pages Istelyn offered, the bishop

bowed and backed off a few paces, unwilling to meet the young monarch's eyes any longer. With a sinking feeling in the pit of his stomach, Kelson scanned the top sheet, his lips compressing in a thin, white line as he read. The gray eyes grew colder by the second as he flicked over the too-familiar seal at the bottom of the page and then skipped to the second sheet.

His face blanched as he read, and it was with a visible control of emotion that he kept his hands from crumpling the parchment then and there. Veiling the icy Haldane eyes beneath long lashes, he began to bend the parchment sheets into a fat roll, not looking up as he spoke.

"Leave us, please—all of you." His voice was chill, deadly, not to be disobeyed. "And Istelyn, you are to speak of this to no one until we give you leave. Is that clear?"

Istelyn paused to bow as he moved toward the doorway. "Of course, Sire."

"Thank you. On second thought, Morgan and Father Duncan, please stay."

The pair had been moving toward the doorway with the others, but paused to exchange puzzled glances before turning to regard their undoubtedly distressed sovereign lord. Kelson had turned his back on the departing lords and stood rising up and down slightly on the balls of his feet, tapping the roll of parchment lightly against the palm of his left hand.

Morgan and Duncan returned to stand expectantly by their former places, but when Nigel paused as though to join them, Duncan lifted a restraining hand and shook his head. Morgan, too, moved as though to bar the way, and with a resigned shrug Nigel turned on his heel to follow the others from the pavilion. His departure left only the three of them within the blue canvas walls.

"Are they all gone?" Kelson whispered. He had not moved during the silent exchange with Nigel, and his only movement now was the slight tap-tap of the parchment roll against his hand—that and his controlled breathing.

Duncan raised an eyebrow at Morgan and glanced again at the king.

"Yes, they're gone, Sire. What is it?"

Kelson turned to eye both of them, the gray Haldane eyes lighting with a fire the two men had not seen since Brion's time. Then he half-crumpled the parchment sheets and flung them to the floor in disgust.

"Go ahead, read them," he blurted, turning then to fling himself across his bed on his stomach. He slammed a lean fist into the mattress with all his might.

"Damn those bishops to thrice-cursed perdition, what are we to do? My God, we are undone!"

Morgan blinked at Duncan in blank amazement, then moved closer to the king in concern as Duncan retrieved the discarded documents.

"Kelson, what is it? Tell us what has happened. Are you all right?"

With a sigh, Kelson rolled over to prop himself on his elbows and gaze up more blandly at the pair, the anger in his eyes now damped to a slight, cold fire.

"Forgive me, you shouldn't have seen that show of temper." He lay back on the bed and stared up at the ceiling of the tent. "I am a king. I should know better. It's a fault, I know."

"And what of the fault with the message?" Morgan urged, glancing at Duncan's calm face as he scanned the documents. "Come, tell us what has happened."

"I'm excommunicated, that's what's happened," Kelson replied in a matter-of-fact tone. "In addition, my entire kingdom is under Interdict, and any who continue to pay me fealty are likewise excommunicated."

"Is *that* all?" Morgan exhaled, a long, relieved sigh, and beckoned Duncan to bring the documents Kelson had discarded in such heat. "By your reaction, I thought it to be truly horrible news."

Kelson sat up straight in the center of the bed. "*Is that all?*" he repeated incredulously. "You obviously don't understand. Father Duncan, explain it to him in words of one syllable. I am *excommunicated*, and everyone who remains with me! And Gwynedd is under *Interdict*!"

Duncan folded the parchment sheaf in half and creased the center sharply, tossed it lightly to the bed. "Worthless, my prince."

"What?"

"It is worthless," he repeated calmly. "The eleven bishops sitting in conclave at Coroth still have not gleaned a twelfth: a requirement that is as firmly fixed in our canon law as any dogma of faith. The eleven at Coroth cannot bind you or anyone else unless they gain a twelfth."

"A twelfth—by God, you're right!" Kelson exclaimed, scrambling upright to snatch up the offending documents and stare at them again. "How could I have forgotten?"

Morgan smiled and returned to his chair, where a half-finished cup of wine awaited him. "It is understandable, my prince. You are not as accustomed to anathema as we are. Remember that Duncan and I have been truly and legally excommunicated for nearly three months now, and are little the worse for wear—which brings us back to our original discussion."

"Yes, of course." Kelson got to his feet and returned to his chair, still shaking his head as he stared at the documents in his hand. Duncan, too, returned to the circle of chairs and sat down, helping himself to a small apple as Kelson finally put the parchment sheaf aside.

"What you are implying, then," the king said, "is that this makes it all the more urgent that you get to Dhassa as quickly as possible. Am I correct?"

"You are, my prince," Morgan said with a nod.

"But suppose Arilan's colleagues won't follow his lead? They are our only hope for reconciliation with the rest of the clergy, and if they should fail us, especially with this new Interdict and excommunication hanging over us—why, we'd never be able to make Loris and Corrigan listen."

Morgan made a steeple of his forefingers and tapped them

lightly against his lips for a moment, then glanced at Duncan. The priest had not changed his relaxed position next to him, and appeared to be chewing unconcernedly on a bite of apple, but Morgan knew that he was thinking much the same thing. Unless they could eventually reach an agreement with Loris and Corrigan, the ringleaders of the curial hostility against Duncan and himself, Gwynedd was doomed. Once the spring flooding was done, Wencit of Torenth would be sweeping into Gwynedd along the Rheljan Range, using high Cardosa as a base. And with internal factions warring in the south and no reinforcements available, it would be a relatively simple matter to cut off Kelson's three armies and destroy them at leisure. The controversy in Corwyn must be resolved, and soon.

Morgan shifted forward in his chair and retrieved his helmet from the floor where he had dropped it. "We shall do the best we can, my prince. In the meantime, what are your plans while we're gone? I know how this inactivity must be fretting you."

Kelson studied a ruby on his forefinger and shook his head. "It is." He looked up and managed a slight smile. "But for the time being, I shall just have to put up with my impatience and stand where I am, won't I? As soon as you have reached agreement with the Six in Dhassa, will you send word?"

"Certainly. And we are still agreed on our rendezvous point?"

"Yes—and I should like to send Derry north for part of the way with you, too, if you don't mind. I need word of the three armies."

"Agreed." Morgan nodded, fingering the chin strap of his helmet. "If you like, we can arrange for you to keep in touch with him through his medallion, the way we did before. Is that agreeable?"

"Of course. Perhaps Father Duncan could brief him, then, and make preparations for you to leave. You'll need fresh horses, supplies. . . ."

"I'll be happy to see to it, Sire," Duncan said, draining the last of his wine and picking up his helmet as he got to his feet. "I shall look in on Bishop Istelyn and reassure him, as well."

Kelson stared after the departing priest for a long moment, then returned his gaze to Morgan, studying the trim form relaxed in the chair there, the hooded gray eyes that watched him in much the same way. As he glanced down at his own hands, he was surprised to find that his fingers were trembling, and he twined them together in annoyance.

"Ah—how long do you think it will take to reach the bishops and . . . resolve things?" he asked. "I'll—need to know when to meet you with the army."

Morgan smiled and lightly touched the pouch at his belt. "I carry your Lion Seal, my prince. I am your Champion, sworn to protect you."

"That isn't what I asked, and you know it!" Kelson said. He rose and began to pace nervously. "You're about to throw yourselves on the mercy of a handful of bishops who could just as easily cut your throat as hear you out, and you prattle on about being my Champion, sworn to protect me. The Devil take you, Morgan, I want to know how you *feel* about this thing. Do I have to spell it out? I want to know if you trust Arilan and Cardiel!"

Morgan's eyes had followed the young king in his pacing, and now swept him from head to toe as he came to a halt behind his chair and leaned both hands against the back. The gray Haldane eyes were dancing with intelligence, apprehension, and a little annoyance, and Morgan suppressed a smile. Kelson, though he was king in his own right and held the throne by powers as awesome as any Morgan could muster up, was still a boy in many ways. At times, his brash outspokenness reminded Morgan a little of his own youth.

But Morgan also had the good sense to know when his king was serious, as he had known for the boy's father. This was one of those times. He let his glance drop to the helmet he still held in his lap, then met the king's gaze once more.

"I have met Arilan only once, my prince—at least to talk to—and Cardiel, never. But as I see it, they may be our only hope. Arilan has always seemed to be at least tolerant where Deryni are concerned; he stood by you at your coronation and did not denounce me or Duncan, even though he must have suspected that there was magic afoot besides yours and Charissa's. I am also told that he and Cardiel were among our staunchest supporters when the Interdict question arose regarding Corwyn. I think we have no choice but to trust them."

"But, to walk right into Dhassa, when there is a price on your heads . . ." Kelson began.

"Do you really think anyone is likely to recognize us?" Morgan snorted. "Look at me. When has the Duke of Corwyn ever worn a beard, or gone about in peasant garb, or even been to Dhassa, for that matter? And what excommunicate fugitive in his right mind would even consider entering the holiest city in Gwynedd when he knows that everyone in the kingdom is looking for him?"

"Alaric Morgan would." Kelson sighed resignedly. "But suppose that you do reach Dhassa safely, you enter the city, you somehow manage to get inside the episcopal palace undetected—then what? You just told me that you've never been to Dhassa. How do you even begin to find Arilan and Cardiel? And if you're captured before you can find them, then what? Suppose some overzealous guardsman decides he wants all the glory for himself, and kills you before you're even taken before the bishops?"

Morgan smiled and wrapped his hands complacently around his helmet. "You forget one thing, my prince. Duncan and I are Deryni. The last time I heard, that still counted for something."

Kelson stared at Morgan speechlessly for an instant, disbelief and astonishment writ all across his face, then threw his head back and laughed delightedly as he sat down again.

"You are very good for me, Alaric Morgan, do you know that? Without preaching, you somehow manage to tell your king that he has been thinking like a fool, but without being the least bit annoying about it. I think it comes of letting me ramble on and on until I run down and realize how ridiculous I've been. Why is that?"

"Why do you ramble on and on, my prince? Or why do I let you?"

Kelson grinned. "You know what I mean."

Morgan stood and brushed dust from his clothing again, then polished across the front of his helmet with his sleeve.

"You are young, you have a natural curiosity, and you lack the experience that only years can bring, my prince," he said easily. "That is why you ramble on and on. As for why I let you . . ." He considered it for a moment. "I let you because it is the best cure I know for anxiety: to get one's fears out in the open and face up to them. Once you realize which are the irrational fears and which are the real ones, you have come a long way toward conquering both kinds. Fair enough?"

"Fair enough," Kelson replied, getting up and moving with Morgan toward the exit. "You *will* be careful, though, won't you?" The statement ended on a doubtful note.

"On my honor, I will, Sire."

CHAPTER THREE

"He shall dwell on high: his place of defense shall be
the munitions of rocks: bread shall be given him;
his waters shall be sure."

ISAIAH 33:16

ON the vast plain below the city of Cardosa, the army of
Bran Coris Earl of Marley had been camped for nearly a
month. They were two thousand strong, these men of Marley, and fiercely loyal to their young commander, but they
had been waiting beside the swollen flood runoff for more
than a week now, anticipating the cessation of the flooding,
yet dreading the moment when Wencit of Torenth would
send his men streaming down the Cardosa defile.

What most frightened the waiting soldiers was that
Wencit's forces could fight with magic—or so it was believed. Yet the men of Marley would stand by their young
earl despite the danger, the almost certain death, for Lord
Bran was a charismatic leader and an able tactician. More-
over, he had always been extremely generous to those who
supported him. There was no reason to believe that success
in the Cardosa campaign would not yield similar largesse.
And in the end, what more could a soldier ask, besides re-
warding service and a leader he could respect? They did not
dwell on the possibility of defeat.

It was early morning, and the camp had been stirring for several hours. Lord Bran, a tartan blanket draped around the shoulders of his blue undress tunic, lounged against one of the outside support-poles of his pavilion and sipped at a goblet of mulled wine as he scanned upriver toward the distant mountains, gleaming in the early morning sun. His gold-brown eyes narrowed slightly as he tried to see beyond the mist. A hard set to the handsome mouth betokened stubbornness and determination. He hooked a thumb in the jeweled belt at his waist and glanced to one side at the sound of footsteps approaching.

"Any special orders for today, m'lord?"

The speaker, Baron Campbell, was a longtime retainer of the earl's family. As he approached, helmet tucked diffidently under one arm, he hiked part of his azure and gold plaid farther back onto his shoulders.

Bran shook his head. "Any change in the river soundings this morning?"

"We're still reading close to five feet, even at the fords, m'lord. And there are sink holes that could swallow up man and horse with nary a trace. I doubt the King of Torenth will be coming down off his mountain today."

Bran swirled the wine in his cup and took another swallow, then nodded. "Then we'll proceed as we have been: regular patrols and lookouts on the western perimeters, and a skeleton watch on the rest of the camp. And ask the bowyer to see me sometime this morning, will you? The grip still isn't right on my new bow."

"Aye, sir."

As Campbell saluted and turned to relay Bran's orders, another man in the gray garb of a clerk approached from a neighboring tent with a sheaf of parchments in his hand. When Bran glanced idly in his direction, the man made a self-conscious bow before extending a brown feather quill toward the earl.

"Your correspondence is ready for signature, my lord. The couriers are awaiting your orders."

With a slight nod, Bran took the letters and glanced through them briefly, a look of boredom on his face, then handed his goblet to the man to hold while he scrawled his mark at the bottom of each page. When he had finished, he returned the documents to the clerk in exchange for his goblet, and would have returned to his idle scanning of the mountains except for the insistent throat-clearing of the man.

"Ah, my lord . . ."

Bran glanced back at the man, mildly annoyed.

"My lord, your letter to the Countess Richenda—don't you wish to seal it?"

Bran's glance flicked to the parchment in the clerk's hand, then back to the man's face with a bored sigh. Slipping a heavy silver signet from his thumb, he dropped it into the man's outstretched hand and said, "See to it, will you, Joseph?"

"Yes, my lord."

"In fact, deliver the letter in person. If you can persuade her, I think it would be a good idea to move her and my heir to some neutral place, perhaps Dhassa. They'd be safe with the bishops."

"Very well, sir. I'll leave at once."

As Bran nodded acknowledgement, the clerk closed the ring in his hand and bowed, then backed off to make way for an older man in captain's uniform, who gave a casual salute as he approached. He was wrapped from neck to knee in a rough wool cloak of faded blue, with a blue plume a-tremble atop the steel helmet under his arm, and Bran allowed himself an easy nod.

"Morning, Gwyllim. Some problem I should know of?" he asked.

Gwyllim shook his head lightly. "Not at all, m'lord. The men of the Fifth Horse request the honor of your review this morning." He glanced at the mountains his lord had been surveying. "It will probably be a sight more entertaining than watching those accursed mountains, at any rate."

Bran chuckled and set aside his goblet. "No doubt it will. But be patient, old friend. There will be action enough even for you, once this stalemate ends. Wencit of Torenth will not stay on his mountain forever."

"Aye, you're—here, what's this?"

Gwyllim had turned his attention toward the pass again as he spoke, and now he straightened and peered more intently into the morning mist. Bran, noting his companion's new interest in the landscape, turned his gaze in the same direction, then snapped his fingers for the page who had been hovering just beyond earshot all the while.

"Eric, my glass, quickly. Gwyllim, sound the alert. This may be it."

As the boy scampered to do the earl's bidding, Gwyllim summoned several of his men waiting a few dozen yards away and began issuing orders. Bran shaded his eyes and continued to watch where a slow-moving mounted column was beginning to emerge from the mist, its riders picking their way carefully along the flood-washed trail. The lead rider was garbed all in white, and carried a lance with a white banner hanging limply from the top. His accompanying escort, perhaps a dozen of them, were heavily cloaked in a dull russet-orange and mounted on bright bays. Frowning, Bran put a spyglass to his eye and studied them more closely.

"Torenth's livery and badge on the escort," he said in a low voice, scanning the approaching column as Gwyllim returned to his side and Campbell joined them. "And a parley banner in the hands of the lead man. Two others at the end, not in livery, who may be the negotiators." He lowered the glass and looked at the riders again, then handed the glass to Campbell and stepped to the side of the tent to snap his fingers and gesture once again.

"Bennett, Graham, take an escort to meet them. Honor the truce as long as they do, but watch them closely. This may be a Torenthi trick."

"Aye, m'lord."

As the parley party continued to descend the mountain, the escort Bran had ordered rode past his tent in a jingle of bits and mail and leather harness, and several more of his staff officers drifted toward his tent. It was clear that the alert status had now been put in abeyance, but something was bound to happen when the earl spoke to the Torenthi emissaries.

Bran watched as the two groups of riders met, perhaps three hundred yards out from the edge of the camp, then ducked into his pavilion to emerge seconds later with a dagger at his belt and a silver circlet on his head. His officers grouped themselves around and behind him in a show of strength as the surrounded parley contingent approached at a walk.

Now that the newcomers were within hailing distance, Bran could see that he had been right about the men not in livery. The taller and more resplendent of the two, in a black brocaded cloak and crimson tunic, had a vaguely foreign air about him as he swung down from his bay and strode toward them, one of the sergeants at his side. His clothes were damp from the ride down the flooded defile, but the lean, bearded face was inscrutable as he pulled the black-plumed helmet from his head and cradled it in the hollow of his right arm. His hair was long and black and caught at the back in a silver clasp. A flame-bladed dagger of silver was thrust casually under his wide silk sash, worn to be drawn from the left. Other than that, he appeared to be unarmed.

"May I take it that you are the Earl of Marley, in command of this army?" the man asked in a faintly condescending tone.

"I am."

"Then my message is for you, my lord," the man continued, bowing slightly from the waist. "I am Lionel, Duke of Arjenol. I serve His Majesty King Wencit, who commands me to bear his felicitations to you and yours."

Bran's eyes narrowed as he studied the speaker, and he hooked his thumbs in the jeweled belt encircling his waist.

"I have heard of you, my lord. Are you not kinsman to Wencit himself?"

Lionel inclined his head minutely and smiled. "I have that honor, my lord. She who is my wife is sister to our beloved king. I trust that you will assure our safety while we are within your camp?"

"So long as you honor the truce proclaimed by your standard, you need not fear. What message do you bear from your king besides his felicitations?"

Lionel's dark eyes swept Bran and his men as he bowed once again. "My lord Earl of Marley, Wencit Furstán Padishah, King of Torenth and Tolan and the Seven Tribes to the East, desires the honor of your presence at his temporary headquarters in the city of Cardosa. There he would meet with you to discuss the possibility of a cessation of hostilities and mutual withdrawal from the area in dispute, or perhaps some other solution that your lordship might care to suggest. His Majesty has no quarrel with the Earl of Marley, and would not wish to do battle with one whom he has esteemed for many years. He awaits your immediate reply."

"Don't do it, m'lord," Campbell rumbled, stepping closer to Bran as though to shield him. "It's some kind of trick."

"It is no trick, my lord," Lionel interjected. "So that you may be assured of His Majesty's sincerity, he has commanded that I and my escort remain as hostages against your safe return. You may bring one of your officers with you, if you desire it, as well as an honor guard of ten men. You are free to leave Cardosa and return to your camp at any time should you feel that further discussion would not be worth your while or in your best interests. I believe the offer is more than generous, my lord. Do you not agree?"

Bran studied the man unwaveringly for several seconds, his face unreadable, then motioned for Gwyllim and Campbell to follow him into the tent. Inside, the walls were hung in blue and ochre velvet, rich furs on the carpets and draped across the carved camp chairs. Bran crossed to the center of the tent and toyed with the hilt of his dagger, then turned to study the faces of his two captains.

"Well, what do you think? Ought I to go?"

The two exchanged furtive glances before Campbell spoke.

"Begging your pardon, m'lord, but I still don't like it. What can we possibly gain from such a parley, besides a new chance for treachery? Regardless of what this Duke Lionel says, I don't think for a minute that Wencit plans to withdraw. There is no question that he can win if he decides to come down off his mountain; it's just a matter of how many men he'll have to lose in order to do it. And if he uses magic . . ."

"Faithful Campbell," Bran smiled grimly, "ever the gadfly, reminding me of the truths I would rather avoid. Gwyllim?"

Gwyllim shrugged thin shoulders under his blue woolen cloak. "Campbell is right in part, my lord. I think we have known all along that we cannot hold the pass for long, if Wencit decides to come down. I wonder what sort of agreement he hopes to reach? Also, I am inclined to agree with Campbell that it smells like a trap. I hesitate to advise you one way or the other."

Bran ran his fingers across the helmet and mail lying on one of the chairs, let his hand caress the fur draped beneath it.

"Who was the other baron with Lionel—the one who stayed mounted? Do either of you know him?"

"Merritt of Reider, my lord," answered Campbell. "He holds sizeable lands to the northeast, adjoining Tolan. I'm surprised that Wencit would send them on a mission like this, especially if he plans something devious."

"Precisely what I was thinking," Bran said, continuing to stroke the fur absently as he stared at the wall of the tent. "It also occurred to me that this might be Wencit's way of telling us that he *is* serious about this parley. So serious that he would risk a brother-in-law and a powerful ally as hostages to reassure us. Being realistic about my own value, I doubt that Wencit would risk the two out there just to capture or destroy me. If that were all he wanted, there are a dozen less dangerous and less expensive ways to try."

Gwyllim cleared his throat uneasily. "M'lord, have you considered the possibility that Wencit might wish the hostages to do something here in the camp while you are away? If they're Deryni, for example, there is no telling what kind of damage they could do. Perhaps not even anything we could detect until you were safely returned and they were on their way back to their master."

"It's true, m'lord," Campbell agreed. "What's to prevent the hostages from wreaking havoc while you're away? I don't trust them!"

Bran rubbed his hands across his face and stared up at the ceiling for a long moment while he considered what the two had said. Finally he turned with a sigh to face them again.

"I cannot argue with your logic—either of you. But somehow I have the feeling that there is no treachery involved, at least in this particular case. If Lionel and Merritt *are* Deryni, they have had ample time out there to destroy us, if that were their sole intent. And if they are *not* Deryni, they would be foolish to try anything devious, right here in our midst.

"Just to reassure you, though, suppose that I have Cordan prepare a strong sleeping draught to be given to all the contingent who remain behind. If Lionel will agree to this precaution, I think it would be relatively safe for me to proceed to the parley that Wencit requests. After all, their agreement will require no little demonstration of trust on their part as well as ours, do you not agree?"

Gwyllim shook his head doubtfully, then shrugged in resignation. "It's still a risk, sir."

"But a reasonable one, I think—and it may buy us some time. Campbell, find Cordan and see to the potion, will you?

Gwyllim, you'll be riding with me to Cardosa. Help me into my mail."

Minutes later, Bran and Gwyllim stepped from the tent and moved toward the waiting Torenthi emissaries. Bran had donned his mail and a cloak of royal blue over his blue tunic, with his blue eagle device picked out in blue stitchery on the breast of his leather surcoat. Bright mail showed at his throat and below the short sleeves of the surcoat, and an ivory-hilted broadsword hung from a white leather baldric across his chest. Gwyllim followed half a pace behind him, Bran's blue-plumed helmet under his arm and his master's leather riding gloves clutched in his left hand. Bran's golden eyes danced with cunning as he stepped into the sunlight.

"I have decided to accept your king's invitation, my lord," he said easily.

Lionel bowed and controlled a small smile. Merritt and several of the liveried men-at-arms had dismounted during Bran's absence and now stood clustered at Lionel's back.

"However," Bran continued, "there are certain conditions which I must impose before I proceed to Cardosa with your standard-bearer, and I am not certain you will agree to them."

Campbell, a man-at-arms, and a slender man in field surgeon's garb slipped into the group clustered around Bran, and Lionel's eyes darted toward them suspiciously. The surgeon was holding a large earthen drinking vessel with knobbed handles on either side. Merritt stepped closer to Lionel and murmured something in his ear, and Lionel frowned as he returned his attention to Bran.

"Name your conditions, my lord."

"I trust that you will not take offense at my caution, my lord," Bran said with a nod, "but I must be assured that there will be no untoward behavior on the part of you or any of your men while I am away."

"You have been given that assurance, my lord," Lionel said evenly.

Bran lifted a hand and lightly shook his head. "And I honor your word, my lord," Bran replied, "but my men desire further assurance, if I am to be absent. Therefore, in order to guard against treachery while you are here and I am not, I have had my master surgeon prepare a simple sleeping draught, of which you, Lord Merritt, and the remaining guards will partake before I leave. You see, I have no way of knowing your true motives at this point, not being able to see into your minds. You could even be Deryni sorcerers, for all I know. Do you agree to these terms?"

Lionel's face had stiffened as Bran spoke, and he glanced uncomfortably at Merritt and his men before replying. It was obvious that neither he nor Merritt was eager to spend the next hours drugged to senselessness in Bran's camp. Yet, to refuse Bran's terms would be to admit that they did not trust him, and perhaps that Wencit's invitation was not all that it seemed. Lionel obviously had been given his orders, and his tone was cold and formal as he addressed the young earl.

"You will forgive my momentary hesitation, my lord, but we had not anticipated such counter-terms. We understand your caution, of course, and wish to assure you that it was not the intention of His Majesty to bring disaster upon you through magic; if he had so wished, he could have done it without risking our lives. However, you will understand if we, in turn, now exercise a certain caution of our own. Before we may agree to your terms, we must be reasonably convinced that your draught is, indeed, only the sleeping potion you claim."

"I concur, of course," Bran said, motioning his surgeon to approach. "Cordan, who is to test your potion for His Grace?"

Cordan nudged a soldier standing at his side and stepped forward, bowing as the soldier came to attention.

"This is Stephen de Longueville, my lord," he murmured. He held the earthen cup in steady hands, his eyes not leaving Bran's.

"Excellent. My lord duke, is this man acceptable to you?"

Lionel shook his head. "Your surgeon could have prepared him in some special way, my lord. If you meant to poison us, he could have been given an antidote. May I make my own selection?"

"Certainly. I must ask that you not choose one of my officers, since I shall require their services while I am away, but any of the others is acceptable. Feel free to choose whomever you wish."

Lionel handed his helmet to one of his men, then turned on his heel and strode back to the mounted Marley riders still surrounding his own escort. He scanned the men carefully, then stepped to the side of one of the riders and laid his hand on the horse's bridle. The horse tossed its head and snorted.

"This man, my lord. There is no way he could have been prepared in advance. Let him sample the draught you would have us drink."

Bran nodded and gave a curt hand signal, and the man swung down from his horse. As he crossed the grass toward Bran, Lionel followed at his elbow, watching him closely. When the man pulled off his helmet and attempted to hand it to one of his fellows standing in the earl's menie, Lionel interposed and took the helmet himself, passing it on to the man for whom the soldier had intended it. The duke was taking no chances that something could be slipped to his test subject without his knowledge.

Motioning Merritt to guard the man, Lionel crossed to Bran and took the earthen cup from Cordan. His black eyes measured Bran for a long moment as he held the cup between them; irritation hinted in his lean face. Then he raised the cup slightly in salute and strode back to where Merritt and the soldier waited. One of Lionel's men dismounted and took the cup to inspect it, sniffing at the contents suspiciously. Only then was Bran's soldier brought closer to place his hands on the vessel. Lionel and Merritt stationed themselves on either side of the man to watch,

Lionel casting a suspicious glance at Bran as they prepared to administer the test.

"What is the required dosage?"

"A goodly swallow is sufficient, my lord," Cordan replied. "The drug is potent and acts very quickly."

"Indeed," Lionel murmured, returning his attention to the man and the cup. "Very well, my good fellow. Drink deep if you dare. Your commander is said to be a man of his word. If he is, you shall awaken later, no worse for the wear. Drink up."

The man, guided by the cupbearer, brought the vessel to his lips and took a mouthful, raising his eyebrows at the obviously pleasant flavor, then glanced at Lionel and swallowed. He had time to lick his lips once in appreciation— Cordan was known for his use of fine wines in his potions. Then he reeled and would have fallen, had not Lionel and Merritt caught him under the elbows and eased him down. By the time he reached the ground, the man was fast asleep, and no amount of shaking or calling would rouse him.

Lionel's cupbearer passed the cup to Merritt and examined the man, peering under the slack eyelids and locating a strong pulse, then nodded reluctantly. Lionel got slowly to his feet and gazed across at Bran, his face grim but resigned.

"It appears that your master surgeon is, indeed, accomplished, my lord. Of course, on the basis of what we have just seen, we cannot rule out a longer-term poison, or the possibility that you might administer something else while we slept, or even murder us where we lay. But, then, life is full of gambles, is it not? And His Majesty will be expecting either your return or mine. Even I am reluctant to keep him waiting."

"Then you will accept my terms?"

"So it seems." Lionel bowed. "I trust, however, that we shall be permitted to sleep somewhere other than on the ground, like your trusting friend." He glanced down at the sleeping guard with a sardonic smile. "When we do return to Cardosa, His Majesty would be most distressed, were he to learn that my colleagues had been obliged to sleep in the dirt."

Bran bowed slightly and held back the flap of his tent, returning Lionel's smile. "Come, then; you shall sleep in my own pavilion. I would not have it said that Eastmarch men do not know how to accommodate noble company."

As Bran and his party stood aside, Lionel inclined his head and then signaled the rest of his contingent to dismount, led them into the tent. He surveyed the rich appointments in appreciation as he removed his gloves, exchanging resigned glances with Merritt and a few of his comrades, then selected the most comfortable of the several chairs in the space and sat down.

Taking his helmet back, he laid it on the floor at his feet and stashed his gloves inside, then propped his booted legs on a leather footstool and sat back in preparation. His long black hair gleamed in the glow of the light that streamed through the open entryway, and he toyed with the hilt of the flame-bladed dagger thrust through his sash as his men arranged themselves on the furs at his feet.

Merritt took the chair beside Lionel's, his homely face tense and apprehensive, and the man with the cup stood uneasily beside the tent's center pole. As Bran and Gwyllim entered the shelter of the tent, the Torenthi standard-bearer moved into the doorway to watch, his face whiter than the white standard he still bore. Only he and the cupbearer could be certain they would return to Cardosa, once the rest drank the cup.

Lionel studied the five men ranged trustingly at his feet, then signed for the cupbearer to go to each of them in turn. Each man kept his eyes locked on Lionel's as he sipped from the cup. The first of them slumped to a supine position as the cup came to Merritt. The cupbearer paused in alarm as two more passed out, and Merritt half-rose from his chair; but Lionel shook his head slightly and signaled for Merritt to drink.

With a resigned sigh, Merritt obeyed, soon nodding off in his chair as another of the men on the floor succumbed. When all were still, a few of them snoring, the cupbearer knelt at Lionel's knee and offered up the cup in trembling hands, unable to meet his lord's eyes. Lionel's look was almost tender as he took the cup and turned it idly in his long fingers.

"They are fine men, my lord Bran," he said softly, glancing up at Bran with hooded eyes. "They have trusted me with their very lives, and I have gambled with those lives held in trust. If you, through any action, cause me to be forsworn—if any harm should come to any man here—I swear that I will avenge them even from the grave. Do you understand me?"

"I have given you my word, sir," Bran said neutrally. "I have said that no harm would befall you or them. If your master's intentions are as honorable, you need have no cause for fear."

"I do not fear, my lord; I warn," Lionel said softly. "See that you keep your word."

With a glance at the cupbearer, he raised the cup in salute and murmured, *"C'raint!"* Then he drank from the cup and gave it back into the cupbearer's hands. As he sat back in the chair, he shivered slightly, as though against a sudden chill, though it was warm enough in the tent. Then he laid his head against the back of the chair and slipped into unconsciousness. The cupbearer set the cup on the carpet beside him and felt for his master's pulse; then, satisfied that there was nothing more he could do, he rose shakily to his feet and made a curt bow toward Bran Coris.

"If you are ready to fulfill your part of the agreement, my lord, we should be on our way. We have a difficult ride ahead of us, a large part of it through icy water. His Majesty will be waiting."

"Of course," Bran murmured, scanning the sleeping hostages with admiration as he donned his helmet. He certainly could not fault their discipline.

"Look after them, Campbell," he said, pulling on gloves and moving toward the entrance to the tent. "Wencit will want them back in good health, and we would not wish to disappoint him."

CHAPTER FOUR

"And I will give thee the treasures of darkness,
and hidden riches of secret places."

ISAIAH 45:3

THE walled city of Cardosa lies nearly a mile above the Eastmarch plain, on a high plateau of sheer-faced rock. It has
been the seat of earls and dukes and, sometimes, of kings,
and it is guarded west and east by the treacherous Cardosa
Pass, the major passage through the Rheljan Mountains.

Late each autumn, toward the end of November, the
snows sweep in from the great northern sea, cutting off the
city and burying the pass in snow. This condition persists
well into March, until long after winter has fled the rest of
the area. Then the melting snow turns the Cardosa Pass into
a raging cataract for the next three months.

But the thaw is not uniform, even in the pass. Because of
the mountains' run-off pattern, the eastern approach is ne-
gotiable weeks before the west: a quirk that has been a major contributing factor in the city's changing ownership over
the years. It was this that enabled Wencit of Torenth to
capture the winter-hungry city without opposition—high
Cardosa, depleted by the previous summer's dispute and exhausted by the snows, which could not wait for relief troops

and supplies from royal Gwynedd. Wencit could supply these things; and so Cardosa surrendered.

Thus it was that as Bran Coris and his nervous escorts made the final, wet approach to the city's gates, the city's new ruler relaxed at leisure in the apartment he had chosen in the city's state house and prepared to greet his reluctant guest.

Wencit of Torenth grimaced as he struggled with the fastening of his doublet's high collar, craning his neck as he made the final adjustment. At a discreet knock at the door, he smoothed the gold-encrusted velvet over his chest with an impatient gesture and thrust a jeweled dagger into his sash. The ice-blue eyes registered a hint of mild annoyance as he glanced in that direction.

"Come."

Almost immediately, a tall, gangling young man in his mid-twenties stepped through the doorway and bowed. Like most members of the royal household, Garon wore the brilliant blue-violet livery of Wencit's personal service, with the leaping black hart of Furstán emblazoned over the left breast in a white circle, along with a flat-linked chain of office. His expression was one of acute interest and anticipation as he watched his royal master begin rolling up documents from the writing table by the window and slipping them into leather storage tubes. When he spoke, his voice was low and cultured.

"Sire, the Earl of Marley is here. Shall I send him in?"

Wencit gave a curt nod as he finished storing the last of the documents, and Garon withdrew without further words. As the door closed, Wencit began pacing the heavily carpeted floor with nervous energy, hands clasped behind his back.

Wencit of Torenth was a tall, thin, almost angular man in his late forties, with hair of a brilliant rust-red, untouched by gray, and pale, almost colorless eyes. Wide, bushy sideburns and a sweeping moustache of the same fiery red emphasized the high cheekbones, the triangular shape of the face. When he moved, it was with an easy grace not usually associated with a man of his size and stature.

The overall effect had led his enemies, who were many, to compare him to a fox—that is, when they were not making other, less complimentary comparisons. For Wencit was a full Deryni sorcerer of the ancient breed, his lineage descending from a family that had stayed in power in the east even through the Restoration and the Deryni persecutions that had followed. In many respects, Wencit *was* a fox. Of a certainty, there was no doubt that, when he chose, Wencit of Torenth could be as cunning, cruel, and dangerous as any member of the vulpine race.

But Wencit was well aware of his effect upon most humans, and knew how to downplay the more frightening aspects of his lineage when it suited him. Accordingly, he had chosen the day's attire with particular attention to detail. His fine doublet and hose were of the same shade of russet velvet and silk as his hair, the monocolor effect heightened rather than broken by the rich gold embroidery of his doublet, the glow of golden topaz at throat and ears and hands. An amber mantle of heavy, gold-embroidered silk spilled from his shoulders, rustling faintly as he moved, and a coronet set with tawny yellow gems rested on the oak table where he had been working, mute reminder of the rank and importance of the man entitled to wear it.

But Wencit made no move to take up the crown and complete his regal image, for Bran Coris was not his subject. Nor was the impending meeting in any way official, at least in any ordinary sense—which, perhaps, was fitting, because there was little that was ordinary about Wencit of Torenth, either.

After another discreet knock at the door, Garon again stepped just inside the room and bowed. Behind him in the doorway stood a youngish man of medium height and build, clad in a damp leather surcoat and mail and a soggy blue cloak. The plumes on the helmet under the newcomer's arm were drenched and bedraggled looking, the gloves dark with damp. The man himself looked both puzzled and wary.

"Sire," Garon murmured, "the Earl of Marley."

"Do come in, my lord," Wencit acknowledged, gesturing toward the rest of the room with a flourish. "I must apologize for your obviously wet ride up the pass, but I fear that even Deryni cannot control the vagaries of weather. Garon, take the earl's cloak and bring him a dry one from my wardrobe, if you please."

"Very good, Sire."

As Bran warily entered the room, Garon took the sodden cloak from his shoulders and spread it on a nearby chair, then disappeared through a side door, emerging seconds later to lay a fur-lined cloak of mossy green velvet around the visitor's shoulders. Then, after fastening the clasp at Bran's throat, he took his helmet and bowed himself out of the room.

Still uneasy, Bran clutched the cloak around him, grateful for the favor in his chilled condition, but he did not take his eyes from his host. Wencit smiled disarmingly and put on one of his more reassuring demeanors as he gestured casually toward a chair by the heavy table, nearer the fire.

"Sit down, please. We need not stand on ceremony."

Bran eyed Wencit and the chair suspiciously for a moment, then frowned anew as Wencit crossed to the fireplace and began tinkering with something Bran could not see.

"Forgive me if I seem unappreciative, my lord, but I fail to see what we can have to say to one another. You are surely aware that I am the junior of the three commanders ranged along the Rheljan Mountains to oppose you. Any arrangement that you and I might reach would not be binding on my colleagues or on Gwynedd."

"I never thought it might," Wencit said easily. He crossed to the table with a small pot of steaming liquid from which he filled two fragile porcelain cups. Then he took the nearer of the two chairs and gestured once more for Bran to be seated.

"Won't you join me for a cup of darja tea? It is brewed from the leaves and flowers of a lovely bush which grows here in your Rheljan Mountains. I think you will enjoy it, especially as cold and damp as you must be."

Bran moved nearer the table and picked up a cup to inspect it, a wry smile twitching at his lips as he returned his gaze to Wencit.

"You play the perfect host, sir, but I think not. The hostages you sent did me the honor of drinking with me," he glanced lightly at the steaming cup, "but then, I told them what was in the cup they drank."

"Indeed?" Wencit's fair brows lifted. And though the voice was gentle and cultured still, it was suddenly tinged with steel. "I am led to surmise that it was not simple wine or tea which passed their lips; and yet, you would hardly have been so foolish as to harm them and then boast of it to me in my own house. Nonetheless, you have piqued my curiosity, if that was your intention. What did you give them?"

Bran sat down, the cup still in his fingers, but set it gently on the table in front of him. "You will appreciate that I had no way of knowing whether your emissaries might be Deryni, instructed to work mischief in my camp while I exchanged pleasantries with you. So I had my master surgeon prepare a simple sleeping draught for them. Since the gentlemen assured me that they were not Deryni, and did not intend me mischief, I doubt not that they will be safe, if somewhat drowsy, when I return. It is no more precaution than you yourself might have taken, had you been in my place."

Wencit put down his cup and sat back in his chair, smoothing his moustache to cover a smile. Even when he picked up his cup to sip again, a trace of the smile lingered on his lips.

"Well played, Earl of Marley. I admire both prudence and daring in those with whom I wish to deal. However, allow me to reassure you that your cup holds no such additive. You may drink without fear. You have my word on it."

"Your word, Sire?" Bran ran a gloved fingertip around the rim of the cup in front of him and glanced down at it, then gently pushed it a few inches away. "Forgive me if I seem rude, my lord, but you've not yet given me a satisfactory reason for this parley. I cannot help wondering what the King of Torenth and a rather minor lord of Gwynedd have in common."

Wencit shrugged and smiled again as he studied his guest. "On the contrary, my young friend, I think the notion at least bears further exploration. If, once you have heard me out, you have no interest in what I have to say, nothing is lost except a little of our time. On the other hand—well, perhaps we shall discover that we may have more in common than you think. I feel confident that we will discover a number of areas of mutual interest, if once we put our minds to it."

"Indeed," Bran replied, a trifle incredulously. "Perhaps you would care to be more specific. I can think of a number of things you might do for me, or for any other man you chose to favor. But damn me if I can think of a single thing I have that you could want."

"Must I want something?" Smiling faintly, Wencit made a bridge of his fingers and studied his guest through shrewd fox-eyes. Bran, for his part, sat back in his chair and returned Wencit's gaze unflinchingly, a gloved right hand resting patiently under his chin, silent. After a moment, Wencit nodded.

"Very good. You know how to wait. I admire that in a man, especially a human." He studied Bran for several seconds more, then continued.

"Very well, Bran Coris Earl of Marley. You are correct, in a way; I do want something from you. I shall exert no undue coercion to bend you to my will; I do not coerce those with whom I hope to be friends. On the other hand, you could expect to be handsomely compensated for any cooperation that you might render. Tell me: what do you think of my new city?"

"I care little for your use of the possessive," Bran observed dryly. "The city belongs to King Kelson, despite its current occupation. Come to the point."

"Now, don't belie my first impression," the sorcerer chided. "I have my reasons for progressing slowly. And I shall disregard your quip regarding my city. Local politics do not interest me at the moment. I am thinking in far broader terms."

"So I have been informed," Bran replied. "However, if you contemplate further expansion to the west, I would suggest that you reconsider. Granted, my small army could not resist you for long. But the loss of life would be high on your side as well. The men of Marley do not sell their lives cheaply."

"Hold your tongue!" Wencit snapped. "If I wished, I could crush you and your army like insects, and you know it!" He reached out to touch his finger to each of the points of the coronet in turn, watching Bran like a cat as he tempered his next words. "But fighting with your army was not what I had in mind—at least not in the sense you are thinking. Alongside, more like. Actually, I had it in mind to move a little south of you, into Corwyn and Carthmoor and then the rest of Gwynedd. I thought you might be interested in . . . oh, the northern regions: Claibourne and the Kheldish Riding, for a start. There are ways I could help you accomplish this."

"You would have me turn against my allies?" Bran shook his head. "I think it unlikely, sir. Besides, why should you wish to give an enemy two of the richest provinces in the Eleven Kingdoms? It makes me wonder what I am not being told about your little plan."

"Ah, but I do not count you as my enemy," Wencit replied. "For the present, let us merely say that I have been watching your progress for some time, and that I believe it might be . . . reassuring to have a man of your caliber holding the northern-most provinces. Of course, there would be a dukedom in it for you, as well as other . . . considerations."

" 'Considerations?' " Though Bran's tone was still suspicious, it was evident that he was becoming intrigued. A spark of calculating greed had kindled behind the honey-colored eyes. Wencit chuckled softly.

"So, you *are* interested. I was beginning to fear that you could not be corrupted."

"You are speaking of treason, sir. Even if I were to agree, what makes you think I could be trusted?"

"You are not without your own kind of honor," Wencit observed. "And as for treason—ah, that is such a weary term. I know for a fact that you have opposed Alaric Morgan in the past—and King Kelson, too, for that matter."

"Morgan and I have had our differences," Bran allowed. "But I have always been loyal to my king. As you say, I am not without my own kind of honor. Besides, I would hardly consider myself in the same league with our good Deryni duke—or Kelson, either, for that matter."

"Kelson is a mere boy." Wencit said evenly. "A boy with power, yes. But still only a boy. And Morgan is a Deryni half-breed, and a traitor to his race."

" 'Ah, traitor is such a weary term,' " Bran quoted without a flicker of emotion.

Wencit measured the younger man through pale, narrowed eyes, then stood abruptly, though he let his features soften. When Bran made as though to rise as well, Wencit waved him back and went to a small, carved chest on a shelf across the room. Lifting its lid, he withdrew something bright and sparkling, which he enclosed in his left hand before closing the chest and returning to his chair. Bran watched with suspicion but also curiosity.

"Well, well," Wencit said dryly. He propped his elbows on the carved arms of the chair and leaned back, his hands clasped before him. "Now that we have determined that you possess a ready wit, suppose you tell me how you feel about Deryni."

Somewhat taken aback by the question, Bran could only stare blankly at Wencit for several seconds.

"In general, or in particular?" he finally replied.

"In general, first." Wencit shifted the object between his palms back and forth from one hand to the other without allowing Bran to see it. "For example, your Church Militant ruled in 917, at the Council of Ramos, that the use of Deryni magic is anathema and sacrilegious. The Duchy of Corwyn is now under curial Interdict because its duke, an acknowledged Deryni, was excommunicated for using his magic and now refuses to surrender himself to the judgment of that Curia. For that, I cannot say I blame him.

"However, if you yourself entertain any religious or moral scruples about spellbinding, it would be wise to mention them now, before we proceed much farther. You cannot fail to be aware that I am very much a practicing sorcerer. I expect my allies to be able to function within that framework. Your Curia would not understand. Does that bother you?"

Bran's expression remained guarded, but it was evident that his interrogator had struck a responsive chord. In addition, he was finding it difficult to restrain his curiosity about the object in Wencit's hands. Suddenly aware that his gaze had turned to the hands again, he brought his attention back to Wencit with a conscious effort.

"I am hardly your ally, sir, and I do not fear the Gwynedd Curia," he answered carefully. "As for magic, the question is academic. Magic is a means of power—other people's power—nothing more. I have had no personal contact with it."

"Would you like to?"

The color drained from Bran's face. "I—I beg your pardon, sir?"

"Would you like to deal with magic?" Wencit repeated. "Or would it make you uncomfortable to use it yourself?"

Bran licked at lips suddenly gone dry, but he answered without hesitation. "Since I am human, and not of a family possessing Deryni power, I have never had the opportunity to find out. If I *were* given the opportunity, though—no, I don't think it would bother me in the least. And I don't believe in Hell."

"Nor do I." Wencit smiled. "Suppose, then, that I were to tell you that you are, in fact, Deryni—at least in part. And that I could prove it."

Bran's golden eyes went wide and his jaw dropped. Totally unprepared for this development, he was not even aware that in that moment he had begun shifting from adversary into vassal.

"The possibility frightens you, doesn't it?" Wencit continued in the same conversational tone. "Close your mouth, Bran. You're gaping."

Bran obeyed instantly, struggling to regain his composure. Swallowing only with difficulty, he managed to murmur, "The reaction you saw was surprise, not fright, my lord. You—you aren't jesting with me, are you?"

"Suppose we find out?" Wencit said, smiling inwardly as he caught the changed form of address.

"My lord?"

"Whether or not you are part Deryni," Wencit answered easily. "If you are, it will make it that much easier to give you the power necessary to be an effective ally. And if you are not . . ."

"If I am not?" Bran repeated in a low tone.

"I think we need not worry about that possibility yet," Wencit said.

He sat forward slightly and opened his hand. In his palm lay a large amber crystal about the size of a walnut, attached to a fine golden chain. It was roughly polished, not faceted, and seemed to glow from within. Wencit grasped the chain delicately between thumb and forefinger and drew it away from the stone, but he allowed the crystal itself to remain resting in the palm of his hand. As Bran stared at the crystal, he became certain that it was glowing.

"This is a *shiral* crystal," Wencit murmured softly. "Such crystals have long been known among those of my kind for their sensitivity to the psychic energies associated with the

Deryni bloodline. You can see that, as I hold it in my hand, it seems to glow. Only a small amount of concentration is necessary to produce this response, if one is of the Deryni." He glanced mildly at Bran. "Take off your glove."

Bran hesitated for but an instant, then wet his lips nervously and stripped off his right glove. As Wencit extended the crystal at the end of its golden chain, Bran held out his bare hand, flinched as its cool mass came to rest in his palm. As Wencit released the golden chain to let it dangle over Bran's fingers, the light in the crystal died. Alarmed, Bran looked up at Wencit, the unspoken question in his eyes.

"You needn't concern yourself with that," Wencit said. "For now, I ask you to simply close your eyes and concentrate on the crystal. Imagine that the heat from your hand is warming the crystal, making it glow. Picture light being absorbed into the crystal and radiating outward. Just do as I ask," he urged, at Bran's obvious nervousness. "Just close your eyes and relax."

As Bran obeyed, closed eyelids trembling, Wencit turned his attention to the *shiral* crystal lying inert in his subject's hand. When nothing happened for several seconds, Wencit's brow creased in a frown; but then he cupped his hands over the crystal to shade it, not touching it or Bran's hands—and was rewarded with a faint glimmer deep in the crystal's heart. Pursing his lips thoughtfully, Wencit lightly brushed Bran's hand with one hand, while the other closed on the dangling chain and withdrew the crystal. The younger man started and opened his eyes just in time to glimpse the crystal still glowing as the older man twirled the chain idly between thumb and fingertips.

"It—it worked," Bran whispered in awe.

"It did—though it appears that you are not true Deryni after all." Wencit noted the stricken look on Bran's face and smiled, knowing he now owned the man. "But you needn't worry. You have the potential to assume full powers, as did the humans of old when they accomplished the Restoration. That is, perhaps, better in many ways, for you would have been obliged to *learn* to use native Deryni powers. The assumed ones come full-blown and ready to deploy."

"Which means?"

Wencit stood casually and stretched, the *shiral* crystal dangling from its chain in his hand. "Which means that the next step is to Mind-See you, to evaluate your potential and to set up the conditions under which I can bestow power on you. You needn't fret yourself with the details. The kings of Gwynedd have been doing it successfully for generations, so there is no danger. I trust that you are prepared to stay the night."

"I hadn't planned to, but—"

"But under the circumstances, you will," Wencit finished for him, smiling faintly. He came around to the other side of the table and sat easily on the edge, to Bran's left. "I shall even send your captain back to reassure your men. 'Tis a pity that you put my emissaries out of commission. Duke Lionel, my brother-in-law, possesses assumed Deryni powers similar to those you will shortly receive. I could have relayed the information through him, had you not dosed him with that sleeping potion. As it is, he will be groggy and testy and utterly impossible to live with for several days, until the effects wear off completely. Still, that is sometimes the price one must pay for progress, and he knows it. Sit back and relax, please."

"Wh-what are you going to do?" Bran murmured, apprehensive, for he had totally lost the sorcerer's line of logic in his bewilderment.

"I told you: Mind-See." Wencit twisted the golden chain so that the *shiral* crystal spun between him and Bran. "Now, I desire your assistance in this. Relax and do not resist me, or you will be left with a beastly headache when we're done. Your cooperation will make it easier for both of us."

Bran squirmed in his chair, uneasy, looking as though he wanted to protest or even bolt. Wencit frowned, and his face went stern, his voice cold.

"Listen to me, Earl of Marley. If we are to be allies, you

must begin trusting me sometime. This is the time. Do not make me force you."

Bran took a deep breath and exhaled softly, further defiance deflating. "I'm sorry. What am I to do?"

Wencit's visage softened and he set the crystal spinning again, his other hand firmly pushing Bran's shoulders back in the chair.

"Just relax and trust me. You have nothing to fear. Take another deep breath and let it out. Watch the crystal. Watch it spin and listen to the sound of my voice. As you watch the crystal spinning, spinning, your eyelids begin to grow heavy—so heavy that you cannot keep your eyes open. Let them close. And as the feeling of lethargy and calm comes over you, accept it. Take it in. Let it envelop and enfold you. Let your mind go blank and picture, if you will, a dark room of velvet night, with a dark door in the dark wall. And then imagine that dark door slowly opening, and cool darkness beyond. . . ."

Bran's eyes had closed, his breathing slowed, and Wencit lowered the crystal as his voice droned on. His words became fewer and farther apart as his subject relaxed. Then he reached out and touched the man's eyelids with thumb and forefinger, murmured the words of magic that sealed the trance. He was silent for a long moment, his own coldly glowing eyes hooded and distant. Then he lowered his hand and spoke softly.

"Look at me now, Bran Coris."

Bran's eyes fluttered open and he looked around, remembering with a start just what it was that was supposed to have happened. When he saw that Wencit had not moved, that his benevolent expression was unchanged, he willed himself to relax and assess the situation as best he could. This time, as he looked up at the sorcerer king, he felt no apprehension. He sensed instead that some sort of unforeseen rapport had been formed; that though the man before him now knew all there was to know about Bran Coris Earl of Marley, it did not matter.

It was not a feeling of bondage; Bran would have chafed under that. Nor would Wencit of Torenth have desired that in one who was to be his ally. It was more a sense of comprehension, even fulfillment; a satisfying and even reassuring feeling, not at all repelling, as a part of him had feared it might be. Though his mind still reeled at the raw power of what had been done to him, he sensed that new knowledge had been imparted, could he but recall it; a subtle scent of empowerment, too tenuous to be assessed as yet. He decided that he liked what he felt.

His attention snapped back to reality as Wencit stood up.

"You did very well," the sorcerer remarked, reaching behind Bran to tug on a brocaded bell cord. "We shall work well together, you and I. When I send for you in the morning, we shall proceed in greater depth,"

"Why not now?" Bran asked, lurching to his feet and staggering, much to his surprise.

Unconcerned, Wencit reached out to steady him. "Because of that, my impatient young friend. Magic is very tiring for the uninitiated, and you have had a full dose for today. In a very little while, you shall find yourself unable to keep your feet for another instant. I shouldn't want Garon to have to carry you to your quarters."

Bran put a dazed hand to his forehead. "But, I—"

"Not another word," Wencit said firmly, stepping back a pace. The door opened behind him and Garon entered, but Wencit did not look in his direction, preferring instead to watch Bran's every move as the young lord tried to orient himself.

"Garon, please take Lord Bran to guest quarters and put him to bed," Wencit said softly. "He is very tired after his long journey. See that his men are provided for, and that his captain is permitted to return to camp to reassure his army."

"Certainly, Sire. This way, if you please, my lord."

As Garon led the bewildered Bran Coris to the door, Wencit watched thoughtfully. Then, when the door had closed behind them, he strolled to the door in a leisurely fashion and shot home the bolt. As he returned to sit at the oak table, he addressed the empty air in a conversational tone.

"Well, Rhydon, what did you think?"

At his words, a narrow panel in the wall opposite opened briefly to admit a tall, dark man in blue. The panel closed silently behind him as he crossed nonchalantly to the chair recently vacated by Bran and leaned with both hands against the high, carved back.

"What did you think?" Wencit repeated, lounging back in his chair to study his colleague.

Rhydon shrugged noncommittally. "Your performance was flawless, as usual. What more can I say?" The tone was light, but the pale gray eyes beneath the hawk visage mirrored more than the spoken words.

Wencit knew that look and nodded. He placed the *shiral* crystal on the table beside the golden coronet and carefully adjusted the chain, then looked up shrewdly at Rhydon once more.

"You are concerned about Bran Coris. Why? You surely do not think he presents a danger to us?"

Rhydon shrugged again. "Call it native cynicism—I cannot say. He seems safe enough. But you know how unpredictable humans can be. Look at Kelson Haldane."

"He is half-Deryni."

"So is Morgan. So is McLain. Forgive me if I sound skeptical, but perhaps you have not been aware of the Camberian Council's attention to that fact. Morgan and McLain, as supposed half-Deryni, are probably the two most unpredictable men in the Eleven Kingdoms right now. They keep doing things they should not be able to do. And that I *know* you are aware of." He came around and sat in the other chair, then picked up Bran's untouched cup of darja and drained it at a single draught. Wencit snorted derisively.

Rhydon of Eastmarch was no longer a handsome man. A saber scar slashing from the bridge of his nose to the right-hand corner of his mouth had forever rendered that an impossibility. But he was a striking man. Dark hair graying at the temples and a luxuriant salt-and-pepper moustache framed a lean, oval face; a small beard softened the pointed chin. The mouth was full and wide but generally set in a firm line, with hints of predatory cruelty. In all, an almost sinister aura—one that the rapier mind behind the face relished and cultivated. A Deryni lord of the first magnitude was Rhydon of Eastmarch; a man in every way Wencit's equal and complement; a man never to be trifled with.

He and Wencit gazed across the table for a long moment before Wencit recalled himself to matters at hand.

"Very well," he said, abruptly straightening and pulling several of the leather document tubes toward him. "Do you wish to observe Bran's initiation tomorrow, or have I convinced you that he is no longer dangerous? To us, at least."

"I am not totally convinced that any human is without danger," Rhydon quipped, "but no matter. I leave him to your judgment." He rubbed a slender forefinger down the bridge of his nose in an automatic gesture, unconsciously following the long scar that lost itself in the thick moustache. "Are those our battle plans?"

Wencit pulled a map from one of the tubes and spread it on the table. "Yes, and the situation improves hourly. With Bran's defection about to split Kelson's strength along the border, we can cut off northern Gwynedd. To the south, Jared of Cassan and his army should be easy picking when we shift south in a few days."

"What about Kelson?" Rhydon asked. "When he finds out what you plan, he will have the entire royal army breathing down our necks."

Wencit shook his head. "Kelson will not know. I am counting on poor communication and difficult travel conditions at this time of year to keep him ignorant of our plans until it is too late to do anything. Besides, the civil and religious turmoil in Corwyn should keep him amply occupied until we are ready to take him."

"Do you anticipate trouble when we do?"

"From Kelson?" Wencit shook his head and smiled. "I hardly think so. Despite what the statutes say about the legal age of kings, Kelson at fourteen is still a boy, half-Deryni or no. And you must admit that being half-Deryni has not particularly helped our ambitious princeling lately. In fact, increasing numbers of his loyal subjects are beginning to wonder if it is a good thing at all, to have a boy-king whose blood harks back to the blasphemous and wicked Deryni race."

"Your carefully placed rumors, of course, have had nothing at all to do with this shift of confidence."

"How could you think such a thing?"

Rhydon chuckled mirthlessly at his companion's feigned look of mild affront, and crossed elegantly booted legs. "Then, tell me what you have planned for the wonder-prince, my lord king. How may I assist you further?"

"Rid me of Morgan and McLain," Wencit replied, at once deadly serious. "As long as they stand beside Kelson, excommunicate or not, they stand a threat to us, both by the aid they can give him and by the powers they personally wield. Since we cannot predict their strength or their influence, we have no choice but to eliminate them. But it must be done legally. I want no trouble with the Council."

"Legally?" Rhydon raised a skeptical eyebrow. "I am not certain that is possible. As half-breeds, Morgan and McLain are immune to arcane challenge by any other full Deryni. And the chances of having them legally executed by secular or ecclesiastical authorities are so remote as to be almost nonexistent. You know they are under Kelson's personal protection."

Wencit picked up a thin stylus and tapped it absently against his teeth, then turned to gaze thoughtfully out the window. "Yes, but there may be another way, one that the Council could not possibly fault. In fact, the Council itself might be the instrument of their destruction."

Rhydon straightened attentively. "Do elaborate."

"Suppose the Council were to declare Morgan and McLain fair game for arcane challenge? Suppose their immunity were taken away?"

"On what grounds?"

"On the grounds that the two of them exhibit full Deryni powers at times," Wencit said with a sly smile. "They have, you know."

"I see," Rhydon murmured. "And you wish me to go to the Council and ask them to entertain the motion? You know that is out of the question."

"Oh, not you, personally. I know how you feel about the Council. Ask Thorne Hagen to do it. He owes me several favors."

Rhydon hissed derisively.

"No, I mean it. Tell him, if you like, that this is not a request but a direct order from me. I think he'll cooperate."

Rhydon chuckled, shaking his head, then stood and straightened his sleeves with a flourish. "He has little choice, when you put it that way. Very well, I shall see to it." He glanced around and rubbed his hands together in anticipation. "Is there anything else you require of me before I go? Perhaps a minor miracle or two? The granting of your heart's desire?"

With the last word, he extended his hands and made a slow pass in the air before him, murmuring a few low syllables under his breath. As he completed the movement, a full, hooded cloak of softest deerskin appeared from nowhere to settle around his shoulders in a whisper of indigo leather. Wencit had taken an incredulous pose with hands on hips as his colleague performed the spell, and shook his head in consternation as Rhydon fastened the clasp.

"If you are quite finished playing with your powers, the one request will be enough, thank you. And now, I'll thank you to be on your way and let me work. Some of us must, you know."

"Ah, I am wounded beyond mending," Rhydon said dryly.

"However, since you request it, I shall go to see your good friend Thorne Hagen. Then I shall return to inspect this Bran Coris creature with whom you seem so enraptured. Perhaps there is some merit in him after all—though I doubt it. Perhaps I shall even endeavor to assess the danger for you: the danger you are convinced does not exist."

"Do, by all means."

Rhydon left in a swirl of indigo leather, and when he was gone Wencit returned to his maps, poring over the red and blue and green lines that outlined his strategy. The ice-pale eyes glittered with power as his fingers roamed the creamy parchment, new tension in the set of his shoulders as he planned and schemed.

"One ruler must unite the Eleven Kingdoms," he murmured to himself as he traced the lines of advance. "One ruler over all the Eleven Kingdoms. And it shall not be the boy-king who sits on the throne at Rhemuth!"

CHAPTER FIVE

"Behold the great priest, who in his days pleased God."

ECCLESIASTICUS 44:16, 20

EARLY in the evening of that same day, two others discussed the fate of the renegade Deryni. The men were prelates, self-exiled members of that same Gwynedd Curia mentioned by Wencit with such derision earlier in the day. These same prelates had been largely responsible for the schism that now split Gwynedd's clergy along diverging lines.

Thomas Cardiel, in whose private chapel the two spoke, had never been regarded as a likely candidate for rebellion. Incumbent of the prestigious See of Dhassa for nearly half a decade, and only a year past his fortieth birthday, he had never expected to become a leader in the events that had taken place two months before. When elected to the episcopate, he had been a seasoned if youthful cleric of steady disposition and unimpeachable loyalty to the Church he served, eminently suited for the neutral role traditionally expected of the Bishop of Dhassa.

Nor had his colleague, Denis Arilan, ever dreamed where the convocation of two months prior might lead. At thirty-eight, Gwynedd's youngest bishop had begun to carve out an imposing niche for himself from the time he first entered seminary. But now, unless events changed dramatically for the better, neither he nor Cardiel was likely to have much of a career beyond this point. Indeed, they would be fortunate to survive the coming weeks.

From the perspective of most of their more senior colleagues, the sins of Cardiel and Arilan were great, for they and four of their fellow bishops had defied the Curia of Gwynedd in open synod, declaring their intention to split the Curia if the contemplated Interdict of Corwyn was not abandoned.

But the Interdict had not been abandoned. Archbishop Loris, having already decided to force the issue through, had called the bluff of the Six. Now Gwynedd's loyalties were divided between two rival curias: the Six in Dhassa, who had expelled Loris and his followers from the city's gates; and the ten others siding with the archbishop, who had withdrawn to Morgan's captured capital at Coroth, who sided with the rebel Warin de Grey and claimed to retain the true authority of the Church. Reconciliation, if it could be achieved at all, would not be easily won.

Focused and intent, Bishop Cardiel paced back and forth before the altar rail of the tiny chapel, reading and re-reading a sheet of creased parchment. He shook his steel-gray head uncomprehendingly as his eyes scanned the text, releasing a perplexed sigh as he skipped back to the top of the page. His companion, Denis Arilan, sat seemingly at ease as he watched from a front pew, one arm stretched along its back, though his own tension was betrayed by the incessant drumming of his fingertips on the wood.

Cardiel shook his head and rubbed a hand across his chin, sighing yet again. A dark amethyst winked on his right hand as it caught the dim candlelight.

"This just does not make sense, Denis," he said, looking up. "How could Corwyners have turned on Prince Nigel, of all people? Has this taint that has touched Kelson also stained his uncle? Nigel is no Deryni."

Arilan stopped his finger-drumming long enough to gesture helplessly, then realized what he had been doing and did not resume. He, too, had been chagrined at the news of the rout at Jennan Vale two days earlier, but his keen mind was already examining all the known aspects of the situation, trying to piece together some plan of action. Running a restless hand across his dark hair, he swept off his violet silk skullcap, which he fingered briefly before tossing it onto the bench beside him. Violet glittered on his hand and on his heavy silver pectoral cross as he folded his arms across his chest.

"Perhaps we have been in error, holding our army here at Dhassa," he said finally. "Perhaps we should have gone to Kelson's aid months ago, when this thing first happened. Or perhaps our duty lies at Coroth, to soothe the ruffled feathers of the archbishops. Until there is reconciliation with them, there can be no true peace in Corwyn." He glanced down at his cross before continuing in a lower voice.

"Ah, Thomas, we have trained our people well, we shepherd-bishops of Gwynedd. When the thunder of anathema rumbles, the sheep obey—even if the anathema is ill-advised, and the sheep badly led, and those against whom the anathema is threatened are innocent of the charges levied against them."

"Then you think that Morgan and McLain are innocent?" Cardiel asked.

Arilan shook his head as he studied the toe of a velvet slipper protruding from beneath his cassock. "No. They are technically guilty. There is no question of that. Saint Torin's *was* burned. Men *were* killed. And Morgan and Duncan *are* Deryni."

"And if there *were* extenuating circumstances, and the two *could* explain . . ." Cardiel ventured.

"Perhaps. If, as you suggest, Morgan and Duncan acted out of self-defense, to extricate themselves from a situation that came about through treachery and entrapment, then it may be that they can be forgiven their guilt in the Saint

Torin matter. Even murder, if done in defense of one's life, can be justified." Arilan sighed. "But they are still Deryni."

"Aye, that's true."

Resignedly, Cardiel half-sat against the marble altar rail in front of Arilan and refolded the parchment, a wistful expression on his face. Light from the Presence lamp hanging a few feet past his head cast a ruddy glow on his steel-gray hair, the purple of his skullcap. After slipping the missive under his purple cincture, he leaned both hands against the rail behind him and scanned the vaulted ceiling above before finally dropping his gaze to Arilan's once more.

"Do you think they will come to us?" he asked quietly. "Do you think Morgan and Duncan will dare to trust us?"

"I don't know."

"If only we could talk to them, if we could find out what really happened at Saint Torin's—we might act as intermediaries with the archbishops, and perhaps end this ridiculous dispute." Cardiel shook his head. "God knows, I had no wish to split the Curia down the middle on the eve of war, Denis—but neither could I support Loris's Interdict for Corwyn." He paused, then continued in a lower tone.

"I search my heart and try to think what I might have done differently, to avoid arriving at the crossroad where we now stand, but I keep coming up with the same answer. Logic tells me I did the only thing I could do and still remain true to myself and my holy vows. But another small part keeps nagging that there *must* have been some other way. Silly, isn't it?"

Arilan shook his head. "Not silly at all. Loris made a powerful appeal to emotion, with his shouts of heresy and sacrilege and murder. He made it sound as though Interdict was the only conceivable punishment suitable for a duchy whose duke had offended God and men.

"But you were not dismayed. You stripped away the histrionics, the verbal harangues calculated to conjure up hysteria, and stood steadfast to the tenets by which you have always lived. It took courage, Thomas." Arilan smiled gently and raised an eyebrow. "I'll own, it took courage to follow you. But there is not one of us who did who regrets that decision, or who will not stand by you, whatever you decide to do next. We all share responsibility for this schism."

Cardiel smiled weakly and lowered his gaze. "Thank you. I value that, coming from you. The trouble is, I haven't the slightest notion what we should do next. We are so alone."

"We are hardly alone," Arilan pointed out dryly. "We have the entire city of Dhassa behind us—and your personal militia. They were not swayed by Loris's rantings. Granted, they know that Morgan and Duncan were responsible for the destruction of Saint Torin's—and it will take a while for some of them to forgive that, no matter how justified Morgan and Duncan appeared to be. But their loyalty to Kelson remains unshaken despite all that. Look at the size of our army."

"Yes, look at it," Cardiel said. "And that army is doing Kelson absolutely no good where it now stands, camped outside the gates of Dhassa. I am not certain we dare wait much longer for Morgan and McLain to show up. I am thinking seriously about sending another dispatch to Kelson and telling him we will meet him where and when he orders. The longer we wait to move, the stronger Warin's rebels and the more obstinate the archbishops."

Arilan shrugged. "I'll grant you that. But I really think you should delay a while longer. A few days either way will make little difference as far as Warin and the archbishops are concerned. But if we can clear the air with Morgan and Duncan before joining with Kelson, it would do a great deal to allay any suspicion of us. We could then march on Coroth and Loris and present a united front, with some real hope of effecting a reconciliation. For, make no mistake, when we refused to agree to the Interdict, we also sided indirectly with Morgan and Duncan and the entire Deryni cause, whether unwittingly or not. Resolving that breach can only be accomplished by proving that we were right about Morgan and Duncan's innocence to begin with."

"Well, I hope to God that we *can* prove it!" Cardiel muttered. "Personally, I like most of what I've heard about Morgan and McLain. I can even understand why McLain hid his Deryni powers all these years. And while I can't condone his entry into the priesthood, knowing as he did that he was Deryni, he appears to have been a very good priest."

"Which, in itself, may say something of note about the Deryni," Arilan said with a faint smile. "Remember when you asked me, several months ago, whether I believed the Deryni to be inherently evil?"

"Of course. You said that there were undoubtedly *some* evil Deryni, just like anybody else. You also said that you didn't believe Kelson or Morgan or McLain were evil."

Arilan's eyes glinted a deep blue-violet in the dim light. "I still believe that."

"So? I'm not certain I take your point."

"Do you not? You said yourself that Duncan appears to have been a very good priest, despite the fact that he is Deryni. Doesn't the fact that he *became* a priest, in direct defiance of civil and canon law, and that he is a *good* priest in spite of this, perhaps suggest that the Council of Ramos was in error? And if the Council was in error in this very important area, why not in others?" He arched an eyebrow at Cardiel. "It could force us to reevaluate the entire Deryni-human question."

"Hmm. I hadn't thought of it in those terms. Extending your logic, we could eliminate bars to the priesthood, bars to holding public office and owning land. . . ."

"And so much for any great Deryni conspiracy," Arilan said lightly, with the trace of a smile.

Cardiel pursed his lips, then shook his head with a frown. "It may not be as simple as that, Denis. I heard an odd rumor a day or so ago. I meant to mention it to you earlier. It's whispered that there may, indeed, be a Deryni conspiracy—and a formal one at that. According to rumor, there is a council of highborn Deryni who purport to speak for their race, who somehow monitor the activities of known Deryni. They haven't moved outwardly as yet, but—"

He straightened and began twisting his hands together, his gray eyes grave and worried as he toyed with his amethyst.

"Denis, suppose there *is* a Deryni conspiracy? And what if Morgan and McLain are a part of it? Or Kelson, God help him? It has been more than two hundred years since the Interregnum ended, two centuries since human rule was restored to most of the Eleven Kingdoms. But the people haven't forgotten what life was like under the dictatorship of sorcerers who used their powers for evil. What if we are coming to something like this again?"

"What if, what if?" Arilan's voice became clipped and a little impatient as he locked eyes with Cardiel. "Thomas, if there *is* a Deryni conspiracy, it lies in the mind and plans of Wencit of Torenth. It's very likely that he and his agents are responsible for the rumors you've been hearing.

"As for the threats of a Deryni dictatorship, that is a precise description of Wencit's rule in Torenth: his family has ruled thus for both of the past two centuries you speak of. *That*, my learned friend, is the only Deryni conspiracy you are likely to see in the near future. And as for some secret council of Deryni . . ." He shrugged, his manner somewhat subdued. "Well, I have yet to see any evidence of their actions, if they exist."

Cardiel blinked rapidly several times as Arilan came to a verbal halt, somewhat taken aback by the intensity of his colleague's reply. Then the blue-violet eyes softened, the cold fire fading, and the bishop averted his eyes. With a sigh almost of relief, Cardiel picked up his cloak from the seat by Arilan and ventured a timid smile as he flung the garment around his shoulders.

"You know, you do worry me sometimes, Denis. I can never quite predict how you're going to react. And somehow you manage to reassure me while at the same time frightening me half to death."

"Do I?" Arilan smiled faintly and reached up to squeeze Cardiel's arm reassuringly. "Forgive me, old friend. I sometimes let myself get too caught up."

"Yes, you do," Cardiel said with an answering smile. "Will you join me for some refreshment? Worrying about the Deryni always makes my throat dry. It makes my head hurt as well, but I don't suppose there's much to be done about that—though some nice Fianna red might help. My predecessors have always kept fine cellars."

Arilan chuckled as he rose to walk with Cardiel to the door. "In a little while, perhaps. I thought I might meditate for a while before retiring. My temper is a definite fault."

"Then I wish you success chastising your temper," Cardiel said. "And if you do get things straightened out with *Him*," he nodded toward the crucifix hanging above the altar, "why don't you join me? I shan't sleep for a while—not after this."

"Perhaps later. Good night, Thomas."

"Good night."

As the door closed behind Cardiel, the younger bishop gazed after him for a long moment, then straightened his cassock and walked back up the short nave to retrieve his own cloak, donning it with a whisper of moiré silk and tying the violet ribbons close around his throat before replacing the purple skullcap on his dark hair.

Glancing around the chapel once more, as though committing every detail to memory, he finally nodded respect to the main altar and moved across the transept to the left, halting before a side altar. The marble slab was unadorned except for a white linen cloth and a single white vigil light, but it was not the altar Arilan was interested in anyway. Surveying the marble floor beneath him, he moved onto a vaguely rounded pattern in the mosaic inlay and felt the vague tingle that told him he was properly positioned.

Then, with a last glance at the closed door leading from the chapel, he gathered the folds of his cloak close around him and closed his eyes, shaping his intent deep within his mind and envisioning his destination—and disappeared from the chapel in Dhassa.

Minutes later, the door to the chapel opened, and Cardiel

poked his head inside. He had opened his mouth to say something, expecting to see Arilan's lean figure kneeling somewhere in the chapel confines. But he mouthed empty air as he realized there was no one in the chapel to say it to.

His brows furrowed in consternation, for he had not gone very far from the chapel before turning back to tell Arilan one last rumor he had heard. And now Arilan was gone, when he had said he was going to meditate.

Ah, well. Perhaps the younger bishop had meant that he was going to meditate in his own room, in which case Cardiel would not disturb him. Yes, that must be it, Cardiel told himself. Arilan was probably kneeling in his own chambers right now.

Very well. The other rumor could wait until morning.

But Bishop Denis Arilan was not in his room. Or even in Dhassa.

CHAPTER SIX

". . . the words of the wise and their dark sayings."

PROVERBS 1:6

THORNE Hagen, Deryni, rolled over and opened one eye, disappointed to find it so dark in the room. Across the smooth white shoulder of his bed-mate he could see a mist-wreathed sun sinking slowly behind Tophel Peak, its fading light casting a faint wash of color on the pale castle ramparts. He yawned delicately and flexed his toes, permitting his gaze to wander back to the creamy shoulder beside him, then reached across to stroke the tousled chestnut curls. As his fingers traced the curve of the girl's spine, she shivered sensuously and turned to gaze at him in adoration.

"Did you rest well, my lord?"

Thorne smiled back at her lazily, allowing his gaze to glide over her with the ease of long practice.

"Sorry, little one, but it's time you were on your way. The Council does not wait, even for high Deryni lords." He leaned closer to kiss her forehead in a fatherly gesture. "I shan't be too late, though. Why don't you come back around midnight?"

"Of course, my lord." She bounded up and began pulling

on a flowing yellow robe, her dark eyes caressing him as she crossed toward his door. "Perhaps I shall even bring you a surprise!"

As the door closed behind her, Thorne shook his head and sighed contentedly, a silly grin playing across his face. He scanned the darkening room with bemused contentment, then got up and padded toward his wardrobe door. As he walked, he muttered a phrase under his breath and made a casual, sweeping gesture with the fingers of his right hand. Candles flared to life around the chamber, instantly dispelling some of the gathering twilight, and Thorne ran a hand through his thinning brown hair as he glanced at the image reflected in the costly wall-mirror of burnished copper.

He certainly looked fit. His body was almost as hard and firm at fifty as it had been a quarter of a century ago. Of course, he had lost some hair and added a few pounds since then; but he preferred to think the changes added maturity to his looks. Pink cheeks and blue eyes seemingly frozen in perpetual astonishment had been a curse through most of his youth; he had been nearly thirty before people would even believe he was of legal age.

At last, however, that was working to his advantage. For while Thorne Hagen's contemporaries had aged and were now firmly ensconced in late middle age, Thorne, with the proper attire and the clean-shaven demeanor he preferred, could easily pass for a man of thirty. And there was no doubt, he thought, as he recalled the charming creature who had just left him, that the appearance of youth did have its advantages.

Briefly Thorne considered calling his body servants to help him bathe and dress for the Council session, then decided against it. He had a little extra time. With care, he should be able to work that water spell that Laran had been trying to teach him for the past month. He was peeved that he could not seem to master the spell. There seemed to be a certain point of coordination beyond which he simply could not go. But only practice and perseverance would get him past that point.

Moving into the center of the room, Thorne planted his bare feet about a shoulder-width apart and drew himself to his full height, joining his palms above his head to form a wedge-shaped silhouette in the flickering candlelight. As he began chanting the words of an incantation under his breath, water vapor began to condense around him like a miniature thunderstorm, complete with tiny lightning. He closed his eyes tightly and held his breath as the water scrubbed across his body, wriggling slightly in pleasure at the tingle of the tame lightning bolts. Then, still in complete control at this point, he tensed himself for the difficult part of the spell.

Lowering his hands to chest-level, palms vaguely defining a head-sized space before his breast, Thorne gathered up the tame lightning and rain and willed it to gather between his two hands: a tiny storm cloud crackling and spitting in the candlelight. He cracked his eyes open and saw it hovering there, and had just begun to maneuver it carefully toward the window to dump it when a brilliant flash lit the room from behind him, in the direction of his Transfer Portal. He whipped his head around to see who was there— and, in that instant, lost control of the spell.

Miniature lightning spat from cloud to sorcerer in a painful arc, breaking his concentration; the captive rain fell to the floor with a magnificent splash, drenching the marble flagstones, a priceless tapestry rug, and Thorne's dignity; and as Rhydon of Eastmarch stepped from the Transfer Portal, Thorne began cursing fluently, his baby-blue eyes flashing with anger and indignation.

"The Devil *take* you, Rhydon!" Thorne sputtered, when he at last became coherent. "Can't you ever announce yourself? I would have done it that time. Now you've made me flood the entire room!"

He backed out of the puddle and stamped his bare feet, trying in vain to shake them dry and maintain some shred of dignity in his nakedness, glaring at Rhydon as his fellow sorcerer crossed the room and did his best not to smirk.

"Sorry, Thorne," Rhydon said with a chuckle. "Shall I clean it up for you?"

"Sorry, Thorne, shall I clean it up for you?" Thorne mimicked. The small, greedy eyes clouded in the baby face. "You probably can, too. There isn't *anyone* who can't do this spell except me!"

Schooling his expression to suitable contrition, Rhydon spread his hands above the wet floor and murmured several short phrases, his gray eyes hooded as he spoke. The dampness disappeared, and Rhydon shrugged and raised an apologetic eyebrow as he glanced back at Thorne. The interrupted sorcerer said nothing, but his look was petulant as he turned on his heel and stalked into his wardrobe chamber. After a few seconds, the rustle of fine fabrics issued faintly from the open doorway.

"I am truly sorry to have disturbed you, Thorne," Rhydon said conversationally, walking around the room and examining the various artifacts there. "Wencit wanted me to ask a favor of you."

"For Wencit, perhaps. Not for you."

"Now, don't pout. I said I was sorry."

"All right, all right." Pause. Then, grudgingly curious: "What does Wencit want?"

"He wants you to persuade the Council to declare Morgan and McLain liable to challenge, as full Deryni are. Can you do it?"

"Liable to challenge as—are you serious?" After another brief bout of rustling, Thorne continued, his anger apparently past. "Well, I can try. But I hope Wencit remembers that I haven't as much influence as I once did. We changed coadjutors last month. Why don't you introduce the subject yourself? You're full Deryni. You are still permitted to speak before the Council, even if you aren't a member of the Inner Circle anymore."

"You have a short memory, Thorne," Rhydon said mildly.

"When last I stood before the Council, I vowed never to set foot in that room again, or in any room where Stefan Coram was present. I've not broken that vow in seven years, and I don't intend to start tonight. Wencit says that you must be the one to raise the issue."

Thorne emerged from the wardrobe chamber, adjusting the meticulous folds of a violet robe beneath his mantle of gold brocade. "All right, all right. You needn't get puffed up about it. It's a pity, though. If it hadn't been for Coram, you might have been coadjutor yourself by now. Instead, you and Wencit—well, you know."

"Yes, we do make a likely pair, don't we?" Rhydon purred, regarding Thorne through slitted gray eyes. "Wencit is a fox; he makes no secret of it. And I—as I recall, Coram likened me to Lucifer that day: the fallen angel cast into the outer darkness, away from the Inner Circle." He smiled darkly and inspected his fingernails as he leaned against the mantelpiece. "Actually, I've always been rather fond of Lucifer. He was, after all, the brightest of all the angels before his fall."

The fire flared behind Rhydon, illuminating him for an instant in an aureole of crimson, and Thorne gulped audibly. Only with an effort did he resist the urge to cross himself in a warding-off gesture.

"You mustn't say such things," he whispered self-consciously. "Someone might hear."

"Who, Lucifer? Nonsense. I'm afraid, my dear Thorne, that our good Prince of Darkness is only a make-believe devil, a fairy-tale legend with which to frighten naughty children. The real devils are men, like Morgan and McLain. You would do well to remember that."

Scowling, Thorne gave his mantle a last, fretting adjustment, then bound a narrow gold fillet across his forehead with fingers that trembled slightly.

"Very well: Morgan and McLain are devils. You have said it; therefore, it must be true. But I can hardly tell that to the Council. Even if Morgan and McLain are what you say they are—and I do not know this, for I have never met the gentlemen—they are also only *half*-Deryni, and therefore immune to arcane challenge by any of us. I shall need to present very good reasons for changing that status."

"Then you shall have them," Rhydon said, rubbing at the scar beside his nose in an unconscious gesture. "You need only remind the Council that both Morgan and McLain appear to be able to do things they oughtn't. And if that doesn't convince them, you might also add that if this continues, the pair could present a threat to the very existence of the Inner Circle."

"But they don't even *know* of the Council!"

"So one assumes," Rhydon replied crisply. "But secrets have a bad habit of eventually getting out. And you might also remember, strictly for your own edification, that Wencit wants this action passed. Need I elaborate further?"

"That—ah—won't be necessary." Thorne cleared his throat nervously and turned away to peer at his reflection in the mirror, controlling the tendency of his hand to tremble as he made a final adjustment to his collar.

"Very well. I have said I would do as you ask," he continued more steadily. "I trust that you, in turn, will remind Wencit of the risk I take by speaking in his behalf. I do not know what he has planned for Morgan and McLain, nor do I wish to know. But the Council is intended to be a neutral body; it looks harshly on any of its members taking sides in politics. Wencit could have been on the Council himself, you know, if only he had been a little more obedient." He ended on a petulant note.

"Obedience is not one of Wencit's stronger virtues," Rhydon warned softly. "Nor is it one of mine. However, if you have some quarrel with either of us, I am certain that an opportunity can be arranged whereby *someone* will gain satisfaction. They say that the time is ripe for challenges."

"You surely don't think that *I* would challenge . . . ?" A trace of the old night terror flickered momentarily in the pale blue eyes.

"Of course not."

Thorne swallowed with difficulty and regained his composure, then moved briskly onto the carved vines and flowers that adorned the tiles defining his Transfer Portal.

"I shall send you word in the morning," he said, gathering his golden mantle around him with such shreds of dignity as he could muster. "Will that be satisfactory?"

Rhydon bowed wordlessly, his eyes slightly mocking.

"Then I bid you good evening," Thorne said—and vanished.

HIGH on a guarded plateau, in a great, octagonal chamber with a vault like faceted amethyst, the Camberian Council was gathering.

Beneath the purple dome, an expanse of onyx floor tile caught the gleam of hammered metal doors extending from floor to ceiling on one side of the room. Wood-limned panels of ancient ivory, richly carved, angled the other seven walls, light from scores of new wax tapers flickering on the incised figures of men and women famed in Deryni history. Brighter brands, thick as a man's wrist, blazed in golden cressets on the wood between the panels. The center of the room held only a massive, eight-sided table and eight high-backed chairs. By five of the chairs stood Deryni.

Three men and two women stood at ease under the purple dome, all save one garbed in the gold and violet raiment of the Deryni Inner Circle. The lone exception, Denis Arilan, held himself aloof and somber in his black cassock and purple bishop's cloak, nodding occasionally in response to a conversation between the stately Lady Vivienne to his right and a dark, intense young man with almond-colored eyes: Tiercel de Claron.

Across the table, a white-haired man with pale, translucent hands was speaking with a girl half a century his junior. The girl smiled and listened with interest, her tawny-colored hair pulled like a flame at the nape of her neck. Arilan suppressed a yawn, then turned as the golden doors parted to admit Thorne Hagen.

Thorne appeared to be upset, his normally florid face pale save for two spots of color high on his plump cheeks. He glanced away as he saw Arilan looking at him, hurrying across the room to engage in conversation with the girl and the old man at the opposite side of the table. He calmed as he spoke to them, his face resuming its usual, disarming expression, but not before Arilan saw him wipe sweating palms surreptitiously against his thighs, or soon enough to hide the slight tremor in his hands as he hid them in his violet sleeves.

Curious, Arilan turned half-away and pretended to follow the conversation of his two companions, schooling his expression to one of indifference, but his mind was not on the hunting tale Lady Vivienne was relating.

Something had shaken Thorne's composure tonight, but what? No human, surely. And if Deryni, then Thorne certainly had nothing to fear in this, of all places. Even if Thorne had provoked the ire of another Deryni, he was safe in here. No Deryni might raise power against his fellows while in the confines of this chamber. Indeed, unless a majority of those present willed it so, and the subject was also willing, no magic might function here at all. The bond of protection was sealed by a blood-oath required of every member, raised and renewed with the acquisition of each new initiate to the Inner Circle. No danger lay here for Thorne Hagen.

Arilan ran his fingertips along the edge of the ivory table with a slight smile, feeling the cold sleekness of the gold that banded it and divided the table into eight wedges.

Of course, there was always another possibility. Sooner or later, Thorne would have to leave the Council chamber. And once outside, there were Deryni not associated with the Inner Circle, who did not acknowledge the Council's dictates, and would have no respect for Thorne's Council office. There were and had always been renegade Deryni like Lewys ap

Norfal, Rhydon of Eastmarch, Rolf MacPherson of the previous century—men who had rejected the Council's authority, or been expelled from its ranks, or even risen in outright
rebellion. Could some rogue Deryni be threatening Thorne
Hagen? Was there some plot against the Council?

Arilan glanced at the man again and did his best to put
aside his reservations, realizing that he had nothing to go on
except his own speculations, at this point. Perhaps Thorne
had merely had a spat with his latest mistress, or quarreled
with his castle warden. Anything was possible.

At a slight rustle of brocade behind Arilan, he turned to
see the final two members of the Council entering through
the great golden doors, each bearing the ivory wand of a
coadjutor. Barrett de Laney, senior of the two men and presiding lord of the Council this evening, cut an impressive
figure, his well-shaped head handsome despite its total lack
of hair, emerald eyes aglow in the finely chiseled face. His
companion, Stefan Coram, was equally striking, pale hair
gone prematurely silver, elegant and blade-like in his confidence as he glided at Barrett's elbow, though even he paled
beside the older man for sheer *presence*.

Poised and solicitous, Coram conducted Barrett to the
chair between Laran and Tiercel, then moved on to his own
place at the opposite side of the table. When each of them
had placed his wand on the table, Coram spread his hands to
either side, one palm up and one down. As the rest at table
followed suit, each resting his palm on the palm of his
neighbor, Coram cleared his throat and spoke.

"Attend, my lords and ladies. Attend and draw near.
Heed the words of the Master. Let all be one in spirit with
the Word."

Barrett bowed his head for a moment, as did all of them,
then raised his emerald eyes heavenward to a crystal sphere
suspended from the center of the dome by a long, golden
chain. The sphere trembled slightly in the still, silent air,
and when Barrett spoke it was in the low, liquid syllables of
ancient Deryni ritual.

"Now we are met. Now we are one with the Light. Regard the ancient ways. We shall not walk this path again." He paused and lapsed back into the vernacular. "So be it."

"So be it."

The eight took their seats in a rustle of rich raiment, a few making whispered comments to their neighbors. When they had settled, Barrett sat back and rested both hands on the arms of his chair, apparently composing himself to begin the session. Before he could speak, the slight, silver-haired man to his right cleared his throat and sat forward. The arms on the shield at the back of his chair identified him as Laran ap Pardyce, sixteenth Baron Pardyce. His expression was somber.

"Barrett, before we begin formal proceedings, I wonder if we might address ourselves to a rumor I have heard."

"A rumor?"

"Laran, we haven't time for rumors," Coram interrupted. "We have urgent—"

"No, this is urgent, too," Laran cut in, stabbing the air with a pale, translucent hand. "I think this is one rumor we must put to rest. For I have heard it said more than once that Alaric Morgan, a half-breed Deryni, displays the ancient ability of healing!"

There was a stunned silence, and then:

"Healing?"

"Morgan has healed?"

"Laran, you must be mistaken." A female voice. "None of us can heal anymore."

"That is correct," Barrett agreed stiffly. "All Deryni know that the healing gifts were lost with the Restoration."

"Well, perhaps no one has thought to inform Morgan of this small detail!" Laran snapped. "He *is* only half-Deryni, you know!" He glared at Barrett for just an instant, then shook his silvery head regretfully. "I do apologize, Barrett. If anyone feels the loss of the healing gifts, it is you."

His voice trailed off awkwardly as he remembered how Barrett de Laney had lost his sight over fifty years ago, from

a hot iron held close to the emerald eyes as ransom for a
score of Deryni children saved from the swords of the persecutors. Barrett bowed his head and reached out to touch
Laran's shoulder in a comforting gesture.

"Do not chide yourself, Laran," the blind man whispered.
"There are things more precious than sight. Tell us more of
this Morgan."

Laran shrugged, much subdued. "Unfortunately, I have
no proof. I have merely heard it said—and as a physician,
my curiosity was aroused. If Morgan—"

"Oh, Morgan, Morgan, *Morgan!*" Tiercel slapped the flat
of his hand sharply against the table. "That's all we ever talk
about anymore. Are we determined to summon up a witch
hunt against our own kind? I thought that was one of the
more expendable things we lost with the Restoration!"

Vivienne snorted in derision, her fine gray head turning
toward the young man in disdain. "Tiercel, do act your age.
It isn't as though Morgan was one of us. He is a half-breed
traitor, a disgrace to the Deryni name—the way he cavorts
around the countryside making indiscriminate use of his
powers!"

Tiercel threw back his head and laughed. "Morgan?
Now, there's a thought. Half-breed he is; traitor he may or
may not be, depending upon whose side one is on—King
Kelson, I know, would not agree. But as for disgrace, madam,
our rogue half-breed has never done anything to discredit
the Deryni name that *I* am aware of. On the contrary, he is
the one Deryni I know of who is *not* afraid to stand and declare himself for what he is. Any disgracing of our name was
done long ago, and by men far more expert than an untrained Deryni half-breed like Alaric Morgan!"

"But you *do* see him as a half-breed," Thorne interjected,
seizing the opportunity to press his suit for Wencit. "And
Duncan McLain, too. All of you regard them both as half-
breeds. And yet, time and time again, they react in ways not
consistent with their supposed bloodline. Now they allegedly can heal—something that even we cannot do! Has

anyone ever considered the possibility that they might not be only half-blood after all? That we may be dealing with a renegade pair of full Deryni?"

Kyri, to Thorne's right—she of the tawny hair—frowned lightly and touched his arm. "Surely that cannot be," she said. "How could they be full Deryni? 'Tis inconsistent with what we know of their parentage."

"Well, their mothers are certain," Vivienne scoffed. "And we know that they, at least, were full Deryni. As for the fathers—well, how certain can *anyone* be?"

She cocked an eyebrow, prompting a low, appreciative chuckle that rippled around the table. Tiercel reddened.

"If you intend to cast aspersions on the parentage of Morgan and McLain," he said, "I should like to remind you that there are some of *us* whose ancestry might not bear close scrutiny. Oh, we are all Deryni; no one could argue against that. But who among us can be absolutely certain, beyond any shadow of a doubt, just who his father was?"

"That will be enough," Coram said sharply, laying his hand on his ivory wand in a gesture of authority.

"Peace, Stefan." Barrett's voice. "Tiercel, we shall not indulge in verbal innuendo." He turned his blind face slowly toward the younger man, as though the emerald eyes could see. "The legitimacy of Morgan or McLain's birth—or yours or mine or anyone else's—is not pertinent to this discussion, except as it may touch on the point just raised by Thorne. If, as he has suggested, the two in question have been exhibiting abilities that were deemed lost, that are inconsistent with those normally associated with their supposed bloodline, it behooves us to inquire how this can be possible. The discussion does not require impassioned rhetoric from either side. Is that clear?"

"I beseech pardon if I have spoken rashly," Tiercel said, though the ritual phrase was not consistent with the tight-jawed expression on his handsome face. "But I exercise my right to inquire further regarding what Laran has reported."

He turned his head in Laran's direction. "You say that Morgan is reputed to have healed?"

"So it is said."

"By whom? And whom is he said to have healed?

Laran cleared his throat and glanced around the table. "You will recall reports of an attempt on the king's life on the night before his coronation. To gain entrance to his chambers, the would-be assassins overpowered the night guards and killed or wounded them. Among the wounded was Morgan's aide, Sean Lord Derry.

"One of the attending surgeons states that he examined this same Lord Derry shortly before Morgan came out of the king's chamber, and that the young man was very near death. When Morgan arrived, the surgeon told him as much, then moved on to treat those who could be helped. A few minutes later, Morgan was summoning another surgeon to attend, telling him that the young lord was not wounded so badly as had been feared.

"It was not until some days later that the two surgeons compared notes and discovered that something approaching a miracle had occurred. For though Derry had been wounded to the very brink of death, and no medical procedure known to them could have saved him, yet he lived. He attended Morgan at the coronation the next day."

"What makes you believe that this was evidence of Deryni healing?" Coram said slowly. "And why should that ability surface now, after nearly two centuries?"

"I merely report what I have heard," Laran replied. "As a physician, I cannot explain what happened in any other way. Unless, of course, you prefer to believe that it really was a miracle."

"Ha! I do not believe in miracles," Vivienne said caustically. "What say you, Denis? You are our resident expert in such matters. Is such a thing possible?"

Denis Arilan glanced at Vivienne, sitting to his right, then shrugged slightly. "Biblically speaking, of course miracles are possible." He traced a careful pattern on the tabletop with his fingertip, his amethyst catching the light. "But miracles in more recent times, at least in the past four or five centuries, can usually be explained—or at least duplicated—by some form of our magic. This is not to say that there are no more miracles; only that, by the use of our powers, we can often cause what *appear* to be miracles. As for what you allege of Morgan, I have no knowledge of that. I have met the man only once, to talk to—and he was only young then."

"But you were present at the coronation the day after this alleged healing, were you not, Bishop?" Thorne said slowly. "And according to all reports, Morgan himself was badly wounded in his duel with the Lord Ian. Yet, when the time came to swear fealty, he walked erect and without pain to place his hands between the king's: somewhat blood-stained, to be sure, but not at all like a man who has just had a handspan of cold steel removed from his shoulder. How do you explain that?"

Arilan shrugged. "I cannot explain it. Perhaps what Morgan said of his own wound was true, as well: that it was less serious than it appeared. Monsignor McLain attended him; I was not close by at the time. But perhaps his skill . . ."

Laran shook his head. "I think not, Denis. Even if this McLain is a capable battle-surgeon, as many borderers are, could he have . . . ?" His voice trailed off briefly, then: "Of course, if he, too, has the healing power—why, this is incredible! If two half-breeds can—"

Young Tiercel could contain himself no longer, and sat back in his chair with an explosive sigh. "You people sicken me! If it really is true that Morgan and McLain have rediscovered the lost gifts of healing, then we should be seeking them out on bended knee, *begging* them to share this great knowledge with us—not dragging their names through this senseless inquisition!"

"But, they *are* half-breeds," Kyri ventured.

"Oh, 'half-breeds' be hanged!" Tiercel retorted. "Maybe they are *not*. How *could* they be, and still be able to heal? The ancient records tell us little about the actual process of training or engaging the healing gift, but we do know that it was one of the most difficult of all the Deryni powers to master, and that it required great focus and discipline to control. If Morgan and McLain can do this, I think we must either accept the possibility that they are somehow full Deryni, that there is something in their makeup of which we are still unaware—or else we must reconsider our whole understanding of what it means to be Deryni."

Vivienne rolled her eyes and looked about to interrupt, but Tiercel shook his head and held up a restraining hand.

"No, hear me out. Perhaps Deryniness is not a cumulative thing at all. Perhaps one either *is* Deryni or one is not, and nothing in between. We know that powers themselves are not cumulative between two people, other than to bring one weakened or untrained individual up to his full potential. If this were not the case, Deryni could band together and the larger, stronger groups defeat the smaller ones every time.

"But, no. We know, at least, that battle doesn't work that way. We keep our duels on a one-to-one basis, and we forbid more than one individual to challenge at a time, and the custom is couched in legend, but why did that become the standard? Perhaps because of the very fact that the powers are *not* additive.

"Perhaps inheritance is governed on much the same principle. Other things are inherited in full from one parent or the other. Why not Deryniness?"

There was silence for a long moment as the Council digested what its youngest member had just said, and then Barrett lifted his hairless head.

"We are well instructed by our juniors," he said quietly. "Does anyone know the present whereabouts of Morgan and McLain?"

No one answered, and Barrett's blind eyes continued to sweep the table.

"Has any one of you ever touched Morgan's mind?" Barrett ventured again.

Again, silence.

"What about McLain?" Barrett continued. "Bishop Arilan, we understand that Father McLain was an associate of yours for a time. Did you never have occasion to touch his mind?"

Arilan shook his head. "He was a fellow priest, and there was no reason to suspect that he was Deryni. And I should have risked exposing my own identity, had I tried to read him for any other purpose."

"Well, you may wish that you had," Thorne retorted. "I am given to understand that he and Morgan are on their way to see you. Something about trying to prove their innocence of the excommunication you and your bishops imposed on them. Personally, I shouldn't be surprised if they tried to kill you."

"I doubt there is that danger," Arilan said confidently. "Even if Morgan or Duncan had reason to hate me personally, which they do not, they are astute enough to recognize that this kingdom is on the brink both of civil war and invasion, and that we must resolve the first in order to prevent the second. If the forces of Gwynedd remain divided over the Interdict imposed on Corwyn, we will be unable to repel the invaders. Deryni-human relations will have been set back at least two centuries."

"Forget that for now," Thorne said impatiently. "In case everyone else has forgotten, there is still the problem of what *we* must do about Morgan and McLain. The situation appears to have come to a head at King Kelson's coronation, after which Morgan was censured for using magic openly. That is also why McLain was called to appear before the archbishops: the illicit and unpredictable use of powers neither of them should have, either by the standards of Church and state, which declare that they should have none, or by ours, which ought, at least, to be able to predict their capabilities.

"Now, I am not particularly bothered that there are Deryni running around loose who have not been properly trained in the use of their powers. That has been going on for years, and I see no way to stop it. But Morgan and McLain somehow *have* learned how to use their powers, and apparently are learning more every day. We have turned a blind eye in the past, since we always regarded them as immune to formal challenge, since they were half-breeds. Now that this assumption seems no longer valid, I think we should declare them liable to full challenge proceedings, just as though they were full Deryni. I, for one, do not wish to find myself in a situation where I might be forced to disobey a Council injunction in order to stop them."

"Realistically, I think there is little danger of that," Arilan said. "Besides, the injunction says nothing about self-defense. It was meant to protect those of lesser training and abilities from being attacked by full Deryni whose powers they could not hope to resist. If a lesser Deryni wished to challenge a full lord and got himself killed in the process, that was his choice."

"It would be interesting to find out if they *are* full Deryni, though," Laran mused. "We could limit the challenge to non-lethal combat—except, of course, in self-defense. I think it might be rather interesting to test wits against Alaric Morgan."

"An excellent suggestion," Thorne agreed. "I so move."

"You so move what?" Coram asked.

"I move that Morgan and McLain be accorded full challenge liability—excluding mortal combat save for self-defense. After all, we must clear up this question of the healing."

"But, is it necessary to *challenge* them?" Arilan asked.

"Thorne Hagen has stipulated that there shall be no mortal challenge permitted," Barrett said evenly. "I think it not out of order. Besides, the question is largely academic. No one even knows where they are."

Thorne suppressed a smile and laced his pudgy fingers together. "Then, it is agreed? They may be challenged?"

Tiercel shook his head. "I like it not. I call for a voice

vote, one by one. I claim the ancient right," he added, at Thorne's look of protest. "And let each person state his reasons."

Barrett turned his blind eyes toward Tiercel for a long moment, touching his mind fleetingly, then nodded slowly. "As you wish, Tiercel. It is, indeed, your right. Voice vote. Laran ap Pardyce, how say you?"

"I agree. Limited challenge is acceptable. And as a physician, I am most eager to find out about this healing ability they may or may not have."

"Thorne Hagen?"

"I proposed it, for the reasons I originally specified. Of course I agree."

"Lady Kyri?"

The young redheaded woman nodded slowly. "If anyone can find them, I think the test is justified. I accept the measure."

"Stefan Coram, how say you?"

"I agree that they ought to be tested when the time is right—so long as it is a non-lethal challenge."

"And Bishop Arilan?"

"I disagree." Arilan sat forward in his chair and intertwined his fingers, turning at the amethyst on his right hand. "I believe it not only uncalled for, but dangerous here. If you force Morgan and Duncan to use their powers to defend themselves against their own kind, you play them directly into the hands of the archbishops. If anything, Morgan and Duncan must be persuaded not to use their powers under any circumstances—at least that the archbishops find out about. Kelson needs their aid desperately, if he is to hold the kingdom together and keep Wencit on his own side of the mountains. I am in the midst of this controversy; I know the situation; you do not. Do not ask me to go against something I believe in."

Coram smiled and glanced sidelong at the man beside him. "No one is asking you to challenge them, Arilan. As it is, you will probably be the first to see them in any case.

And we all know that no one could force you to give away their whereabouts against your will."

"I thought you were in sympathy, Coram."

"Sympathy, yes. I feel for their plight: half-breed Deryni obliged to stand as though they were full, against their kinds of both halves, human and Deryni. But I didn't make the rules, Denis. I merely play by them."

Arilan glanced down at his ring, briefly bent his head to touch his lips to the stone, then shook his head. "My answer is still no. I will not challenge them."

"Nor will you tell them of the possibility of challenge," Coram persisted.

"No," Arilan whispered.

Coram nodded in Barrett's direction, sending him a mental image of the action, and Barrett returned the nod.

"Lady Vivienne?"

"I concur with Stefan. The young men must be tried to test their mettle." Her fine, silvery head turned to scan the table. "I wish it understood, however, that this is not out of malice, but in curiosity. We have never had so promising a pair of half-breeds in our midst, despite what I said about them earlier. I, for one, will be interested to see what they can do."

"A measured observation," Barrett agreed. "And Tiercel de Claron?"

"You know I vote against the measure. I shan't repeat myself."

"And I must vote to accept the proposal," Barrett countered, coming full circle at last. "I think there is no need for a formal count." He rose slowly to his feet.

"The measure is sealed. From this time hence, until such time as the Council may reconvene and alter its decree, the two half-breed Deryni known as Alaric Morgan and Duncan McLain are to be liable to full challenge proceedings, saving only mortal combat. This injunction against deadly force does not, of course, preclude self-defense, should either of the aforementioned men attempt to answer such challenge with killing strength. But should any member of this Council, or any Deryni who keeps the Council's tenets, be tempted to disregard this decretal, let him be liable to the censure of the Council. So let it be written."

"So let it be done," the seven others replied in unison.

Hours later, Denis Arilan paced the carpet of his room in the Bishop's Palace at Dhassa. For him, there was little sleep that night.

CHAPTER SEVEN

"Many things beyond human understanding have been revealed to thee."

ECCLESIASTICUS 3:25

MORGAN peered out the window of the ruined tower and scanned the plain far below. Away and to the southeast he could just discern a lone horseman moving rapidly out of sight: Derry, on his way to the northern armies. Below, at the base of the tower, two dun-colored horses pulled hungrily at the new spring grass, their harness worn and common. Duncan was waiting at the foot of the ruined stairway, slapping a brown leather riding crop against one muddy boot. As Morgan stepped back from the window and began his descent, Duncan looked up.

"See anything?"

"Just Derry." He sprang lightly across the last few feet of rubble to land in a clatter beside his kinsman. "Are you ready to move on?"

"I want to show you something first," Duncan said, gesturing with his crop toward the ruins farther back and beginning to lead in that direction. "The last time we were here, you were in no condition to appreciate what I'm about to show you, but I think it will interest you now."

"You mean, the ruined Portal you found?"

"Correct."

Walking carefully, Morgan followed Duncan down the broken aisle of the ruined chapel, hand resting easily on the hilt of his sword. Saint Neot's once had been a flourishing monastic school, renowned in its day as one of the principal seats of Deryni learning, but that had ended with the Restoration. The monastery had been sacked and burned, many of its brothers murdered on the very altar steps they now passed. Now Morgan and Duncan crossed the ruined nave of the school's crumbling chapel to view the remains of something else lost from that time.

"There's the Saint Camber altar you told me about," Duncan said, gesturing with his crop toward what remained of a marble slab jutting from part of the eastern wall. "I reasoned that a Portal wouldn't have been placed out in the open, even in Interregnum times, so I looked further. In here."

As Duncan pointed, he ducked low to ease his way through a small opening in the crumbling wall, precariously supported by fallen and half-rotted ceiling beams. Mounds of rubble littered the floor on the other side, but as Morgan followed his kinsman through, he could see that this had probably been a sacristy or vestry.

He dusted his gloved hands together lightly as he straightened in the ruined chamber, noting the cracked marble beneath his boots, the timber beams still supporting much of the ceiling. Against the far wall, he could make out the remains of an ivory vesting altar, its panels blackened by fire, fragments of chests and moldering vestment presses to either side. More substantial rubble made the footing precarious: blocks of stone fallen from the half-tumbled walls, rotting wood, shattered glass. Footprints of small animals tracked over the heavy layer of dust that covered everything.

"Over here," Duncan said, motioning him to a spot before the ruined altar and squatting down on his haunches. "Look. You can see the outline of the slab that marked the Portal. Put your hands on it and probe it."

"Probe it?" Morgan dropped to his knees beside his cousin and rested a gloved hand on the square, glancing at Duncan in faint question. "What am I supposed to feel? You said it had been destroyed."

"Just probe the slab gently," Duncan urged. "The brethren left a message."

Morgan raised an eyebrow skeptically, then let his mind go blank, willing his senses to extend gradually to the slab beneath his hand.

Beware, Deryni! Here lies danger!

Startled by the intensity of the contact, Morgan drew back his hand and glanced at Duncan in question, then briskly pulled off his right glove and placed his hand flat on the slab, fingers splayed, again reaching out with his mind.

Beware, Deryni! Here lies danger! Of a full one hundred brothers only I remain, to try, with my failing strength, to destroy this Portal before it can be desecrated. Kinsman, take heed. Protect yourself, Deryni. The humans kill what they do not understand. Holy Saint Camber, defend us from fearful evil!

Drawing a deep, steadying breath, Morgan withdrew from the contact and looked across at Duncan. The priest was solemn, his eyes intensely blue in the shadowed chamber, but a ghost of a smile played about his lips as he stood up.

"I would say that he succeeded," Duncan said, glancing wistfully around the chamber. "It probably cost him his life, but he destroyed the Transfer Portal. Strange, isn't it, how we're sometimes forced to destroy the things we hold most dear? We, as a race, have done that. Look at the knowledge lost, the bright heritage tarnished. We are a shadow of the people we once were."

Morgan got to his feet and clasped Duncan's shoulder in a gesture of reassurance. "Enough of that, Cousin. Our Deryni ancestors brought a large amount of their fate upon themselves, and you know it. Come. We'd better ride on."

They squinted against the brightness as they left the ruined chamber and emerged into the nave once more. The sunlight streaming through the empty clerestory windows set the dust motes dancing in its beams, throwing everything into sharp relief of light and sooty shadow. The two men were just approaching the ruined western doorway, where their horses waited beyond, when the air in the doorway suddenly seemed to shimmer, as if from heat.

"What the—"

The pair pulled up short, gaping as a figure took shape in the doorway, silhouetted against the brightness: the cowled form of a man in gray monk's robes, with a wooden staff in his right hand and a nimbus of golden light around his head that outshone even the sunlight. It was the figure that both men had come to associate with Saint Camber of Culdi, the ancient patron of Deryni magic.

"Dear God in Heaven," Duncan whispered, crossing himself, as Morgan put out an arm and both of them backed off a step.

The figure in the doorway did not disappear; on the contrary, it stepped through the opening and took several steps toward them. Morgan retreated yet another step, reluctant to contend with the strange being, whoever he might be, then jerked back with a grunt of dismay as his left shoulder encountered something sleek and unyielding, something that had given off a golden flash when he brushed against it.

His shoulder seemed to tingle for several seconds, and he rubbed it gingerly as he eyed the stranger. Duncan moved closer to his kinsman, both hands lifted in a vaguely warding-off gesture, and did not take his eyes from the newcomer either. As both watched in awe, the stranger raised his left hand to push back the cowl from his head. The eyes, at once piercing and caressing, were of the same blued-gray as the sky beyond. The face was both ancient and ageless, the nimbus flaring about his silver-bright head like captive sunlight.

"Do not go against the wards again, or you may be injured," the man said. "I prefer that you do not leave just yet."

The lips moved, but the voice was more inside their heads than actually heard. Morgan glanced uneasily at Duncan to see his cousin staring at the stranger in rapt attention, a look of incredulity on his face. He wondered abruptly if this was the man Duncan had seen on the road to Coroth a few months ago, and knew even as he thought it that it had to be the man. Duncan started to open his mouth to speak, but the man held up a hand for silence and shook his head.

"Please. I have not much time. I have come to warn you, Duncan, and you, Alaric, that your lives are in grave danger."

Morgan could not control a faint snort of derision. "That is hardly a new threat. As Deryni, we were bound to make enemies."

"*Deryni* enemies?"

Duncan only stared at him numbly, but Morgan's gray eyes narrowed shrewdly.

"What Deryni enemies? You, sir?"

The stranger chuckled with a silver laughter, as though pleased with the reply, and for the first time seemed to relax slightly.

"I am hardly your enemy, Alaric Morgan. If I were, why would I come to warn you?"

"You might have your reasons."

Duncan nudged his kinsman in the ribs and cocked his head at the stranger. "Then, who are you, sir? Your appearance is that of Saint Camber, but . . ."

"Come, now. Camber of Culdi died two centuries ago. How could I be he?"

"You answer a question with yet another question," Morgan persisted. "*Are* you Camber of Culdi?"

The man shook his head, slightly amused. "No, I am not Camber of Culdi. As I told Duncan on the road to Coroth, I am but one of Camber's humble servants."

Morgan raised a skeptical eyebrow. Despite the disclaimer of sainthood, the stranger's manner did not suggest that he was anyone's humble servant. On the contrary, he exuded a decided aura of command, an impression that this was a man far more accustomed to giving orders than to receiving them. No, whoever the man was, he was not a servant.

"You say that you are one of Camber's servants," Morgan finally repeated, unable to keep a slight edge of disbelief out of his voice. "Would it be impertinent to inquire which one? Or do you not have a name?"

"I have many names," the man smiled. "But I pray you not to press me on this point. For now, I would rather not lie to you—and the truth could be dangerous to all of us."

"Then . . . you're Deryni," Morgan guessed. "You would have to be, to do all of this—to come and go the way you do." He considered further as the man merely gazed at him in faint amusement. "But no one knows that you're Deryni," he continued after a slight pause. "You've been in hiding, like Duncan was all these years. And you can't let anyone know."

"If you wish."

Perplexed and at a loss, Morgan frowned and glanced at Duncan, suspecting that the man was but toying with him, but the priest shook his head slightly.

"This danger you speak of," Duncan said, edging slightly closer for a better look at the man. "These Deryni enemies: Who are they?"

"I regret that I cannot tell you that."

"You can't tell us?" Morgan began.

"I cannot tell you because I do not know myself," the stranger interrupted, holding up a hand for silence. "What I *can* tell you is this: Those whose business it is to know these things have become convinced that you may possess the full spectrum of Deryni powers, some which even they were not aware still exist."

The two could but gape incredulously as the man moved back into the sunlit doorway once more and pulled his cowl back into place.

"Remember, however, that regardless of your true powers, there are those who would test the theory I have just recounted, and would challenge you to duel arcane to discover your strength." He turned slightly to regard them one final time. "Think on that, my friends. And take care that they do not find you before you are secure in your powers—whatever those powers may be!"

With that, the man gave a curt nod and walked briskly to where the horses were grazing. The animals did not seem to notice his approach; and as Morgan and Duncan moved into the doorway to stare after him, he raised a hand as though in benediction, walked behind the horses, and disappeared.

Stifling an oath, Morgan raced around the animals and searched anxiously for some trace of the stranger, but he could find nothing. Duncan remained in the doorway for several seconds, his blue eyes focused on some distant memory, then joined Morgan and absently began stroking one of the grazing horses.

"You won't find him, Alaric," he said softly. "No more than I could find him after he disappeared on the Coroth road a few months ago." He glanced at the ground and shook his head. "No footprints, no sign to mark his passing. It's as though he was never here. Perhaps he wasn't."

Morgan turned to glance sharply at his cousin, then went back to inspect the doorsill, the gritty floor beyond. There might have been footprints besides their own, but if they had ever existed, they had been effectively obliterated when Morgan and Duncan went in pursuit. Nor was there any sign of the man's passing on the damp, grassy earth.

"Deryni enemies," Morgan breathed, returning to stand quietly by Duncan's side. "Do you realize what that implies?"

Duncan nodded. "It implies that there are far more Deryni than we ever dreamed; Deryni who know what they are and who know how to use their powers."

"And we don't know who any of them are except Kelson

and Wencit of Torenth," Morgan murmured, running both hands distractedly through his windblown yellow hair. "God's Blood, Duncan! What have we gotten ourselves into?"

Just what the two had gotten themselves into was to become more and more apparent as the day wore on.

SEVERAL hours later, Morgan and Duncan guided their horses into a dense thicket just off the Dhassa road and drew rein to listen. Bearded and mud-bespattered as they were, mounted on common horses of no certain ancestry, they had aroused no suspicion from the travelers they encountered on the well-traveled highway. They had passed farmers and soldiers and merchants with pack trains, and once even a pair of mounted messengers wearing the badge of the Bishop of Dhassa himself.

But they had not been challenged. And now, as they made their final approach to the valley that led to Dhassa, the road was momentarily deserted. Beyond the ridge ahead lay the valley and Saint Torin's, and both men sobered as they remembered their last journey to this place.

Saint Torin was the patron saint of Dhassa. Custom decreed that those approaching the city from the south, as Morgan and Duncan now did, must first stop and pay homage to the city's protector before being permitted to cross the lake to the city's gates. In days gone by—up until three months ago, to be precise—there had been a shrine near the lake: a centuries-old structure built entirely of wood native to the area. There, after entering the shrine alone and unarmed and making a token offering, the pious traveler paid his respects and received the pewter cap badge that identified him as a proper pilgrim. With this he might obtain passage on the small ferry skiffs that plied the lake to the city beyond. Only the badge would serve as fare, and the boatmen could not be bribed.

As a consequence, travelers wishing to enter the city

from the south and avoid a two-day ride to the north gate, where the passage was free, gladly paused to pay their respects to Saint Torin. To most, the time saved was well worth a prayer.

But the price for Morgan and Duncan, three months before, had been far higher; and they had never reached Dhassa at all. There had been a trap awaiting Morgan when he entered the shrine: a treacherous needle tipped with the Deryni mind-muddling drug merasha, so placed that Morgan was virtually certain to snag his hand on it.

He had done so, and the drug had done its work. When he awoke, powerless and confused, he had found himself prisoner of the rebel Warin de Grey and one of the archbishops' retainers. Only Duncan's timely intervention had saved Morgan from a slow and terror-filled death.

Nor had the rescue been without its price to Duncan. For in the course of the battle which ensued, Duncan had been obliged to reveal his Deryni identity, to use forbidden Deryni magic to make good their escape. In their flight from the death-filled shrine, flames had been kindled by falling torches, turning the ancient wood structure into a raging inferno.

It was this event, coupled with deeds before the burning, which had brought the winds of anathema howling about the heads of the two who now approached. And it was this set of deeds which they hoped to expiate, could they once reach the relative refuge of the Bishop of Dhassa's presence, to throw themselves on his mercy.

The two men sat silently for a long while in the thicket, listening, sniffing the air, then easing themselves quietly from saddles to the ground. They had seen blue smoke rising in the noon heat beyond the ridge ahead: the smoke of many campfires. Now, as they listened and tested the wind with their extended senses, they could hear the sounds of animals tethered beyond the ridge, the murmur of voices in the valley far below, could catch the pungent scent of woodsmoke on the still spring air.

With a sigh of resignation, Morgan glanced at his kinsman and gave a wry smile, then tethered his horse and began slowly working his way up the slope toward the crest of the ridge, Duncan following. There was ample forest cover as they climbed the ridge, thinning to brush and tall spring grass as they approached the crest. For the last dozen yards, they crawled through the tall grass on hands and knees, gradually sinking to their bellies as they neared the edge.

Blinking like lizards in the brilliant sunlight, they raised their heads cautiously to peer over the edge. The valley below was lightly forested, but the trees concealed little from the two observing from atop the ridge. As far as the eye could see, to the south and to the eastern valley wall, the valley floor was alive with armed men and their encampment; with tents and pavilions, cook-fires and forges, picket lines of tethered horses, pens of animals for provisioning.

Heraldic banners stirred outside the more ornate of the tents, their colorful devices bright and shimmering in the noonday sun. A few were familiar to the two who watched, but many more could not be identified. Only the occasional banners of violet and gold, the rich pennants of purple surmounting the regular battle standards, identified this encampment as an episcopal army. From the condition of the camp, they had been there for some time; by all indications, they expected to be there a good while longer.

As Morgan suppressed a sigh of dismay, Duncan nudged his elbow and gestured to the left with his chin. Far in that direction, almost out of their range of vision, Morgan could just make out the former site of Saint Torin's. A blackened pit yawned where the shrine once had stood: a charred tangle of beams and collapsed walls were all that was left of the once-famous place of pilgrimage.

But there were soldiers swarming there as well, clearing out the debris and digging in the ruins. Over to the right, more soldiers were cutting new beams and timbers. Apparently the bishops had put at least some of their army to work rebuilding Saint Torin's while they waited for war.

Shaking his head grimly, Morgan inched backward until he could safely scramble to a crouch, then began to make his way back down the slope, straightening as he went. Duncan followed. When they had reached the comparative safety of their horses, Morgan sighed and leaned one arm across his saddle, glancing at Duncan.

"Well, we certainly can't slip past the entire episcopal army," he said in a low voice. "Any ideas on what to try next?"

Duncan toyed with a strap on his horse's stirrup and frowned. "It's hard to say. Apparently they aren't requiring travelers to go through the shrine anymore, because there isn't any. But I doubt they're letting just anyone cross the lake to Dhassa, either."

"Hmm. I wonder." Morgan scratched a forefinger thoughtfully across his beard and grimaced.

"How about trying to bluff our way through?" Duncan suggested, after a pause. "In these clothes, and bearded as we are, I doubt anyone would recognize us. You saw how little reaction we got on the road this morning. We could even try to steal a boat tonight, if you think the broad daylight idea is too daring."

Morgan shook his head. "We daren't risk even that. We *must* reach the dissident bishops. If we were captured before we could get to them, and had to use our powers to extricate ourselves, we'd never be able to convince the bishops of our sincerity."

"Then what do you suggest? Take two days to ride to the northern approach to the city? That's hardly feasible."

"No, there has to be another way." Morgan paused. "Ah, you don't suppose there are any Transfer Portals around here, do you? I wonder how the ancients built them."

Duncan snorted. "As well wonder why we can't fly! What we could do, though, while we're trying to figure out a solution, is to talk to a few local citizens and find out what the situation in the valley really is. If worse comes to worst, we can always appropriate another Torin badge and try the broad daylight approach. I still have mine, you know."

At Morgan's look of surprise, Duncan pulled the object in question from his belt pouch and began attaching it to the front of his leather cap. Morgan watched the operation in silent appreciation for his kinsman's foresight, then nodded slowly as he considered the last suggestion. Within minutes, they were moving back toward the road to choose a suitable informant. It could do no harm to pretend devotion to the local saint.

They did not have long to wait. After letting a caravan of pack animals and their guards pass unchallenged, their vigil was rewarded by the approach on foot of a fat, balding man in the robes of a minor clerk. The man wiped his sweating face with the sleeve of his habit as he came abreast of where the two lurked; and since there was no one else in sight on the road, and they had not much time, Duncan cast a final look at his cousin and stepped into the road to bow with a flourish.

"Good morrow, sir clerk," he said courteously, sweeping his leather cap from his head and smiling engagingly, making certain the man saw the Torin badge. "I wonder, could you tell me whose army lies camped in the valley below?"

Duncan's sudden appearance startled the man; and as he drew back in surprise, his eyes going wide, he backed directly into Morgan, whose hand closed over his opening mouth.

"Just relax, my friend," Morgan murmured, extending his powers as the man began to struggle. "Step backward and don't resist. You won't be harmed."

The man obeyed tremblingly, his eyes going slightly glassy, and Morgan half-dragged him back in the brush until they were safely shielded from the road. When they had reached suitable cover, Duncan touched his fingertips lightly to the man's temples and murmured the words that would seal the trance, smiling faintly as the man's eyes fluttered closed and he sagged against Morgan's support. When they had eased him to the ground and propped him against a tree, Morgan sat back on his haunches with a grin as Duncan made sure of their control.

"That was too easy," Duncan murmured, glancing up with a gleam in his eye. "I feel almost guilty."

"Let's see if he can tell us anything worthwhile, before you gloat," Morgan said, touching his fingers lightly to the man's forehead. "What's your name, my friend? Come on, you're all right. You can open your eyes."

The man's eyes flicked open and he looked up at Morgan in mild surprise. "I be Master Thierry, good sir, a clerk of the household of Lord Martin of Greystoke." His eyes were wide and guileless, with no trace of fear showing through the Deryni-induced trance.

"Are those Bishop Cardiel's troops assembled in the valley?" Duncan asked.

"Aye, sir. They be camped there more than two months now, waiting on word from the king. 'Tis said His young Majesty will come soon to Dhassa, to be absolved of the fearful evil he has taken upon himself."

"Fearful evil?" Morgan questioned. "What kind of fearful evil?"

"The Deryni powers, sir. An' they say he has given succor to the wicked Duke Alaric of Corwyn an' his cousin, the heretic priest, when all know that those were excommunicated when the bishops met in April last."

"Ah—yes, we know about that," Duncan said uneasily. "Tell me, though, Thierry, how does one get into the city now? Are pilgrims still obliged to pay homage to Saint Torin?"

"Ach, of course Saint Torin must still be honored, sir. Ye wear the badge. Ye should know. His pilgrim tokens are distributed near where stood the paddock of the old chapel. Fearful rogues they were, who burned it down this spring. Duke Al—"

"Who guards the ferries?" Morgan interrupted impatiently. "Can the boatmen be bribed? What kind of guard is kept on the quays?"

"*Bribed*, sir? The boatmen of Saint—"

"Relax, Thierry," Duncan said, touching the man's forehead and exerting control. "Is it possible for two men to cross the lake without being challenged at the quay?"

Thierry had slumped back against the tree at Duncan's touch, and now resumed his previous matter-of-fact recitation. "No, sir. The guards have orders to search all travelers and to detain those who look suspicious." He paused wistfully. "I must say that you do look suspicious, sirs."

"Indeed," Morgan muttered under his breath.

"Beg pardon, sir?"

"I said, is there any way to get to Dhassa besides across the lake? Aside from riding around to the other gate, that is."

Thierry knew of none. Nor did the next three travelers whom Morgan and Duncan interrogated and left sleeping beneath the trees. Happily, their fifth informant, a grizzled master cobbler, was more useful. His response to the fateful question began in much the same way; but this time, it had a slightly different ending.

"And do you know of any other way to the city besides crossing the lake?" Morgan asked patiently, never dreaming that he would receive an affirmative answer.

"Nae more, sor. There used to be, but that's been twenty years now."

"There used to be?" Duncan murmured, sitting up straighter and glancing quickly at his cousin.

"Aye, there was a wee track through the high pass to the north," the man said pleasantly. "Hardly more than a game trail, it was. But that was washed out by the floods when I was just a lad. 'Tis just as well. Otherwise, impious souls might try to reach the holy city without paying their respects to our patron. That, of course, would be—"

"Oh, unthinkable, of course," Morgan agreed, edging closer to gaze into the man's eyes. "Now, just where was this trail, Dawkin? How can we get to it?"

"Och, ye cannae get through. I told ye, it's washed awa'.

If ye would to enter Dhassa, ye must take the ferry—unless, of course, ye wish to ride to the northern gate."

"No, I think we'll try to find this old trail," Morgan said with a small smile. "Now, tell us how to find it."

"If'n yer sure." The man shrugged with apparent lack of concern. "Ye go back to tha road and follow it for 'bout half a mile, then take a trail that heads north. After a few hundred yards, the trail enters a defile that splits north an' west. Ye take the north fork; the west fork leads to the village of Garwode. After that, ye're headed toward th' old trail."

"You've been a great help, Dawkin," Morgan said with a grin, nodding toward Duncan.

"Oh, it won't do ye a bit of good," the man chattered on, as Duncan leaned toward him. "The trail's now't but a track, an' it's washed out. Ye cannae get through . . ."

His voice trailed off and his head lolled onto his chest as Duncan exerted control, and he lapsed almost at once into comfortable snores. With a smile, Duncan got to his feet and glanced down at the man; then, on second thought, he bent to remove the Torin badge from the man's shirt. He handed it to Morgan with a wry grin as they made their way back to the horses, and Morgan polished it against his sleeve before affixing it to his cap. The stolen pewter winked warm and silvery in the leaf-filtered sunlight as the two mounted up.

"Remind me to offer a special prayer of thanks for Master Dawkin, Duncan—the next time we visit Saint Torin's officially."

"I shall, indeed." Duncan chuckled. "The next time we visit Saint Torin's officially."

An hour later found the two riders high in the mountains walling Lake Jashan and Dhassa from the rolling plains to the west. After taking the fork in the defile that Dawkin had described, they had made their way down a gentle slope to a grassy meadow beyond, where half a dozen scrawny sheep and goats cropped contentedly at the rich mountain grass. They saw no one in the vicinity, and the animals had paid them little attention beyond eyeing the horses warily for a few minutes. It had taken a while to locate the trail that led from the other side of the meadow, but at last it was found and the two proceeded on their way.

The trail, once found, was little more than the track Dawkin had described, and obviously little used. The new green growth of spring grass had hardly been disturbed, and field flowers seemed to spring in riotous profusion from every patch of earth and rock cranny. The trail worsened as they rode, the ascent steepening and the footing becoming less certain. The horses were still able to pick their way without too much trouble, but far ahead they could hear the sound of rushing water. Morgan, in the lead, chewed at his lip thoughtfully as he listened, finally turning back to glance at Duncan.

"Do you hear that?"

"It sounds like a waterfall. What do you want to bet that—"

"Don't say it!" Morgan replied. "I was thinking the same thing."

The sound of rushing water grew louder as they rounded the next bend in the trail, and they were not surprised to find their way barred shortly by a rather sizeable stream. A cascade roared down the mountainside to their left and formed a fast-flowing torrent that disappeared into the forest to their right, in the direction of Lake Jashan. There appeared to be no way around it.

"Well, what have we here?" Morgan said, drawing rein to survey the flood.

Duncan reined his horse beside Morgan's and studied the falls dismally. "In case you require a reply, that is called a waterfall. Any brilliant ideas?"

"No brilliant ones, I'm afraid." Morgan moved his horse a few yards downstream to study the current patterns. "How deep do you think it is?"

"Deep enough," Duncan replied. "Well over our heads. Besides, the horses could never get across in that current.

We'd be swept away and battered to death—if we didn't drown outright."

"You're probably right," Morgan said. He reined in his horse once again, then turned in the saddle to peer up at the falls.

"How about going above the falls? We might be able to get across, even if the horses couldn't."

"It's worth a look, I suppose."

Swinging a leg over his saddle, Duncan jumped to the ground and shrugged his leather cloak back on his shoulders, letting his mount's reins dangle. As he began scrambling up a fairly easy game track toward the falls, Morgan, too, dismounted and secured his mount, following close behind his kinsman.

They had traversed perhaps two-thirds the distance up the face of the cliff when Duncan froze momentarily, then scrambled onto an outcrop and turned to give Morgan a hand up. The ledge where the two found themselves seemed quite ordinary at first; but then Duncan drew Morgan's attention to what had first caught his eye: a deep cleft in the rock, rising vertically for more than thirty feet until it was lost in a veil of mist from the thundering falls. They needed several treacherous steps to reach a point from which they could both peer into the cleft.

The opening was narrow, no more than five feet at its entrance, but from where they stood they could not see the back wall, lost in the shadows. The side walls, as far as the eye could see, were covered with a verdant growth of lichen and moss, the velvety perfection broken only by an occasional patch of ruby or topaz. In the floor of the cleft, which lay a few feet below the level at which they stood, a thin trickle of icy water welled out of a crack in the stony floor, the water so cold that the air above it condensed into shimmering mist where a narrow shaft of sunlight struck it.

The two of them gazed at the swirling mist in awe for several seconds, neither quite willing to break the mystical mood the place had cast. Then Duncan sighed, and the spell was broken. Together they peered more closely into the cleft beyond, returning their focus to their original concern.

"What do you think?" Morgan whispered. "Could it go all the way through?"

Duncan shrugged and lowered himself gingerly into the cleft to take a closer look, but after only a cursory incursion into the shadows, he turned and came back, shaking his head as he accepted Morgan's hand up.

"No joy there, I'm afraid. It doesn't go much farther than what you can see from here. Let's see what's at the top."

The prospects farther up were no better than below. The water was fast-moving and tumbled over jagged rocks and enormous boulders in the streambed. It looked shallower here, probably little more than waist-deep, but the current was treacherous. One false step could sweep a man's legs from under him and carry him over the falls to the rocks below. The watercourse farther upstream was even worse, with steep banks sloping sharply upward on either side, with no room for a man to even stand at water level, much less cross it. Some other way would have to be found, perhaps farther downstream, below the falls.

With a quick grimace of frustration, Morgan turned to begin climbing back down the cliff face, Duncan waiting above him to follow. But no sooner had Morgan begun his descent, than Duncan glanced below and froze, reaching to touch Morgan's shoulder in alarm.

"Alaric, get down!" he whispered, flattening himself against the rock and restraining his cousin with a warning hand. "Get down, and then don't move. Look behind you, quietly!"

CHAPTER EIGHT

*"Make thy shadow as the night in the midst
of the noonday . . ."*

ISAIAH 16:3

HUGGING the cliff face, Morgan turned his head slowly and peered over the edge to where Duncan pointed. At first he could see nothing out of the ordinary: merely one of the horses placidly cropping grass beside the stream bank below.

Then he realized he couldn't see the other horse—and caught a flash of movement farther underneath him, closer to the falls. He leaned out farther to see what the motion had been, then froze in astonishment. He could hardly believe what he saw.

Four children, their heads tousled and damp, homespun tunics plastered close to their bodies, were leading the second horse into the water at the edge of the waterfall. The horse was hoodwinked with what looked like the blanket from the saddle's pack, and one of the children held his hand on the animal's nose to keep it from nickering as they urged it into the cold stream. The oldest of the four appeared to be a boy of about eleven; the youngest could not have been more than seven.

"What the devil?" Morgan murmured, hazarding an astonished glance at Duncan.

Duncan pursed his lips grimly, then moved as though to start down the slope after them. "Come on. The little thieves are going to steal both horses if we don't stop them." Morgan could only barely hear him above the roar of the water.

"No, wait." Morgan grabbed Duncan's cloak and halted him in mid-motion, watching as children and horse waded toward the falls in a patch of calm water. "You know, I think those beastly urchins have a way across. Look."

Even as Morgan spoke, horse and children disappeared behind the falls. Morgan glanced around, then scrambled partway down the side of the cliff, beckoning Duncan to join him behind a rocky outcropping. As they took cover, horse and children reappeared at the other side of the falls, drenched and shivering, but none the worse for wear. The youngest of the four, a girl by the long braids dripping down her back, scrambled up the embankment with some assistance from her companions, then took the reins and led the snorting horse up and out of the water. As the girl calmed the frightened animal, pulling the blanket from its head to begin wiping it down, the other three children disappeared into the falls once more.

With a look of firm resolve, Morgan slapped Duncan on the shoulder as a signal to go, then began clambering down the side of the cliff, keeping to the shadows as much as possible and trusting the roar of the waterfall to cover the sound of their descent. His face was grim but pleased as he and Duncan ducked into cover near the remaining horse, and he controlled the urge to smile again as the three children came out of the falls and hauled themselves dripping onto the bank.

The three glanced back at their friend across the stream, who was letting the captured horse graze while she scanned the cliff far above their heads—looking for *them*, Morgan realized. Then the other three began moving stealthily toward the remaining horse.

Morgan let them all get within touching distance of the animal, one of them actually taking the reins and reaching to stroke the beast's nose. Then he and Duncan broke from cover and started grabbing children.

"Michael!" squealed the lone child on the opposite bank. "No! No! Let them go!"

In a flurry of screams, frantic squirming, and flailing arms and legs, the children tried to escape. Morgan succeeded in getting a strong grip on the first boy, who had been gentling the horse, and had a hold on a second for an instant. But the second boy was also the oldest, and strong, struggling hard; and after a few frantic squirms, he was able to wrench loose to flee shrieking toward the falls.

Duncan, his hands controlling the third child, made an effort to capture the second as he shot past, but ended up with only a handful of wet tunic to show for his trouble. The boy—for there was no mistaking that fact with the tunic missing—streaked for the falls and jumped into the water like an eel, disappearing behind the falls before either of the men could take more than a few steps in that direction.

The two children the men had managed to hold onto continued to struggle and scream, and Morgan was forced to silence his with a hastily applied touch. The girl on the opposite bank had scrambled into the saddle of the stolen horse and was guiding it toward the falls, reaching a hand down for her escaping comrade as he scrambled from the water in the buff.

Morgan had no choice but to call up a spell. Magic would but terrify the children more at this point, but he could not permit them to escape and tell tales of the two men trying to ford the stream. Morgan let his child slip limply to the ground and raised his arms.

As the two on the other side tried to flee, drumming thin, bare legs against the heavy saddle in an effort to make the big horse move, a wall of incandescence suddenly sprang up before them, blocking their way. The children pulled their mount to a plunging halt, their eyes wide as saucers as the light extended to a semi-circle hemming them against the bank of the stream. Duncan calmed the child in his grasp and laid his limp form across the saddle of the remaining horse, then nursed a bloodied hand to his lips, bent to plunge it into the rushing water.

"One of the little beggars bit me!" he murmured, as Morgan put his child across the saddle beside the first and glanced anxiously across at the other two children.

"Just stay where you are and you won't be harmed," Morgan called, raising his voice to be heard over the roar of the falls, and brandishing a finger at the two. "I'm not going to hurt you, but you can't leave yet. Just stay where you are."

As the children watched, wide-eyed and terrified despite Morgan's reassurances, Duncan took the reins of the remaining horse and led it toward the falls, hooding it with the tunic he had pulled from the fleeing boy. Morgan walked beside the animal, steadying the two sleeping children in the saddle and watching the other two warily. He gasped involuntarily as he entered the icy water, nearly losing control of the restraining light-ring for an instant, then inched along beside the animal and into the falls. There was a narrow ledge behind the roaring wall of water, waist-deep and covered with green slime and treacherous, stream-polished pebbles that slid under a man's boot or a horse's hoof. But they were able to pick their way across without serious incident.

As the nervous horse lurched up the bank, Duncan caught the two children as they slid from the saddle and laid them gently on a patch of grass in the sunshine. Morgan calmed the horse, then raised one eyebrow and strode toward the two children on the other horse. The pair sat stiff in the saddle, petrified but defiant, as Morgan walked through the wall of light and reached a wet hand to the bridle. As he looked up at them, the light behind him died.

"Now, do you want to tell me what you intended to do with my horse?" he asked calmly.

The front child, the girl, glanced behind at her partner and whimpered, then looked wildly back. The older one's arms tightened around the girl's waist reassuringly as he returned Morgan's gaze, a hard gleam flashing through the fear.

"You're Deryni, aren't you? You're spying on my lord bishops."

Morgan suppressed a smile and pulled the first child from the saddle, without resistance from the boy. The girl went limp as Morgan touched her, from fear rather than any manifestation of Deryni power, and the boy sat a little straighter in the saddle, indigo eyes going cold in the tanned young face. Morgan handed the little girl over to Duncan, exchanging his human armload for a handful of wet tunic, which he tossed to the boy. His gray eyes were slightly amused as the boy took the tunic without a word and slipped it over his head.

"Well?" the boy demanded, tugging his tunic into place with a defiant gesture. "*Aren't* you Deryni? Aren't you spying?"

"I asked you first. What were you going to do with my horse? Sell it?"

"Of course not. My brothers and I were going to take it to our father, so that he could ride with the bishops' army. The captains told him that our cart horse was too old, and couldn't keep up on a long march."

"You were going to take it to your father," Morgan said, nodding slowly. "Son, do you know what they call people who take things that don't belong to them?"

"I'm not a thief and I'm not your son!" the boy retorted. "We looked around and didn't see anyone, so we thought the horses must have strayed from the encampment down below. They *are* fighting horses, after all."

"Are they, now?" Morgan mused. "And you thought it quite likely that such horses would be wandering loose." The boy nodded gravely.

"You're lying, of course," Morgan said flatly, grasping the boy by the bicep and swinging him down to the ground.

"But, then, that's to be expected. Tell me, are there any more obstacles between here and the Dhassa gates, or—"

"You *are* spies! I knew it!" the boy blurted, starting to fight as his feet hit the ground. "Let me go! Ow, you're hurting me! Stop it!"

Shaking his head in annoyance, Morgan deftly twisted one of the boy's arms behind his back and held it, increasing his pressure until the boy doubled over with the pain. When he had ceased struggling, his attention wholly on the hurting arm—which he had discovered did not hurt if he stopped struggling—Morgan released him abruptly and swung the boy around to face him.

"Now, relax!" Morgan commanded, turning his gray gaze on the boy to Truth-Read. "I haven't time to listen to your hysterics."

The boy tried to resist, but he had no chance against Morgan's compulsions. Blue eyes met gray ones defiantly for just an instant; but then the young will yielded and the blue eyes blinked and went a little glassy. As the boy calmed enough to be Read, Morgan straightened and released the boy's arm, letting out a relieved sigh as he tightened his belt and brushed a drying strand of hair back from his face.

"Now," he said, again looking the boy in the eyes, "what can you tell me about the rest of the trail? Can we get through?"

"Not on horses," the boy said calmly. "You could probably get through on foot, but the horses—never. There's a slide area ahead: mud and shale. Not even the mountain ponies can get across."

"A slide area? Is there any other way around?"

"Not to Dhassa. The way you came leads back to Gar-wode. Hardly anyone ever uses this trail, because you can't get through with pack animals or baggage."

"I see. Anything else you can tell us about the slide area?"

"Not really. The worst part is about a hundred yards across, but you can see the other end of the trail before you start across. It'll be muddy this time of year. You'll just have to pick your way across as best you can."

Morgan glanced at Duncan, who had moved to his side during the interrogation. "Anything else?"

"How about the gates at Dhassa?" Duncan asked. "Will we have any trouble getting in?"

The boy glanced at the Saint Torin badge pinned to Duncan's cap, then shook his head. "Your badges will pass you. Just mingle with other people who get on the ferries. There are scores of strangers in Dhassa these days."

"Excellent. Any more questions, Duncan?"

"No. What are we going to do with them, though?"

"We'll leave them here with the horses and a few false memories to explain how they got them."

"You're going to let them *have* the horses," Duncan said incredulously.

Morgan touched the boy's forehead lightly and caught him as he crumpled, then picked him up to move him beside the other children.

"We can't take them with us, it seems."

"But—you're encouraging their thievery!" Duncan began.

Morgan shrugged as he laid the boy beside the other children. "You heard what he said about why he was stealing the horses."

"Yes. So that their father can join the bishops' army and maybe kill us later on!"

"Not if we win over the bishops." Morgan smiled as he smoothed a lock of hair off the boy's forehead and straightened up.

"Feisty little devil, isn't he?"

Duncan gave a grudging smile. "I wouldn't be surprised if he were the one who bit me."

"Humph, I'd probably have bitten you, too," Morgan said. He touched the boy's forehead again for just an instant, setting the memories straight, then pulled the saddlebags from his saddle and slung them over his shoulder with a grin.

"Ready to go sliding, Cousin?"

THE sliding about which Morgan joked so lightly came very near to costing them their lives. The portion of trail affected by the slide, though shorter by a third than they had been led to expect, was also at least twice as treacherous and steep. Besides being slick with sand and shale, it was also muddy.

Nor was this a thick mud, which might impede motion, should a climber start to slip. Instead, it was a viscous quagmire, capable of turning semi-liquid in the twinkling of an eye. Duncan's saddlebags were lost in the crossing, and very nearly Duncan himself. But once the slope had been traversed, the way onward was as easy as the boy had predicted. When, around midafternoon, they reached the Dhassa side of Lake Jashan, they found it a comparatively easy task to slip through the gates among a group of new arrivals just off the ferries. Today and the next were market days, and there were, indeed, many strangers in Dhassa. Dhassa's newest arrivals had little difficulty making their way from the gates to the crowded market square outside the Bishop's Palace.

Morgan picked up several pieces of fruit from a market stall and flipped a small coin to the proprietor, then pushed his way back into the crowd and continued to watch and listen. He and Duncan had been in the square for nearly an hour now, mingling with the local citizens and asking the occasional question; but thus far, they had been unable to discover a way to get into the Bishop's Palace undetected. It was essential that they guard their tongues, for there were soldiers scattered all through the crowded marketplace. But they dared not wait too long to act, or the square would clear with the coming darkness and they would risk exposure. As things now stood, they had no place to go once darkness fell.

The sights and smells and sounds of market day pervaded the square in a tangle of brilliant color, boisterous voices and complaining pack animals, the smells of spice and dung and new-baked bread, meat roasting on spits, the squeals of pigs and sheep, the frantic cackling of chickens and other feathered things.

Morgan glanced idly at a troupe of jugglers performing outside a silk-hung pavilion, catching a whiff of overly sweet perfume as a soldier lurched through an opening in the curtains. An airy, tinkling music and the sound of female laughter floated from beyond the silk, and the man had a slightly glassy look to his eyes as he staggered into the crowd and was lost from sight. A pair of saucy serving maids jostled him from behind, their laden baskets pushing a wide swath through the crowd, but the girls were unkempt and dirty looking; definitely not to Morgan's taste.

Morgan shifted the saddlebags slung across his shoulder, then bit into one of the apples in his hand, savoring the tart crispness between his teeth. Continuing to glance around as he walked, he spotted his cousin a few stalls down, buying fresh bread and a slab of crusty country cheese. Duncan paused to peer at the stall of the sweet smells and tinkling music for just a moment; then he frowned and began to move away.

Morgan suppressed a grin and began to stroll in the direction Duncan had gone, watching and munching as he walked. At length, Duncan settled on a ledge beside a public well and began eating bread and cheese, cutting off thick chunks of the cheese with his dagger. Morgan made his way to the well and deposited saddlebags and fruit on the ledge beside Duncan. As he leaned against the wall and continued to scan the busy market square, it was a distinct effort to keep his manner casual. One could never tell who might be watching.

"Busy place, isn't it?" he said in a low voice, finishing his apple and tossing the core to where a heavily laden donkey could reach it. He tore off a chunk of bread and cut himself some cheese, gray eyes continuing to scan as he tucked into the more substantial fare. "I hope you've found out more than I did."

Duncan swallowed a mouthful of bread and cheese and looked around cautiously. "Little of any immediate use, I'm afraid. But I'll tell you this: the bishops are going to have trouble on their hands, if they don't do something fairly soon. Popular support is with Cardiel and his army right now, but there are many who aren't happy about his plans. They consider it a disgrace that leaders of the Church should quarrel among themselves to the point of schism, and I can't say that I blame them. Especially on the eve of war."

"Humph." Morgan cut off another piece of cheese and glanced behind him before leaning closer to Duncan. "Did you hear about old Bishop Wolfram?"

"No, what happened?"

"There was an assassination attempt a few weeks ago. It didn't succeed, but—" He broke off as a pair of soldiers strolled nearby, and took another bite of bread, chewing nonchalantly until the two men were out of earshot.

"Anyway, that's why the gates to the palace are so closely guarded. Cardiel doesn't dare risk anything happening to one of his bishops. If one of the Six were to be killed now, Loris and Corrigan in Coroth would appoint his successor. And we all know to whom that successor would owe his loyalty."

"Thereby giving Loris the twelve voices he needs to make his decretals legal in fact as well as in name," Duncan whispered.

Morgan finished his cheese and dusted his gloved hands against his thighs, then turned to dip water from the well. His eyes flicked to the palace gates as he drank, and then to the towers of the palace beyond. He filled the dipper again and handed it across to his cousin, sinking down on the ledge once again as Duncan drank.

"Y'know," Morgan murmured, studying the crowd in the square, "I think the crowd is beginning to thin. We're going to be conspicuous soon, if we don't decide what to do."

Duncan handed the dipper back to Morgan and wiped his mouth against his sleeve. "I know. Fewer soldiers, and more and more clergy."

Bells began to chime in a tower far away and to the rear of them, and were soon echoed by the great bells within the walls of the Bishop's Palace. Duncan paused as the bells began to ring, his eyes still scanning the crowd, then slowly straightened, an intense look coming upon his face.

"What is it?" Morgan murmured, careful not to betray his emotion by voice or gesture. There were soldiers striding by again.

"The monks, Alaric," Duncan whispered, nodding toward the gates. "Look where they're going."

Morgan turned slowly and let his eyes follow the direction of his kinsman's gaze. A postern gate had opened in the lower left portion of the huge palace gates to permit a handful of cowled monks to enter. He glanced back at Duncan to find his cousin stuffing the last of the bread and cheese into the saddlebags. As he looked askance, Duncan shot him a quick, conspiratorial wink and took the last apple, polishing it against his sleeve. Mystified, Morgan picked up the saddlebags and followed as Duncan started to stroll slowly in the direction of the gates. He touched his cousin's right elbow in question as the two of them headed along the edge of the square.

"Do you see where the monks are going?" Duncan murmured around a bite of apple.

"Yes."

Duncan took another bite and continued walking. "And they aren't being challenged, are they?" he said. "Now, look where they're coming from, around to your left. Mind you don't stare."

Morgan glanced casually in the direction indicated and finally saw a door leading into a deeply shadowed background, apparently the side door to a monastic church. Periodically, the door would open to disgorge one or two monks in cowled black habits. As far as Morgan could see, all the monks who left the church were heading toward the palace gates. And none of them were being turned away.

"Where are they all going?" Morgan murmured, as his cousin finished his apple and hitched up his sword under his cloak. The main doors to the church were farther to the left, below the stubby stone towers, and they could see townspeople going in, several monks standing at the church doors to greet those who entered.

"I should have realized," Duncan said under his breath, "that in any city where there's a large monastic community, it's customary for the brethren to attend services in the bishop's basilica, if there is one. They're on their way to Vespers."

"Vespers," Morgan breathed. He kept silent as they continued to walk toward the church, now heading away from the palace gates. Then: "Duncan, we are not going to attend Vespers in that church, are we?" It was less a question than a statement.

Duncan shook his head lightly, and Morgan had to control a smile.

"That's what I thought."

Ten minutes later, two more monks joined the line of brethren filing slowly into the Bishop's Palace. They walked briskly to catch up with their fellows, these two laggard monks in their tall, black cowls and floor-length robes. They bowed their heads humbly as they passed between the sentries guarding the postern gate, hands piously folded in long, loose sleeves. Inside, as they passed sedately along the glistening corridors, an occasional footstep sounded oddly hollow amidst the sandaled tread of their brother monks.

But the two moved with care, anxious to do nothing that might cause them to stand out from their fellows, for these were no ordinary monks. They bore steel beneath their coarse black robes: swords girded close against their sides, and daggers in boots and sleeves and belts, and bright mail beneath the riding leathers the robes covered.

And something more telling there was, to distinguish

these particular monks, had anyone known. For the two at the end of the line were Deryni, and carried magic in their souls.

Morgan and Duncan drew aside as the rest filed into the basilica, blending into the shadows of a cul-de-sac at the end of a nearby corridor. After a short while, they could hear the sound of the monks' voices raised in song and praise, and then the sung responses of the service itself. Several times the doors opened to admit latecomers, and once Duncan thought he heard Cardiel's voice within.

Finally the office of Vespers ended, and the doors were flung wide. Servants of the bishop's household, pages and squires, several lords and their ladies, and several prelates filed from the chapel, some engaged in low conversation, all heading in different directions where the corridor branched before the doors. In the midst of them all came Bishops Cardiel and Arilan themselves, followed shortly by a number of priests and clerks and then more lords and their ladies.

Duncan nudged Morgan in the ribs as the two bishops appeared, for he knew Arilan and had seen Cardiel at a distance before. But Morgan froze with an intake of breath at the sight of a woman and child who followed a short distance behind the lords and ladies. The woman, dressed all in sky blue, was speaking in a low voice to another, darker lady, her hand on the shoulder of a boy about four years of age. She was tall and slim, her carriage regal without being imposing, and Morgan's eyes widened almost involuntarily as he drank in every detail of her presence.

Deep, wide eyes of a cornflower hue, set in a heart-shaped face framed by gossamer silk; hair the color of flame in sunlight, swept wing-like past her temples and caught in a loose knot at the nape; the nose delicate and slightly upturned; the cheekbones high and touched with a blush of rose; the mouth full, generous, tinged with color and inviting; the redheaded child at her side was sleepy-eyed, his silken hair tousled.

Except in his dreams, Morgan had seen the pair only

once, what seemed like an eternity ago, in a coach outside the ruined shrine not far from here. But on that occasion their image had been graven on his memory for all time to come. He reminded himself that the woman was married, the child some other man's son, then wondered anew who they might be.

He felt a slight pressure at his left elbow and turned to find Duncan looking at him rather oddly. Morgan flashed him an apologetic look as he gathered his wits about him, then hazarded one last glance back at the corridor before returning his attention to the two bishops. But the woman and her child were gone.

As Duncan drew his hood farther onto his forehead and stepped out sedately, Morgan followed, trying to assume as near a copy of Duncan's humble walk and manner as possible. The two bishops had rounded the turn of the next intersection, but they came back into sight as Morgan and Duncan followed at a discreet distance until the two prelates disappeared through a set of double doors. Uncertainly, the two Deryni came to a halt a short distance from the doors and considered their next move.

"What's in there, do you know?" Morgan whispered.

Duncan shook his head. "I've never been here before either. It could be the Curia chamber, for all I know. We'll just have to chance—"

He broke off as a group of soldiers came around the corner and halted in front of the doors. As one of them knocked respectfully, another glanced aside and saw the two monks loitering there. With a slight frown, he turned to murmur something to one of his companions, then headed toward them purposefully. Morgan and Duncan, with an exchange of apprehensive glances, attempted to appear as innocuous as possible.

"Good evening, Brothers," the soldier said, eyeing them curiously. "May I ask what you're doing here? Unless you have permission from your superior, you're not permitted in this part of the palace. You know that."

Duncan bowed slightly, keeping his face carefully averted. "We have urgent business with His Grace of Dhassa, sir. It is vital that we see him."

"I'm afraid that won't be possible, Brother," the soldier said, shaking his head. "Their Excellencies are already overdue at a convocation meeting."

"We only need a moment of his time," Duncan ventured, glancing at Morgan and wondering how they were going to extricate themselves from this one. "Perhaps if we could speak with them as they walked . . . I know they will wish to see us."

"I hardly think that likely," the soldier began, beginning to get a little irritated with these two insistent monks. His prolonged conversation had attracted the attention of several of his colleagues, including the officer of the guard. "However, if you'd care to give me your names, I could——"

"What seems to be the trouble, Selden?" the guard officer asked, approaching slowly with several of his men at his back. "You brothers know you're not meant to be here. Didn't Selden tell you that?"

"Oh, he did, sir," Duncan mumbled, bowing again. "But——"

"Sir," one of the guards staring at Morgan interrupted suspiciously, "that man looks like he has something under his robe. Brother, what is th——"

As the man reached for his elbow, Morgan's hand instinctively moved toward the hilt of his sword, and he stepped back. The movement was sufficient to swirl the robes closer around the sheathed blade, silhouetting it beneath the cloth, and to show the toe of a riding boot instead of the sandals that should have gone with monastic attire.

Several of the soldiers gave a concerted gasp as the implication registered, and then they were rushing to grab Morgan's arms, pinning him against the wall and entangling his sword arm. He was aware that Duncan, too, was under assault; and then someone got a grip on the shoulder of his robe and yanked until the fabric parted with a muffled, ripping sound. Morgan's hair gleamed like a sleek golden helmet as the cowl fell away.

"God in Heaven, this is no monk!" one of the soldiers gasped, recoiling involuntarily from the impact of the cold gray eyes.

Even as Morgan was borne to the floor by the massed weight of five or six bodies, he continued to struggle, almost throwing off their restraints at one point. But then he was pinned, helpless, swords leveled at throat and side, one blade pressing dangerously hard against his jugular.

Abruptly he stopped fighting and let them disarm him, biting his lip as they removed even the stiletto in its slim wrist sheath. As they pulled away the black robes and discovered the mail beneath his riding leathers, he forced himself to relax, hoping to allay any senseless brutality. His captors appeared to appreciate the cooperation, for they merely consolidated their hold on him, one man sitting on each of his limbs while a fifth continued to hold a dagger to his throat. He decided against trying to raise his head to see what had happened to Duncan. He dared not risk getting his throat cut before he could talk his way out of this mess.

The guard officer straightened, breathing hard, and sheathed his sword in disgust as he glared down at the two prisoners.

"Who are you? Assassins?" He prodded Morgan in the ribs with the toe of his boot, none too gently. "What's your name?"

"My name is for the bishops only," Morgan said softly, staring up at the ceiling and forcing himself to remain calm.

"Oh, it is, is it? Selden, search him. Davis, what about the other one?"

"Nothing to identify him, sir," a guard replied from Duncan's side.

"Selden?"

Selden fumbled with the pouch at Morgan's belt, then opened it and extracted a number of small gold and silver coins and a small doeskin bag with drawstrings. The bag was heavy in his hand as he lifted it from the pouch, and the guard officer saw something change in his captive's face as the guard handed it up.

"Something more important than gold, isn't it?" the officer guessed shrewdly, loosening the ties and opening the bag.

Two golden rings tumbled out into his hand as he turned the bag bottom-up. One was a heavy gold band set with an onyx, the black stone etched with the golden Lion of Gwynedd: the ring of the King's Champion. The other showed an emerald gryphon set in an onyx face: the seal of Alaric Morgan, Duke of Corwyn.

The man's eyes widened as he recognized the devices, his mouth going agape. Then he glanced down at his captive once more, squinting through the beard. A gasp escaped his lips as he recognized the man lying at his feet.

"Dear God, it's Morgan!" he whispered, his eyes going wider still.

CHAPTER NINE

*"Mine own conscience is more to me than
what the world says."*

CICERO

"MORGAN!"

"My God! The Deryni among us!"

Several of the men crossed themselves furtively, and those holding the prisoners shrank back, but none of them loosened their holds.

Just then, one half of the double doors to the room opened, and a priest poked his head out. He took one look at the soldiers massed outside the doors, gasped as he saw the two men pinned spread-eagled on the floor among them, then ducked quickly back inside to return momentarily with a tall man in a violet cassock, with a silver pectoral cross gleaming on his breast. The face of the Bishop of Dhassa was calm and serene beneath the steel-gray hair as he, too, took in the scene with a glance, his pale eyes coming to rest at last on the officer of the guard.

"Who are these men?" Cardiel asked quietly. Gold and amethyst glinted as he rested his hand on the latch of the heavy door, and the guard officer swallowed nervously as he gestured toward his two prisoners.

"Th-these intruders, Your Excellency, they—"

Without further words, he came closer to extend a shaking hand holding the two rings he had taken from Morgan. Cardiel took the rings and inspected them, then glanced carefully at the two, who returned his gaze measure for measure. Then, abruptly, Cardiel turned inside to call, "Denis?" before stepping out into the corridor. Seconds later, Bishop Arilan appeared in the doorway, his face a study in control as he saw and recognized the two prisoners. Cardiel opened his hand to show the rings, but Arilan gave them only a perfunctory glance.

"Father McLain and Duke Alaric," he said carefully. "I see that you have reached Dhassa at last." He folded his arms across his chest, his bishop's ring flashing cold fire in the stillness. "Tell me, have you come to seek our blessings or our deaths?"

His face was stern, the deep blue-violet eyes cold, and yet there was something in his face that Duncan could read to be satisfaction rather than enmity, almost as though he were putting on an act for the benefit of the guards.

Clearing his throat, Duncan attempted to sit upright but almost had to give it up until Arilan signed for the guards to allow it. Duncan slowly drew himself to a sitting position on the corridor floor, two of the guards retaining control of his wrists and another continuing to pin his legs. They were taking no chances. Beside him, Morgan, too, was permitted to slowly wriggle upright, similarly restrained.

"Your Excellency, we crave your pardon for the manner of our coming," Duncan said, "but we had to see you. We have come to give ourselves into your authority. If we have acted wrongly, either now or in the past, we beg to be shown our errors and forgiven. If we have been falsely accused, we hope for the opportunity to show that to you, also."

Several of the guards looked at him sharply as the statement registered, but Arilan seemed implacable. His gaze shifted from Duncan to Morgan and back again. Then he turned and pushed the double doors apart, standing aside in the doorway to face the guards once more.

"Bring them inside and then leave us, please. Bishop Cardiel and I will hear what they have to say."

"But, Your Excellency, these men are outlaws, dangerous, damned by your own decree. They destroyed Saint Torin's, they killed—"

"I know what they have done," Arilan said, "and I am perfectly aware that they are outlaws. Now, do as I say. You may bind them, if it will ease your fears."

"Very well, Excellency."

As the soldiers gingerly pulled the two captives to their feet, several brought forth strips of rawhide and bound their hands tightly in front of them. Cardiel watched silently, following Arilan's lead as his colleague moved back into the room. The priest who had answered the door hurried to pull two heavy chairs away from the fireplace to face into the room. Then, as the guards ushered their prisoners into the room, nervously glancing at Arilan for guidance, the priest stole a covert look at Duncan. Father Hugh de Berry and Father Duncan McLain had been friends since boyhood, seminarians together, ordained on the same day; but he bowed his head in dismay, sick at heart, as Duncan glanced in his direction and attempted a smile of reassurance. Only God knew what the fates now had in store for the man he had thought he knew.

Arilan crossed briskly to one of the chairs and sat, waving dismissal to his secretary and the guards. Father Hugh started to withdraw immediately, but several of the guards hesitated around the doorway. Cardiel, who had lingered nearer the doors, reassured the men with the promise that they might remain on guard outside, and that he would call them if there was any need. He stood adamant until the last one had left the room, then closed the doors securely and locked them. As he took his place in the chair beside Arilan, the younger bishop made a bridge of his fingers and sat looking over them at the prisoners for a long time. Finally, he spoke.

"So, Duncan, you have come back to us. When you left

our service to become the King's Confessor, we lost an able assistant. Now it appears that your career has gone in directions neither of us dreamed."

Duncan bowed his head uncomfortably, well aware of the formal phrasing in Arilan's "we" and "us." The bishop's statement had been relatively neutral, but its deeper meaning could be read in many ways, some of them not at all hopeful. Duncan would need to tread very carefully, indeed, until he ascertained just where the bishop's sympathies lay. For now, his demeanor was stern. Duncan glanced at Morgan and knew that his cousin was waiting for him to speak.

"I am sorry if I have disappointed you, Excellency," he murmured. "I hope to offer an explanation that will at least meet with your understanding. In time, I dare to hope for your forgiveness."

"That remains to be seen. We are in accord on the reasons for your coming, though, are we not?"

Morgan cleared his throat. "Excellency, we were under the impression that the king would be in contact with you, and that he would have advised you of the reasons for our coming."

"He has," Arilan agreed. "However, I had hoped to hear confirmation of those reasons from you. It is your intent, is it not, to attempt to clear your names of the charges levied by the Curia this spring and to seek absolution from the excommunication which was laid upon you at that time?"

"That is our intent, Excellency," Duncan murmured, sinking to his knees and bowing his head once more. Morgan, with a glance at his cousin, followed suit.

"Good. Then we understand one another. I think it would be well if Bishop Cardiel and I heard your individual accounts of what happened at Saint Torin's, each separately." Arilan rose. "My Lord Alaric, if you will come with me, we shall leave Bishop Cardiel and Father McLain to the privacy of this room. This way, if you please."

With a glance at Duncan, Morgan rose from his knees and followed Arilan through a small doorway to the left.

Beyond the door was a small anteroom, its walls pierced only by a single leaded glass window rather high up. A rack of candles burned on a writing table against the wall with the window, and a straight-backed chair stood before the table.

Arilan pulled the chair away from the table and turned it around, then sat, motioning for Morgan to close the door. Morgan obeyed, then turned to stand awkwardly before the bishop. There was a low bench not far from Arilan's chair, against the opposite wall, but Morgan was not invited to sit and did not dare to presume.

Carefully veiling his apprehension, he dropped to one knee at Arilan's feet and bowed his golden head, resting his bound wrists across his upraised knee. He searched briefly for the right words with which to begin, then raised his eyes to Arilan's. Gray eyes met blue-violet ones in a steady, even gaze.

"Is this to be a formal confession, Excellency?"

"Only if you wish it," Arilan replied with a slight smile, "and I suspect that you do not. But I must have your leave to discuss what you tell me with Cardiel. Will you release me thus far from the seal of the confessional?"

"For Cardiel, yes. There is no longer any secret to what we did, since all now know us to be Deryni. But I may have to tell you things which are best kept private from most."

"That is understood. What of the other bishops? How much may I tell them, should such telling become necessary?"

Morgan lowered his eyes. "I must trust your discretion in that matter, Excellency. Since I must make my peace with all of you, I am hardly in a position to dictate terms. You may tell them as you see fit."

"Thank you."

Arilan's pause became an awkward silence, and Morgan realized that he was expected to begin. He wet his lips nervously, painfully aware how much depended upon what he said in the next minutes.

"I beg you to bear with me, Excellency," he murmured. "This is very difficult for me. The last time I knelt in confession, it was at the feet of one who had sworn to slay me. Warin de Grey held me captive beneath Saint Torin's, and Monsignor Gorony with him. There I was forced to begin a similar recitation of sins which I did not commit."

"No one forced you to come here, Alaric."

"No."

Arilan waited for a moment, then sighed. "Am I meant to infer, then, that you claim to be innocent of all the charges brought against you in the Curia?"

Morgan shook his head. "No, Excellency. I fear that we did do most of the things of which Gorony accused us. What I wish to clarify is why we did the things we did, and to ask whether, in your judgment, we could have done any differently, if we hoped to survive the trickery prepared for us."

"Trickery?" Arilan made a steeple of his forefingers and rested them lightly against his lips. "Suppose you tell me about trickery, then, Alaric. I understand that a trap was set. Tell me about it."

Morgan stole a fleeting glance at Arilan but realized that he could not meet those eyes if he hoped to recount the Saint Torin affair accurately. With a deep sigh, he lowered his gaze. When he began to speak, his voice was very low, and Arilan had to lean closer to hear what he said.

"We were on our way to plead with the Curia not to lower the Interdict," Morgan said. He raised his eyes as far as Arilan's chest and held them fixed there on the center of the cross the prelate wore. "We were convinced, as we still are, that the Interdict was wrong—as you and your colleagues here at Dhassa apparently have since decided as well. We hoped that if we appeared before the Curia, we might be able to reason with you, to at least take the burden of your wrath upon ourselves instead of letting it fall on my people."

His voice assumed a hollow tone as he prepared to let the memory of his ordeal surface in all its detail.

"Our way lay through Saint Torin's, through the shrine as any other pilgrims—for even then, I was suspect, and could not officially enter Dhassa as Duke of Corwyn without Bishop Cardiel's permission. I knew that he would never dare to give that permission with the Curia in full session here."

"You misjudge him, but go on," Arilan murmured.

Morgan swallowed and continued. "After Duncan had visited the shrine and returned, I went in. There was merasha on a needle on the gate. Do you know what that is, Bishop?"

"Yes."

"Thank you," Morgan whispered. "That will make this somewhat easier. I—I scratched my hand on the gate, and the drug overcame me. I passed out—and when I came to my senses, I was in the hands of Warin de Grey and a dozen or so of his men. With him was Monsignor Gorony. They told me that the bishops had decided to give me to Warin, if he could capture me, and that Gorony had been sent only to lend some semblance of legitimacy to the act—to minister to my soul, should I choose to acknowledge my 'sins' and seek absolution.

"They—were going to burn me, Excellency," Morgan said haltingly, hardly able to force out the words. "They had the stake all ready for me . . . and the chains. They never had any intention of letting me clear myself. I—I didn't know that at the time, however." He paused to wet his lips again, to swallow painfully.

"They—questioned me; the substance of that interrogation is mostly a blur. Finally, Warin decided that it was time to kill me. I was helpless in his power; I could barely stay conscious, much less use my powers to protect myself.

"And then he said that I had this one last, partial reprieve: that though my life was to be forfeit, I was to be permitted to at least try to redeem my soul by confessing to Gorony. The only clear thought I remember in that instant of desperation was that I must stall for time, that if only I could stay alive long enough, Duncan would surely find me. So I—I . . ."

"And so you knelt to Gorony," Arilan supplied.

Morgan closed his eyes and nodded painfully as he remembered. "And would have confessed to almost anything to keep death at bay, was ready to invent sins to prolong the time until . . ."

"I quite understand," Arilan said softly. "What did you tell him?"

Morgan shook his head. "I had time for nothing. At that moment, God must have heard my prayers. Duncan came hurtling down through an opening in the ceiling, and his sword cut a swath of death through that place."

IN the next room, Bishop Thomas Cardiel sat stiffly in a window seat, Duncan kneeling at his feet. Duncan, though his wrists were bound, had laced his fingers together in an attitude of prayer, his hands resting lightly on the cushion of the seat beside Cardiel. Duncan's head was slightly bowed, but his voice was steady. Cardiel's gray eyes were focused incredulously on the top of his head as he listened to Duncan's tale.

"So I'm not certain how many I killed: four or five, I suppose. I wounded several more. But when Gorony tried to knife me, I grabbed him for a shield. I don't think it even occurred to me that he was also a priest until I was half-way across the room with him. Alaric was in a bad way, had killed at least one man that I know of, and I had to protect him. Gorony was my surety until I could get Alaric to the door and out of that place. And of course, the whole shrine was burning."

"That was when you revealed that you are Deryni?" Cardiel asked.

Duncan nodded slowly. "As Alaric tried to open the door, we realized that it was locked from the outside, and that this was *Warin's* surety. Alaric and I both had used our powers to unlock doors before, so I knew that it could be done, but he was in no condition to even attempt such a thing.

"I had a choice to make, and I made it. I used my powers to get us out of there. Gorony saw the whole thing, of course, and shrieked it out. And then Warin started screaming about blasphemy and sacrilege.

"That was when we left. There was nothing we could do about the burning shrine, so we got to our horses and rode away. I think the fire was what saved us, in the end. There was no pursuit. If there had been, I am almost certain we would have been taken. Alaric was very weak."

He bowed his head and closed his eyes, trying to shut out the memories, and Cardiel shook his head in amazement.

"What since then, my son?" he asked gently.

MORGAN'S voice had regained its customary crispness as he finished his confession, and he dared to look up at Arilan again. The prelate's face was serene, thoughtful, but Morgan almost thought he could detect a note of admiration on the handsome face. After a moment, Arilan's gaze drifted to his hands folded in his lap, to the bishop's ring flashing fire there. Then he stood up, turning away slightly, his voice matter-of-fact.

"Alaric, how did you manage to get into Dhassa? Your garb when you were first captured indicates that you must have divested some of Thomas's poor monks of their habits. You didn't harm them, did you?"

"No, Excellency. You'll find them sleeping off a Deryni spell in the vaults beneath the main altar. It seemed, I regret, the only way to accomplish our purpose without doing them real harm. I assure you, they'll suffer no ill effects."

"I see," Arilan said. He turned to stare thoughtfully down at the kneeling Morgan, then clasped his hands behind his back and looked up at the high window.

"I cannot grant you absolution," he said.

Morgan's head shot up, a hot retort on his lips.

"No, don't interrupt," Arilan interjected, before Morgan could speak. "What I mean to say is that I cannot grant you absolution yet. There remain certain details of your story that I must investigate further. But come; this is not the time to talk of such matters. If Cardiel and Duncan are finished," he crossed behind Morgan to ease the door open, then pulled it wide, "and I see that they are, we should rejoin them so that further actions may be considered."

Morgan scrambled to his feet, studying Arilan quizzically as the bishop passed into the larger room. Duncan was sitting in the window seat, his eyes downcast, and Cardiel had retreated to another window, head resting against a forearm thrust across the window jamb. Cardiel looked up as the two appeared, and started to speak, but Arilan shook his head.

"We'd best talk privily, Thomas. Come. The guards can stay with them."

As Arilan threw open the doors, the guards streamed in, hands on the hilts of their weapons, but at Arilan's gesture they drew back, merely stationing themselves around the room to stare apprehensively at the two prisoners. As soon as the doors had closed behind the departing bishops, Morgan moved slowly to the window seat, keeping his bound hands well in sight of the guards, and eased himself down beside his cousin. He could hear Duncan's light breathing beside him as he leaned his head against the glass panels behind and closed his eyes to concentrate.

I hope we've done the right thing, Duncan, his mind whispered in the deadly silence. *Despite our good intentions, if Arilan and Cardiel didn't believe us, we may have signed our own death warrants. How do you think Cardiel took it?*

I don't know, Duncan replied after a long moment. *I really don't know.*

CHAPTER TEN

"I form the light, and create darkness."

ISAIAH 45:7

"SO, what of Morgan and Duncan?" Arilan asked.

The two rebel bishops were standing once more in Cardiel's private chapel, the doors closed and barred from within, and an anxious escort from Cardiel's household guard waited outside. Arilan leaned casually against the altar rail to the left of the center aisle, idly fingering the cross and chain around his neck. Cardiel, restless with nervous energy, was pacing the marble floor and carpet before him, striding back and forth in the narrow transept and gesturing expansively as he spoke.

"I simply am not sure, Denis," he said perplexedly. "Though I know I should be more cautious, I am inclined to believe them. Their stories are plausible—much more so than many I have heard. And aside from the differing points of view, they even agree with what Gorony told us on the day it all happened. Frankly, I don't see how they could have done any differently and still lived to tell of it. I probably would have done the same thing."

"Even to using magic?"

"If I were capable, yes."

Arilan bit on one of the links of his chain reflectively. "An interesting observation. Thomas, you surprise me. It appears that the question is not so much *what* they did, but how they did it. The real issue is magic, and the wanton use of it."

"Is it wanton to defend oneself when attacked?"

"Perhaps, if one uses magic to do it. At least that is what we have always taught and been taught."

"Well, perhaps we have been wrong." Cardiel scowled. "It wouldn't be the first time. You know, if Morgan and Duncan were not Deryni, they would have been absolved by now, after coming to us the way they did—if they had even been excommunicated in the first place, that is."

"But they *are* Deryni, they *were* excommunicated, and they have *not* been absolved," Arilan pointed out. "You must admit that the first seems to have a bearing on the second and third.

"And yet, should it? Is it right to deal a different kind of justice to a man just because he happens to be born of the wrong set of parents, because of something over which he has no control, which he cannot change?"

Cardiel shook his head stubbornly. "Certainly not. That would be as ridiculous as your saying you're a better man than I because your eyes are blue and mine are gray—things which neither of us can change." He stabbed the air with an emphatic forefinger. "Now, you may be better than I because of what you *see* with your eyes, or what you do with what you see. But the color of the eyes, or the fact that your mother had one blue eye and one green eye, hasn't a blessed thing to do with it!"

"My mother's eyes were gray," Arilan said with a smile.

"You know what I'm talking about."

"Yes, I do. But blue eyes versus gray eyes is one thing; good versus evil is quite another. What it comes down to is whether the good or evil of a man has anything to do with the fact that he happens to be born Deryni."

"You don't think my analogy holds true?"

"I didn't say that. Thomas, I told you before that I was not convinced that all Deryni are evil. But how do you convey that simple truth—if, indeed, it is truth—to the common man, who has been taught to hate Deryni for the past three centuries? More specifically, how do you convince him that Alaric Morgan and Duncan McLain are not evil, when the voice of the Church has said otherwise? Are *you* totally convinced?"

"Perhaps not," Cardiel murmured, not meeting Arilan's eyes. "But sometimes, perhaps we must believe in the uncertain. Perhaps we must take some things on faith, even in the real world, away from the metaphysics of religion and doctrine and subjects that we usually associate with what priests teach."

"Simple faith," said Arilan. "I wish it were that simple."

"It *has* to be that simple. I know that *I* have to believe it, at least for now; that I *want* to believe it, desperately. Because if I'm wrong about the Deryni—if they really *are* as we have believed for all these centuries of hatred—then all of us are lost. If the Deryni as a race are evil, then Morgan and McLain will betray us, as will our king. And that will leave the way open for Wencit of Torenth, who is also Deryni, to ride over us like the revenging wind."

Arilan stood with his eyes downcast for a long time, his manner solemn as he toyed with the cross on his breast. Then, with a resigned sigh, he beckoned to Cardiel and walked with him, hand on shoulder, toward the left side of the chapel, where a mosaic pattern in the floor awaited.

"Come. There is something you should see."

Puzzled, Cardiel glanced at his colleague in question as they halted before the stark side altar. The white vigil light cast a silvery glow on the heads of the two prelates. Arilan's face was unreadable.

"I don't understand," Cardiel murmured. "I've seen—"

"You've not seen what I would show you," Arilan said

almost sharply. "Look up at the ceiling there, where the beams cross."

"But there's nothing . . ." Cardiel began, tilting his head back to squint in the dimness.

Arilan closed his eyes and let the words begin to shape inside his head, felt the tingle of the Portal beneath his feet. Pulling Cardiel abruptly against him in an iron grip, he reached out with his mind and wrenched the spell into being.

He heard Cardiel gasp. And then they jumped, and the chapel vanished, and they were standing in total darkness.

Cardiel staggered drunkenly as the darkness hit, arms reaching out blindly as he regained his balance. Arilan was gone from behind him, and he could see nothing in the blackness. His mind churned chaotically, trying to put some rational explanation to what he had just experienced, trying to orient itself to the darkness, the utter silence. He straightened in the blackness, cautiously, one arm sweeping the air before him while the other guarded his eyes. Finally, he got up the courage to speak, a terrifying suspicion growing in his mind.

"Denis?" he whispered meekly, almost afraid he would receive an answer.

"Here, my friend."

There was a faint rustle of fabric a few yards behind him, and then a flare of white light. Cardiel turned slowly, his face draining of color as he spied the source.

Arilan stood in a soft glow of silver, his face framed in a silvery aureole, which waxed and waned and flickered almost as a thing alive. His expression was calm and serene in the silver light, the violet-blue eyes gentle and reassuring. In his hands he held a sphere of bright, cold fire whose quicksilver glow spilled sharp radiance on his face, his hands, and down the violet folds of his bishop's cassock. Cardiel stared at him in astonishment for perhaps five heartbeats, his eyes growing wider, his pulse pounding in his ears.

Then the room was spinning and the darkness was swirling around him and he was falling. He was next aware that he was lying on something soft yet unyielding, eyes tightly closed, and that a gentle hand was raising his head to put a cup to his lips.

He drank, hardly aware that he did so, then opened his eyes as cool wine trickled down his throat. Arilan was bending over him anxiously, a blown-glass goblet in his hand. He gave a wan, tentative smile as Cardiel opened his eyes.

Cardiel blinked and peered at Arilan again, but the image did not disappear. There was no silvery nimbus around his head, however, and the room was now lighted by perfectly ordinary candles in many-armed candlesticks. A low fire burned in a fireplace off to the left, and he could make out the dim shapes of furniture around the perimeter of the room. He was lying on a fur of some sort. As he raised himself to his elbows, he could see that it was the skin of a great black bear, the head grimacing fiercely to one side. He rubbed a hand across his forehead, his eyes still wide with shock. Memory returned in a rush.

"You," he whispered, looking slowly at Arilan with awe and a little fear. "Did I really see . . . ?"

Arilan nodded, his face carefully neutral, and stood. "I am Deryni," he said softly.

"You're Deryni," Cardiel repeated. "Then, all of the things you said about Morgan and McLain—"

"—were true," said Arilan. "Or else they were things it was imperative you consider before making a decision on the Deryni question."

"You're Deryni," Cardiel repeated, slowly regaining his composure. "Then, Morgan and McLain—they don't know?"

Arilan shook his head. "They do not. And though I regret the mental anguish I have undoubtedly caused them through my secrecy, they are not to be told. Only you, among humans, know my true identity. It is not a secret I share lightly."

"But, if you're Deryni . . ."

"Try, if you can, to imagine my position," Arilan said with a patient sigh. "I am the only Deryni to wear the episcopal purple in nearly two hundred years—the only one. I am also the youngest of Gwynedd's twenty-two bishops, which again puts me in a historically precarious position." He lowered his eyes before continuing.

"I know what you must be thinking: that my inaction for the Deryni cause has probably permitted countless deaths, untold suffering at the hands of persecutors like Loris and others of his ilk. I know, and I ask the forgiveness of every one of those unfortunate victims in my prayers each night." He raised his eyes to meet Cardiel's unflinchingly. "But I believe that the greater virtue sometimes lies in knowing how to wait. Sometimes, though the price be almost unbearable, and though a man's mind and soul and heart cry out in protest, even then must he wait until the time is right. I only hope that I've not waited too long."

Cardiel looked away, unable to bear the blue-violet gaze any longer. "What is this place? How did we get here?"

"We came by means of a Transfer Portal," Arilan replied neutrally. "The way lies through the floor design in your chapel. It is very old."

"Deryni magic?"

"Yes."

Cardiel eased himself to a full sitting position, turning that bit of information over in his mind. "Then, is this where you came after I left you in the chapel the other night? When I looked in a few minutes later, you were gone."

Arilan crooked a hint of a smile. "I see that I was wise not to linger." He sighed. "Thomas, I *am* sorry, but I cannot tell you where I went." He held out his hand to assist Cardiel to his feet, but Cardiel ignored it.

"Cannot or *will* not?"

"*May* not," Arilan replied sympathetically. "At least not yet. Try to be patient with me."

"Implying that there are others with authority over you?"

"Implying that there are things I may not tell you," Arilan whispered, a pleading look on his face as he continued to extend his hand. "Trust me, Thomas? I swear I'll not betray that trust."

Cardiel stared for a long time at the outstretched arm, at the eyes slightly fearful in the long-familiar face. Then he reached out slowly to grasp Arilan's hand, letting the younger bishop pull him to his feet. They stood hand-clasped that way for several seconds, each reading what he could in the other's eyes. Then Arilan smiled and clapped Cardiel on the shoulder.

"Come, my brother, we have work to do this night. If you truly mean to receive Morgan and Duncan back among us, then they must be told, and preparations made. Also, there remains the matter of our recalcitrant brethren of the convocation, who will be wondering what makes us so long overdue. They must still be persuaded, though I suspect they'll follow your lead readily enough."

Cardiel ran a nervous hand through steel-gray hair and shook his head incredulously. "You do move quickly when you want to, don't you, Denis? You'll pardon me if I seem to react a bit stupidly for a few minutes, but this is going to take a little getting used to."

"Of course it is." Arilan chuckled, guiding Cardiel back to the center of the room where a design embossed the floor. "And we might as well start by getting back to your chapel. The guards will be getting edgy."

Cardiel glanced apprehensively at the floor. "The Transfer Portal you spoke of?"

"Indeed," Arilan replied, moving behind Cardiel to place his hands on the other's shoulders once more. "Now, just relax and let me do the work. There's nothing to it. Relax and let your mind go blank."

"I'll try," Cardiel whispered.

And the floor tipped out from under him and Arilan in a soft, black blur.

IN the next hour, Morgan and Duncan were told of the bishops' decision.

It was not a cordial meeting; all were too wary, too guarded for that. The former fugitives had been outcast from the Church for too many months not to feel some mistrust of a pair of that Church's most powerful prelates; and the feeling was somewhat mutual.

But the bishops' attitude was not hostile. It was as if the two were testing the penitents, probing their reaction to the decision. They had, after all, been charged with the spiritual well-being of these dissident sons of the Church.

Cardiel was markedly silent and said little, which Morgan thought a bit strange when he remembered some of the brilliant letters that had come to Kelson from the man's pen in the past three months. The Dhassan bishop kept glancing at Arilan with a strange, questioning expression, which Morgan could not interpret: a look that sometimes raised the hackles on Morgan's neck, though he could not say just why.

Arilan, on the other hand, was now relaxed, witty, and seemingly unaffected by the gravity of the situation. He was also quick to point out, however, just before the four entered the room where the convocation waited, that the real dangers were only beginning. There were still half a dozen bishops in the chamber who must be convinced of the innocence and penitence of the two Deryni lords—and then the eleven grim men in Coroth. And all of this must be resolved before they could even think about any confrontation with Wencit of Torenth.

There were a few mild protests when the four entered the chamber. Siward had gasped; Gilbert had crossed himself furtively, his small, pig-eyes darting to his companions for support; and even the peppery old Wolfram de Blanet, staunchest opponent of the Interdict, had gone a little white. None of them had ever knowingly been in the presence of even one Deryni, much less two.

But they were reasonable men, these bishops of Gwynedd. And while not entirely convinced of the beneficence of Deryni in general, they were at least willing to concede that perhaps these particular Deryni had been more wronged than wronging. The excommunication must be lifted and absolution given, now that repentance had been shown.

The situation was by no means resolved with that decision. For, while the bishops at Dhassa were, for the most part, reasonably educated and sensible men, not overly given to superstition and certainly not inclined to hysteria, convincing the common folk would be quite another matter, and one which must be carefully considered. The average man had long harbored the belief that the Deryni were an accursed race, whose very presence in a place could bring ruin and death. And while Morgan had managed to keep a relatively neutral name while in the service of Brion and Kelson, and Duncan's reputation had been impeccable until the Saint Torin affair, these facts had been largely overshadowed in the greater knowledge that both men were Deryni.

For that reason, a more tangible affirmation must be offered to show that Morgan and Duncan had, indeed, mended their Deryni ways. So simple a measure as absolution and penance would not do for the common folk: the townspeople, soldiers, artisans, and craftsmen who make up and support an army. Their simple faith demanded a more exacting reconciliation, more substantial proof of the humility and repentance of the two Deryni lords. A public ceremony was called for, which would graphically demonstrate to the people that the bishops and the two Deryni were now in complete accord in the sight of Almighty God.

It would be nearly two days before final battle plans could be formalized; two days before the bishops' army could be ready to move out, in any case. Also, Morgan and Duncan had brought word that Kelson could not be at the planned rendezvous point before the end of the fourth day anyway. It took but two days to reach that point.

Taking all of that into account, the time for formal reconciliation had been set for the evening hours two nights hence, on the eve of departure for the meeting with the king. During those two days, the two Deryni would confer with the bishops and their highest military advisors and plan the strategy of the war to come. And Bishop Cardiel's monks would go out among the people and spread the word of Morgan and Duncan's surrender and subsequent repentance. The evening of the second day would see their official reception back into the Church, before as many of the army and citizenry as could crowd themselves into Dhassa's great cathedral. There, in a solemn display of episcopal authority, Morgan and Duncan would be taken back into the fold with all the pageantry the Church could muster. The people would approve.

TWO days later, at the edge of the great Llyndruth Plain below Cardosa, Sean Lord Derry pulled off his helmet and wiped a tanned forearm across his brow. It was warm here at Llyndruth Meadows, the air already charged with the sticky heat of approaching summer. Derry's hair was damp where the helmet had matted it to his head, and his body itched between the shoulder blades beneath its leather and mail.

Restraining a sigh, Derry shrugged his shoulders to ease the itch and slung the helmet over his left arm by the chin strap. As he started back toward the clearing where he had left his horse tethered, he moved stealthily, treading as soundlessly as possible in the new spring grass. He had chosen this meadow return with care, for the footing among the trees was treacherous with the threat of snapping twigs and branches left from the long winter. To be captured now could mean a painful and lingering death at the hands of those who camped on the plain below.

Derry reviewed what he had learned as he worked his

way in the direction of the thicket. Off to the east, the Rheljan Mountain Range reared its jagged peaks more than a mile above the plain, sheltering the walled city of Cardosa in the cut of the Cardosa Pass. Wencit of Torenth was there, or so men said. But to the west, Derry's right, the Llyndruth Plain stretched on for miles and miles. And just over the ridge behind him lay the massed armies of Bran Coris, the traitorous Earl of Marley, now the ally of that same Wencit of Torenth whose presence at Cardosa threatened the very existence of Gwynedd.

The picture taking shape in Derry's mind was not a pleasant one; nor could he expect it to improve in the near future. After leaving Morgan and Duncan two days earlier, Derry had headed northeast through the greening, boulder-strewn hills of northern Corwyn, making his way toward Rengarth and the supposed campsite of Duke Jared McLain and his army.

But there was no ducal army at Rengarth; only a handful of peasants who told him the army had gone north five days before. He rode on, and the gently rolling green of Corwyn slowly gave way to the bare, silent plains of Eastmarch. Instead of the expected army, he found only the aftermath of a terrible battle: terrified villagers huddled in the ruins of sacked and burned-out towns; the hacked bodies of men and horses lying unburied, rotting in the sun, the McLain tartan on their saddles dark with blood and gore; broken standards of red, blue, and silver trampled in the dusty, blood-drenched fields.

He questioned those of the villagers he could lure out of hiding. Yes, the duke's army had come this way. They had joined with another army that had seemed friendly at first. The two leaders had clasped arms across their saddles as the two armies met.

But then the carnage had begun. One man thought he had seen the green and yellow banner of Lord Macanter, a northern border lord who had often ridden with Ian Howell, late the Lord of Eastmarch. Another told of a preponderance of royal blue and white among the standards: the Earl of Marley's colors.

But whoever led the opposing army, the blue-and-whites fell upon the duke's men without mercy, cutting down the ducal army almost to the man, and taking captive those they did not slay. When the battle was over, some remembered black-and-white banners among the riders of the rear guard, and the leaping hart badge of the House of Furstán. Treachery was definitely afoot.

The trail of blood and death ended at Llyndruth Meadows. Derry had arrived at dawn to find the army of Bran Coris encamped in concentric circles around the mouth of the great Cardosa defile. He knew he should report what he saw and get out while he could, but he knew that there would be no chance to speak with Morgan by the prearranged Mind-Speaking until later tonight; and Derry might learn much more by then.

Discreet wandering among the outlying camps of the army revealed even more disturbing information. For apparently Bran Coris had switched his allegiance to Wencit of Torenth on the very eve of war, not more than a week ago, tempted and held by dark promises whose implications were too horrible to even contemplate. Even Bran's men grew uneasy when they talked about it, *if* they talked about it; though they, too, were lured by the promise of fame and fortune which Wencit seemed to offer.

Now, if only Derry could stay free long enough to tell Morgan tonight. If only he could last until a few hours after sunset, it would be a simple matter to slip into that strange Deryni sleep by which he and his lord could communicate even at this distance. The king must be told of Bran's treachery before it was too late. And something must be done to determine the fate of Duke Jared and the remnants of his army.

Derry had re-entered the trees and was almost to his horse when the faint crackle of a breaking twig put him on his guard. He froze and listened, hand creeping to the hilt of his broadsword, but heard nothing further. He had nearly decided that the sound had been nothing, that his taut nerves were playing tricks on him, when he heard a horse snort and shuffle its feet in the clearing ahead.

Could the animal have smelled him?

No, he was downwind of the thicket. The situation was showing all the signs of a trap.

A faint rustling sound repeated itself slightly to his left, and he was sure of the trap. But he could not hope to escape without a horse. He had to brazen it out. There lay his only chance.

Hand resting warily on sword hilt, he strode into the clearing ahead where his horse was tied, making no effort now to go quietly. As he had feared, there were soldiers there waiting for him: three of them. He rather expected that there were others that he could not see: perhaps even bowmen with feathered death aimed at his back right now. He must act as though he belonged here.

"Are you looking for something?" Derry asked, coming to a cautious halt a few yards inside the clearing.

"What's your regiment, soldier?" the foremost of the three men asked. His tone was casual and only faintly suspicious, but there was something vaguely menacing in the way his thumbs were thrust under his belt to either side. One of his companions, the shortest and heaviest of the three, was more openly hostile, and toyed with the hilt of his weapon as he glared across at Derry.

Derry put on one of his more innocent expressions and spread his arms in a wary gesture of conciliation, his helmet dangling by its leather chin strap.

"Why, the Fifth, of course," he dared, guessing that there had to be at least eight horse-regiments in Bran's army. "What is this, anyway?"

"Wrong," the third man glared, his hand also going to the sword at his belt as his eyes flicked over Derry's form. "The Fifth wears yellow buskins; yours are brown. Who's your commanding officer?"

"Now, gentlemen," Derry soothed, edging his way backward and calculating the distance to his horse. "I don't want any trouble."

"You've already got that, son," the first man muttered, thumbs still hooked nonchalantly in his belt. "Now, are you going to come peacefully or not?"

"Not, I should think!"

Flinging his helmet into the face of the startled man, Derry whipped his sword from its scabbard and lunged forward, dispatching the short, fat soldier with his first deft thrust. Even as he wrenched his blade free, the two remaining guardsmen were shouting and attacking, leaping over the body of their slain comrade to charge him with drawn swords. He could hear shouts in the distance and knew that help was being summoned. He must get away *now*, or it would be too late.

He dropped momentarily to one knee and came up slashing with the dagger he had drawn from his boot top, raking the blade across the knuckles of one of his attackers. The man screamed and dropped his weapon, but Derry was beset by the fellow's partner and another pair of swordsmen before he could press the advantage. A glance hazarded over his shoulder revealed half a dozen more armed men approaching at a dead run, swords already drawn, and Derry cursed under his breath as he slashed his way to his horse's side.

He lashed out with the dagger and one booted heel as he tried to scramble to the horse's back, but someone had loosened the girth and the saddle went out from under him. Even as he flailed for balance, reaching hands were grabbing at him, pulling at clothes and hair, hooking into his belt to drag him from the saddle.

He felt a lancing pain in his right bicep as someone's dagger caught him, and his sword slid from fingers that were suddenly slippery with blood: his own. Then he was being borne to the ground under a crush of mailed bodies, his limbs pressed down spread-eagled against the new spring grass, the breath being choked out of him.

CHAPTER ELEVEN

*"The tents of robbers prosper, and they that
provoke God are secure."*

JOB 12:6

DERRY winced and stifled a groan as rough hands rolled
him to his back and began probing his wounded arm.

He had passed out briefly as the men manhandled him
from his horse, regaining consciousness as he was half-
dragged and half-carried to where he now lay on a patch of
damp grass. Three armed soldiers pinned his limbs to the
ground: three grim men in the harness of war, badged in the
royal blue and white of the Earl of Marley.

One of the men held a dagger's blade casually at his captive's throat. A fourth man in the tunic of a field surgeon
knelt by Derry's head, clucking to himself disapprovingly as
he bared the wound and began to dress it. Derry's concentration brought a score of additional men into focus, standing watchfully around and staring down at him. With a
sinking feeling, Derry realized that escape was now close to
impossible.

When the surgeon finished binding up the wound, one of
the standing guards pulled a length of rawhide from his belt
and looped deft coils around Derry's wrists, securing them

in front of him. After testing the bonds, he straightened and stared at the prisoner suspiciously, almost as though he recognized him, then disappeared from Derry's range of vision. Derry lifted his head and tried to orient himself as the men who had been holding him got to their feet and joined the watching circle.

He was back in the camp, lying partially in the shade of a low, brown leather tent. He did not recognize the specific place and did not expect to, since he had seen only a small part of the encampment; but there was no doubt in his mind that he was deep within it.

The tent was of the sort used by the plainsmen of Eastmarch, low and squat but finely finished: an officer's tent by the look of it. He wondered briefly whose tent it was, for he had certainly seen no one of appropriate rank so far. Perhaps these men did not realize the importance of their prisoner. Perhaps he could avoid meeting someone of higher rank who might recognize him.

On the other hand, if they did not realize who he was and believed him to be but a common spy, he might not even get a chance to talk himself out of this one. They might execute him without further ado.

But they had bandaged his wound—a senseless waste of effort if they only meant to kill him. He wondered where the men's commander was.

As though in response to his thought, a tall, middle-aged man in mail and a blue and gold plaid strode to the green beside the tent and tossed a crested helmet to one of the watching soldiers. He had the lean, assured carriage of aristocracy, a sureness of movement that immediately marked him as an accomplished warrior. Jewels glittered on the pommel of his sword and subtly within the links of a heavy gold neck chain. Derry recognized him immediately: Baron Campbell of Eastmarch. Now, would Campbell recognize him?

"Well, what have we here? Did the king send ye, lad?"

Derry frowned at the condescending tone, wondering

whether he was being baited or whether the man already knew who he was.

"Of course the king sent me," Derry finally decided to say, permitting a trace of indignation to show in his voice. "Is this how you always treat royal messengers?"

"So, it's a royal messenger you're claiming to be, is it?" the man asked, cocking his head wistfully. "That isn't what the guards told me."

"The guards didn't ask," Derry said contemptuously, raising his head in defiance. "Besides, my messages were not intended for guards. I was on my way to Duke Ewan's army in the north, on king's business. I stumbled on your encampment quite by mistake."

"Aye, 'tis indeed a mistake, lad," Campbell murmured, his eyes sweeping Derry suspiciously. "Ye were taken whilst prowling around the edge of the camp, ye lied to the men who asked your identity, killed a soldier who tried to take you into custody. And ye have no credentials or messages on you, nothing to indicate that you are what you say you are, and not a spy. I think that you *are* a spy. What's your name, lad?"

"I am not a spy. I am a royal envoy. And my name and my messages are not for your ears!" Derry said hotly. "When the king finds out how you have treated—"

In a flash, Campbell was on his knees beside Derry, his hand twisted in the neck of Derry's mail and pulling it choking-tight as he stared his captive in the face.

"You will not speak to me in that tone, young spy! And if you hope to see a ripe old age, which appears unlikely the more ye talk, ye'd best hold yer tongue unless you have civil words upon it! Do I make myself perfectly clear?"

Derry winced as the man tightened his grip on the mail, biting back a smoking retort that surely would have been the end of him, if he had voiced it. With a slight inclination of his head, he signaled his acquiescence and took a deep breath as the man released his throat. Even as he wondered what he was going to do next, Campbell took that decision out of his hands.

"We'll take him to his lordship," he said, getting to his feet with a sigh. "I have nae the time to fool with him. Mayhap the Lord's Deryni friends can weasel the truth out of him."

As his words sank in, Derry was dragged to his feet and herded along a muddy path toward the center of the camp. There were questioning looks as they went, and several times Derry thought he saw faces turn toward him with near-recognition in their eyes. But no one approached them, and Derry was too busy trying to stay on his feet to look at anyone too closely. Besides, it didn't much matter whether he was recognized now or not. Bran Coris would know him instantly, and what he was about. Nor was the reference to Bran's Deryni allies comforting.

They skirted a sparse grove of oaks to emerge in the headquarters area, where a splendid tent of royal blue and white dominated the center of a broad patch of velvet green. Other tents of only slightly lesser size and splendor surrounded the central area, their brilliant colors and standards vying with one another for attention. Not far away, the wash of the great Cardosa River ran its swollen course across the plain, the water high and muddy-brown in this run-off season.

Derry's escort yanked him along as his steps faltered, at last throwing him to his knees before a black and silver tent next to Bran's royal blue one. His wounded arm had started to ache abominably from the men's rough handling, and his wrists chafed in their rawhide bonds. From inside the tent, he could hear men's voices arguing loudly, though the words were muffled and indistinguishable behind the thick fabric of the tent walls.

Baron Campbell paused for just a moment, apparently weighing the advisability of entering, then shrugged and disappeared through the open tent flap. From within came an explosive exclamation of indignation, a murmured curse in an accent foreign to Derry's ears, and then the sound of Bran Coris's voice.

"A spy? Damn it, Campbell, you interrupted me to say you've captured a spy?"

"I'm thinking he's more than a spy, m'lord. He's—well, you'd best see for yourself."

"Oh, very well. Duke Lionel, I'll return shortly."

Derry's heart sank as Campbell emerged from the tent, and he averted his face as a slender figure in a blue tunic stepped into the sunlight behind Campbell. Derry heard a muffled intake of breath from Bran's direction, and then he was aware of two pairs of boots standing a few paces before him, one pair black and shining and spurred with silver.

It would do no good to postpone the inevitable. With a resigned sigh, Derry lifted his head to behold the familiar face of Bran Coris.

"Sean Lord Derry!" Bran blurted. The golden eyes went cold. "So! How *does* my dubious colleague, outside the king's Council chambers? You haven't deserted your precious Morgan, have you?" Derry's eyes flashed defiance. "No, I didn't think so. My Lord Lionel, come and see what the Duke of Corwyn has sent us," he called. "I do believe it's his favorite spy."

As he spoke, Lionel Duke d'Arjenol emerged from the tent and joined Bran, staring hard at Derry all the while. He was tall and regal and looked vaguely foreign, dark beard and moustache trimmed close to his face to emphasize thin, cruel lips.

A robe of faintly rustling white silk flowed from the duke's broad shoulders to sweep the toes of claret velvet boots. But there was the gleam of a mail-backed crimson tunic where the robe parted in front, the flash of a curved dagger thrust through his sash. The hair was long and black, pulled in a lock at the back of his neck and held across the brow by a broad fillet of silver. Jeweled wrist guards glittered red and green and violet as he folded silk-sleeved arms across his chest.

"So, this is Morgan's minion," Lionel said, his cool gaze sweeping Derry with disdain.

"The Earl of Derry," Bran replied with a nod. "Kelson appointed him to Lord Ralson's vacant Council seat last fall. He was Morgan's military aide for some time before that. Where did you find him, Campbell?"

"On the ridge just south of here, m'lord. A patrol spotted his horse and just waited for him to come back. He cut up some of our men when they tried to take him, though. Peter Davency is dead."

"Davency? Heavy-set fellow, rather quick-tempered?"

"The same, m'lord."

Bran hooked his thumbs in the jeweled belt at his waist and stared down at Derry for a long time, slowly rising up and down on the balls of his feet, jaw clenching and unclenching as he stared. For a moment, Derry feared that Bran would kick him, and he steeled himself for the blow; but it did not come. After what seemed like an eternity, Bran curbed his anger and turned slowly to face Lionel, not daring to look at Derry any longer.

"If this man were wholly my prisoner, he would be dead by now for what he has done," Bran said, his voice hardly more than a whisper. "However, I am not so blinded by anger that I cannot realize the value he may have to you and Lord Wencit. Will you ask your kinsman what he wishes me to do with this offal?"

With a curt bow, Lionel turned on his heel and glided into the tent, Bran following a step behind. They paused just inside the opening, their shapes silhouetted against the inner darkness. Just before Bran twitched the tent flap over the opening, a faint play of light flared somewhere above the men's heads, suggesting that they intended using some kind of magic to contact Wencit. After a few minutes, Bran emerged from the tent alone, his manner thoughtful and a bit amused.

"Well, Sean Lord Derry, it appears that my new allies are inclined to be merciful. You are to be spared a spy's execution and instead are to be the guest tonight of His Majesty, King Wencit, in Cardosa. Personally, I cannot vouch for the quality of entertainment you will find there; Torenthi sport can be a bit bizarre for my tastes, I must confess. But perhaps you will enjoy it. Campbell?"

"Aye, m'lord."

Bran's face hardened as he stared down at the helpless Derry. "Put him on a horse and get him out of here. The sight of him sickens me!"

MORGAN paced the length of the tiny anteroom in the bishop's palace in Dhassa and rubbed a hand across his newly shaven jaw, then turned to peer impatiently through the bottom of the high, grilled window. Outside, darkness was falling, the night mists moving in swiftly as they often did in this mountain country, cloaking all of Dhassa in an eerie, clammy shroud. Though it was not yet fully dark, torches were beginning to appear in the lowering dimness, their wavering flames pale and ghostly against the twilight.

The streets that had teemed with soldiers an hour earlier were almost silent now. Over to the left, he could see an honor guard lined up before the doors of Dhassa's cathedral, and scores of mailed and cloaked fighting men and city burghers making their way into the high nave beyond. Occasionally, when a lull came in the arrivals at the cathedral, he could see through the open doors and into the great nave itself, catching the gleam of many candles lighting the place nearly as bright as day. In a little while, he and Duncan would be entering that cathedral with the bishops. He wondered what their reception would be.

With a sigh, Morgan turned away from the window and glanced across the room to where Duncan sat quietly on a low wooden bench. A candle burned at Duncan's end of the bench, and the priest seemed absorbed in the content of a small, leather-bound book with gilt-edged pages. Like Morgan, he was robed in penitential violet, clean-shaven, his face oddly pale where his beard had been. He had not yet bothered to secure the front of his robe, for it was warm in the tiny chamber, close with the night air that drifted on the mists outside. A white tunic, hose, and soft leather boots shone stark beneath the robe, the pristine whiteness unrelieved by any jewel or adornment.

With another sigh, Morgan glanced down at his own robe and tunic, at the gryphon and lion rings winking on his hands, then moved slowly to Duncan's side of the room and looked down at him. Duncan did not seem in the least concerned that his kinsman had been pacing in precisely the same manner for the past quarter hour, or even to have noticed that he had finally stopped.

"Don't you ever get tired of waiting?" Morgan asked.

Duncan looked up from his reading with a faint smile. "Sometimes. But it's a skill that priests must learn quite early in their careers, or else become good actors. Why don't you stop pacing and try to relax?"

So, he *had* noticed.

Morgan sat heavily on the bench beside Duncan and leaned his head against the wall behind, arms folded across his chest in an attitude of utter tedium.

"Relax? That's easy enough for you to say. You like ritual. You're used to dealing with ecclesiastical pageantry. Me, I'm as edgy as a squire at his first tournament. Not only that, but I think I'm going to die of hunger. I haven't had a thing to eat all day."

"Nor have I."

"No, but you're better used to it than I. You tend to forget that I am a degenerate nobleman, accustomed to indulging myself whenever the whim strikes me. Even some of that wretched Dhassa wine would be almost welcome."

Duncan closed his book and leaned back against the wall with a smile. "Think about what you're saying. Think what wine would do to our clear-headedness after two days with only bread and water—and nothing today. Besides, knowing Dhassa wine, I personally would rather die of thirst."

"I concede you the point." Morgan smiled and closed his

eyes. "Goes to show you what fasting will do. It doesn't mortify the soul, it corrodes the brain."

"Well, perhaps the bishops wouldn't be averse to a touch of *something*," Duncan said with a chuckle. "More bread and water, maybe? I hardly think they'd want us fainting away during the ceremony, for lack of food."

Morgan grinned, getting up to resume his pacing. "Shows how much you know. Fainting might be the best thing we could do out there. Just think: The penitent Deryni, weakened by fasting, their spirits chastened and their hearts purified, faint away in the presence of the Lord."

"Actually, that's an interesting—"

A soft knock at the door interrupted whatever Duncan had thought might be interesting, and he broke off expectantly, glancing toward Morgan as he got to his feet. Bishop Cardiel swept into the room in a rustle of purple silk, the hood of his cape thrown back on his shoulders. He waved dismissal to the black-cowled monk who had accompanied him as Duncan and Morgan bent to kiss his ring, then pulled the door softly to. Then he reached beneath his cloak to produce a folded piece of parchment.

"This came an hour ago," he said in a low voice, handing it to Morgan and glancing out the window uneasily. "It's from the king. He wishes us well in tonight's endeavors and looks forward to meeting us at Cor Ramet the day after tomorrow. I hope we shall not have to disappoint him."

"Disappoint him?" Morgan, who had moved closer to the candle to scan the letter, looked up with a start. "Why? Is anything wrong?"

"Nothing is wrong—yet," Cardiel said. He held out his hand for the letter and Morgan gave it over without a word. "Does either of you have any question about what is to happen tonight?"

"Father Hugh briefed us several hours ago, Excellency," Duncan said carefully, studying Cardiel's face. "My lord, if there is some difficulty that concerns us, we should know about it."

Cardiel eyed them both for a long moment, then turned to rest one gloved hand against the high windowsill. He stared at the barred window for several seconds, as though choosing his words with care, then turned his head partially toward the two in the room. His steel-gray head was silhouetted against the darkening sky, his cloak parted slightly by his uparised arm. Beneath the cloak, a spotless alb gleamed like silver against the gray stone wall, and Morgan suddenly realized that the bishop had interrupted his vesting to come to them. He wondered what Cardiel was trying to say.

"You made a good impression this afternoon in the procession. Are you aware of that?" the bishop said lightly. "The people love to see penitents make public demonstration of their contrition. It makes them feel more righteous. Fortunately, the majority of those who will attend us tonight are willing to believe in the sincerity of your reconciliation."

"However . . ." Morgan ventured.

Cardiel lowered his eyes and smiled in spite of himself. "Yes, there is usually a 'however,' isn't there?" He looked up, directly into Morgan's eyes. "Alaric, try to believe that I do trust you—both of you." He glanced at Duncan. "Unfortunately, there are many who will attend tonight who remain unconvinced. No matter how repentant you may appear to be, I'm afraid it would take a miracle to persuade some of them that you mean no harm."

"Are you asking us to provide a miracle, Excellency?" Morgan murmured, returning Cardiel's gaze.

"Good heavens, no! That's the last thing I want." Cardiel shook his head emphatically. "In fact, that is perhaps the crux of what I must say to you now." He laced his fingers together and stared down at his bishop's ring.

"Alaric, I have been Bishop of Dhassa for four years now. During those four years, and during the tenures of at least the last five of my predecessors, there has never been a breath of scandal associated with the See of Dhassa."

"Perhaps you should have considered that point before joining the schism, my lord," Morgan said softly.

Cardiel looked pained. "I did as my conscience bade."

"Your mind agrees," Duncan said. "But your heart is afraid of what two Deryni might do. Is that it?"

Cardiel glanced up at them and stifled a nervous cough. "I—perhaps." He cleared his throat. "Perhaps it is." He paused.

"Duncan, I require your promise that you'll not use your powers tonight—either of you. Whatever happens, I must have your solemn assurance that you'll do nothing, nothing whatsoever, to make you appear different from any other penitent who has ever entered my cathedral to make his peace with the Church. Surely you understand the importance of what I am asking."

Morgan looked at the floor and pursed his lips thoughtfully. "I assume that Arilan knows you've come to us?"

"He does."

"And the subject of conversation?"

"He agrees. There must be no magic."

Duncan shrugged and glanced at Morgan. "Then, it appears that you must have our word on it, my lord. You have mine."

"And mine," Morgan said, after an almost imperceptible pause.

Cardiel gave a low sigh of relief. "Thank you. I shall leave you alone for a few more minutes, then. I suspect you will wish to prepare yourselves for the ceremony. Denis and I will return for you shortly."

As the door closed behind Cardiel, Duncan glanced at his cousin. Morgan had turned away as the bishop left, and now the single candle at the end of the bench was casting long, dancing shadows on the stone walls, planing Morgan's face into a mask of concentration. Duncan stared at him for a long moment, a thread of unease rippling through his mind, then started to move across the chamber to Morgan's side.

"Alaric?" he said in a low voice. "What—"

Morgan snapped out of his reverie and held a finger to his

lips, then eyed the door as he crossed to the bench and dropped to his knees in front of it.

"Duncan, I fear that I have been a stranger to prayer in these past weeks," he murmured, motioning for Duncan to join him, and glancing at the door again. "Will you pray with me?"

Wordlessly Duncan knelt at his kinsman's side, his eyes narrowing in question as he made the sign of the cross. He started to speak again, hazarding another glance at the door, but he saw Morgan's lips shape the single syllable, *No*, and he bowed his head instead. Watching Morgan from the corner of his eye, he formed his words so that he was certain only Morgan could hear. He was reluctant to use mind-speech when they had promised Cardiel they would use no magic.

"Will you tell me what's going on?" he murmured. "I know you're concerned that we may be watched, but there's more to it than that. You were reluctant to give your promise to Cardiel. Why?"

"Because I may not be able to keep that promise," Morgan whispered.

"Not keep it?" Duncan replied, remembering just in time to keep his head bowed. "Why on earth not? What's wrong?"

Morgan leaned forward slightly to glance at the door past Duncan, then sat back on his heels. "Derry. He was supposed to contact us either last night or tonight. Last night he didn't. When the time comes tonight, we'll be right in the middle of the ceremony."

"Sweet *Jesu*!" Duncan exploded under his breath, crossing himself as he remembered he was supposed to be praying, and bowing his head once more.

"Alaric, we can't listen for Derry's call in the cathedral— not after we promised Cardiel that we wouldn't use our powers. If we're caught—"

Morgan nodded slightly. "I know. But there isn't any other way. I'm afraid something may have happened to

Derry. We'll just have to take the chance and hope we won't be caught."

Duncan buried his face in his hands and sighed. "I sense that you've thought about this at length. You have a plan?"

Morgan bowed his head again and edged slightly closer to Duncan. "Of sorts, yes. There are several places in the liturgy, both in the ceremony itself and in the Mass which follows, when we won't have many responses to make. I'll try to listen for Derry, while you keep watch. If it looks like we're about to be detected, I'll break off. You can—"

He broke off and bowed his head deeply as he heard the latch being lifted on the door. Then both men crossed themselves and rose as Cardiel stepped into the open doorway, followed closely by Arilan. Both men were solemnly vested in violet, croziers in hands and jeweled miters on heads. In the corridor behind them stood a long line of black-cowled monks, each holding a lighted candle.

"We are ready to begin, if you are," Arilan said. The violet silk of his cope caught the deep blue-violet of his eyes and turned them to sparkling jewels in the candlelight, like the amethyst on his hand.

With a bow, Morgan and Duncan moved to join the procession. It would soon be quite dark.

IT was already dark in the Rheljan Mountains when Derry and his captors at last reached Cardosa. Derry had been tied across a saddle like a piece of baggage rather than being permitted to ride upright like a man—an embellishment calculated, he was sure, to further divest the prisoner of any false sense of dignity. Riding up the defile in this position, his head half-way down his horse's side, had been a wet, cold, and often terrifying experience; for the horses had, at times, plunged through water almost up to their withers. Several times Derry's head had been under water, lungs strained almost to the bursting point as he tried to keep from drowning. His wrists were numb and raw from the chafe of the rawhide thongs that bound him, his feet like lead from the cold and lack of circulation.

But these small details seemed to bother Derry's escort not in the least. As soon as the little band had reined in, just within a small, dark courtyard, Derry's bonds were cut and he was pulled roughly from the saddle. His wounded arm had gone stiff during the long, cramped ride, and he nearly passed out with the pain as his wrists were roughly bound in front of him once more. The fire of circulation returning to cramped and tortured limbs was almost more than he could bear, and he was almost glad for the support of the two guards who held his elbows to either side.

Derry tried to take notice of his surroundings, hoping that this would help him to ignore the pain. He was outside Esgair Ddu, the black-cliff fortress that protected the walled city of Cardosa. He could see the stark, barren ramparts looming above his head as he forced himself to remain standing, but he was not permitted a more leisurely inspection of the place. A pair of guards in the black and white Furstán livery came and took him from his original escort, and he was hurried down a flight of rough stone stairs. He tried to force himself to pay attention to the route they took, mentally charting each twist and turn in the dim corridor through which they dragged him. But his feet would hardly obey him, and he was too tired, and his pains too great, to pay heed the way he ought to.

When at length they came to an iron-bound door, and one man held him up while the other worked the key in the lock, it was all he could do merely to remain conscious. He was never certain how he got from the doorway to the carved armchair in which they sat him.

The men lashed his wrists to the chair arms and passed leather straps around waist and chest and ankles. Then they left him. Slowly his more immediate pains subsided, to be replaced by a dull, aching fatigue and an even more mind-numbing dread. After a few minutes, he finally opened his eyes and forced himself to take stock of the room.

The chamber appeared to be one of Esgair Ddu's better dungeons. By the light of the single torch set in a cresset to his left, he could see that the floor, though strewn with straw, was at least not muddy, and the straw was clean. Nor were the walls dank and dripping—a feature which, in his meager experience with dungeons, he had often dreaded.

But the walls were still dungeon walls, adorned here and there with iron rings set at strategic locations, with bright, well-used chains, with other instruments whose purpose Derry preferred not to think about. Along similar lines, there was also a rather large leather-bound trunk set against the wall to Derry's right: a squat, sinister-looking thing that seemed out of place. It bore an engraved crest below the hasp on the trunk: an ornate, vaguely alien badge etched in gold against the dark, polished leather. But the light was too dim, the trunk too far away, for Derry to be able to read the crest clearly. He had the feeling, however, that the trunk was a recent addition to the room, and that he did not want to meet its owner. He forced himself to leave the trunk and continue his inspection of the room.

There was a window in the place, he realized now. He had almost missed it in the dim light, set deep in the wall opposite him. But almost immediately he saw that it would do him little good. It was high and narrow, several feet wide on the inside, but narrowing to hardly more than a hand-span or so at the outer limit. An iron lattice guarded the window rather than the more usual bars, and Derry realized, as he peered at the grille, that even if he could somehow remove it, he could never slip through the narrow window itself. Besides that—if he had not lost all sense of direction—the window looked out over a sheer cliff face, completely smooth. Even if he could get through the window, there would be no place to go once he got there—unless, of course, he chose another sort of escape. The rocks at the base of Esgair Ddu could give release of a kind, if it came to that.

Derry sighed and turned his attention back to the

chamber itself. It served no useful purpose to contemplate the sort of freedom that might lie outside that window, since he could never get through there to begin with. Besides, apart from his personal aversion to the very thought of suicide, he knew that he was of no use to anyone dead. Alive, if he could withstand whatever his captors had in store for him, there was always the possibility that he could somehow escape, however slim that chance. Alive, he might yet be able to tell Morgan what he had learned, before it was too late.

The thought brought with it the stunning realization that he *had* the means to tell Morgan, if he could but use it. Morgan's Saint Camber medallion still hung undiscovered around his neck. As long as they did not take that from him, there was a chance that he could still make contact with Morgan on schedule.

He did a rapid mental calculation and decided that it was about the time when Morgan would be expecting his call; forced out of his mind what would happen if he were wrong. The spell would work; it *must* work—though, trussed and helpless as he was, he wasn't sure exactly how he was going to do it yet.

Taking a deep breath to calm himself, and praying that he would be permitted the time to do what he had to do, Derry wriggled his torso in its bonds and concentrated on locating the medallion against his chest. Morgan had told him that he should hold the medallion in his hands when trying to establish contact, but since that was out of the question, he would have to hope that the touch of medallion on bare chest would suffice.

There! He could feel the medallion, warmed to body temperature, resting slightly left of center. Now, if only such a touch were sufficient, as well as the touch of hand. . . .

Derry closed his eyes and tried to visualize the medallion as it lay against his chest, imagining that he was holding it in his hands, the incised carving sleek beneath his right thumb. Then he calmed his mind and let the

words of the spell Morgan had taught him begin to roll
through his mind, concentrating on his memory of how
he had cupped the Camber medallion in the hollow of his
hand.

He felt himself verging on the sleep-like trance that accompanied the spell, started to let himself slip into its cool
depths—then tensed at the sound behind him of the door
bolt scraping in its guides. Hinges creaked as the door
swung back, and he could hear booted footsteps approaching. He controlled the impulse to twist his head around in
an effort to see.

"Very well, tell him I'll take care of it," said a cool, cultured voice. "Deegan, did you have something?"

"Only this dispatch from Duke Lionel, Sire," a second
voice replied, an underling by the tone.

There was a murmur of assent, followed by the brittle
crack of a seal being broken, the faint rustle of parchment. Derry's stomach had begun a queasy churning as
the voices spoke, for there was only one man in Esgair Ddu
who would be addressed as "Sire." As he registered this
grim fact, someone stepped into the doorway with another
torch, casting grotesque, misshapen shadows on the dungeon wall.

The hackles rose at the back of Derry's neck, and he felt
his heart begin to race. He told himself that the shadows
did not reflect their owners' true appearance, that it was a
trick of the torchlight that struck such a note of mortal fear.
But another corner of his mind whispered what he already
knew: that one of the men had to be Wencit of Torenth.
Now he would never get through to Morgan.

"I'll deal with this later, Deegan. Leave us now," the
smooth voice said.

There was the rattle of parchment being folded, of
leather creaking and harness jingling as someone withdrew.
Then the door hinges were rasping closed, the bolt being
shot into place. The torchlight began to intensify to his left,

though he was certain that someone came from the right as well.

The faint rustling of the footsteps in the straw set frantic alarm bells clanging in Derry's head.

CHAPTER TWELVE

"Be not far from me; for trouble is near;
for there is none to help."

PSALMS 22:11

IN the cathedral in Dhassa, the ceremony of reconciliation
for the two repentant Deryni was underway. After entering
the cathedral in full procession, in the company of eight
bishops and untold numbers of priests, monks, and other as-
sistants, Morgan and Duncan had been solemnly presented
to the presiding Bishop Cardiel and had formally declared
their desire to be received back into the communion of Holy
Mother Church. After that, they had knelt together on the
lowest step of the altar and listened while Cardiel, Arilan,
and the others intoned the prescribed formulae to accomplish their purpose.

It had been a time of concentration and of danger, for the
two were required to respond often and intricately to the
liturgy so sung and spoken. At last a portion approached
when there would be little for the penitents to outwardly
say or do. The two avoided looking at one another as each
was led by two priests to the wide riser before the final approach to the altar and assisted to lower himself to the carpet,

there to lie prostrate while the next portion of the ceremony continued.

"Bless the Lord, O my soul," the bishops chanted, "and forget not all His benefits: Who forgiveth all thine iniquities; Who healeth all thy diseases; Who redeemeth thy life from destruction; Who crowneth thee . . ."

As the psalm droned on, Morgan shifted his position from where his head rested lightly on his clasped hands and moved them slightly so that he could see his Gryphon ring. Now, while the bishops were absorbed in their sacerdotal function, he must try to contact Derry, even if only fleetingly. For if all were well with Derry and he could make contact, it would be a relatively simple matter to arrange for another contact later this evening, when circumstances were not so dangerous.

He opened his eyes a slit and saw that Duncan was watching him covertly, that no one seemed to be paying much attention to them for the moment. He would have perhaps five minutes. He prayed that it would be enough.

Closing his eyes, he felt the brief touch of Duncan's presence signaling ready, then slitted his eyes open once again to use his Gryphon as a focal point. Slowly he permitted his senses to close out the candlelight, the drone of the bishops' voices, the pungent incense smoke swirling around him, the rough scratch of wool carpeting under his chin. Then he was slipping into the initial levels of trance, his mind reaching out for some fleeting contact with the mind of Sean Lord Derry.

". . . Against Thee, Thee only, have I sinned and done this evil in Thy sight, O Lord," Cardiel sang, "that Thou mightest be justified when Thou speakest, and be clear when Thou judgest . . ."

But Morgan did not hear.

DERRY tried to mask any hint of his very real fear as the two men stepped from either side of him in the narrow dungeon.

The man on the left was tall and hawk-visaged, with a terrible scar knifing down the aristocratic nose until it disappeared in the neatly trimmed moustache and beard, the dark hair touched with silver at the temples, the eyes pale as silver in the torchlight. He it was who bore the torch whose fire-fled shadows had sparked such dread in Derry minutes before, who terrified Derry anew as he turned casually to set the torch in a wall bracket not far from the one already there.

But this was not Wencit. Derry knew that instinctively, after only a glimpse of the second man. For the man who glided past his right side to pause directly in front of the chair was as different from the tall, scarred stranger as two men could be: trim and angular yet graceful, red of hair and moustache, pale blue eyes gazing unblinking at the frightened captive who sat immobilized before him. Wencit's attire was informal, a flowing robe of slubbed amber silk pulled on over rich satin damask of the same golden hue. A wide, linked belt of gold girdled his narrow waist, with a jeweled dagger thrust carelessly into the top. Rings glittered on the long, ascetic fingers, but other than those, Wencit wore no jewels. Tawny velvet slippers with pointed toes showed beneath the hem of the long tunic, the fabric gold-embroidered across the instep. So far as Derry could see, the dagger was Wencit's only weapon. Somehow the thought did little to put his mind at ease.

"So," the man said. It was the same voice that Derry had identified as Wencit's earlier, and this but confirmed his growing fear. "So, you are the illustrious Sean Lord Derry. Do you know who I am?"

Derry hesitated, then permitted himself a curt nod.

"Splendid," Wencit said, much too amiably. "Tell me, have you made the acquaintance of my esteemed colleague? Permit me to introduce Rhydon of Eastmarch. The name may be familiar to you."

Derry glanced instinctively at the other man, who was leaning casually against the wall to his left, and the man dipped his chin in acknowledgement. Rhydon was dressed much like Wencit but in midnight blue and silver instead of the amber gold. The more somber attire, the shadow-side of Wencit's sunlit hues, seemed to suggest that it was Rhydon who should be more feared, made Wencit seem almost a trifle soft and even effeminate by comparison.

But, no! Derry sharply reminded himself that he must not allow himself to be lured into that illusion. Wencit was to be feared more than ten Rhydons, regardless of Rhydon's reputation as a Deryni of the highest powers. Derry must not let them throw him off his balance. It was Wencit who was to be feared.

Wencit gazed at his prisoner for a long moment, noting Derry's reaction to the darker man, then smiled faintly and crossed his arms on his chest. The soft rustling sound of the long silk robe instantly brought back Derry's attention. Wencit's broadening smile worried Derry even more than had his sterner countenance.

"Sean Lord Derry," Wencit said again. "I have heard much of you, my young friend. I am given to understand that you once served as Alaric Morgan's military aide, that you now sit on the Haldane kinglet's royal council. Well, not precisely *now*, I suppose." He watched Derry bite his lip at that.

"Yes, indeed, I have heard a great deal about the derring-do of Sean Lord Derry. It appears that we shall soon be in a position to learn whether that sterling reputation of yours is merited. Pray, tell me about yourself, Sean Lord Derry."

Derry tried not to let his consternation show, but he feared he was not succeeding. Very well, let Wencit know that it was not going to be easy. Why, if Wencit thought he was going to give in without a fight, he was sadly mistak—

Very suddenly Wencit moved a step closer. Derry tensed and froze, but he forced himself to meet the sorcerer's gaze defiantly, hardly daring to breathe—and was surprised when Wencit drew back slightly, was a bit dismayed to see that the sorcerer had dropped one hand to the hilt of the dagger at his waist.

"I see," Wencit said, casually withdrawing the dagger to turn it between his two hands. "You presume to resist me, eh? I think it only fair to warn you that I am delighted. After everything I had heard about you, I was beginning to fear you would disappoint me. I so dislike disappointments."

Before Derry could react to that declaration, Wencit suddenly crossed the remaining two paces to Derry's chair and laid the edge of his dagger hard against Derry's throat. Derry's eyes closed briefly as he braced himself for death, but he knew this was not yet his time—as did Wencit. The Torenthi sorcerer watched Derry's face carefully for some sign of yielding as he exerted pressure, but there was none, and none expected.

With a slight smile, Wencit withdrew the blade and set its tip under the top lacing of Derry's leather jerkin—and cut the thong. Derry started as the leather gave, but he forced himself to remain impassive as Wencit continued moving slowly down the row of lacings, cutting each in turn.

"Do you know, Derry," *cut*, "I have often wondered what it is about Alaric Morgan that inspires such loyalty in his followers," *cut*. "Or Kelson and those other rather strange Haldane predecessors of his," *cut*. "Not too many men could sit here silently as you do," *cut*, "refusing to talk, though they surely can guess what unpleasantness awaits them," *cut*, "and still remain loyal to a leader who is far away and can never hope to help them out of this, even if he knew."

Wencit's blade hooked in another thong and moved to cut, but this time the blade was stopped by something that clinked metallic. Wencit had reached mid-chest level, and he raised an eyebrow in feigned surprise as he looked up at Derry.

"Why, what is this?" he asked, cocking his head wistfully. "Why, Derry, there seems to be something stopping my blade, doesn't there?" He tried a few more sharp, downward strokes, again with no other result than a dull clink.

"Rhydon, what do you suppose it is?"

"I'm sure I don't know, Sire," the darker man murmured, collecting himself and strolling to Derry's other side.

"Nor I," Wencit purred, using the dagger as a retractor to pull aside the edge of the jerkin until a sturdy silver chain was revealed. The ends of the chain disappeared under Derry's shirt. "Why, look at this."

With a questioning glance at Derry, Wencit flicked the end of his blade under the chain and began slowly withdrawing it until a heavy silver medallion appeared.

"A holy medal?" Wencit asked, his mouth twitching at the corners. "How touching, Rhydon. He carries it next to his heart."

Rhydon chuckled. "One is tempted to ask what saint he believes could protect him from you, Sire. But I daresay, there is none."

"No, there is not," Wencit agreed, glancing at the medal, then lifting it closer with the tip of his blade for a better look. "Saint *Camber*?"

His eyes seemed to darken to pools of indigo as he glanced up at Derry's face, and Derry felt his heart miss a beat. Slowly, deliberately, Wencit bent to scan the words incised around the rim, scorn edging his voice as he read them aloud.

"*Sanctus Camberus, libera nos ab omnibus malis*—deliver us from every evil. . . ."

Very deliberately, not taking his gaze from Derry's, Wencit closed his hand around the silver disc and wrapped the chain around two fingers, pulling it taut around Derry's neck until their faces were but a hand-span apart.

"Art thou Deryni, then, youngling?" Wencit whispered harshly, his words chill as ice. "Thou invokest a Deryni saint, my foolish young friend. Dost believe he can protect thee from *me*?"

Derry's stomach did a slow, queasy roll as Wencit gave the chain a slight twist.

"Wilt not answer, Sean Lord Derry?"

The terrible eyes seemed to be boring into Derry's, and the young Marcher lord wrenched his gaze away with a shudder. He heard Wencit's snort of disgust, but he would not permit himself to be drawn back into that potent glance.

"I see," Wencit breathed softly.

The pressure on the chain around Derry's neck lessened slightly. But then Wencit's hand was moving in a lightning blur, snapping the chain and jerking Derry's neck with the sudden tension before one of the metal links gave. With a gasp, Derry stared at the sorcerer again, at the broken chain spilling from between long, white fingers. The back of his neck stung where the chain had burned him with the friction of passing, and he realized, with a sinking sensation in his stomach, that Wencit now held the Camber medallion.

Now he could never hope to stand up to Wencit. His link with Morgan was broken. The magic was gone. He was all alone now, and Morgan would never know.

He managed to swallow, though with difficulty, and tried, unsuccessfully, to calm his pounding heart.

AS the long prayers ended in Dhassa Cathedral, Morgan dragged himself from the depths of trance and forced himself to open his eyes. He must be very careful, for in a very short time he was going to have to get to his feet and proceed with the ceremony, make coherent responses. There must be no sign that the past five minutes had been in any way out of the ordinary. No one must suspect.

He thought, though, that he had briefly touched Derry's mind. He wished he could be certain. He had been left with the distinct impression that Derry had tried to reach him but had been interrupted. And then, just now, he had been nearly overcome by a mind-numbing flare of fear as he tried to extend even further; and he very nearly had been unable to come back unaided.

He made himself draw a deep, settling breath and slowly

let it out, applying one of the Deryni aids to banish fatigue, and forced himself to lift his head, to rise to his knees as the priests lifted him up. He caught Duncan looking at him as he stood to be divested of the violet robe covering his white tunic, and tried to flash him some sign of reassurance; but Duncan knew that something was wrong. He could sense the tension in every line of his kinsman's body as the two of them knelt again before the high altar. Morgan tried again to gather his wits about him as Cardiel began another prayer.

"*Ego te absolvo . . .*" I absolve you, Alaric Anthony and Duncan Howard, and do absolve and deliver you from all heresy and schism, and from every and all judgment, censure, and pain for that cause incurred. So do we restore you into the unity of our Mother, Holy Church. . . .

Morgan humbly bowed his head and folded his hands in an attitude of piety and tried to formulate some new plan of action. Having made contact once, however fleeting, he knew that he would have to try again, that something must be drastically wrong wherever Derry was.

But what? And how much harder did he dare to try, here within the confines of the cathedral?

The priests were at his elbows again, pressing him forward, and to his left he could see Duncan receiving the same guidance. He moved to the first step before him and knelt again, Duncan to his left. Cardiel stood directly before them. Now came the imposition of hands, the central part of the ceremony. Morgan bowed his head and tried to clear his mind, to make his response not altogether unworthy, and listened as the age-old phrases rolled from Cardiel's lips, his outstretched hands slowly descending toward their heads.

"*Dominus Sanctus, Patri Omnipotenti, Deus Aeternum. . . .*" Holy Lord, Father Omnipotent, Eternal God, who coverest the earth with Thy favor, Thee we Thy lowly priests as suppliants ask and entreat, that Thou wilt deign to incline the ear of Thy mercy and remit every offense and forgive all the sins of these, Thy servants, Alaric Anthony and Duncan Howard; and give unto them pardon in exchange for their afflictions, joy for sorrow, life for death.

Cardiel's hands came to rest lightly on their heads.

"Lord, grant that they, though fallen from the celestial heights, may be found worthy to persevere by Thy rewards unto good peace and unto the heavenly places unto life eternal. *Per eumdem Dominum nostrum Jesum Christum Filium tuum, qui tecum vivit et regnat in unitate Spiritus Sancti Deus, per omnia saecula saeculorum. . . . Amen.*"

There was a great shuffling of feet and clearing of throats and rustling of garments as the congregation got to its feet, and Morgan let his attending priests guide him and Duncan to the side of the chancel. Now would follow a special Mass of thanksgiving, in celebration of their return to the fold. Morgan glanced covertly at his kinsman as they took their places at a wide prie-dieu, where they were expected to remain during the Mass. His eyes sought Duncan's as they knelt side by side.

"Something has happened," Morgan murmured, his voice barely audible. "I don't know what, but I'm going to have to try to find out. And I'm going to have to go deeper into trance to do it. If I go too deep, and lose track of what's going on here, bring me back, and we'll use the ruse we discussed earlier. I'll even arrange to faint, if necessary."

Duncan nodded slightly, his eyes grave as he scanned the cathedral. "All right, I'll do my best to cover you. But be careful."

What might have been a faint answering nod descended into Morgan's hands as he closed his eyes, feigning an attitude of prayer. Again he triggered the first stage of the Thuryn trance, this time going almost immediately into deeper and deeper levels, reaching, questing . . .

WENCIT opened his hand and gazed at Derry's Camber medallion again, then passed it to Rhydon, who slipped it into a pouch at his belt. The Deryni sorcerer still seemed calm, composed, but Derry thought he detected a touch of irritation, a hint of unease. The torchlight cast ruddy highlights on Wencit's hair, making him seem even more malefic in the wavering shadow-play, and Derry was suddenly reminded that he was playing for his life. The thought sobered him as nothing else could have done at that moment, for he could no longer entertain any doubt that Wencit would kill him without a qualm if it suited his purpose. He felt the icy gaze upon him again and forced himself to meet it, tried to will his growing dread to recede.

"So," Wencit said with a sinister calm to his voice, "I wonder what we should do with this bold interloper, Rhydon. This spy in our midst. Shall we kill him?" He leaned both hands on the arms of Derry's chair, his face very close to Derry's.

"I suppose we *could* feed him to the caradots," Wencit continued conversationally. "Do you know what a caradot is, little lordling?"

Derry swallowed with difficulty but would not trust himself to answer. He had a suspicion. Wencit smiled.

"I gather that you are not acquainted with caradots," Wencit murmured, looking pleased. "I fear 'tis a subject sadly lacking in your education, young Derry. This Morgan of yours has been very lax. Rhydon, would you be so good as to show him a caradot?"

With a sly, languid nod, Rhydon moved closer to Derry's left side and drew himself erect, then traced a peculiar symbol in the air with his forefinger as Wencit moved behind the chair to Derry's right. At the same time, Rhydon murmured words of an ancient spell under his breath, uttered in an alien tongue whose sound grated on the senses.

The very air crackled at the sorcerer's fingertips, and a noxious scent of molten lead tickled at Derry's nostrils. In that instant, which seemed all too endless, Derry caught a glimpse of a creature straight from Hell: a shrieking, mawing terror of green and crimson and gore, with a gnashing, ravening mouth and undulating tentacles that reached hungrily toward his face, closer, closer . . .

Derry screamed, squeezing his eyes closed and struggling hysterically in his bonds as he fancied he could feel the creature's acid breath on his face. He heard the monster roar, the hot, leaden smell almost overpowering in his nostrils.

Then there was only a sudden, deathly silence, a breath of fresh breeze; and he knew that it was gone. He opened his eyes to find Wencit and Rhydon gazing down at him in wry amusement, Rhydon's pale eyes still veiled with a hint of dark, unspeakable power. Derry's breath came in ragged, terror-fueled shudders as he stared up at the pair of them in horror. Wencit's mouth twitched in satisfaction, a patronizing little smirk, as he turned to Rhydon and made him a short, casual bow.

"I thank you, Rhydon."

"It was my pleasure, Sire."

Derry swallowed hard, not trusting himself to do more, and tried to still the gibbering fear that still nipped at the edge of his mind. He told himself that they would not let that thing have him, at least not until they learned from him what they wanted to know, but the thought did little to ease his fear. Gradually he willed his ragged breathing to slow. His head ached with the effort the whole thing had cost him.

"So, my young friend," Wencit said silkily, leaning his hands on Derry's chair arms once more, "do we feed you to the caradots? Or do we find some better use for you? I rather got the impression that you didn't like our little pet . . . though I'm certain he liked you."

Derry swallowed again, overcoming a wave of nausea, and Wencit chuckled.

"No caradots? What do you think, Rhydon?"

Rhydon's voice was sleek and cold. "Methinks a more suitable fate might be found for him, Sire. I like this sport as well as you, but we must not forget that Sean Lord Derry is an earl and the son of an earl, a man of gentle birth. Hardly proper caradot fare, do you not agree?"

"But the beast seemed so taken with him," Wencit pouted, his eyes laughing as Derry shrank back in the chair. "Still, you are doubtless right. Sean Lord Derry alive is a far more valuable commodity to me than Sean Lord Derry dead—though he may wish for death before this night is done." He straightened to fold his arms across his chest and stare down at Derry with an indulgent smile.

"Now, you will begin by telling us everything you know of King Kelson's strength, both military and arcane. And when you have finished that, you will tell us all there is to know about this Morgan of yours."

Derry stiffened in outrage, his blue eyes flashing defiance. "Never! I'll not betray—"

"Enough!" Wencit did not raise his voice, but his single word lashed Derry into silence. "Do not tell *me* what you will and will not do!" So saying, he leaned down closer to Derry with a terrible intensity. For an instant, the gaze caught and held, the pale eyes swimming in Derry's vision like twin pools of molten metal. Then Derry was wrenching his gaze away, turning his head to squeeze his eyes shut in desperation, knowing—but not knowing how he knew—that Wencit had tried to Truth-Read him. He could not bear the touch of that alien mind.

He risked opening his eyes a crack and saw Wencit straightening in faint disbelief, the rust-colored brows slightly furrowed. The sorcerer eyed him suspiciously for a moment, then crossed the chamber to the leather-bound trunk set against the right-hand wall. Lifting the lid, he rummaged inside for a long moment.

When he straightened and turned, one hand held a small crystal vial filled with a white, opalescent liquid. His other hand held one of earthenware, from which he decanted four golden drops of a clear fluid into the opalescent white. The opaline fluid turned a glittering, swirling red, like luminous blood, as Wencit held it to the torchlight. He swirled the contents of the vial with slow, circular movements of his hand as he turned and strolled back toward his captive.

" 'Tis a pity you have decided not to cooperate, my young friend," Wencit said, leaning one elbow on the back of Derry's chair and holding the vial to the light to admire the color—in front of Derry's face, where he could also see it. "Still, I suppose you have no more choice than I. They have managed to shield you well, this Morgan and his upstart prince. But alas, Deryni-given powers are subject to the same limitations as those Deryni-born—alas for you, that is. The contents of this vial will strip away all resistance."

Derry swallowed dry-throated and stared at the vial. "What is it?" he found himself whispering.

"So, curiosity is not dead after all, is it? Frankly, though, you would know little more after I told you than before. The merasha is fairly common, but the rest . . ." Wencit chuckled as Derry clenched his teeth in apprehension. "Yes, you've heard about merasha, haven't you? No matter. Rhydon, hold his head."

As Derry's head whipped around to search wildly for the second Deryni, he was already too late. Rhydon's hands were immobilizing his head in a vise-like grip, pinning his head brutally against Rhydon's chest. Rhydon knew the pressure points and applied them, and Derry felt his mouth opening, helpless as a baby's.

Then the crimson fluid was rushing down his throat, searing his tongue and choking him as he fought not to swallow. He felt the blackness swoop down on him as Rhydon applied more pressure to force him to swallow. And then he was gulping it down, despite his best efforts to the contrary—once, twice, finally exploding in a frantic cough as his head was released.

His tongue was numb, a flat, metallic taste in his mouth, his lungs burning with the fire of the fluid that had passed so near. He coughed again and shook his head in an attempt to clear it, tried to will himself to vomit back what Wencit had forced upon him, but it was no use. As his coughing ceased and the fire subsided, he sensed his vision blurring, his limbs going slack. There came a great roaring in his ears, as though the most powerful wind in all creation were trying to blow him from time and space. Colors flashed and fused before his eyes, and yet it seemed to be growing darker.

He tried to lift his head, but it was too much effort. He tried to force his eyes to focus but could not. He saw the tips of Wencit's velvet slippers by his chair legs as his head lolled helplessly to the right; heard the hated voice murmur something he should have been able to understand but could not.

Then the darkness claimed him.

THE cathedral had grown hushed as the Mass approached its climax, and Morgan tried desperately to force himself back to consciousness. He had caught a fleeting taste of the darkness just before it overwhelmed Derry, though he could not pinpoint its source or its subject, only knew that it had to be somehow connected with Derry, and that something was horribly wrong.

But he could learn no more. He tensed with the effort of disentangling himself from that instant of terror, reeling slightly on the prie-dieu as he slipped at last from his trance. Duncan felt him waver and cast him a furtive glance as he tried to remain unobtrusive.

"Alaric, are you all right?" he asked. His blue eyes said, *Are you playing, or is this for real?*

Morgan swallowed and shook his head, trying to regain his equilibrium, but his recent exertions, coupled with his recent fast, really had addled his wits. Given time, he could recover, he knew; but here, surrounded by men who were already predisposed to suspicion, he was altogether vulnerable. He sat back on his hunkers and groped blindly for the support of Duncan's arm as his senses reeled again, knowing he would not be able to stay conscious much longer.

Duncan glanced at the bishops, several of whom were staring in their direction, then leaned closer to Morgan's ear.

"They've noticed, Alaric. If you really need help, tell me. The bishops are—uh-oh, Cardiel has stopped the Mass. He's coming this way."

"Take over, then," Morgan whispered, closing his eyes and swaying again. "I really am going to pass out." He swallowed. "Be caref . . ."

His whisper trailed off in mid-syllable as he crumpled against Duncan's shoulder and went limp. Duncan eased him to the floor and felt his forehead, then looked up to see Cardiel, Arilan, and two of the other bishops staring down at them in various attitudes of concern. He must divert their attention as quickly as he could.

"It's the fasting; he's not accustomed to it," he said, bending over the unconscious man to loosen his collar. "Can someone please bring him some wine? He needs nourishment."

A monk was dispatched to fetch the wine, and Duncan ventured a quick, clandestine probe of Morgan's mind. Morgan really *had* fainted; there was no doubt about that now. His face was pale, his pulse rapid and ragged, his breathing shallow. Duncan knew he would eventually come around of his own accord, none the worse for the experience, but he dared not prolong this scene any longer than necessary. Cardiel had crouched beside him, also reaching out to touch Morgan's wrist, Arilan and another of the bishops behind him. And several of the barons and generals and warlords nearest the chancel had left their places to stand uncertainly in the aisle, some fingering the hilts of swords and daggers suspiciously. These men must be reassured, and at once, or there would be trouble.

With a look of concern that was not entirely feigned, Duncan took Morgan's head between his hands, thumbs massaging at the temples, at the same time silently applying the Deryni spell to banish fatigue. He felt Morgan's stirring in his mind long before the slack body moved slightly.

Then Morgan gave a low moan and rolled his head to one side, eyelids fluttering as consciousness returned. A monk knelt with a hanaper of wine, and Duncan lifted his cousin's head against his knee to bring the wine to his lips. Morgan's eyes slowly opened.

"Drink this," Duncan ordered.

Morgan nodded meekly and allowed himself to be given several swallows of the wine, steadying Duncan's grip on the hanaper with both hands, then passed one hand before his eyes as though to clear away a troublesome memory. As he did, his other hand contracted almost infinitesimally on Duncan's, reassuring him that the danger was past. Morgan was once more in control.

Morgan took another swallow of the wine, swirling it around his tongue and judging it too sweet, then pushed the hanaper aside and sat up. The bishops hovered over him with a mixture of concern, indignation, and suspicion, and several of the barons crowded closer to the altar rail to hear what Morgan would say by way of explanation.

"You must pardon me, my lords. A silly thing to do," he murmured, allowing the real fatigue that remained to tinge his speech with hesitation. "I fear I am not accustomed to fasting . . ."

He let his voice trail off dazedly, permitting himself to swallow with effort, eyes downcast, and the bishops nodded. The effects of fasting were something they could understand. Under the strain of the past three days, it was not altogether inappropriate that the Duke of Corwyn should faint away at Mass. Cardiel touched Morgan's shoulder lightly in acquiescence, then stood to reassure the waiting barons and warlords as Morgan and Duncan resumed their places at the prie-dieu.

Arilan stayed looking down at them for long seconds as they knelt again, returning to his place only when Cardiel mounted the altar steps once more. The objects of his scrutiny noted this hesitation and exchanged wary glances as the Mass got underway once more.

From that point, however, the Mass continued to its conclusion without further incident. The two penitents received communion and a blessing, final prayers were said, and at length populace and prelates filed from the cathedral, with Cardiel, Arilan, and the two Deryni ending up in the sacristy with the rest of the bishops. Arilan removed his miter and retired to the tiny vesting chapel off the sacristy while the rest of the prelates finished their business in the room and finally were gone. Only then did he rejoin them, still vested, to move slowly to the door and bolt it.

"Is there something you wish to tell me, Duke of Corwyn?" he asked softly, not turning toward them from his place before the bolted door.

Morgan glanced at Duncan, then at Cardiel, who was standing quietly to one side and looking very uncomfortable.

"I am not certain that I understand your implication, my lord," Morgan replied carefully.

"Is it usual for the Duke of Corwyn to faint at Mass?" Arilan asked, turning to face Morgan with cold, blue-violet eyes.

"I—as I have said, my lord, I am unaccustomed to fasting. It is little done in my household. And the late hours we have kept these three days, the little sleep, the lack of food—"

"—do not constitute an acceptable excuse!" the bishop snapped, crossing to look Morgan in the eyes. "You gave your word. You lied to us. You used your Deryni powers in the very cathedral, even though we forbade it both of you! I trust that you can produce a justification that seemed valid at the time!"

CHAPTER THIRTEEN

"And I will camp against thee round about,
and will lay siege against thee . . ."

ISAIAH 29:3

MORGAN returned Arilan's cold stare unflinchingly for several seconds, then nodded slowly.

"Yes, I used my powers tonight. I had no choice."

"No choice?" Arilan echoed. "You dared to risk this entire operation, the work of weeks of careful planning, by your disobedience, and you say you had no choice?"

He turned on Duncan and held his gaze also. "And you, *Father* Duncan. As a priest, I would have thought your word would mean more to you than that. I suppose you had no choice either?"

"We did what had to be done, Excellency. If there had not been grave cause, we would not have considered breaking our promises to you."

"If there was grave cause, I should have been informed of it. If Cardiel and I are to lead this force effectively, we must know what is happening. We cannot have the two of you making what could be critical decisions without our knowledge."

Morgan only barely held his temper in check. "You would

have been told in due time, my lord. As it was, the decision had to be ours to make. If you were Deryni, you would understand!"

"*Would* I?" Arilan breathed.

He turned away abruptly, hands clasping tightly together, and Morgan hazarded a glance at Duncan. In doing so, he could not help noticing Cardiel, who had gone almost as white as the alb he had just removed. His expression was strained, his eyes riveted on Arilan. Before Morgan could reach any conclusion regarding the bishop's reaction, Arilan turned and took two long strides toward him, stopped to face him down, hands on hips.

"Very well, Alaric. I had not thought to tell you yet, but perhaps it is time after all. Surely you did not think that you and Duncan were the only Deryni in Gwynedd?"

"The only—" Morgan broke off in consternation, finally understanding why Cardiel was staring at his colleague so intently. "But, you . . ." he murmured.

Arilan gave a curt nod. "That is correct. I am Deryni also. Now tell me why I should understand what the pair of you did tonight."

Morgan found himself speechless. Shaking his head in denial and disbelief, he staggered backward several steps and found a chair behind his knees. Gratefully he sank down on it, unable to take his eyes from the Deryni bishop. Duncan, who had retreated as far across the room as he could go, merely stared at Arilan and nodded slowly, as though putting together pieces of a puzzle he had held for a long time and never knew they formed a picture. Cardiel said nothing. Arilan, with a faint, almost self-conscious smile, turned and began removing his vestments, watching all of them out of the corner of his eye.

"Well, can't one of you say something? Duncan, you must surely have suspected. Am I that good an actor?"

Duncan shook his head, trying to keep an edge of bitterness from his voice. "You are among the best I have ever seen, Excellency. I know from personal experience how difficult it is to live a lie, to keep the secret you and I have kept. But, tell me, did it never bother you to stand idly by while our people suffered and died for lack of your assistance? You were in a position to help them—yet you did nothing."

Arilan lowered his eyes, then removed his stole and touched it to his lips, hung it carefully on a wooden peg before replying. "I did what I dared. I would it had been more. But being both priest and Deryni is not an easy role, as I'm sure you will agree. So far as I know, you and I are the only men to be ordained in several centuries. I dared not jeopardize what greater good I might achieve by revealing myself prematurely. You can understand that, can't you?"

Duncan did not answer, and Arilan ventured a sympathetic hand on his shoulder. "Duncan, I know how it must have been for you. It will not always be as it has been."

"Perhaps you're right. I don't know."

With a patient sigh, Arilan turned his attention back to Morgan, who had not moved. The duke had regained most of his composure while the two priests spoke, and now he lifted his gaze to Arilan almost defiantly. The bishop understood immediately, and moved closer to Morgan's chair.

"Is it so hard to trust, Alaric? I know that your path has not been easy either. We priests have no monopoly on sorrow."

"Why should I trust you?" Morgan said. "You deceived us before; why not again? What reassurance do we have that you'll not betray us?"

"Only my word—and it is at least as good as yours." Arilan smiled wanly. "Or no, there is another way. Why don't you let me show you why you should trust? Let me share a little of the other side with you, if you are not afraid. You may be surprised at what you see."

"You would enter my mind?" Morgan breathed.

"No, you would enter mine. I shall allow it. Do you accept?"

Even as Morgan started to shake his head in instinctive refusal, Arilan abruptly dropped to one knee before him, a hand resting lightly on the arm of Morgan's chair as he gazed into Morgan's eyes. It was not an offer of physical contact—a condition that Morgan had always thought essential for a first Mind-Touch between strangers. But he sensed that Arilan did not seem to expect that this would be necessary.

Very tentatively, Morgan sent out a questing tendril of thought—and at once found himself skimming along the outermost levels of Arilan's consciousness, floating without effort along vistaed halls of ordered, reasoned intellect whose fascination he could not resist. He caught glimpses of Arilan as a young man in seminary, in his first parish, in the chambers of the Curia last March, opposing the Interdict. How much there was that he had not expected!

Then he was back in his own mind, and Arilan was merely looking up at him. Without a word, the bishop stood and resumed removing his vestments, finally finishing in his familiar purple cassock and cloak. Only then did he meet Morgan's eyes again, his manner now totally serene and matter-of-fact, as though nothing had happened.

"Shall we go?" he said easily, gliding to the door and shooting back the bolt.

As Arilan pulled the door wide and stood aside, Morgan nodded sheepishly and got to his feet, Duncan and Cardiel falling in quietly behind him.

"And you might tell us, as we walk, of what you learned in the cathedral tonight," Arilan added, spreading his arms to include them all in his comradely embrace. "After that, I think we all had best retire to rest. We march at first light, and we wouldn't want to keep Kelson waiting."

TWO days later, Kelson received the homage of the rebel bishops at Dol Shaia, and himself knelt to the formal absolution they pronounced to free him of the taint of consorting with former excommunicants and heretics. Two days after that, they were at the gates of Coroth.

Strangely enough, Kelson had not seemed terribly surprised to learn that Arilan was Deryni. He had been aware, from the minute that Morgan and Duncan and the rebel bishops joined him, that something vital had changed. Other than Cardiel, none of the other bishops knew of Arilan's newly revealed status; but even so, there was a subtle difference in the way they deferred to him as opposed to Cardiel, almost as though they felt his power without actually being aware.

Kelson, long a student of the subtle nuance in speech and movement, had even noticed a difference in Morgan and Duncan's attitude toward Arilan; something that even he, after long association with both men, could not fully explain.

Once Arilan was revealed to him, however, it was a simple matter merely to take the information in stride, accepting Arilan's Deryniness as an old and established fact. This ready acceptance worked much to his favor, for by the time the royal army came within sight of Coroth late the next afternoon, the four Deryni were a team. Kelson felt relaxed and confident as they drew rein at the top of a rise and watched the army deploying around Morgan's occupied city.

They had flushed out several bands of gray-clad rebel horsemen as they advanced toward Coroth, so any element of surprise they might have had was long gone by the time the first royal advance scouts sighted the city.

Now the plain outside Coroth lay empty, deserted, the late-afternoon breeze rippling the sea grass to a gently undulating ocean of pale green. To the southeast, down a wide stretch of ocean strand, they could see the flat crinkle of the sea, green and silver in the mist-shrouded afternoon sun. The tang of salt was in the air, along with the slightly sharp scent of decaying seaweed, a whiff of the castle middens with their ripe decay.

Kelson surveyed the scene for several minutes, eyeing the blank castle walls, the empty expanse of plain and sand dunes, bare except for the rapidly advancing royal army. Far to the northwest, he could see the violet banners of Cardiel's Joshuic Foot, war standards slowly giving way to spears and then to armed foot soldiers with tall, kite-shaped shields as they came over the rise.

Closer on his left flank, Prince Nigel's crack Haldane archers were taking positions at a point of vantage atop a cluster of sand dunes. The regiment's drummers, garish in their lowland dress of green and violet stripes, were hammering out a fast, complicated marching beat, twirling their sticks above their heads and shouting occasionally as they marked time with their feet. Each archer was partnered with a foot soldier armed with spear and shield, whose duty it would be to protect his archer during a rain of enemy bow-fire. All the men in the regiment wore the green and violet feather cockades of the Haldane Archers Corps in the front of their hard leather fighting caps.

At Kelson's back, the flower of Gwynedd's cavalry waited, knights and squires, pages and men-at-arms pulling quickly into position behind their king. The banners of the Lords of Horthness and Varian, Lindestark and Rhorau, Bethenar and Pelagog, floated above the heads of the royal knights: leaders of the greatest houses in Gwynedd, scions of families loyal to the Crown through all of Gwynedd's noble history, since the inception of the Eleven Kingdoms. Morgan's black gryphon banner could be seen off to the right, where Morgan was conferring with several of his officers on some minor point of strategy.

And riding toward Kelson was Duncan, accompanied by a squire carrying his McLain banner of sleeping lions and roses, the banner marked with the red label of three points that identified him as the heir to Cassan and also, since the death of his elder brother Kevin, Earl of Kierney. Duncan wore a fighting harness as he joined Kelson atop the command rise, only a small, plain silver pectoral cross denoting his priestly calling in the midst of McLain plaid and fighting gear.

The Deryni priest nodded greeting to Kelson as he drew

rein, then turned to watch Morgan now riding toward them. The gryphon banner joined sleeping lion and roses and the Gwynedd lion, followed shortly by Arilan's episcopal banner of Rhemuth and Cardiel's Dhassa banner. Nigel's crescent-charged demi-lion was also approaching.

"Well, what think you, Morgan?" Kelson asked. He pulled off his helmet and ruffled at damp raven hair with one gloved hand. "You best know the strength of your own seat. Can it be taken?"

Morgan sighed and slouched in the saddle, resting crossed forearms across the high, tooled pommel.

"I should hate to try to take it by force of arms, Sire. Any wall can be breached, given time and the proper equipment. I would prefer to have my city back intact, of course, but I realize that may not be possible. We haven't a great deal of time."

Arilan cocked an eye at the lowering sun, increasingly shrouded in mist, then turned in his saddle to glance at Kelson. Leather creaked as he moved, and his bishop's cope gleamed in the weakening sunlight. Both he and Cardiel were mailed and armed beneath their bishops' robes: two fighting bishops ready to fight for the Church Militant. Arilan's keen eyes sought out Kelson's in question.

"It will soon be dark, Sire. Unless you mean to engage in night battle, we should begin making arrangements for camp."

"No, you're right. It's too late to make our move today." Kelson flicked a fly away from his horse's ears. "I do want to parley with them, though. There is a chance, though only a slim one, that we can reach agreement without raising a sword."

"Very little chance of that, I should think," Duncan retorted. "Not while Warin has anything to say about it, at least. The man is obsessed with his hatred of Deryni. He'll take a lot of convincing."

Kelson frowned. "I know, but we have to try. Cardiel, call the rest of the bishops to assemble with us here in front of the lines. Morgan and Father Duncan, I'd like you to spread the word that we'll be camping here tonight, and have the men start making preparations. You might also set the watches before we try to parley. I don't want the outlying camps harassed during the night by rebel patrols."

"Aye, my prince."

HIGH on the rampart walls, the activities of the royal army were being watched by other eyes. In the shelter of a merlon near the great portcullis gate, Warin de Grey and several of his lieutenants peered down from the castle wall and observed the preparations being made. Warin's gray eyes searched the plain carefully, noting and recording the banners of the great lords assembled there, mentally tallying the hundreds of soldiers who appeared to be encamping on the plain below.

Warin had not the appearance one might expect in a man who had brought half of Corwyn to its knees. He was only middling of height, with close-trimmed hair and beard of a nondescript dun color. Gray was his tunic and cap, gray the cloak he now pulled more closely around his narrow shoulders. Only the stark black of the falcon badge emblazoned on the chest of his leather tunic broke the monotony of it all, black and white against the dull, plain gray. Steel gleamed at throat and wrists and on greaved legs, but even that was muted, satin-bright. Only the eyes were truly outstanding about this man now known as the Lord Warin: the eyes of a mystic, a seer, some said, a saint.

With those eyes, Warin could bore into a man's soul, they said; could heal in the manner of the ancient prophets and holy men. Out of the north had he come, preaching a violent end for those of Deryni blood, calling for holy war to rid the people of the Deryni scourge that had lain too long upon the land.

Warin was appointed by God—or so he believed. At any rate, his successes, the charismatic leadership he seemed to display over his men, all appeared to point to the truth of that statement. Even the Curia of Gwynedd had been swayed to his cause, though Gwynedd's Primate, Archbishop Edmund Loris, had been himself a foe of the Deryni for lo, these many years.

Now militant rebels and curial forces stood shoulder to shoulder behind the walls of Castle Coroth, ready to wage war against the city's lawful lord and her king. They had captured the castle through the trickery of a few key men inside the walls, had taken proud Coroth without a single death or major injury.

Morgan's staunchest adherents now lay in the dungeons deep below Coroth Keep, fed and cared for, but nonetheless prisoners of the fanatical religious forces that had occupied the city. Warin's charisma had swayed even the citizens of Coroth, winning them over from their age-old loyalty to duke and king.

Now, peering down from his sheltered vantage point atop the walls of Coroth, Warin surveyed the enemy anew. A scabbard scraped against the wall behind him, and one of his lieutenants coughed to clear his throat.

"They bring many men, Lord. Will the walls keep them out?"

Warin nodded. "For now, Michael. At least for now. This Morgan was no fool when he fortified his city. He is certain to have defended it against every kind of attack he could foresee. How, then, can he breach his own defenses?"

A second man, Paul de Gendas, shook his head. "I like it not, Lord. You know what kind of villain this Morgan is. Remember what he did at Saint Torin's, while not even in full command of his powers. Now he is joined by more Deryni: the priest McLain, the king himself, perhaps even the king's uncle and his uncle's sons. All of the Haldane line are to be feared, Lord."

"Be not anxious," Warin said softly. "I have reason to believe that even Deryni powers cannot broach these walls without considerable difficulty. Where are my lord archbishops, by the way? Have they been informed of what is happening here?"

"They're coming, Lord," said a third man, bowing slightly in response to the question. "His Grace of Valoret was infuriated when he heard."

"No doubt he was," Warin murmured, allowing the briefest of smiles to cross his lips. "His Grace of Valoret is a man of violent appetites. Happily, he is not afraid of Morgan face-to-face. He will be our most formidable spokesman this afternoon."

Around him, all along the wide battlements, archers and spearmen were taking their positions on the castle ramparts. Great piles of stones had been readied in the days just past, and now strong men in sweat-stained jerkins stood ready to hurl the missiles down on unprotected attackers, should the need arise. As Warin turned to scan the towers to his rear, he saw the archbishops' colors break from the top of the highest tower. His own falcon standard already whipped in the brisk sea breeze on a less lofty tower. And as he watched, the banners of nine more bishops appeared along the ramparts proper, interspersed with the lesser banners of nobles who had been persuaded to join the holy cause.

Warin returned his attention to the plain below and noted that the enemy leaders were assembling before the massed army, a white-cloaked rider approaching the king. At that moment, Warin was joined by Archbishops Loris and Corrigan and several of the lesser bishops. Loris was dressed in a plain working cassock of somber purple, a cloak of the same fabric pulled around his shoulders against the chill sea air. A skullcap made a halo of what wispy white hair could escape from beneath its confines, and Warin found himself idly wondering what kept the cap on in this breeze. A silver pectoral cross and a bishop's ring were Loris's only adornment against the somber violet of his robes, and his face was set and pale.

Corrigan, at his side, had put on flesh since Dhassa, three months prior, and his pale, fearful eyes darted nervously past Loris and Warin to the array on the plain below.

Warin's lieutenants bowed from the waist as the prelates joined them, and Warin inclined his head in greeting. Loris gave a curt nod as he moved closer to the parapet wall.

"I was on my way when your messenger arrived," he said, eyeing the army that surrounded them on three sides. "How do you think they will move?"

"They appear to be preparing to parley, Excellency. I doubt they would attack this close to dark. There at the front, though, you can see the king in the crimson, there beside a white rider. And over there, Bishops Cardiel and Arilan and the rest of the rebels, the prince Nigel. And of course, Morgan and the priest McLain are with them, as we expected they would be. Apparently they have induced the rebel bishops to believe in their innocence, since they wear normal battle attire."

"Their 'innocence,' indeed!" Loris snorted. "God knows, I don't have to tell you of their 'innocence,' Warin. You were at Saint Torin's!"

"So I was, my lord," Warin said mildly. "And the fact remains that the 'innocents' are now camped before us, and apparently wish to parley. Is this agreeable to you?"

Loris flounced to the edge of the parapet and leaned out briefly for a better look, then rejoined Warin. A small party was detaching itself from the rest and beginning to ride slowly toward the city walls. The white-cloaked rider now bore a white parley banner.

"Very well, we will at least listen. Signal your men to hold their fire and honor the flag of truce."

As Loris spoke, the white-cloaked rider broke from the parley party and began riding a slow zig-zag pattern toward the castle walls. Bareheaded and, to all outward appearances, unarmed, he bore a banner of white silk, the staff gleaming silver and gold in the wan sunlight that yet remained. As

Warin lifted a spyglass to his eye, reading the device on the rider's surcoat, he identified the youth to be Prince Nigel's eldest son.

Warin put the glass from his eye and watched as the young man drew rein perhaps fifty yards from the wall. Warin raised a hand to stay his men from hostile action, and bows and spears were lowered all along the wall. The young rider resumed his approach, this time at a walk, to draw rein perhaps twenty yards out from the walls. Warin watched as the youth scanned the parapets, guessing that he was looking for someone of rank to address.

"I bear a message for Archbishop Loris and the man called Warin de Grey," the lad called, his raven head raised defiantly to search the faces appearing along the battlement.

Loris stiffened slightly, then moved forward, Warin at his elbow. The lad saw them and made his horse prance sideways, closer to their position. Even Warin had to admit that he was a fine rider.

"My lord Archbishop?" the lad called. His tone was slightly sharp, his boy's voice high-pitched with nervousness.

"I am Archbishop Loris, and Warin de Grey stands beside me. What message have you?"

The young man bowed slightly in the saddle, then gazed up at the two. "My lord cousin, Kelson King of Gwynedd, bids me say that he wishes parley with you. He asks only that the truce marked by this banner be upheld so that he and several of his retainers may approach to speaking distance. Will you grant this request in honor?"

Loris cast a sidelong glance at Warin, then nodded. "I will grant it in honor," he replied formally. "But tell His Majesty that unless he has a mind to make peace with the Church he has forsworn, and to surrender into our jurisdiction the two Deryni he harbors, this talk will do little good. There are certain things about which we are adamant."

"I will so inform him, my lord," the lad said with a bow. With that, he wheeled his horse and cantered back to his escort, the white silk banner snapping in the breeze. Warin and Loris watched him go, watched as he and his escort approached the crimson-clad figure waiting in the front lines of the enemy army. Then Loris made a fist and hit his hand lightly against the stone merlon beside him.

"I like it not, Warin," he murmured. "I like it not at all. You'd best send your lieutenants among the men, just in case there is treachery afoot. I fear I do not trust our king any longer."

WITH the royal army, Kelson gazed up at the two figures standing on the distant castle parapet, sacerdotal purple and rebel gray, then replaced his crowned helmet and signed for the parley-banner to strike out again. As the lad rode out—he was but a year younger than Kelson—the king touched spurs to his mount and began to follow, flanked on his left by Morgan and on his right by Bishop Cardiel. The royal standard-bearer cut ahead of them and moved into position directly in front of Kelson and a little to the right, and two noble men-at-arms ranged themselves at the king's back. The wan sunlight gleamed on the narrow gold coronet circling Kelson's helmet, on the green-plumed helm of Morgan, and on Cardiel's simple miter.

As he rode, Kelson glanced up at the golden Haldane lion snapping in the breeze, aware of the lion device repeated on the crimson surcoat he wore. Morgan, on his left, wore a cloak of brilliant green over his leather surcoat and mail. Cardiel, to his right, carried a bishop's crozier footed in his stirrup instead of a lance. Ahead, his cousin Conall bore the white parley banner as though it, too, were a royal one, his raven head held high and proud. As they approached the wall to where Conall had halted before, Kelson looked up to see Loris staring down at him, Warin beside him, and swallowed a little nervously as the rebel leader's eyes touched his for just an instant.

Then the standards, white and crimson, were drawing

aside to flank him and his noble escort, and other faces were peering through gaps in the crenellated battlement above. Squaring his courage with a slow, measured breath, the temporal ruler of Gwynedd stared up at the spiritual ruler of Gwynedd and spoke.

"Good greeting to you, my lord Archbishop. My thanks for your permission to approach."

Loris inclined his head slightly. "When a king approaches in true contrition, Sire, what priest could refuse?"

"Contrition, Archbishop?" Kelson glanced to Cardiel for reassurance, then returned his attention to Loris. "My Lord, I will not quibble over words. I have resolved to reconcile our differences and be one again in mind for Gwynedd. This internecine bickering must cease, and now, or we shall all be overcome by the peril in the north."

Loris folded his arms across his chest and raised his chin a trifle higher. "I will be pleased to make a reconciliation with you, Sire, if you will do me the courtesy to explain why you consort with heretics and traitors. Or can you have forgotten what has brought us where we are? Those who ride beside you know whereof I speak."

Cardiel cleared his throat and eased his horse a pace forward. "My lord, I and my brothers in Christ are satisfied that Duke Alaric and his cousin have returned to us in true contrition. They have been received back into the communion of Holy Mother Church, and with that, all strife among us is resolved."

"That is absurd," Loris said flatly. "Morgan and McLain were excommunicated by lawful action of the Gwynedd Curia. Even they are aware of that. You and your rebellious colleagues were party to that action." He glanced toward the assembled bishops back at the front lines, dismissing their presence with a contemptuous wave of his hand. "And now you presume to rescind the action of that Curia by the will of six men? I will not hear of it."

"We are eight now, my lord, not six. Two more have joined us, who were not present that day. And we freely acknowledge that we were in error. Accordingly, the Duke of Corwyn and Father McLain have been reinstated in our grace, as have His Majesty and all his loyal followers who suffered by our judgment."

Loris half-turned away in disgust. "That is preposterous. You cannot overturn the Curia's ruling. Why should I even listen to you? You are clearly mad!"

"Then, listen to your king, Archbishop," Kelson said, his eyes narrowing dangerously as he stared up at Loris. "We have another quarrel with you: namely, the actions of your supposed supporter and ally, Warin. His bands have been marauding through Corwyn for nearly six months now, intimidating my barons, burning fields, preaching insurrection against me—"

"Not against you, Sire," Warin said stiffly. "Against the Deryni."

"And am I not half-Deryni?" Kelson countered. "And if you preach against them, do you not also preach against me?"

Warin stared down at Kelson with cold gray eyes. "It is regrettable that you bear Deryni blood, Sire; but we choose to overlook that, because you are our king. We crusade against the true Deryni, like the one who sits there at your side. You should not be in such company, Sire."

"Do you presume to rebuke your king?" Kelson snapped. "Warin, I have not the time nor the inclination to debate the Deryni question with you. Wencit of Torenth is poised on our borders, ready to invade—and he is an evil man, even were he not Deryni. The civil strife that you and the archbishops have raised must please him beyond all accounting."

Loris shook his head angrily, striking a defiant pose. "Do not blame *us* for Wencit of Torenth, Sire. Wencit is not the issue. I will not compromise the will of the Lord, not even for the will of the king."

"Then, you had best hear me as king," Kelson said evenly. "As you have pointed out, I am lawful king in Gwynedd.

You yourself poured the consecrated oil upon my head and crowned me; and what has been done in that manner cannot be undone by men.

"Therefore, by the authority which you bestowed upon me in the name of our Lord, I command that you lay down your weapons and surrender this city to its lawful lord. Later, when there is more time, we will discuss your differences in this Deryni matter."

There was the rumble of dissent behind Loris, and the prelate shook his head. "I recognize your authority, Sire, but I regret that it is impossible for me to obey you in this matter. I cannot surrender the city. Further, I must urgently suggest that you and your party withdraw before some of my people anger at your words and shame us all by an attempted regicide. Much as I am forced by conscience to disobey you, I would not have your royal blood upon my hands."

Kelson stared up at the archbishop for a full ten seconds, speechless with anger, then wheeled his horse sharply and began galloping back toward his lines. His companions rode hard behind him, keeping careful watch for some overzealous bowman such as Loris had warned of. Only when they had reached the safety of his own army did Kelson rein in and trust himself to speak. He did not seem even to be aware of his other generals and warlords crowding around to hear what had happened.

"Well, Morgan? What should I have said to that insolent priest?" Kelson pulled off his helmet in a furious gesture and threw it to a waiting squire. "Well, speak, King's Champion. What ought I to have said? The sheer gall of that man, threatening *me*!"

"Peace, my prince," Morgan murmured. Kelson's horse was dancing and curvetting, reacting to Kelson's anger, and Morgan laid a hand on the reins to still it. "My lords, pray, excuse us," he said to the watching officers. "There is no immediate cause for alarm. Nigel, if you would continue to oversee the making of camp, my lord bishops, the same.

Duncan, you and Arilan and Cardiel, come with us, please. His Majesty has need of our counsel."

"I am not a child," Kelson murmured. He jerked the reins away from Morgan and glanced at him sharply. "I'll thank you not to treat me like one."

"But my Liege will surely listen to the counsel of his trusted advisors," Morgan continued, crowding his horse against Kelson's and herding it away from the officers, in the direction of the royal pavilion. "Duncan, you are aware of most of the layout of Castle Coroth, are you not?"

"Certainly," Duncan agreed, aware that Morgan was trying to get Kelson out of the center of attention. "My prince, I believe that Alaric has a plan."

Kelson reluctantly let himself be guided off to the side, where soldiers had finished erecting his pavilion and were setting up other tents, then glanced at Morgan once again, his anger apparently abated.

"I'm sorry, I didn't mean to make a scene," he said in a low voice. "It's just that Loris infuriates me so. Do you really have a plan?"

Morgan inclined his head, a faint smile on his lips. "I do." He glanced around covertly, then dismounted and motioned the rest to do the same. When they had all entered the royal pavilion, he gestured for them to take seats, then stood with his hands on his hips.

"Now, we can do nothing yet, since we require the cover of darkness and time to prepare for what I have in mind. But once night falls, here is what I propose."

CHAPTER FOURTEEN

"Behold my servant, whom I uphold; mine elect,
in whom my soul delighteth."

ISAIAH 42:1

THAT night, a thousand watch fires burned on the windswept plain before Coroth, their flickering lights like a thousand eyes watching the besieged city. Outside the king's tent, five specially prepared horses waited, their harness and hooves muffled against telltale sounds, their trappings dull and dark.

Nigel's son Conall stood watch over the horses. It would be his task to bring the animals back, once he had completed his mission. The boy gathered a black cloak around himself and scuffed the toe of a boot against the sandy soil beneath his feet, then looked up abruptly as the tent flap was withdrawn. His father stood in the opening, back still to the outside, and Conall moved a little closer as Morgan, Duncan, the king, and finally the two bishops came into the space before the tent.

"You understand my orders, in case we fail, then, Uncle," the king was saying.

Nigel nodded gravely. "I understand."

"And you, Bishop Arilan," the young king continued. "I know I can count on you."

"I doubt my aid will be necessary, Sire," the bishop said, permitting a smile to cross his lips. "Your plan seems sound. But you know how to reach me, should the need arise."

"We will pray that will not be needed," Kelson replied. He dropped to one knee, as did Morgan and Duncan. After a slight hesitation, Conall, too, knelt, and Cardiel bowed his head.

"God go with all of you, my prince," Arilan murmured, blessing them with the sign of their faith. *"In nomine Patris, et Filii, et Spiritus Sancti, Amen."*

The blessing completed, the men rose and began mounting up, taking reins silently in gloved hands. As Morgan began to lead out, Duncan following, Arilan laid a hand on Cardiel's bridle and motioned him to bend nearer.

"God keep you, my friend," he said in a low voice. "I should hate to see you perish before your time. We have much work to do, you and I."

Cardiel nodded gravely, not trusting himself to speak, and Arilan smiled.

"You do know why it is *you* who are going instead of I, do you not?"

"I understood that you are to aid Prince Nigel, should the need arise. Someone has to be here to assist him, should anything happen to Kelson, God forbid."

Arilan smiled and inclined his head slightly. "That is part of the reason. However, has it occurred to you that, of the four going on this mission, you alone are fully human?"

Cardiel stared at his colleague for a moment, then lowered his eyes. "I had gathered that it was because I am at least the outward leader of the rebel bishops, and that the others might listen to me. There is another reason as well, though, isn't there?"

Arilan clasped his friend on the shoulder in reassurance. "There is, indeed, another reason—but no sinister purpose,

I assure you. I am merely hoping that you will have the opportunity to observe some very fine Deryni practitioners in action. And while I know that you believe what I have told you about the Deryni, at least with your mind, I want you to see it at first hand, and believe with your heart as well."

Cardiel raised his eyes to meet Arilan's and smiled a wan smile. "Thank you, Denis. I—I shall try to keep an open mind—and heart."

"I ask no more," Arilan said with a nod.

Nodding in return, Cardiel turned his horse's head and followed after the others at a trot. Even as he rode, he seemed to melt into the flickering shadows cast by the myriad campfires. Arilan continued to smile as he turned back to Nigel, who still waited in the entryway to the royal tent.

PERHAPS half an hour later, the five riders drew rein in a deep defile southwest of Castle Coroth and dismounted. They had ridden far to the west initially, then had cut in a southerly direction until they could make their way along the shelter of the rocky coastline.

Now, perhaps half a mile from the outermost defenses of the city, Morgan motioned for silence in the slight moonlight, fastening his reins to the saddle of another horse and then repeating the process until all four of the extra horses were in a single line. When that had been accomplished, he returned to the head of the line, where Duncan was giving young Conall a leg up, and handed him the lead rein of the extra horses.

"Godspeed, young prince," he whispered. "Be certain you don't cut inland until you reach the place where we entered on the way here. I don't want you spotted from the castle."

"Aye, Your Grace. Take care."

"And you. Off with you, then," Morgan whispered, slapping the flank of the boy's horse in acknowledgement and stepping back. "Duncan, my lords, let's go."

As Conall turned his horse and began to make his way back up the beach, the string of horses following docilely behind, Morgan strode to a tumble of wave-smooth rocks near the high-water mark and began climbing into them. The others followed him to the edge of the rocks and stood watching, dark cloaks wrapped close, until Morgan finally raised a dark, gloved hand in the moonlight and motioned them to follow.

Scrambling after him, they soon spied a deep, narrow cleft, nearly hidden amidst the rocks and the tangle of shoreline scrub encroaching from the sand dunes inland and above their heads. Into this cleft Morgan lowered himself, feet first, disappearing into some hidden recess even as they watched. The three remaining, Duncan, Kelson, and Cardiel, exchanged uncertain glances; then Duncan climbed up and stuck his head inside to look around. It was pitch-black inside, and he gasped when Morgan's face suddenly appeared in the darkness below.

"*Jesu*, you gave me a fright!" Duncan muttered, as the others crowded nearer. "You just disappeared."

Morgan grinned, his teeth flashing white in the moonlight. "It's a bit of a drop, but come ahead. Send Kelson first."

"*Me?*"

"Hurry up, hurry up. Duncan will give you a hand, and I'll help you down. We don't need any injuries."

As Morgan disappeared from sight, Kelson obeyed, bracing himself on his elbows and then letting Duncan lower him by his hands. His face flashed pale in the moonlight as he glanced anxiously toward the promised floor he could not see. Then, abruptly, he disappeared as Duncan released him.

There was a muffled *oof!* from the darkness below, a muted scuffling, and then Duncan could see Kelson's face beside Morgan's in the darkness below.

With a grin, Duncan motioned Cardiel to follow. Very shortly, all four of them were standing in the nearly total darkness of the subterranean chamber. Morgan let them all stand for several seconds while their eyes adjusted to the lack of light, then felt along the wall until his hand found an opening into even deeper darkness. Grinning, he returned to his three colleagues and gathered them closer around him.

"So far, so good. It's exactly as I remembered it. I don't dare show a light until we get around a bend or two, though—you can never tell who might be patrolling above—so we'll just link on one another's belts and go a while in darkness. I can feel my way for the first few dozen yards."

There were grunts of assent, and then the four were inching forward in single file, Morgan in the lead and followed by Kelson, Cardiel, and Duncan. As they edged into the deeper darkness, Kelson cast one last look back at the wan moon- and starlight framed by the entrance to the chamber, then began resolutely to follow Morgan.

After what seemed like an eternity, but in fact encompassed only minutes, Morgan halted. The blackness was total now, no hint of light reaching them from where they had come.

"Everyone all right?" Morgan whispered sotto voce.

Hearing murmurs of assent, he disengaged Kelson's hand and stepped away from them. Kelson strained to see in the darkness, then raised an eyebrow in understanding as a faint glow began to emanate from behind Morgan's body. He heard Cardiel gasp, but by then Morgan was turning to face them, a sphere of softly glowing verdant light cupped in the hollow of his left hand.

"Relax, Bishop," Morgan murmured, making his way back to Cardiel with the light in his outstretched hand. "It's only light, neither good nor evil. Here, touch it. It's cool, perfectly harmless."

Cardiel stood his ground as Morgan approached, watching Morgan's face, not the light itself. When the young general at last halted before him, only then did the bishop lower his eyes to look at the light again. It was cool and green, a softly shimmering glow like that which had sur-rounded Arilan's head the night he revealed himself as Deryni.

Very tentatively Cardiel put out his hand. There was nothing there to touch per se; only the cool illusion of a breath of breeze as his hand passed through where the light should be and then touched Morgan's hand. At that touch, Cardiel let his eyes lift to meet Morgan's and forced himself to smile.

"You must forgive me if I seem a little squeamish, but—"

Morgan smiled. "Believe me, I quite understand. Come. It isn't far, now that we have light."

Morgan was as good as his word. It was not far—except that the end of the tunnel came all too soon, in a pile of rock and rubble tumbled into a wide tidal pool that Morgan clearly had not expected. With a pass of his hand above the sphere of green light, Morgan made it hover in mid-air, then moved to the wall of rock and motioned Duncan and Kelson to join him.

The three laid their hands on the rocks and closed their eyes, minds probing outward and beyond to the clear corri-dor beyond. As they worked their way down the obstacle, finding no opening, Morgan opened his eyes and edged closer to the tidal pool, staring into the depths for some minutes, then began stripping off his cloak and gloves.

"What are you doing?" Cardiel asked, moving to Mor-gan's side and also peering into the pool.

His question brought the other two as well, and they, too, watched as Morgan stripped off mail and leathers until he was left with only a sleeveless linen singlet and his belt dagger.

"I think there's a passage underneath," Morgan said, low-ering himself into the water and easing himself over to the rock face blocking their way. "I'll be back shortly."

With that, he took a deep breath and ducked his head under water, up-ending and sending himself downward with a stroke of his arms and a powerful frog kick. The three watched as he disappeared into the murky depths, then waited as he did not surface.

With a frown, Duncan herded the light sphere closer and peered into the pool. Finally, they saw bubbles breaking the surface a few yards out from where Morgan had disappeared, and then a sleek golden head broke the surface. Morgan grinned as he shook the hair from his eyes and swam toward them.

"I found a way through," he said, shaking his head again to clear the water from his ears. "It's only a few feet long, but it's at least my height down. Bishop Cardiel, can you swim?"

"Well, I—yes, a little. But I never . . ."

"That's all right, you'll do fine. I'll help you." Morgan grinned and reached up to slap the bishop's ankle reassuringly. "Kelson, I'll let you go first. It's dark on the other side, of course, but the edge of the pool is only a few yards away. As soon as you make shore, conjure up a light and then get back in the water to help the bishop. I'll wait with him until you've had a chance to finish."

Kelson nodded, shrugging out of the last of his outer garments as Morgan finished.

"What about our weapons? We can't take them with us, and we may need them on the other side."

"We can get more in my tower chamber. We'll go there first," Morgan replied, reaching out a hand to assist Kelson into the water.

"All right, show me this underwater passage of yours."

With a nod, Morgan took a deep breath and dived, Kelson following right beside and slightly behind him. Both disappeared from sight almost immediately, and after several seconds Morgan alone surfaced. Duncan was ready by then, so Morgan motioned him into the water and repeated the process.

When he surfaced, a white-faced Cardiel was standing on the edge of the pool, clad only in a long white singlet. He carried no weapon, but he had tucked the long tail of the singlet up between his legs and secured it under a cord belt around his waist. Stripping down had revealed a very plain wooden crucifix hanging on a cord around his neck, which he fingered anxiously as Morgan swam to the edge of the pool and grinned up at him.

"Now?" Cardiel murmured sheepishly.

Morgan nodded and held out a wet hand, still smiling, and Cardiel, with a sigh, lowered himself to sit on the edge of the pool. He shivered as his legs entered the cold water, his eyes wide and faintly luminous in the greenish light shed by Morgan's glow sphere.

Patiently, Morgan held out his hand, nodding encouragement as Cardiel grasped his wrist and slid into the water with a sharp gasp. Then they were treading water above the place where Duncan and Kelson had disappeared. Cardiel swallowed nervously and craned his neck out of the water in an effort to peer downward as Morgan beckoned the light closer.

"Do you think you can make it?" Morgan asked in a low voice.

"Have I any choice?" the bishop retorted. He was pale with fright, but he appeared resigned to his fate. "Just show me what I'm to do."

Morgan nodded. "The entrance is a goodly distance down, directly below and ahead of you there. Do you see it?"

"Not really."

"Never mind. Just do what the others did. I'll dive with you and propel you along. The main thing to remember is not to breathe until we're on the other side. All right?"

"I'll try," the bishop said doubtfully.

With a silent prayer to whatever saint protected inept bishops, Morgan beckoned his light closer and made a pass over it. The light dimmed as Morgan touched Cardiel's shoulder in signal to go. With an audible gulp, Cardiel screwed his eyes tightly closed, held his breath, and tried to dive, Morgan right beside him.

But it became immediately obvious to Morgan that this

was not going to work. Though Cardiel kicked with all his might, and flailed earnestly with his arms, he could not go deeply enough. Morgan grasped the bishop by the waist and tried to propel both of them downward toward the sought-after passage, but it was no use. Cardiel simply did not know enough about what he was doing.

With a slight shake of his head, Morgan began tugging Cardiel back toward the surface. The light had gone out as they dived, and thus they surfaced in total darkness, Cardiel thrashing his arms in a panic until Morgan could put reassuring arms around his shoulders and buoy him up.

"Easy, my lord, you're all right."

Cardiel panted for breath, his breathing ragged and labored as he trod water beside the young Deryni.

"Did we make it through?" he asked.

Morgan was glad that Cardiel could not see his face in the darkness.

"I'm afraid not," he replied, trying to sound more positive than he felt. "But we'll make it this time, don't worry. You need to kick off harder this time."

There was a short, painful silence, and then Cardiel coughed, the only sound in the echoing cavern save for the occasional splash from them treading water.

"I am sorry, Alaric. I—I warned you that I was no swimmer. I don't think I can go that deep."

"You're going to have to," Morgan said in a low voice. "Either that, or I'm going to have to leave you behind. And I can't do that."

"No, I suppose not," Cardiel agreed in a weak voice.

Morgan sighed. "All right, let's try it again. This time, I want you to take a very deep breath and then let out most of it before you dive. That will help you to get the depth we need. I'll help you get up the other side."

"But if I breathe out all my air before I dive, won't I drown?" The bishop's question had a plaintive ring to it. Morgan could tell that the man was more frightened than he would ever admit.

"Don't worry. Just don't breathe in," he murmured, grasping the bishop's shoulder. "Now, a deep breath, exhale—and go!"

He heard the bishop's gasp for air, the slow exhale, and then Cardiel was sinking, making a feeble attempt at a proper dive into the darkness below. Morgan grasped his shoulders and propelled him along, guiding him toward where he knew the opening to be, but as they reached the near side opening of the passage, he felt Cardiel begin to panic.

With a resigned shake of his head, he forced the bishop's body into the opening and propelled it on through. But as he followed him out the other side, he felt Cardiel cease his struggling and go limp. With a silent call to Duncan and Kelson, he began towing Cardiel toward the surface where he could see a faint light, praying that Cardiel had not inhaled too much water.

But however much or little water Cardiel had breathed, he was quite unconscious when Morgan brought him to the surface. As Morgan's head broke the water, he simultaneously shook the hair from his eyes and shouted for Duncan and Kelson to assist him.

The two were already in the water and were grasping at Cardiel even as he called out, but even so, it took them precious seconds to drag the limp bishop to the edge of the pool and haul him out of the water. Morgan turned him on his stomach and began pressing the water from his lungs with strong, rhythmic movements, shook his head as water poured from the bishop's mouth and nose.

"Damn!" he cursed, as the man refused to breathe on his own. "I told him not to breathe down there! What does he think he is, a fish?"

He turned Cardiel face-up, but the bishop's chest was still motionless. Muffling another curse under his breath, he began slapping the man's face, Kelson chafing at his wrists while Duncan blew directly into his lungs.

After what seemed like an eternity, Cardiel's chest heaved once out of sequence with Duncan's breathing, and the three resumed their efforts. Eventually they were rewarded by a faint cough, which erupted quickly into a wracking paroxysm of uncontrollable hacking. Cardiel rolled onto his side and spewed out more water, then finally opened his eyes and turned his head to gaze up at them weakly.

"Are you sure I didn't die?" he croaked, "I was having the most terrible nightmares."

"Well, you almost did die," Morgan said gruffly, shaking his head with relief. "Someone must surely favor you in Heaven, my lord."

"Pray God they always do," Cardiel murmured, crossing himself quickly. "Thank you, all of you."

He struggled to a sitting position with a little help from Duncan and coughed again, then gestured for them to help him to his feet. Without a word, but with a pleased smile at the bishop's pluck, Morgan held out his hand and helped Cardiel to rise. Within a few minutes, the four of them were standing at a fork in the rough stone corridor. Darkness lay beyond in the corridor to the left, but the one to the right was blocked by a dense fall of rock. Probing it gingerly with hands and powers, Morgan straightened resignedly and dusted his hands together.

"Well, that's unfortunate. I had hoped to use that passage to get us to my quarters, after we clothe and arm ourselves in my tower room."

"Can't we get to the tower room from here?" Kelson asked.

"Oh, certainly. But we can't get anywhere else from there. We'll have to go into the regular corridors and risk being spotted. Come on, now. We've got a bit of a maze ahead of us, and then some steps. Be quiet, as our voices may carry."

After a few yards, Morgan led them up a long, extremely narrow stairway, no wider than a man's shoulders. The stairway spiraled gently to the right, a steep, stony passageway that seemed to go on forever. But finally Morgan came to a halt and motioned them to silence.

Hushing the hand-fire to a low, eerie glow, he stepped ahead of them for perhaps six steps, just far enough so they could not see precisely what he did in the stairway ahead of him. The remaining three caught traces of a low-muttered phrase that they could not quite understand. Ghostly lights played on the passage walls, shielded behind Morgan's body.

But then the lights died and Morgan was turning to beckon them after him. A door swung open ahead, giving direct access to the tower room: Morgan's private sanctuary, where no man might enter without his express consent.

The room was ghostly silent as they entered, lit only by the starlight and waning moonlight that filtered faintly through the skylight and the seven green glass windows piercing the tower walls. As Morgan padded across the tapestry carpet, bare feet making no sound, he gestured absently with one hand, blanking the windows and bringing the fire to life on the hearth.

As the others paused, blinking in the sudden firelight, Morgan scooped up a brand from the fire and lit candles on a free-standing candelabrum and on a small circular table near the fireplace. The flickering light winked and gathered in a fist-sized amber sphere in the center of the table, a polished orb supported by a golden gryphon. Cardiel caught his breath in wonder as he spied the sphere, starting toward it in fascination until Duncan's low-voiced call brought his attention away.

Then he and the others were rummaging in coffers and chests, stripping off wet garments and exchanging them for dry. When they had finished, only Morgan and Duncan looked as though they were properly dressed. Kelson had managed to find a short tunic of Morgan's that made a passable one of knee-length on him, and a dark cloak that trailed the ground only a little. Morgan completed the ensemble by handing him a plain circlet of hammered silver.

Bishop Cardiel had contrived to put together an outfit all of black, though there the resemblance to clerical attire ended. The tunic was tight in the waist, and the boots were a bit narrow for his feet, but a long black cloak covered a multitude of sartorial anomalies. He dried his wooden crucifix as best he could, then buffed his bishop's ring against his dry tunic and touched it to his lips for reassurance. Around him, Morgan and Duncan were buckling on swords and daggers from the store of weapons kept in the chamber.

Finally, Morgan cautioned for silence and beckoned them toward the main door: a wide, deep-carved thing of dark-stained oak signed with a great green gryphon. He put his eye to the gryphon's eye and peered through to the other side, then held a finger to his lips for silence and eased the door open. There was another door beyond that, and he listened at that second door for a long while before returning and closing the first one securely behind him.

"There's a guard out there, just as I feared," he whispered. "Duncan, will you come and listen with me? If he's receptive enough, we may be able to control him through the door. Otherwise . . ."

"It's worth a try," Duncan said with a nod, before Cardiel could think too much about what had just been said. So saying, he joined Morgan close before the door.

The two stood with heads and hands against the second door for a long time, eyes closed, their breathing light and controlled. But finally Morgan shook his head and opened his eyes, drawing a thin-bladed stiletto and testing its point against the end of his thumb. His lips mouthed *Ready?* to Duncan, and the priest nodded grim assent as his hand moved to the lock on the door.

As Kelson and Cardiel moved closer, drawn by morbid fascination, Morgan sank to one knee and ran the fingers of his left hand along the door until he found a narrow crack. The blade of the knife was put to the crack, poised for just an instant, then thrust through in a clean, sure stroke.

The blade glinted darker when it was withdrawn, accompanied by a faint moan and a sliding sound from the other side of the door. With a shake of his head, Duncan set his shoulder against the door and pushed it open against some resistance. Slumped outside lay the limp body of a rebel guard, blood welling slowly from a red-stained spot on his lower back. Morgan felt at the man's throat, then grasped him under the arms and began pulling him into the chamber. Cardiel's face clouded as the body was deposited on a portion of floor uncovered by carpet, and he signed the air above the man's head with a cross before stepping across to join the others.

"I'm sorry, but it was necessary, Bishop," Morgan murmured, closing the door behind them and motioning them to follow. Cardiel said nothing, but merely nodded and did as he was told.

Five minutes of stealthy meandering took them to a series of ornately carved panels at the end of a hallway. A torch burned in a brass cresset beside the panels, and Morgan snatched it up in one gloved hand as the fingers of the other moved across the panels in a quick, agile pattern.

The center panel slid aside, receding far enough for them to pass through, one at a time. Morgan motioned them through, then followed and closed the panel behind them. He led them several dozen yards before pausing to turn toward them once again.

"Now, listen, and listen carefully, because I probably won't have time to repeat this. The place where we are now is the beginning of a series of secret passages that honeycomb the walls of this castle. The branch we're going to take leads to my personal living quarters, where I'd be willing to wager that either Warin or the archbishops have taken up residence. Now, stay silent until I say otherwise. Agreed?"

There was no dissent. Silent as the grave, the four began moving once more, coming at length to a portion of the passage that was heavily carpeted and hung with thick draperies along the walls. Morgan handed the torch to Duncan and moved to the left-hand wall, where he drew aside a fold of the drape and peered through a peephole. Carefully he scanned the room beyond, taking in all the familiar accoutrements of the chamber that had been his own until a few short months ago, then drew back with a look of grim determination. As he had suspected, Warin de Grey now occupied the chamber and seemed to be in conference with some of his men.

With a curt gesture, Morgan pointed out several other peepholes, then motioned for Duncan to douse the light. They would try to learn what the rebel leader was saying to his men before barging in unannounced.

"Well, we don't really know *what* he can do, now do we?" one of the men with Warin was saying plaintively. "I know we have a holy mission, and I'm prepared to die for our cause, if need be, but what if the duke conjures magic against us? We dinnae have any defense against that, save our faith."

"Is that not enough?" Warin replied, sitting back in the chair beside the fireplace and lacing his fingers together.

"Well, yes, but—"

"Trust the right of our mission, Marcus," a second man said. "Did God not protect us when Lord Warin had the Deryni cornered at Saint Torin's? His magic was of no avail that day."

Warin shook his head and stared into the flames. "A poor analogy, Paul. Morgan was drugged when we captured him at Saint Torin's. I even believe he told the truth that day— that he could not have used his magic while he was under the influence of the mind-twisting Deryni drug. Otherwise, his cousin would not have revealed himself. Duncan McLain had kept his secret far too long to reveal himself for any other than dire reasons."

"Then, we dinnae know what the duke might do," Marcus interjected. "Mayhap he could bring this whole castle tumbling down around us, if he chose. He could—"

"No, he is a rational man, for all that he is Deryni. He would not destroy his own house unless there were no other way. He—"

There was a staccato knock at the door, followed by a repeat of the knock before anyone could react. Warin broke off what he had been about to say and glanced at his two lieutenants.

"Come," he called.

The knocking was repeated, more insistently this time, even as Paul strode quickly to the door.

"I doubt they can hear you, Lord. This room is well soundproofed. I'll let them in."

As Paul reached the door, the knock was repeated, even more urgently, if that were possible, and as he drew back the latch, a sergeant in the garb of Warin's militia almost fell into the room.

"Lord, Lord, you must help us!" he sobbed, dashing across the room to throw himself at Warin's feet. "Some of my men were stacking stones near the north rampart, when the entire pile collapsed."

Warin sat upright in his chair, staring at the man intently.

"Was anyone hurt?"

"Yes, Lord: Owen Mathisson. Everyone else managed to get out of the way in time, but Owen—his legs were caught under the slide, Lord. His legs are crushed!"

Warin stood as four more men shuffled in through the still-open door carrying the limp form of the unfortunate Owen. As they entered, the sergeant grasped the hem of Warin's robe and touched it to his lips, crumpled it against his chest as he whispered, "Help him, Lord. If you will it, he can be saved."

The four men paused uncertainly in the center of the room, and Warin nodded slowly, motioning them to lay the injured man on the state bed at the other side of the room. The men quickly left their limp burden where they were told, then withdrew at Warin's signal. As Warin moved closer to the bed, he motioned Marcus to close the door behind the departing soldiers, gazing down at the man with compassion.

Owen Mathisson had been a strong man, but that had

not saved him when the rocks began sliding down on him. From the waist up he was still intact, no mark upon him to show that he had suffered any injury. But his legs inside his leather leggings were twisted and contorted into angles never meant for human appendages. He groaned as he became aware of his surroundings again, and Warin motioned for Paul to bring the candles closer, laying his hand on Owen's forehead as the man's gnarled face grimaced in pain.

"Can you hear me, Owen?"

Owen's gaze wandered slightly, then focused on Warin's face. A whisper of recognition flitted past, just before he closed his eyes again.

"Forgive me, Lord. I should have been more careful."

Warin glanced over the man's battered form, then returned his attention to the man's face.

"Are you in great pain, Owen?"

Owen swallowed hard and nodded, jaws set tight against the pain, then opened his eyes to stare at Warin again. There was no need for verbal confirmation of what Warin saw in those pleading eyes.

Warin straightened and glanced down at the man's legs again, then reached his hand toward Paul.

"Your dagger."

As Paul handed over the weapon, Owen's eyes widened and he looked as though he might try to rise, but Warin pushed him gently back on the bed.

"Peace, my friend. This is not the coup. I fear it will cost you your breeches, but I pray not your life. Bear with me."

As the man lay back, stunned, Warin caught the blade of the dagger under the bottom of one scuffed and bloodstained leather legging and began to cut, extending the gap all the way to the man's waist. At his first touch, Owen cried out in pain as the shattered limb was moved; then he mercifully passed out. The second legging was opened in the same manner to reveal the twisted, bloody limbs.

Warin dropped the knife on the bed beside Owen and silently gazed down at the injuries for a moment, then motioned for Marcus and Paul to help him straighten out first one leg, then the other. When it was done, he paused for just an instant, hands clasped together, then addressed the three men watching.

"He is very badly injured," he said in a low voice. "If he is not helped soon, he will die." There was a long silence in which the only sounds were their breathing, before Warin continued.

"I have never attempted to heal so great a hurt before." He paused. "Will you pray with me, my friends? Even if it is God's will that this man be made whole again, I shall need your support."

As one man, Paul, Marcus, and the sergeant dropped to their knees to watch in awe, hands clasped fervently at their breasts. Warin continued to stare at his patient for a moment, almost as though there were no one else in the room, then looked up and spread his arms to either side.

"*In nomine Patris, et Filii, et Spiritus Sancti, Amen. Oremus.*"

As Warin began to pray, shifting to the common tongue, his eyes closed and a faint aura began to take form around his head. His words were murmured, hushed, in the stillness of the chamber, so that the watchers behind the panels could not hear all that he said. But they could not mistake the aura surrounding the rebel leader as he prayed, or ignore his calm assurance as he stretched forth his hands over the injured man's legs and touched them.

In silence they watched as Warin's hands passed along the surface of the man's legs, watched as the jagged breaks, discernible even from across the room, grew smooth under his touch.

Then the rebel leader was murmuring an end to his prayers, lifting the man's legs—first one and then the other. The legs were whole again, straight, as though they had never felt the ruin of the crushing stones.

"*Per Ipsum, et cum Ipso, et in Ipso, est tibi Deo Patri omnipotenti in unitate Spiritus Sancti, omnis honor et gloria. Per omnia saecula saeculorum, Amen.*"

As Warin's words whispered into silence, Owen's eyes flicked open and he carefully sat up. He stared in amazement at his legs, running his hands up and down them in anxious reassurance as the others rose from their knees. Warin watched him for a moment in silence, then crossed himself piously and murmured, *"Deo gratias."* The miracle was complete.

Behind the panels, Morgan prepared to make his move. Motioning Duncan and Kelson to draw near, he whispered a few words, then straightened and glanced through the spy hole again. As he did so, Duncan drew his sword and slipped away in the darkness to the left. Morgan let the wall-hanging fall and motioned Cardiel to come to him.

"We'll go in now, Excellency. Follow my lead as much as possible. They have unwittingly set the stage for a very effective entrance, and I want to preserve the mood for as long as possible. Agreed?"

Cardiel nodded solemnly.

"Kelson?"

"Ready."

As Warin and his lieutenants murmured over the restored Owen, helping him to his feet, some slight sound must have come from the direction of the fireplace. Only Paul was facing in that direction, and as his glance shifted toward the sound, he froze and gasped unbelievingly, his eyes wide with horror.

"My lord!"

At his exclamation, Warin and the others turned to see a shadowed doorway opening in the wall to the left of the fireplace, only faintly visible by the light of the low fire burning on the hearth. Blank disbelief froze them all in their places as Kelson emerged from the opening, his young face unmistakable in the red firelight. A collective gasp of anguish accompanied the appearance of Morgan, right behind the king; they did not recognize the third figure, whose steel-gray hair caught the firelight as the opening closed behind him.

All at once, Warin was glancing around wildly, his men

scrambling toward the door only to pull up short at the sight of Duncan standing against the green-glowing doorway, a naked sword held across his body in a non-threatening but vigilant pose.

Warin froze and stared at Duncan wild-eyed for an instant, remembering his last encounter with this proud young Deryni who now stood so confidently before him, then closed his eyes and tried with a visible effort to compose himself. Only then did he turn to face his nemesis and his king.

CHAPTER FIFTEEN

"Curse not the king, no not even in thy thought."

ECCLESIASTES 10:20

"TELL your men to surrender, Warin," Kelson said. "I am assuming command here."

"I cannot permit that, Sire." Warin's brown eyes met the king's without a flicker of fear. "Paul, summon the guards."

"Paul, stay away from the door," the king said before the man could move to obey.

The rebel lieutenant froze at the sound of his name on the royal lips, then glanced beseechingly at Warin. Behind Duncan, the door still glowed with a faint, greenish light, and the priest minutely shifted his grip on his bared sword in a gesture calculated to instill hesitation.

Warin glanced at the door, the look of indecision and fear on Paul's face, the unreadable eyes of Morgan standing close by the king. Then, with a sigh, he dropped his gaze to the floor at his feet, his shoulders drooping dejectedly.

"We are undone, my friends," he said in a weary voice. "Put aside your weapons and stand away. We cannot resist Deryni sorcery with mere steel."

"But, my lord," one of the men started to protest.

"Enough, James." Warin lifted his gaze to Kelson's once more. "All know the fate of men who defy their king and fail. At least you and I and the others will die in the certain knowledge that we fought on the side of God. And you, O King, will pay a high price for our lives in the Hereafter."

There was a scarcely concealed murmur of consternation from the four men grouped behind him, but then they began slowly unbuckling sword belts and baldrics. The dull thud of sheathed steel on carpet was the only sound in the firelight as the men put down their weapons and bunched closer behind their leader. Even so, their manner was defiant.

Kelson noted this and many other things as he signed for Duncan to collect the weapons. And while the new captives were at least partially diverted by Duncan's movement, he caught Morgan's subtle nod toward the low armchair by the fireplace.

With a slight inclination of his head, Kelson moved toward the chair, waiting while Morgan turned it to face Warin and his men, then sitting and adjusting the folds of his borrowed cloak. When Kelson had seated himself, Morgan retired to a position just behind and to the right of the king's chair. Cardiel remained in the shadows to the left of the fireplace. The tableau immediately took on the aspect of a king holding court, even in the very informal setting of a castle bedchamber, and in borrowed clothes. Nor was the effect lost on Warin's men, who watched apprehensively to learn what this bold young king would do.

"We do not require your life or the lives of your men," Kelson said to Warin, deliberately adopting the royal "we." "We require only your loyalty from this time on—or, if not your loyalty, at least your willingness to consider what we are about to tell you."

"I owe no allegiance to any Deryni king," Warin said baldly. "Nor am I any longer intimidated by your royal birth. You Deryni are very bold when you have your magic to defend you."

"Indeed?" said Kelson, raising an arched brow. "We seem to recall that you once placed our General Morgan at your mercy in a similar manner, stripped him even of most human faculties, that he might not defend himself in any fashion. The tendency to press one's advantage is a human trait as well as a Deryni one, it seems."

"I do not associate with those who traffic in magic," Warin retorted, beard jutting stubbornly as he half-turned away.

"Do you not?" Morgan's retort was more a statement than a question, and he controlled an impulse to smile, for Warin had just given him the very opening they needed. "How, then, do you manage to keep faith with yourself? The gift of healing is, after all, a kind of magic, is it not?"

"Magic?" Warin bristled as he whirled back to face Morgan. "That is blasphemy! How dare you profane so holy a sign of God's favor by comparison with your foul and heretical powers?! Our Lord was a healer. Why, you are not worthy even to breathe the same air as He!"

"That may well be," Morgan replied neutrally. "Such is not for me to judge—or you, I think. But, tell me. What is your understanding of the gift of healing?"

"My—?" Warin blinked and hurriedly glanced at the others, but could discern no hint as to the purpose of the question. "Why, Holy Scripture tells us that Our Lord healed the sick, as did His disciples after He was gone. Surely, even you are aware of that."

Morgan nodded. "And my Lord Bishop Cardiel, do you concur with Warin's answer?"

Cardiel, who by choice had remained in the background until now, started as his name was spoken, then moved hesitantly into the firelight beside Morgan. The flickering light caught a heart of amethyst in his ring as he fingered the wooden crucifix around his neck and gazed across at the rebel leader.

"It has always been my belief that Our Lord and His disciples healed the sick and the lame," he agreed cautiously.

"That is my belief as well," Morgan said, turning back to Warin. "May I take it, then, that both of you would agree that healing is a God-given gift, one not to be trifled with?"

"It is," Cardiel said.

"Certainly," Warin replied, not batting an eye.

"And your *personal* power of healing," Morgan said softly. "Would that also be considered a gift of God?"

"My pers—"

Kelson allowed himself a perturbed sigh and crossed his legs in exasperation. "Come now, Warin, don't be coy. We know that you can heal. We saw you, minutes ago. We also have certain knowledge that you healed a man in Kingslake last spring. Do you deny it?"

"I—certainly not." Warin reddened a little as he held himself more erect, chin lifting. "And if the Lord has appointed me to be His instrument, who am I to question His word?"

"Yes, I know," Morgan said, nodding impatiently and holding up a hand for silence. "What you are saying, then, is that healing is a sign of God's favor."

"Yes."

"And that only those favored by God can heal?"

"Yes."

"Then, suppose that a Deryni were able to heal?" Morgan asked quietly.

"A Deryni?!"

"*I* have healed, Warin. And there can be no doubt that I am Deryni. Do you suppose it is possible, then, that God does favor at least some Deryni by giving them the healing gift? For that matter, perhaps the healing gift is actually a Deryni power. . . ."

"That cannot be," Warin whispered.

His men stood stunned, and Warin himself had turned as pale as whey, his face so blanched of color that the blank, uncomprehending eyes were the only things even remotely alive in the frozen face. There was a flurry of furtive whispering among Warin's men at their leader's reaction, quickly cut off when Warin suddenly reeled against one of them and had to clutch at his arm for momentary support. Then the rebel leader, no longer quite so rebellious, was blinking life back into his face, staring disbelievingly at Morgan with a look almost of terror on his face.

"You are mad!" he whispered when he was finally able to speak. "The Deryni corruption has addled your mind. Deryni cannot heal!"

"I healed Sean Lord Derry as he lay dying of an assassin's blade in Rhemuth last fall," Morgan said quietly. "Later, in the cathedral, I healed my own wounds. I speak the truth, Warin, though I cannot explain how I have done this. Both human and Deryni have felt my healing."

"That is impossible," Warin murmured, almost to himself. "It cannot be. The Deryni are spawn of Satan. So we have *always* been taught."

Morgan laced his fingers together and studied his two thumbnails. "I was taught that as well, by some. At times, I have almost been willing to believe it, when I consider the terrible punishments meted out to Deryni in past years.

"But, I, too, was taught that healing comes of God. And if my hands can heal . . . well, then, perhaps God favors me as well, at least in this small way."

"No, you lie!" Warin shook his head emphatically. "You lie—and you attempt to draw me into your lies!"

Morgan sighed and glanced at Kelson, at Cardiel and Duncan, then noticed that Duncan was sheathing his sword, a tiny, odd smile quirking at his lips. The priest raised an eyebrow at his cousin as he strode casually to join his colleagues before the fire. Warin and his men drew back suspiciously, a few of them eyeing the now unguarded door.

"Alaric Morgan does not lie," Duncan said easily. "And if you are willing to *listen* instead of plotting an impossible escape, perhaps I can prove that to your satisfaction."

Warin's men quickly returned their attention to Duncan, and the rebel leader looked suspiciously at the priest.

"What, would you have him heal for us?" Warin asked contemptuously.

"That is precisely what I propose," Duncan replied, his slight smile returning.

Morgan's brow furrowed, and Cardiel shifted uneasily, his hand tightening on his crucifix. Kelson sat spellbound, for even he had never actually seen Morgan heal before. Duncan now had all of their undivided attention.

"Well, Warin?"

"But—whom should he heal?"

Duncan smiled his secret smile again. "I do have a proposal that may resolve our apparent dilemma. Warin, you refuse to listen to us unless Alaric can prove to your satisfaction that he speaks the truth. Alaric, you in turn cannot give Warin the proof he requires without someone to heal. I submit that one of us should allow himself to be slightly wounded, so that you may demonstrate your healing power and Warin may be satisfied. Since it was my idea, I offer myself to be the subject."

"What?" said Kelson.

"It's out of the question," Morgan said flatly.

"Duncan, you *must* not!" came Cardiel's simultaneous reply.

Warin and his men could only stare in utter disbelief.

"Well, why not?" Duncan asked. "Unless one of you has a better alternative, I think we have no choice. We are deadlocked unless one of us can break the impasse. And it needn't be a serious wound. A scratch would suffice to prove our point. What say you, Warin? Would this satisfy you?"

"I—" Warin was speechless.

"And just who do you propose shall make this 'scratch'?" Morgan finally asked, his gray eyes clearly showing his disapproval.

"You, or Kelson—it makes little difference," Duncan replied, keeping his tone light.

Cardiel shook his head adamantly. "I cannot permit it. You are a priest. To shed a priest's blood—"

"I am a *suspended* priest, Excellency. And you know that I must do what I must do."

He hesitated for just an instant, then pulled his dagger from his belt and extended it across his forearm toward the three of them, hilt first.

"Come. One of you do the deed, and let's be done with it. Otherwise, I may lose my nerve."

"No!" Warin said suddenly. He took several steps toward the four but then stopped, strained but erect as he stared fearfully across at them.

"You have some objection?" Kelson asked, standing slowly in his place.

Warin wrung his hands together and then began pacing the room explosively, shaking his head and gesturing to punctuate his speech.

" 'Tis treachery, treachery! I dare not trust you! If I did, I should never know if you had staged the entire thing for my benefit, if you had only *appeared* to wound this man and then *appeared* to heal him. That is no proof. Satan is a master of lies and illusions."

Duncan glanced at his companions, then abruptly turned and extended the dagger's hilt toward Warin.

"Then, *you* draw my blood," he said evenly. "*You* make the wound whose healing will convince you that we speak the truth."

"I?" Warin paled. "But, I have never—"

"Surely you do not claim that you have never shed blood," Morgan retorted. "I very much doubt that. But if 'tis true, then it is even more important that you do the deed. If you want proof, you shall have it. But you yourself must be a part of the proving."

Warin stared at them searchingly, clearly grappling with some inner demon, then took a step backward and eyed the dagger distastefully.

"Very well, I will do it. But not with that dagger. I must have one of our own, that I know to be untainted by Deryni sorcery."

"As you wish," Duncan said.

As he sheathed his dagger and began unbuckling his sword belt, Warin edged cautiously toward the pile of weapons confiscated earlier and sank to one knee beside it. He glanced over the assortment of weapons for several seconds, then selected a slender, cross-hilted dagger with ivory fittings. Firelight flashed on the polished blade as he unsheathed it and kissed the relic enclosed in the hilt. Then he rose wordlessly.

"I must ask," said Duncan, "that you limit yourself to a wound which you yourself could heal." His linen shirt was half-unlaced, and he pulled it from the waistband of his breeches preparatory to removing it. "Also, if you choose to deliver a potentially lethal wound, I must insist that it be a slow one. I shouldn't like to bleed out before Alaric can bring his powers into play."

Warin glanced away uncomfortably, tightening his sweaty grip on the dagger's hilt. "I shall not wound you beyond my own power to heal."

Nodding his acceptance, Duncan pulled his shirt off over his head and handed it to Morgan, who draped it over the back of the chair Kelson had vacated. The priest was pale but unafraid as he turned to face Warin.

Warin was trembling as he brought the dagger to waist level and approached—cautious, reluctant, yet drawn in horrified fascination that this enemy would permit what he was about to do. The thought crossed his mind that he could, if he chose, kill at least this one Deryni, but another part of him strangely shrank from that thought, as though already entertaining the possibility that these particular Deryni were telling the truth, terrifying though that was to contemplate.

When he had come within an arm's length of Duncan, he stopped and forced himself to meet the calm blue eyes that gazed back at him, then shifted his focus downward. The priest's torso, rarely exposed to the sun, was a pale ivory, almost like a woman's, though there the similarity ended.

The shoulders were broad and powerful, sleek with well-tempered muscles, with little body hair. A faint scar crossed the ribs below the left breast, another on the right bicep—training scars, probably.

Slowly Warin lifted the dagger point to eye level and brought it lightly to rest against Duncan's left shoulder. The priest did not flinch as the steel touched his skin, but Warin could no longer meet the eyes.

"Do what you must do," Duncan whispered, bracing himself for the thrust.

CHAPTER SIXTEEN

"You have probed me, and you know me."

PSALMS 139:1

SUDDEN pain lanced deep into Duncan's left shoulder, and his body recoiled in a vast shudder. In that first instant of shocked agony, he was aware of Warin's eyes blazing insanely, of Kelson's gasp of alarm, Alaric's arm under his good shoulder as his knees gave way and he began to sag, borne down by the pain.

Then he was collapsing to the floor, and Alaric was snapping at Warin, the gray eyes ablaze with anger, sanity returning to Warin's face as he recoiled in horror from what he had done.

Through the haze of his own disbelief and shock, Duncan felt Alaric's fingers probing at the blade that still pierced into his shoulder, the reassuring strength of his cousin's strong arm supporting his head.

Then Cardiel was moving all the others back—all except Alaric. Besides them, Warin was the closest other one in the room. Alaric bent closer, his eyes like pools of storm, lips moving in words Duncan could not quite understand.

"Duncan? Duncan, focus! Can you hear me? Damn you,

Warin! This is more than we agreed! Duncan, listen to me! It's Alaric."

Duncan found that, by concentrating, he could make the lips' movement match the words that sounded muffled to his ears. He blinked and stared up at his cousin dazedly for what seemed like an eternity, then managed a weak nod. Extending out of range beyond his chin, he could just see the hilt of Warin's little ivory-fitted dagger, the ivory darkly stained with his blood.

He looked again at Alaric, feeling a wave of calm brush his mind as his kinsman's right hand touched lightly on his forehead and then returned to the hilt of the dagger.

"It's a serious wound," the golden Deryni murmured, searching his eyes. "If you can stand the pain, I need you to stay conscious while I work. I'm not altogether certain I can do this alone."

Duncan turned his head slightly to glance at the dagger again, his cheek resting momentarily against his kinsman's hand.

"Go ahead," he whispered. "I'll do my best."

He saw the gray eyes close once in agreement, then felt the arm beneath him raising him slightly so that he was resting against Alaric's chest. The left hand was curved to stanch the wound now, once the dagger was withdrawn by the right. Duncan raised his right hand to Alaric's left, ready to add whatever assistance he could, then braced himself for the withdrawal of the steel.

"Do it now," he murmured.

He gasped at the scrape of metal against bone, the sear of steel in muscle, sinew, nerve, like fire. Then his life's blood was pumping into the still night air, Alaric's agile fingers pressing to the wound, his own right hand suddenly going wet to the feel of his own hot blood. But then Alaric's mind was wrapping around his own, soothing, calming, damping and even quenching the agony.

Something deep inside him detached itself from the pain then. All at once he was able to open his eyes and gaze up into Alaric's deep gray ones, losing himself in their depths. Rapport was found and established in a heartbeat, minds linked stronger than the link of hands could ever be.

Alaric closed his eyes then, and Duncan did the same, sinking to yet another level. Through some faculty far beyond mere hearing, he began to sense a deep, musical thrum. The bond deepened, and an all-pervading peace began to wrap itself around him, almost as though a shadowy hand, without form or substance, were laying itself across his feverish brow. Fleetingly he seemed to sense another Presence linked with him and Alaric, one he had never seen or heard before.

Then, very suddenly, he knew that it was done, that the bleeding stopped. He opened his eyes to find Alaric's golden head still bowed over him, felt the bond begin to dissolve away. He stirred slightly against Alaric's arm as his kinsman opened his eyes, lifting his head far enough to peer down at the three bloodstained hands that rested on his left shoulder. The top hand—Alaric's—lifted; and simultaneously his own and Alaric's other hand fell away.

The wound was gone! All he could see was a very faint line on the skin where the blade had entered—a line that was fast fading—but even of the monstrous quantity of blood that had escaped his body, there was little trace except on their hands. He held up his own bloodied hand, glanced at Alaric's, then let his head loll back against Alaric's shoulder to look up for the first time at the circle of watchers. Warin was closest—drawn, white, awestruck—and beside him Kelson and Cardiel, Warin's men clumped in a scared, incredulous knot a little to the right. Duncan managed a weak smile and lowered his hand slowly, then glanced up at Alaric.

"Thank you," he murmured.

Alaric allowed himself a wry smile and shifted Duncan's weight to help him sit up.

"So," the Deryni duke said, looking directly at Warin. "Can you accept what you have seen? Will you concede that, if your premise of healing being a God-given gift is correct, God also gives to the Deryni?"

A pale Warin shook his head, but in wonder rather than denial. "It cannot be true. Deryni cannot heal. Yet you healed. Therefore healing must be a Deryni power as well. And I, who also heal . . ."

His voice trailed off as the full implications of this line of reasoning began to sink in, and his face went even paler, if that were possible. Noting the reaction, Morgan guessed that he had finally achieved at least part of his original purpose. With an understanding smile, he helped Duncan to his feet and betook both of them to the basin and ewer set on a nightstand, pouring water into the basin so he and Duncan could wash the blood from their hands.

"Yes, you must face that possibility now," he said softly to Warin over his shoulder. "It's a great deal to assimilate, I know—and if you had been told before, you would not have listened. You had to see it demonstrated." He dried off his hands and turned to face Warin. "And here's another possibility that you would have been unable to consider. We believe that you, too, may be Deryni."

"No! That isn't possible," Warin managed to murmur, looking dismayed. "I *couldn't* be!" His voice became more plaintive. "Why, I have hated Deryni all my life. And I *know* that there are no Deryni in my ancestry. It cannot be!"

"Perhaps not," Kelson said, joining Morgan to gaze carefully at Warin. "But many go through all their lives without ever knowing, unless something happens to change all of that. You have, perhaps, heard how my mother discovered her Deryni heritage—and no one *ever* would have suspected Jehana of Gwynedd of being Deryni. She was as adamant on that point as you are, Warin—perhaps more so, in many respects."

Warin's hands were trembling as he wrung them in his agitation, and he looked up beseechingly.

"But, how—how does one find out for certain?" he ventured meekly. "How does one know?"

Morgan spared him a sympathetic smile. "The queen found out by using powers she did not know she possessed, when there was no other choice. On the other hand, there are people who have powers we cannot explain through Deryni blood. You might be one of those. The only way to know for certain is to Mind-See. I can do that for you, if you like."

"Mind-See?"

"You place yourself in a relaxed and receptive state and allow me to enter your mind with mine. I cannot explain how I know, once I am linked with you—but I do know. You will have to accept that I have this ability. Will you permit me to do that?"

"To—to enter my mind? I—" He glanced plaintively at Cardiel, unconsciously falling back upon Cardiel's authority as a bishop. "Is—is this permitted, Excellency? I—I know not how to judge this situation. Guide me, I beseech you!"

"I trust Morgan," Cardiel said carefully. "I have no idea how he does what he does, but I accept the fact that it happens. And although I have not felt the touch of his mind, I am confident of his good intentions."

"Then—you counsel me to accept his offer?" Warin whispered.

"I do," Cardiel said gently. "Warin, you must see the error of what has gone before and join us. We must have unity in Gwynedd to stand against Wencit of Torenth. Surely, you see that."

"Yes. Yes, I do. But, to permit *Morgan* . . ." His voice trailed off, resistance still evident as he hazarded another glance at the Deryni general, and Morgan nodded coolly.

"Believe me, I share your reluctance in this matter. My regard for you is likewise tainted by what has gone before. But there is none other who can do what must be done in this instance. The king, talented though he is, has not the necessary experience. And I fear that you have weakened my cousin to the point that I could not permit him to undertake it. What must be done requires an investment of energy, which, frankly, he cannot spare at this time. So it appears that you are left with only one choice—if you wish to learn the truth, that is."

Warin lowered his eyes, studying his feet for a long moment, then turned slowly to confront his men.

"Tell me truthfully," he said, his voice scarcely more than a whisper. "Do you believe me to be a Deryni, Paul? Owen?"

Paul glanced uneasily at the others, then shuffled a few steps forward. "I believe I speak for all of us, Lord, and what it comes to is that we don't know what to think."

"But what should I do?" Warin whispered, almost to himself.

Paul glanced at the others and then spoke again. "Find out for certain, Lord. Perhaps we have been mistaken about the Deryni. Certainly, if you yourself are one of them, then not all can be evil. We would ride with you to Hell and back—you know that, Lord. But find out!"

Warin's shoulders slumped in an attitude of defeat, but then he slowly turned back toward Morgan, not meeting his eyes.

"It appears that I must submit to you," he said. "My followers must know where I stand, and I confess that I, too, must know. I—what must I do?"

Morgan handed Duncan's shirt back to him, then began turning the chair to face the fire. "It is hardly a matter of submission," he said, motioning the others to stand back out of the line of vision of the chair. "What you will experience is a—a sharing of awareness, both of us working together. If at any time you become afraid, and do not wish to go on, you may break the bond. I promise you, I shall not force you against your will. Sit here, please."

Swallowing with difficulty, Warin looked at the chair now facing the fire, then forced himself to sit gingerly on the edge of the seat. Morgan moved behind the chair and reached his hands to Warin's shoulders, urging him back to sit in the chair properly. The hands remained resting lightly on the rebel leader's shoulders as Morgan began to speak. The others stayed behind the chair as well, so that they could see only Morgan and the back of Warin's head and shoulders. Morgan's voice was low and soothing in the fire-lit darkness.

"Take a deep breath and let it all the way out. Sit back and focus on the fire on the hearth. There is little true magic involved in what we do here . . . perhaps just a trace of that power I used earlier to heal. Relax and watch the flames. Concentrate on the sound of my voice and the touch of my hands. You'll not be harmed, I promise you. Relax and drift with me. Let the soft flicker of the flames be the only movement in your universe. Relax and drift with me . . ."

As Morgan's voice droned on, rising and falling with the flames, he became aware that Warin was, indeed, beginning to drift beneath his hands. He relaxed his hands slightly and Warin did not flinch at the movement—a good sign. Slowly, as Warin came more and more under the spell of the murmuring voice, Morgan began to extend his senses, glancing down at his gryphon signet and triggering the first stage of Deryni mind-linking. Warin had slipped into a light trance by this time, his breathing slow and deepening by the minute, eyelids quivering on the verge of closing altogether.

After a few more seconds the eyelids did close, and Morgan gently eased his hands to either side of Warin's head, masking the movement with a touch of firmer control. Warin did not stir at this new, more intimate probe of mind, and with a slight sigh of relief, Morgan permitted himself to go deeper. Tipping Warin's head back against his chest, he gazed down at the closed eyes through hooded lids, then bowed his head and also closed his eyes—and entered Warin's mind.

It was perhaps a hundred heartbeats before he stirred, and then it was only to lift his head slightly and look toward Kelson and Duncan, his eyes deeply hooded.

"He has a very well-ordered mind, underneath all the

anti-Deryni conditioning," Morgan whispered, "but I am almost certain he is not Deryni. Will you confirm?"

Wordlessly, Kelson and Duncan moved to either side of Morgan and reached out to place their hands on Warin's brow. After a few seconds, they withdrew.

"He was right. I don't think he *is* Deryni," Duncan whispered.

"And yet, we have all seen him heal," Kelson murmured in wonder. "He also seems to have a slight persuasion in the area of Truth-Say. Of all the Deryni talents, those two are probably the most useful to a man like him, who believed he had a divine mission to fulfill. You don't suppose he really *is* a holy man, albeit a misguided one?"

The answering lift of Morgan's eyebrow dismissed the last notion, but he could not disagree with the rest of Kelson's assessment.

"We'll work with what we know. I'm going to show him a little of the true background of the Deryni to help counteract what he's been taught before, then bring him out of it."

He closed his eyes briefly and did what needed to be done, then looked up again, slipping his hands back to Warin's shoulders to give a reassuring squeeze. Warin, as his head was released, opened his eyes, too, turning his head to look up at Morgan in wonder.

"I'm—I'm not Deryni," he breathed, a look of awe on his face. "And yet, I feel almost disappointed. I had no idea . . ."

"But you understand now, don't you?" Morgan said with a weary sigh.

"I just don't see how I could have been so wrong about the Deryni. And my calling—was it ever really there?"

"Your powers are certainly there, and they come from somewhere not Deryni," Duncan said in a low voice. "Perhaps you *were* called, but misread the tasks set out for you to do."

Warin looked up at Duncan as the words sank in, then realized that Kelson was standing beside him, the gray eyes studying him gravely. Abruptly he remembered that he should not be sitting in the presence of the king, and he scrambled to his feet in dismay.

"Sire, forgive me. The things I said to you earlier, the things I've done against you in the months gone by—how can I ever make amends?"

"Be my liege man," Kelson said simply. "Help us to convince the archbishops of what you have just learned, that we all may stand together against Wencit. If you will do this, and your followers also, I will forgive what has gone before. I need your help, Warin."

"And I will freely give it, Sire," Warin said, dropping to one knee and bowing his head in homage. Warin's men, awed by what they had seen, likewise went to their knees.

Kelson touched Warin's shoulder in acknowledgement and offered him his hand to kiss, in token of his homage, then motioned them all to rise.

"I thank you, gentlemen, but we have no time for further ceremony here. Warin, we must next think of a way to spread the news of your apparent change of heart. Have you any suggestions?"

Warin thought for a moment, then nodded. "I think so, Sire. Often, in the past, I have had dreams at critical times. My people know of these dreams, and will believe what I tell them. I have but to say that I have had a vision in the night, that an angel came and told me I must give my allegiance back to you, that Gwynedd not fall. There will be time enough later to reveal the true story. In the meantime, if we release the news immediately, the story should be sufficiently embellished by morning to account for your presence here and give us solid support when we confront the archbishops. Does this meet with your approval?"

"Morgan?" Kelson asked.

"Warin, you have an eye for intrigue—and I am glad that it now serves the king." Morgan smiled. "Can your lieutenants see to it right away?"

The rebel leader nodded.

"Excellent. And when you have finished, I should like for all of you to meet us in the tower stairwell. In the meantime, there are several of my officers whose expertise I require. Are they in the dungeons?"

"Alas, I fear they are," Warin admitted.

"No matter. I know of ways to get them out. Shall we meet, then, in two hours?"

"It will be light in three," Paul de Gendas volunteered.

Morgan shrugged. "That cannot be helped. We must have time to make preparations. In two hours, in the tower stairwell, then. Agreed?"

CHAPTER SEVENTEEN

"And he will lift up an ensign to the nations from far . . ."

ISAIAH 5:26

BY dawn there were few in Castle Coroth who did not know at least something of the strange and wondrous vision dreamed by Lord Warin during the night. Warin's troops, who composed the bulk of Coroth's defenders, still stood in staunch support of their charismatic leader, though they did not pretend to understand this seeming reversal of his former policy regarding Deryni. The handful of ecclesiastical troops who had come with the archbishops to Coroth were wary of outright resistance to the change, in light of the rebels' greater numbers. In the early hours of the morning, several of them had made the mistake of questioning the new orders being handed down. Many had found themselves promptly locked up in the castle dungeons by Warin's loyal followers.

Accordingly, first light found Archbishops Loris and Corrigan and a half-dozen of their colleagues gathered fearfully in the ducal chapel, ostensibly to celebrate morning devotions but in fact to speculate among themselves as to what the night's developments might mean. Most were dubious about the reports that Warin had had a vision; none had any inkling of what had actually occurred.

"The entire thing has gotten out of hand!" Loris was saying. "This Warin de Grey goes too far. The idea of *visions*, in these times! Why, it's unheard of."

His subordinates sat huddled at the far end of the chapel's nave, close to the sanctuary, where Loris was pacing the carpeting in obvious spleen. Archbishop Corrigan, looking haggard and aged beyond his sixty years, occupied a stool a little apart from the others, as befitted his station as Loris's second-in-command. The others—de Lacey, Creoda of Carbury, Carsten of Meara, Ifor, and two of the itinerant bishops, Morris and Conlan—sat facing them anxiously. There was no one else in the chapel, and it was barred from within. Conlan, one of the younger bishops present, cleared his throat in a growl.

"Well, you may say that it is unheard of, my lord, but frankly, it worries me. It appears that Warin is moving toward a more lenient policy toward the Deryni. And what will happen if he decides to support the king?"

"Aye, what *does* happen?" Ifor agreed. "I have even heard that he is considering it. With a royal army camped right at our gates, we are in serious trouble if he does."

Loris looked sharply at both bishops and then harumphed. "He wouldn't dare. Besides, not even Warin commands that much influence among his troops. He cannot change their entire outlook overnight."

"Perhaps not," Creoda wheezed. The old bishop's voice was thin and reedy, and he had to pause often to cough. "Perhaps he cannot, but there is certainly something strange going on this morning. You can feel it in the air. And two of my personal escort, some of the men we brought with us, cannot be found. Many of the guard posts were occupied by unfamiliar faces."

"Humph!" Loris said again. "I don't suppose anyone knows for sure just what Warin's so-called *vision* was all about."

"Not precisely," said de Lacey, toying with the amethyst on his finger. "But my chaplain told me this morning that one of the guards said Warin saw an angel in his dream."

"An angel?"

"That *is* preposterous!" Loris huffed.

De Lacey shrugged. "Preposterous or not, that is what I was told. An angel with horns of light appeared to Warin in his sleep and warned him that he must reconsider what he has been doing."

"Damn him, he goes too far!" Loris exploded. "He cannot just dream a dream and then reverse everything he has stood for. Who does he think—"

At a pounding at the chapel door, all of them fell silent. As the knock was repeated, all eyes turned to Loris. Conlan, at Loris's signal, got to his feet and padded back to the double doorway. Hand on the bolt, he called, "Who is it?"

"Warin de Grey," a familiar voice said. "What is the meaning of this? Why are the chapel doors closed?"

At a sign from Loris, Conlan slid aside the heavy metal bolt, then stood aside in consternation as Warin, his lieutenants, and a full dozen armed men pushed their way into the chapel, the men taking up posts along either side of the room. One of Warin's lieutenants hustled Conlan back to the rest of the bishops as all came to their feet, and Warin followed with another man at his elbow.

"What is the meaning of this?" Loris demanded, drawing himself to his full height in an attempt to overawe.

Warin paused to bow slightly from the waist, his face set and solemn "Good morning, my lord Archbishop," he said, arms stiffly at his sides. "I trust that you and your colleagues slept well."

"Well enough," Loris said coldly. "Why have you interrupted our morning devotions with armed men? Such have no place in a house of the Lord."

"Sometimes such actions are necessary, Archbishop," Warin replied evenly. "I have come to ask that you lift an excommunication."

"With armed men?" Loris began indignantly.

"Hear me, my lord. I wish you to lift the excommunication you placed upon Alaric Morgan, Duncan McLain, and the king, and also the Interdict that you imposed on Corwyn."

"Why on earth would I do that? Are you mad?"

"Not mad, my lord. But I shall be very angry if you do not accede to this request."

Loris sputtered and grew red in the face. "You *are* mad! Conlan, call the guards. We need not subject ourselves to this—"

"Paul, bar the door," Warin countered, cutting across Loris's fulminations. "And you, my lord Archbishop, hold your tongue and listen. Your Majesty, would you care to join us now?"

Warin's words elicited a gasp from the prelates, as a sacristy door beside the altar opened. Through it stepped a red-cloaked Kelson, followed closely by Morgan, Duncan, Cardiel, and several of Morgan's rescued castle officers.

Kelson's raven head was crowned with a golden circlet, and silk and cloth-of-gold gleamed beneath the crimson cloak. Morgan had donned one of his formal gryphon tunics, the winged beast worked in gold and emeralds on the breast of the silken cloth. Duncan was in black, with the bright plaid of his McLain ancestors secured to one shoulder with a heavy silver brooch. Cardiel wore clerical attire again, black under a magnificent cloth-of-silver cope, with a miter of silver and white on his steel-gray hair.

The significance of this unexpected intrusion took but an instant to register with the watching prelates. Conlan and Corrigan had gone noticeably pale, several other bishops crossed themselves furtively, and even Loris was at least momentarily speechless.

Before that could change, Warin and his men sank to one knee in homage, the armed men raising mailed fists to chests in earnest salute. Kelson let his gaze touch on the motionless bishops, who could not seem to move from their places, then signed for Warin and his men to rise. As he and his followers moved across the chapel floor to join Warin, the bishops shrank back uneasily. When Kelson had gained the company of Warin, he turned to face Loris and the others, his people grouping themselves at his back in a show of solidarity.

"So, my lords, have you forgotten the oaths of allegiance you swore to us and our crown?" He surveyed them from beneath the golden circlet with cold gray eyes.

Loris drew himself a little straighter and gathered up the shreds of his dignity with visible effort.

"Sire, with all due respect, you are excommunicate. Excommunication removes from you certain prerogatives that would ordinarily be yours to command. You are dead to us, Sire."

"Ah, but I am not dead, Archbishop, in body or in soul," Kelson countered. "Nor are Morgan, nor Father McLain, nor any of the others whom you have anathematized on the basis of one misunderstood incident. Even Warin now does us honor."

"Warin is a traitor," Loris said coldly, with a sidelong glance at the rebel leader. "He has been deceived by your Deryni tricks. You have corrupted him!"

"On the contrary, Warin de Grey is a loyal subject," Kelson replied. "He now understands the error of his previous belief, and has voluntarily joined us. The unfortunate incident at Saint Torin's, upon which you appear to base your retribution against my loyal subjects, has been explained to his satisfaction and that of the bishops at Dhassa. The matter is closed. If you continue to justify your disobedience by dwelling on that incident, we can only conclude that there is some other overriding motive behind your continued defiance of your king. It is not Warin who is the traitor. He has not chosen to continue to defy us."

"You have done something to him!" Loris whispered, pointing a shaking finger at Warin. "You have used your vile powers to corrupt his mind. He would not have had this change of heart if you had not meddled."

Morgan took a step forward, restrained menace in every line of his body. "Do not forget to whom you speak, Archbishop," he said, his voice silky but deadly. "Even a king's patience can reach the breaking point."

"Ach!" Loris flung up his hands in disgust and rolled his eyes heavenward. "Must we listen to this heretic? I have nothing more to say to either of you. We will not be shaken in our faith."

"Then you will be incarcerated here at Coroth until you reach a change of heart," Kelson said quietly. "We will not brook defiance from any subject, even an archbishop. Guards, take Archbishop Loris into custody and escort him to a suitable place of confinement. Bishop Cardiel, we hereby designate you as acting Primate of Gwynedd, until such time as the Curia can meet officially to either ratify your appointment or choose some other loyal bishop more to their liking. Archbishop Edmund Loris is no longer acceptable in the eyes of the Crown."

"You cannot do that!" Loris raged, as two guards restrained him. "This is absurd!"

"Hold you tongue, Archbishop, or we shall have you gagged. Now, those of you who do not wish to share His Excellency's fate have but two alternatives. If you feel that you cannot, in good conscience, unite with us to repel the invader Wencit, we shall free you to retire to the sanctuary of your respective sees, on condition that you swear neutrality until this conflict is resolved.

"But if you cannot give us that pledge of neutrality, we ask that you not forswear yourselves by pretending that you can. You would be far better off in custody here at Coroth than to face our wrath when we discover that you have broken faith with us.

"For the rest of you—and we pray that there may be some—we offer an opportunity to renounce the actions you have pursued for these past months and restore your good names. If any of you will bend your knee to us now and renew your allegiance to the Crown, we will be pleased to grant full pardon for past offenses and welcome you back into our company. Your prayers and support will be sorely needed when we face Wencit of Torenth a few days hence."

He let his gaze search the faces of the watching prelates once again. "Well, my Lords? Which is it to be? The dungeon, the monastery, or the Crown? You have no other choices."

The conditions Kelson had offered were too much for the infuriated Loris.

"He offers you no *choice*," the archbishop ranted. "There can be no other *choice* where heresy is concerned! Corrigan, you will not betray your faith, will you? Creoda, Conlan, surely you do not mean to bend to this brash young king's mistaken will?"

Kelson gave a curt hand signal, and one of the guards holding Loris pulled a cloth from his tunic so that his colleague could begin gagging the archbishop.

"You were warned," Kelson said, eyeing Loris, then the rest of them, with a cold intensity. "Now, which is it to be? We have not the time to delay any longer while you ponder."

Bishop Creoda coughed nervously and glanced at his colleagues, then stepped forward. "Sire, I cannot speak for my brethren, but I wish no further argument with you. If it please Your Majesty, I shall retire to Carbury for the duration. I do not really know what I believe anymore."

Kelson nodded curtly, then scanned the rest. After a slight hesitation, Ifor and Carsten also stepped forward, Ifor bowing slightly before he spoke. "We, too, ask your indulgence, Sire. We accept your offer, and will retire to our respective sees. You have our word on it."

Kelson nodded. "What of the rest of you? I told you, I haven't all day."

Bishop Conlan, with a decisive movement, crossed to Kelson and dropped to one knee before him. "I kneel to you once more, Sire. I abjure my support of what followed the Saint Torin affair. If you believe in the innocence of Morgan and McLain, that is sufficient for me. We were all of us caught up in what happened there. Pray, forgive us, Sire."

"I forgive you freely, Bishop Conlan." Kelson reached down to touch Conlan lightly on the shoulder. "Do you ride north with us, then?"

"With all my heart, Sire."

"Thank you." Kelson returned his gaze to the rest of them: to Loris, struggling in the hands of his captors, making incoherent noises behind his gag; to Creoda and Ifor and Carsten, who would be going into seclusion; then to the two remaining prelates who had not yet declared themselves.

"De Lacey, I have not heard your answer."

De Lacey averted his eyes for a long moment, then rose stiffly from his seat and slowly sank to his knees in place. "Forgive my seeming indecision, young Sire, but I am an old man, and the old ways die slowly. I am not accustomed to disobeying either my archbishop or my king."

"Unfortunately, it appears that you shall be obliged to disobey one of us, my lord. Who is it to be?"

De Lacey bowed his head. "I shall ride with you, Sire. If I might have a horse-litter instead of a warhorse, however . . . I fear that my bones are too old to travel astride a horse at the pace you will demand."

Kelson inclined his head in agreement. "Captain, see to a litter for His Excellency. And Archbishop Corrigan—what about you? Must I ask each of you individually? Surely you have had time to decide by now."

Corrigan was ashen, his fat face clammy and glistening with perspiration. He cast long looks at his colleagues, at his henchman Loris in the soldiers' bonds, then pulled a large handkerchief from his sleeve and mopped his face as he lumbered slowly toward Kelson. When he had come to within a few paces of the young king, he cast a final look behind him at Loris, then cast his eyes down and studied his hands, twisting his handkerchief between stubby fingers.

"Forgive me, Sire, but I am old and tired and unable to fight any longer. Much as I fear you are wrong, I have not the strength to oppose you—and I fear I could not survive your dungeon. I ask permission to return to my estates outside Rhemuth. I—I am not well, Sire."

"Very well," Kelson said quietly. "If I have your word that you'll not oppose me, you are free to go. My lords, I thank you for not making this any more difficult than it had to be. And now, Morgan, Warin, Lord Hamilton, I wish to be riding out of here by noon, if at all possible. Please see to whatever needs to be done."

IT was late afternoon, not midday, before the combined armies were ready to move out, but Kelson gave the marching orders anyway. By traveling through the night and not stopping until the following midday, they could hope to cross most of Corwyn before having to rest. Then, a short stop until the early morning hours of the next day, and they could be in Dhassa by noon of the second day.

From there, it would take at least another two days to combine this army with the other already waiting outside Dhassa. In all, it would be nearly a week before they could hope to meet Wencit's forces farther north. Kelson prayed that it would be soon enough,

The shadows were lengthening, but no one felt the slightest urge to complain at the late start as the advance battalions pulled out of Coroth and began their trek to the northwest. Royal lion banners vied with the gray and black falcon standards of Warin's former rebels, both flags interspersed with the episcopal purple of Cardiel's elite troops brought down from Dhassa. Supply carts creaked their way along the roads, while mounted cavalry thundered across the grass-green of the fields through which they passed. Pack animals snorted and squealed as their drovers bullied them along in the wake of the main army, gay tassels and braid bright and cheerful in the afternoon sun. The richly embroidered surcoats of Morgan's rescued liegeman were interspersed with the uniform tunics of the Royal Haldane

Lancers, the Joshuic Foot, the Haldane Archers Corps, lord and commoner alike bound in the common tie of loyalty to the young king who rode in the vanguard.

On returning to his camp, Kelson had once again donned the gold-washed mail of the kings of Gwynedd, had laced his boots with cords of gold, bound his slim waist with a belt of snow-white leather edged with gold, on which hung the gold-chased greatsword that his father had carried in war at a similar young age. Kelson's golden helmet glowed like burnished sunlight as he rode out that afternoon, a jeweled golden circlet fixed to the helm and a crimson plume bobbing jauntily from the top.

Around his shoulders was a cloak of scarlet, on his hands gloves of scarlet leather. The white charger between his thighs pranced and arched its neck as Kelson curbed it, red leather reins supple and sleek between its rider's gloved fingers. At Kelson's side rode his lords: Morgan, Duncan, Cardiel and Arilan, Nigel and his son Conall, Morgan's lieutenants, a host of others.

So they were arrayed as they rode out of Coroth that day. So they would appear when they joined battle with Wencit a few days hence. But for now, it was enough that they were united and riding once more, heading toward a rendezvous with other loyal troops, secure in the knowledge that at least a moral victory had been won within Coroth's walls.

There would be other, more glorious days for Kelson King of Gwynedd. But doubtful it was that any of the others would be remembered with quite such fondness in years to come. For the day that King Kelson rode out of Coroth at the head of an army marked his first true military victory, despite the fact that not a sword had been raised. Spirits would still be high when they reached the gates of Dhassa two days hence.

CHAPTER EIGHTEEN

"Yea, mine own familiar friend, in whom I trusted,
who did eat of my bread, hath lifted up
his heel against me."

PSALMS 41:9

THEY arrived in Dhassa as planned, and had been there for a
night and a day making final plans for the Cardosa campaign,
but news from the front was scarce. There had been no word
from the armies of the north for nearly a week—indeed, no
word from anywhere at all north and east of Dhassa—and
concern was growing hourly. Now that the main armies of
Gwynedd were once more united, the outcome of the approaching war was beginning to look more promising as far
as sheer numbers were concerned. But the continuing silence
in the north augured ill for the days ahead. Morgan was especially concerned that he had not been able to reopen communication with Derry.

It was not for lack of trying. The night before, as they
had on numerous occasions since that last fleeting touch the
night of the reconciliation, Morgan and Duncan had joined
their efforts and attempted to make contact with Derry
through the medallion spell they had used successfully so
often in the past.

But all their efforts were for naught. Morgan had been

confident that he could at least discover Derry's location, especially at this relatively close range; but of the young Marcher lord there had been no trace. Even by stretching his powers almost to the limits of his endurance, Morgan had not been able to make the slightest contact.

Reluctantly, he could only conclude that Derry either was dead or else in the grip of something so monstrously powerful that he could neither detect Morgan's call nor be detected. Morgan sadly feared that it was the former: a particularly sobering thought, after the heady successes of the week before.

Nonetheless, the business of planning for war must go on. On the night before the king's armies were to depart for Cardosa, the candles burned late in the bishop's palace at Dhassa. Bishop Cardiel had graciously set aside the great Curia chamber for a meeting place, that Kelson and his generals and military advisors might have a proper place to work. Outside the city walls, in the valley beyond the guardian lake, the soldiers of Gwynedd slept beside a thousand campfires while their leaders plotted and planned.

The king's war council was in session. In the Curia chamber, the dishes and cutlery of the evening's supper had been cleared away some hours ago to make way for the maps and charts and books of military strategy which were the generals' stock in trade. Amidst the dull rumble of half a hundred gruff voices, the head-work of making war continued as bright-colored markers on painted maps were advanced and withdrawn and scarred fingers traced out positions and troop movements. A light collation of cheeses, fruit, and bread had been brought in an hour before, and some of the men picked at the fare distractedly.

But no one was particularly interested in food at this point. Though wine goblets dotted the tables, and might be raised in burly fists from time to time, the atmosphere was essentially a sober one. Generals and tacticians worked shoulder to shoulder with princes of the Church, who sometimes were able to suggest startling innovations, despite their disclaimers of secular knowledge. Even minor officers of foot and horse were recruited for their specialized expertise, when warranted. The hall echoed to the ring of steel-shod heels on marble flags, to the clunking of scabbards against sturdy oak furniture as the men came and went.

The king, for his part, had made it his business to remain on the fringes of what was going on, circulating among the clergy and lesser nobles of his court to soothe pre-battle nerves and leaving all but the most critical decisions in the able hands of Morgan and Nigel and the other generals. To that end, he had elected to remain inconspicuous, clad in the simplest of crimson lion tunics and with raven head bare of any princely adornment, taking special care to reassure those among his nobles who had little to offer besides their goodwill.

When requested, Kelson would break away from whatever he was doing and rejoin the generals to consider some important point of strategy, to make some decision which only he could make. But he was astute enough to realize that, in the main, his generals and military advisors knew far more of war and military cunning than he did, for all the fact that he was the son of Brion Haldane, who had been an almost legendary leader of men. In the short term, it seemed the single most effective thing he could do was keep quiet and offend no one. For, without the support of every man in the royal army, they could not hope to stand against Wencit of Torenth in the week ahead.

Nor was Kelson alone in his determination to smooth ruffled feathers and make peace among the nobles of Gwynedd. Across the room, Morgan and Bishop Conlan were wrangling with three of Morgan's western barons who had joined them at Coroth. Several of the younger lords and Nigel's son Conall watched and listened with wide eyes. Prince Nigel, too, had been a part of the debate until a little while ago, but now he had returned to the main table to arbitrate some minor difference of opinion between Warin and the Earl of Danoc.

Only Duncan seemed not to be caught up in the taut bustle of the night's work, Kelson thought, as he caught a glimpse of the priest gazing moodily out an open window. Duncan had kept himself somewhat apart for much of the evening, declaring himself no authority on military matters, any more than Kelson was. Yet, Kelson knew that Duncan was a trained swordsman, a duke's son, and must have learned the rudiments of strategy at his father's knee before he heard his calling to the priesthood. As two more bishops approached Kelson with some new query, he wondered what was troubling the priest. It was not like the usually gregarious Duncan to be so distant.

Duncan sighed and leaned an elbow against the windowsill, unconsciously shrugging back the plaid that had begun to slip from one shoulder. His blue eyes were hooded as he searched the inky darkness of the mountains east of Dhassa, and the slim, ringless fingers of one hand tapped restlessly against the stone of the casement edging.

If questioned, he could not have said just why he was so pensive tonight. Certainly, the ceaseless wrangling was beginning to wear on all their nerves, and the pressure was increasing hourly as departure time approached. But he was also worried about Derry—and more, about Morgan's growing concern over the missing Marcher lord. All aside from the obvious loss to Gwynedd's service, if ill had befallen Derry, Duncan knew that the young earl's death would have a profound effect on Morgan. Derry, for all his youthful exuberance and even occasional recklessness, had managed to forge a depth of friendship with Morgan that was enjoyed by few humans. If Derry had died as a result of Morgan's instructions to go out "a-spying"—even though the idea had originally been Kelson's—Duncan knew that it would be a long time before Morgan would be able to bring himself to forget.

And then there was the matter of Duncan's own sorrow, of a vocation held and not held, which could not be resolved until he could come to grips with his Deryniness—because he *had* lied about it to get himself ordained, defying canon law and his own conscience.

Wolves howled in the distant hills, and Duncan let his gaze roam the city walls once more. He could see torches approaching the palace gates from the lake, half a dozen dancing points of light borne by men on horseback. As they drew nearer, he watched the postern gate open to admit them, leaning out then to survey a handful of horses crowding through into the narrow courtyard below.

One of the riders—a page or squire, by the look of him—rode low on his horse's neck, his head lolling alarmingly as the horses jolted to a stop. It was difficult to be certain at this distance, but the lad's mount appeared to be footsore and badly winded. More torches flared in the darkness as stablemen approached.

As one of the men grabbed at the reins of the foundering animal, the beast staggered and went to its knees, pitching its young rider out of the saddle to land in a heap. The unfortunate lad picked himself up painfully and held onto one of the guards for support, then glanced up toward Duncan's window before staggering toward the stair on the man's arm. As he did so, his muddy cloak parted to show a flash of the livery underneath.

Duncan clutched at the windowsill and stifled a gasp, staring after the lad as he disappeared into the stairwell entrance. The sky-blue silk of the boy's livery was long-familiar, known from earliest childhood, as was the sleeping lion badge emblazoned on the chest in silver-gray.

But the sky-blue had been grimy and ragged, stained with a hue more red than mud, the lion badge almost obliterated by a great rent that ran from throat to waist. What could have happened? Had the lad brought word from Duke Jared's army?

The flash of a blade dispatching the foundering horse ended Duncan's stunned speculation, and he came to his senses with a start. The lad would be brought directly to Kelson, he was sure. Duncan was just turning to look for

Morgan and the king when the great doors of the chamber were thrown back to admit a guard and a grimy, towheaded page of perhaps nine or ten. Beneath a guard's borrowed cloak, Duncan could see the tattered remains of McLain livery, stained, as he had feared, with the rich red-brown of blood long-dried. The lad sported a great bruise under his left eye, and a crusty, ugly-looking cut on his left elbow, in addition to other scrapes and bruises. His dazed gaze flitted anxiously around the room and he stumbled as he came through the doorway. He would have fallen then and there, had not his escort caught him under his good arm and supported most of his weight.

"Where is the king?" the boy gasped, reeling against his supporter and trying to keep his young eyes in focus. "I must see the king. I have urgent news of—Sire!"

At that instant he spotted Kelson, who had started toward him even as he spoke his first words. The boy reached out a grimy hand and started to sink to his knees, then winced and began to crumple. The guard eased him down, and Kelson was at his side almost at once. Morgan and Duncan pushed their way through the crowd to kneel down on either side, Morgan cushioning the boy's head against his knee. The four were quickly surrounded by a bevy of astonished and apprehensive lords.

"He's passed out from exhaustion," Morgan said to no one in particular, touching the boy's forehead and shaking his head. "He's feverish from his wounds, too."

"Conall, bring some wine," Kelson ordered. "Father Duncan, he wears your father's livery. Do you know who he is?"

Duncan shook his head, white-lipped. "If I saw him before, I have forgotten, Sire. I saw him arrive, though. He rode at least one horse to death to get here."

"Hmm," Morgan grunted, running his hands over the boy's body to ascertain additional wounds or broken bones. "He's certainly been through one devil of a time, I'll say that much for—here, what's this?"

He had felt an odd bulge under the boy's tunic, next to his heart, and further investigation revealed a tattered scrap of silk, tightly folded.

He fumbled as he tried to open it, for the silk was stiff with blood. Kelson reached across and took the other edge, and together they unfolded what was obviously part of a battle pennon. In the center of the silk was a leaping black hart on a white circle. The rest of the banner, where it was not caked with mud and gore, was a brilliant, flaming orange-red.

Kelson whistled low under his breath and released the silk, unconsciously wiping his palms against his thighs in distaste. There was no need for further words, for all knew the leaping hart badge of Torenth and what its presence on the bloody standard suggested. In shocked silence, Kelson turned his eyes on the pale face of the unconscious page. Conall returned with the wine, to observe as Morgan took the cup and held it to the boy's lips. The boy whimpered as his head was lifted slightly and supported against Morgan's left arm.

"All right, let's drink up here, young fellow," Morgan murmured, tipping the cup to let a little of the wine trickle between the boy's teeth.

The boy moaned and tried to turn his head away, but Morgan was relentless.

"No, drink some more. That's a good lad. Now, open your eyes and try to tell us what happened. His Majesty is waiting."

With a suppressed sob, the boy forced his eyes open and squinted up at Morgan, at the face of Kelson opposite, at Duncan peering down from above, then closed his eyes momentarily and bit at his lip. Morgan gave the goblet back to Conall and laid a gentle hand on the boy's forehead.

"It's all right, son. Tell us what happened, and then you can rest."

The boy swallowed and wet his lips before opening his eyes again, then fixed his gaze on Kelson, as though it were only the royal presence that kept body and soul together. It was obvious even to those totally without medical training that he was on the verge of passing out again.

"Sire," he began weakly, "we are undone. Terrible battle . . . traitor in our midst . . . Duke Jared's army, all . . . gone. . . ."

His eyes rolled upward and his voice trailed off as he lapsed into unconsciousness again, and Morgan anxiously felt for a pulse. His expression was grim as he looked up at Kelson.

"He doesn't appear to have any major injuries—a few cuts and bruises, despite the bloody clothes. But he's too exhausted to bring around again. Maybe in a few hours . . ."

His voice trailed off expectantly as he gazed across at the king, and Kelson shook his head.

"It's no good, Alaric. We can't wait that long. A battle, a traitor in their midst, Duke Jared's army 'gone' . . . We've got to find out what happened."

"If I force him back to consciousness, it could kill him."

"Then we'll have to take that risk."

Morgan's eyes flicked to the boy's face, then back to Kelson's. "Let me try another way, my prince. It is not without its own risks, but . . ."

He gazed into Kelson's unblinking eyes for several seconds, and finally Kelson gave a slow nod.

"Can you do it here with reasonable safety?" he asked, inquiring as much after Morgan's safety as that of the boy.

Morgan lowered his eyes. "You must have your information, my prince. And your barons will have to see me in action sooner or later. I think we have little choice."

"Then do it," Kelson breathed, straightening on his knees and glancing around him at his watching lords. "Gentlemen, I beseech you to stand away and give His Grace space to work. The boy's message must be heard, and only my Lord Alaric's gifts can make that possible without endangering an innocent life. There is no danger to any of you."

There was a murmur of consternation among nobles and clergy as Kelson spoke, and several made furtive movements toward the doors until Kelson's sharp gaze swept the room and held each man in his place. Those closest to the tableau moved away a little, as the king had asked, until only Duncan and Kelson himself were still kneeling beside Morgan and the unconscious page. As Morgan shifted to a sitting position, supporting the boy in his lap, the murmuring ceased and the room grew hushed. For all but a few, this would be the first time they had ever seen a Deryni use his powers.

Morgan looked up at them and studied the fearful, sometimes hostile faces. Never had he looked so human, so vulnerable, as he sat in the middle of the floor with the child cradled in his arms. Never had the gray eyes been so guileless in the presence of potential enemies.

But there must be confidence. Now was not the time for old enmities, for fears to crowd beside the trust that must be engendered. Here must be a time of openness, of stark truth. These men must be convinced, once and for all, that the fearsome powers of the Deryni could be used for good. So much depended upon what happened here in the next minutes. There must be no mistakes.

Morgan permitted himself the tiniest of smiles as he carefully chose his words.

"My lords, I fully understand your apprehension," he said in a low voice. "You will have heard many rumors about my powers and the powers of my people, and it is natural that you should at first fear what you do not understand.

"What you are about to see and hear will, undoubtedly, seem very strange to you," he went on. "But so the unknown always seems until it becomes the known." He paused. "Even I cannot predict with certainty just what will happen in the next minutes, for I have no idea what this lad has been through. I ask only that you do not interfere, no matter what happens—that you watch and listen silently. The process is not without its danger for *me*."

As he looked down at the boy again, a faint sigh whispered among the watchers, quickly fading into total silence. Morgan smoothed the unconscious boy's fair hair gently across his forehead, then positioned his left hand so that he could see the gryphon signet close by the boy's chin. With a last glance at Duncan and Kelson, who still knelt silently across from him, he gazed at the gryphon and made a conscious effort to relax, breathing deeply to trigger the Thuryn trance as he had learned long ago.

Then his head bowed and his eyes closed, and his breath came deep and easy. The boy stirred once beneath his hands, then was still.

"Blood."

Morgan whispered the word, but there was an alien quality to the sound that sent a ripple of chill through the watching lords.

"So much blood," Morgan murmured, louder this time. "Blood everywhere." His head slowly raised, though the eyes remained tightly closed.

Duncan glanced sharply at Kelson, then edged closer to his kinsman, his pale eyes fixed on the familiar face now gone strange. He had more than a suspicion now what his kinsman was attempting, and the thought chilled him for all his understanding of the act. He wet his lips nervously, his eyes never leaving the strained face of Morgan.

"Who are you?" he said in a low voice.

"Oh, my God, who's that coming?" Morgan's voice replied, as though he had not heard, a boyish quality evident even as Duncan had suspected.

"Ah, 'tis only my Lord Jared, with his good allies, the Earl of Marley and his friends. . . . 'Boy, bring wine for my Lord of Marley. Bran Coris has come to reinforce us. Bring wine, lad. Show your respect for the Earl of Marley!' "

Morgan's voice paused, then continued in a lower, darker tone, so that his listeners had to move closer to catch all of his words.

"The armies of Bran Coris join with ours. The royal blue

banners of Marley mix and meld with the sleeping lions of Cassan, and all is well.

"But, wait! The soldiers of Bran Coris draw their swords!"

Morgan's eyes popped open, but he continued to speak in the boy's voice, his voice rising in pitch, almost cracking with the strain.

"No! Not treachery! It cannot be! Bran Coris's men ride with the Furstán hart beneath their shield covers! They slay the duke's men! They cut a swatch of carnage through the ranks of Cassan!

"My lord! My Lord Jared! Flee for your life! The Marley's men are upon us in treachery! Fly, oh, fly away, Your Grace! We are undone! Oh, my lord, we are undone!"

With an anguished moan, Morgan's head dropped against his chest, bitter sobs wracking his body. Kelson started to reach out and touch him, but Duncan frowned and shook his head. They watched tensely as Morgan's sobbing finally stopped and he raised his head once more. The gray eyes were blank and strained, the cheeks strangely damp, the expression that of a man who has just looked on Hell. He stared unseeing for several seconds, and then:

"I see my Lord Jared go down beneath a sword," he whispered dully. Duncan controlled a gasp of anguish. "I do not know if he is dead. I fall from my horse and am nearly trampled, but I escape, I play dead."

He shuddered and continued, choking back another sob. "I roll beneath the body of a slain knight, am drenched by his dying blood, but I am not found out. Soon the battle ends and night falls, but even then there is no safety. The Marley's men take prisoners, and Torenthi death squads dispatch the badly wounded. No living man escapes that field of death except in chains.

"When all is quiet, I crawl from beneath my dead knight and stagger to my feet. I start to whisper a prayer for the dead knight's soul, for he has unwittingly saved me from the enemy." Morgan's face contorted and his right hand crumpled the silken banner still across the boy's chest. "But then I see the black hart banner in the dead knight's hands, the blue eagles of Marley sprinkling the leather of his surcoat." He stifled a sob.

"I take the banner as proof of what I have seen, and then I stumble into the night. Two—no, *three* horses die beneath me before I reach the gates of Dhassa with the news."

His eyes glazed slightly, and Duncan thought he was about to come out of it, but then the strange voice spoke again, Morgan's lips curving in a strained smile.

"But, I have accomplished my mission. The king knows of Bran Coris's treachery. Even if my Lord Jared lies dead, our liege lord the king will avenge him. God save . . . the king!"

With that, Morgan's head slumped once more against his chest, and this time Duncan did not stop Kelson as he reached across to lay a trembling hand on Morgan's arm.

After a few seconds, the tense shoulders relaxed and Morgan breathed a great sigh. Then his right hand flexed against the tattered silk he still clutched, and he opened his eyes. He stared at the still form of the boy in his arms for a long moment, remembering the horror he had shared, then disengaged his hand from the silk and laid his hand across the boy's forehead.

The gray eyes closed momentarily and opened again, and then Morgan straightened and raised his eyes to meet Kelson's. His cheeks still glistened with the tears he had shared with the boy, but he made no move to wipe them away.

"He has borne a heavy burden for you, my prince," Morgan said quietly. "Nor do I welcome the news he has brought us."

"One is not expected to welcome the news of treachery," Kelson murmured, his eyes distant and hooded. "Are you all right?"

"Only a little tired, Sire. Duncan, I am sorry about your father. I wish the boy could have seen what became of him."

"I am his only remaining son," Duncan whispered dully. "I should have been out there, at his side. He was getting too old to lead armies."

Morgan nodded, knowing the guilt his kinsman must be feeling, then looked up at the assembled lords and bishops. Two squires came to take the boy away to rest, but they would not meet his eyes as they took the boy from his arms. Morgan got to his feet, steadying himself against Kelson's shoulder, then swept the torchlit room with his cool gaze. The eyes were dark, mostly pupil in the flickering torchlight— inky pools of power and mystery, even though the body behind them was exhausted.

But to his surprise, as his gaze touched the men, they did not shrink from the contact. The bishops shuffled feet, twisted nervous fingers in the folds of purple cassocks, but they did not retreat. The generals and captains, too, stared at Morgan with a new look of grudging respect, fearful but now willing to trust. In all, there was not a man in the room who would not have gone on his knee to Morgan in an instant, had he requested it—notwithstanding Kelson's presence in the room.

Only Kelson, brushing dust from the knees of his hose in a carefully casual gesture, seemed unaffected by the feat of magic they had just witnessed. Anger, not awe, and a little resignation were in his manner as he stepped slightly away from Morgan and surveyed his waiting court.

"As you have surmised, gentlemen, the news of Bran Coris's defection has shocked and angered me greatly. And the loss of Duke Jared will be felt by all of us for many years to come." He flicked a sympathetic glance at Duncan, and the priest bowed his head.

"But I think there is no question what must be done now," the king continued. "The Earl of Marley has allied himself with our bitter enemy and turned against his own kind. For this he will be punished."

"But, what *are* his own kind, Sire?" Bishop Tolliver whispered. "What are *we*, hodge-podge of human and Deryni and half of each? Where is the dividing line? Who is on the side of right?"

"He who serves the right is on the side of right," Cardiel

said softly, turning to face his colleagues. "He who is human and Deryni and half of each. It is not a man's blood that makes him choose good or evil. It is what lies within his soul."

"But we are so different . . ." Tolliver glanced at Morgan in awe.

"It does not matter," Cardiel said. "Human or Deryni, we share at least one common bond—and it is thicker than blood or oath or any spell that one might bind from the outer darkness. It is the sure and certain knowledge that we side with the Light. And he who would side with Darkness can only be our enemy, no matter what his blood or oath or spell."

The other bishops, with the exception of Arilan, glanced among themselves and then were silent. Cardiel, after a slow scan across their faces, turned back to Kelson and bowed.

"I and my brethren will assist you in whatever way we can, Sire. Will the news of Bran Coris change your plans to leave at dawn?"

Kelson shook his head, grateful for the bishop's intercession. "I think not, Excellency. I suggest that all of you get some sleep and make whatever arrangements are necessary for your provisioning now. I shall need the help of every one of you in the days ahead."

"But we are not fighting men, Sire," old Bishop Carsten protested weakly. "What possible use can we—"

"Then pray for me, Excellency. Pray for us all."

Carsten opened his mouth and then shut it again, rather like a fish gulping air. Then he bowed and edged back with the rest of his colleagues. After a pause, those in the rear of the group turned and began making their way from the room. As they filed out, Nigel and the generals returned to their maps and resumed their interrupted discussion, though much subdued.

Kelson watched as Morgan led Duncan back to a window seat and talked with him for several minutes, then joined the fringes of the war council. Markers clicked and voices were raised and lowered with the tension of revising their plans, but after a while Kelson turned away from the council and walked slowly to one of the fireplaces. He was joined shortly by Morgan, who had noticed his withdrawal, even if no one else had.

"I hope that you're not going to try to insist that Bran's defection was all your fault," Morgan said in a low voice. "I've just listened to Duncan tell me how this could all have been avoided, if only he had been at Rengarth with his father's army."

Kelson lowered his eyes, studying a scuff mark on the leather of his wide belt. "No." He paused. "Bran's wife and his heir are here in Dhassa, did you know?"

"I am not surprised. Did they come here for sanctuary?"

Kelson shrugged. "I suppose so. There are a lot of women and children staying here. Bran has a manor not far away, but apparently he decided that Dhassa would be safer for them. I don't suppose he expected how things would turn out. I would like to think that he didn't."

"I doubt that Bran's defection was premeditated," Morgan said, if only to reassure the king. "No man would deliberately send his wife and his heir into hostage bond if he could prevent it."

"But the potential was there—it *had* to be," Kelson murmured. "And I should have recognized it. We all knew that Bran had great passions—and great hatreds. I should never have sent him so close to the front."

"I thought you were not going to blame yourself," Morgan said with a slight smile. "If it's any consolation, I would have done the same thing and been just as wrong. You cannot be right all the time."

"*I* should have known," Kelson repeated doggedly. "It was my business to know. I am the king."

Morgan sighed and glanced distractedly at the war council, wishing he could change the subject.

"You mentioned an heir—do you think he'll give us any trouble?"

Kelson snorted, a sardonic smile coming to his lips. "Young Brendan? I hardly think so. He's only three or four years old." He sobered, staring into the flames in the stone fireplace before him. "I dread telling his countess, though. From all reports, she and her family have always been the soul of Crown loyalty. It will not be easy to tell her that her husband is a traitor."

"Do you want me to come along?"

Kelson shook his head. "No, this is my job. You are needed with the generals. Besides, I have had a bit of practice dealing with hysterical women, if it comes to that. My mother was very good at that sort of thing, you know."

Morgan smiled, remembering the beautiful and stubborn Queen Jehana, now in sanctuary at a monastery in the heart of Gwynedd, grappling with her Deryni soul. Yes, Kelson had had ample experience dealing with distraught women. Morgan had no doubt that Kelson could handle the situation admirably—and alone.

"Very well, my prince," he said with a slight bow. "Nigel and I will wind up things here in the next hour, and then send the men off to get some sleep. I'll send word to your quarters if there's need of your personal attention."

Kelson nodded, glad of the opportunity to slip away without further words, and turned on his heel to leave. As he made his exit, Duncan stirred from his window seat, glanced at Morgan, then crossed the room and left by the same door, heading in the opposite direction.

Morgan watched him go, knowing that his cousin needed to be alone just now, then made his way back to the map table and shouldered his way to a position where he could see and hear. Aides had set up new markers to show Bran Coris's alliance with Wencit of Torenth, and the plains between Dhassa and Cardosa were empty, now that Jared's army no longer occupied them.

Far to the north, the bright orange markers of Duke Ewan's forces were deployed along the farthest reaches of the border; but they were relatively few, and their position could not be counted upon. Indeed, in light of the past hour's news, even Ewan's army might no longer exist. The royal army gathered here at Dhassa might be the only thing now standing between Wencit and the rest of Gwynedd.

"So we know for certain only that Jared was defeated south of Cardosa, somewhere here on the Rengarth plain," Nigel was saying, tracing the location with a forefinger. "We don't know how many men Wencit has, but Bran's forces numbered somewhere in the neighborhood of thirty-five hundred, at last report. So far as we know, they're still camped somewhere along here." He pointed out the eastern border of a plain at the mouth of the Cardosa Defile.

"Now, we have about twelve thousand men, with our combined armies. With a day's forced march, we can swing around the end of the Coamer Range and be in position for the defile by dusk tomorrow. Once we reach that position, though, each of us will have to hold his assigned area at whatever cost. We don't know how many men Wencit has added to Bran's forces."

Grunts of agreement met this declaration.

"Very well, then. Elas, I'll expect you and General Remie to hold the left flank, here. Godwin, you and Mortimer will . . ."

Nigel went on, detailing each general's responsibilities in the final marching order and battle arrangements, and Morgan drew back a little to watch the men's reactions. After a while, one of Nigel's military aides came in with a flat stack of dispatches for Nigel, but Morgan intercepted them and began leafing through them himself, so that Nigel need not be disturbed. The seals identified most of them as routine, and Morgan did not trouble himself with more than a cursory glance at those. But there was one—a stained, brown packet with a yellow seal—that eluded immediate recognition.

With a slight frown of anxious speculation, Morgan broke the seal and opened the letter, stifling a gasp of amazement as he scanned the contents.

Then he was pushing his way back to Nigel's side, gripping the duke's shoulder in excitement as he caught and held the attention of the others with his eyes.

"Your pardon, Nigel, but this is welcome news. Gentlemen, I have in my hand a dispatch from General Gloddruth, who, as most of you know, was with Duke Jared's army at Ren—"

Exclamations of excitement and disbelief cut off further speech, and Morgan had to rap on the table with his knuckles before order was restored. It was with obvious restraint that the men ceased their excited speculation and listened for his next words.

"Gloddruth says that Jared was definitely wounded and captured, not killed," Morgan went on, consulting the letter, "along with the Earl of Jenas, the Sieur de Canlavay, and Lords Lester, Harkness, Collier, and Bishop Richard of Nyford. He says that he and Lord Burchard managed to bring out about a hundred men between them, and he thinks that a few hundred more may have escaped to the west."

There was a ragged cheer at this last, but Morgan held up his hand for silence.

"This is welcome news, of course, but Gloddruth goes on to say that he counts the battle a total rout. They were taken completely by surprise. He estimates that sixty per cent of the army was killed outright, and almost all of the others were taken captive. He will meet us at Drellingham tomorrow, with those he was able to bring out."

"Sixty per cent?"

"The Hell you say!"

"Morgan, where did—"

"What else does it say, Your Grace?"

Morgan shook his head and began easing his way to the door, brandishing the dispatch beside his head. "I'm sorry, gentlemen, you now know as much as I do. Nigel, I'll rejoin you shortly. Duncan and the king will want to know about this."

He could not readily find Duncan. And Kelson was, at

the moment, occupied with matters far more trying, if less urgent, than what had just transpired in the council chamber. After leaving the war council, Kelson had gone, as he had said he would, to search out the apartments of Bran Coris's wife, the Countess Richenda. He had finally located her quarters on an upper floor of the east wing, but it had taken what seemed like an eternity for the lady's servants to rouse their mistress from her sleep.

Kelson waited uneasily in the apartment's dayroom while a few sleepy servants tidied the place and brought in a rack of candles on a floor standard. White moonlight streamed through an open eastern window, creating an eerie, ghostly atmosphere that made Kelson even more uncomfortable than he had been.

At last the door to an inner chamber opened and the lady appeared. Even then, Kelson was not prepared for the young, reed-slim figure in white who glided into the room and made her graceful curtsy.

Beauty he had been prepared for, knowing Bran Coris; and Richenda of Marley had that in abundance, though of a less earthy sort than Kelson had envisioned. The delicate, heart-shaped face was framed by masses of reddish-gold hair bound with a white lace kerchief; the eyes were of a deep, sea-blue shade that Kelson had never seen before. In addition, though he knew that she was Bran Coris's wife and the mother of his young heir, he found it difficult to remember that she was probably a dozen years his senior, not a maiden barely out of girlhood.

But her attire was very austere for one so young: stark white on white, unadorned but for the pattern of the fabric itself, almost as though she had known, before entering the room, of the dreadful news the young king brought. After the servants had been dismissed, she listened calmly as Kelson told of her husband's treachery, her expression hardly changing. When he had finished, she turned away and stared out the window for a long time: a slim shadow of white and gold in the brilliant moonlight.

"Shall I call one of your maidservants, my lady?" Kelson asked in a low voice, concerned that she might faint or become hysterical, as he had heard that noble ladies sometimes were wont to do.

Richenda bowed her head and shook it slowly, pulling the lace kerchief from her long, red-golden hair and letting it fall to the floor. A gold ring set with a heavy seal—her husband's betrothal ring—winked on her left hand as she ran her hands along the stone window-ledge, and Kelson thought he saw something wet mark the stone sill for just an instant.

But the hands quickly covered the teardrop, if such it had been. Nor did the slim fingers tremble as she gazed down at them, unseeing. Richenda of Marley was a daughter of the nobility, bred to dignity and stoic acceptance of her lot in the general order of things. She reminded Kelson a little of his mother.

"I am truly sorry, my lady," Kelson finally said, wishing there was something else he could say to ease her pain. "If—if it will make your sorrow any easier to bear, be assured that I will not hold your husband's treachery against you or your son. You shall have my personal protection for as long as—"

There was a curt, staccato knock at the door, followed immediately by Morgan's low-voiced, "Kelson?"

Kelson turned expectantly at the sound of his name and moved toward the door, not noticing the effect the voice had had on the woman at the window. As Morgan entered, Richenda's face went pale and the fingers of one hand clenched on the sill of the moonlit window. Morgan made a perfunctory bow in her direction but did not really see her, so absorbed was he in delivering his message to the king. As he and Kelson met, the woman watched in amazement, as though unable to believe what her eyes and ears perceived.

"Forgive the interruption, my prince," Morgan murmured, lowering his head to point out the signature as Kelson tilted the page toward the light. "I knew you would wish to see this at once. Duke Jared is captured but alive, at last report. General Gloddruth and a few others managed to escape. The council has been apprised."

"Gloddruth!" Kelson breathed, moving toward the rack of candles and reading eagerly. "And Burchard, too! My lady, you will pardon me, this is important news."

At his words, Morgan glanced up as though just remembering that there was a third person in the room, then met the woman's wide blue eyes and nearly recoiled. For just an instant, his memory flashed back to the previous spring, to the road by Saint Torin's, to a mired coach bound for Dhassa and a lady with hair the color of flame in sunlight; again, to a woman and child seen leaving vespers at the bishop's chapel only last week. It was the same woman, the one he had almost asked Duncan about; the woman whose face had been graven on his memory since that first brief encounter on the Dhassa road.

Who was she? And what was she doing *here*, in the chambers of the Countess of Marley?

He took an involuntary step toward her, then drew up in confusion, hastily covering that confusion with a courtly bow. His pulse was pounding in his ears, and he could not seem to think clearly. It was all he could do, as he raised his eyes to hers, to simply murmur, "My lady."

The lady managed a shaky, hesitant attempt at a smile. "I perceive that it was not a simple hunter named Alain who rescued my coach that day at Saint Torin's," she said softly, her eyes as blue as the lakes of Rhendall.

"M-my lady," Morgan whispered, casting prudence to the winds and shaking his head in wonder. "Yours was the last face I remember before oblivion claimed me on that awful day. I have seen you only once since then, and you did not see me. But in my dreams . . ."

His voice trailed off as he realized that he had no right to be saying these things, and the lady lowered her eyes and toyed with a fold of her gown.

"Forgive me, my lord, but I know not how to call you," she whispered plaintively.

Kelson, finishing his dispatch, looked up with a start to see the two conversing and hurried back to join them.

"My lady, you must forgive my ill manners. I forgot that you have not made the acquaintance of His Grace, the Duke of Corwyn. Morgan, this is Lady Richenda, wife to the Earl of Marley."

At Kelson's allusion to the traitor, though he did not speak the name, Morgan's stomach did a slow, queasy roll, and he had to force himself to remain outwardly calm, not to show his consternation.

Of course, she had to be Bran's wife. What else would she be doing in this room?

Richenda of Marley . . . Bran Coris's wife. What perverse quirk of fate could have brought them together on the Dhassa road only to forever part them here, within Dhassa walls? Richenda of Marley—God, how could he have been so imperceptive?

He cleared his throat nervously and bowed again in acknowledgement, further masking his discomfiture with a slight cough.

"Ah, the lady and I have already met, after a fashion, Sire. A few months ago, I helped free her ladyship's coach from the mud outside Saint Torin's. I was—ah—in disguise at the time. She could not have known who I was."

"Nor he, I," Richenda murmured, lifting her chin bravely but not meeting Morgan's eyes.

"Oh," said Kelson. His glance flicked from one to the other, trying to read the meaning of Morgan's odd reaction more plainly, but then he gave it up with a bright smile.

"Well, I am pleased to hear that you were being chivalrous even in disguise, Morgan. My lady, if you will pardon us, we must take our leave of you now. My Lord Alaric and I have other duties that require our attention. Besides, I imagine that you will wish to be alone for a while now. Please do not hesitate to call on me, if I may be of any assistance."

"You are very kind, Sire," Richenda murmured, dropping a deep curtsy and lowering her eyes once more.

"Ah—yes. Morgan, shall we go?"

"As you will, my prince."

"A moment, Sire."

Kelson turned to find the lady staring at him hopefully.

"Is there something else, my lady?"

Taking a deep breath, Richenda moved a few steps closer to him, her hands clasped nervously at her waist, then sank to her knees before him and bowed her head. Kelson glanced at Morgan in astonishment and question.

"Sire, grant me a boon, I beseech you."

"A—a boon, my lady?"

Richenda raised her eyes to meet Kelson's. "Yes, Sire. Permit me to go with you to Cardosa. Perhaps I can talk to Bran, persuade him to give up this folly—if not for me, then for our son."

"Go with us to Cardosa?" Kelson echoed, casting Morgan a frantic plea for help. "My lady, that is not possible. An army is—no place for a woman of gentle birth. Nor would I expose you to the dangers of battle, even were suitable accommodations available. We are going to *war*, my lady!"

Richenda lowered her eyes but made no attempt to get to her feet. "I am aware of the problems, Sire, and I am willing to endure a few hardships. It is the only way that I can attempt to atone for my husband's treason. Please, do not deny me, Sire."

Kelson glanced at Morgan again for guidance, but the general would not look at him, was staring absorbedly at the parquet floor beneath his boots. For just an instant, Kelson had the fleeting, inexplicable impression that Morgan wanted him to acquiesce, though Morgan certainly had said nothing to indicate it. Kelson looked at Richenda again, kneeling quietly before him, then reached out his hands to take hers and raise her up. He would make one final attempt to dissuade her.

"My lady, you cannot know what you ask. It would not be seemly. For you to travel unchaperoned with an army . . ."

"I could travel under the protection of Bishop Cardiel,"

she said earnestly. "Perhaps you were not aware of it, Sire, but Cardiel is my mother's uncle. Under the circumstances, I think he would not object."

"He is a fool, then," Kelson murmured. He glanced aside, briefly considering, then up at the lady's face with a resigned expression.

"Morgan, have you any major objections?"

"Only the usual ones, my prince," Morgan said quietly, not meeting his eyes. "And the lady seems to have dispensed with those."

Kelson sighed and then nodded. "Very well, my lady, I give you my leave to go, on the condition that Bishop Cardiel will consent. We leave at first light, but a few hours from now. Can you be ready?"

"Yes, Sire. Thank you."

Kelson nodded. "Morgan will see to your accommodations."

"As you wish, Sire."

"Good night, then."

With that, Kelson made her an awkward bow and swept out of the room, his now-forgotten dispatch crumpled in his fist. Morgan moved as though to follow him, but before he closed the door behind him, he turned to gaze once more at the white-clad lady standing in the moonlight. Richenda's face was pale and drawn, but there was a look of determination on her face as she stood framed in the window. She lowered her eyes and made a slight bow as Morgan paused, but she would not look up to meet his eyes again.

With a puzzled sigh, Morgan closed the door behind him and followed Kelson.

CHAPTER NINETEEN

"They encourage themselves in an evil matter; they
commune of laying snares privily; they say,
Who shall see them?"

PSALMS 64:5

AT noon in Cardosa, the sun beat down fiercely in the thin
mountain air, even though patches of snow still lay in the
deep crannies and crevices of the mountains. Earlier that
morning, Wencit, Rhydon, and Wencit's kinsman Lionel
had ridden down the Cardosa Defile to meet with Bran
Coris and those of Wencit's officers who were now assisting
him in the deployment of Wencit's assault forces. The defense works had been inspected, and now Wencit and his en-
tourage drew rein before the great, flame-colored pavilion
where the Torenthi king would make his headquarters once
the enemy arrived.

Soldiers in Wencit's black and white Furstán livery
swarmed around the slight rise where the royal pavilion had
been erected, setting tent poles and lines and seeing to the
installation of those items of personal comfort that Wencit
considered essential to any field operation.

The tent was enormous. A giant, onion-shaped dome of
flame-colored silk, it covered an area easily the size of Wencit's
great hall at Beldour. Inside, the structure was divided into

half a dozen separate rooms, the walls hung with heavy tapestries and furs designed both to beautify and to keep out sound and heat. Within these walls was ample space to hold any sort of conference that Wencit might have wished, but he judged the day too fair to be confined indoors, so had gestured for the major-domo to place chairs on the rich carpet laid before the enclosure.

As servants scurried to set up the chairs and stools required, one of Wencit's personal body servants came to take his master's cloak, which was mud-spattered and waterlogged from the ride down the defile. Another offered a khaftan-like robe of heavy amber silk, which Wencit shrugged on over his damp and stained riding leathers. He sat back in a leather camp chair and permitted yet another servant to exchange his boots for dry slippers, then watched as the major-domo poured steaming darja tea into fragile porcelain cups.

Wencit nodded benignly at his colleagues, inviting them to sit in the chairs that the servants had prepared; then, with his own hand, he took a cup from the tray that the major-domo offered and held it out to Bran Coris.

"Drink and be refreshed, my young friend," he said in a low voice, smiling as Bran leaned forward to take the cup. "I am exceedingly pleased."

As Bran took the cup, Wencit lifted two more and passed them to Rhydon and Lionel, who nodded their thanks before settling back with their tea. The Torenthi king smiled as he inhaled deeply of a fourth cup he took for himself, balancing it between the fingers of his two hands.

"Indeed, I am quite intrigued and impressed with the diversion which you have devised for our adversaries," the sorcerer continued, watching the ripples his breath created on the steaming darja. "You have also done a commendable job of integrating our two forces, of multiplying our strengths and neutralizing any weaknesses. Lionel, we are fortunate to have such an ally."

Lionel lifted his cup in salute, then sipped at the hot tea.

"It is fortunate that our Lord of Marley chose to join us, Sire. He might have proven a troublesome opponent. He has an uncanny ability for making . . . creative use of all available resources." Lionel's dark eyes were capable of flaying a man with a glance when he was angered, but today they were warm, almost cordial, almost as though he and the young human lord had found some subtle bond of kinship. "Even I have learned from him, Sire," Lionel added, almost as an afterthought.

"Have you, indeed?" Wencit chuckled gently.

Bran, basking in the approval of two Torenthi princes, took a careful sip of his steaming tea and relaxed, apparently unaware of the scrutiny he was receiving from Rhydon. After a silent moment while the four men drank, Rhydon spoke.

"Sire, it occurs to me that we have heard no report of the Cassani prisoners since their capture," he said, eyeing Bran over the rim of his cup. "The diversion that Bran and my Lord Lionel have conceived is . . . ingenious. Would that I had thought of it myself. Most assuredly, the effect on morale among King Kelson's supporters will be profound, if not shattering. But the Cassani prisoners—I would point out that some of them are of high rank, indeed, and exceedingly valuable. Or have plans been made for them of which I am not aware?"

Lionel chuckled, a low, dangerous sound, idly fingering the end of his braid. "You seem to suggest that Bran and I must justify our actions to you," he said mildly. "However, you need not concern yourself with the plans for the Cassani prisoners."

"Can it be that you expect my opposition, then?"

"I expect no *interference* from you," Lionel said pointedly. "We have been given leave to use the prisoners to our best advantage—and that is precisely what we shall do. Other than that, you need know nothing more."

Wencit smiled, vaguely amused by the exchange. "Now, Rhydon, you must not quarrel with my kinsman. Even I am not privy to all the details of this campaign; nor do I wish to be. I depend upon my lords of battle and advisors like Lionel to take care of those matters for me. I trust Lionel's judgment just as I trust yours. And if he assures me that he is doing what is most expeditious, then I must assume that he is. Do you dispute me in this matter?"

"Of course not," Rhydon replied, taking another sip of his darja. "It was not intended to make an issue of it. If I have, I apologize to all concerned."

"Apology accepted," Wencit nodded idly.

Rhydon turned his cup in his fingers before continuing. "I have had an additional message from General Licken since this morning's dispatches, by the way. His advance patrols confirm that King Kelson's army should be here no earlier than dusk, depending upon how much our diversion slows him up. We need fear no action before tomorrow morning."

"Excellent." Wencit turned in his chair and motioned to his major-domo, who had been waiting just out of earshot, and the man immediately brought out a large, leather-bound dispatch case studded at the corners with hammered gold. As the man withdrew, Wencit opened the box and leafed through a sheaf of already opened dispatches until he found the one he was looking for, then pulled it out with a grunt of approval. After making a short notation on it, he returned it to the box and pulled out another one, which he scanned briefly.

"Ah, here it is. I received some news this morning which concerns you, Bran," he said, glancing up wistfully. "It seems that the Haldane princeling has learned of your defection and taken your family into custody."

Bran stiffened, then slowly drew himself upright in his chair, his knuckles whitening around the cup he held.

"Why was I not told?"

"You *are* being told," Wencit said, leaning forward to hand the dispatch across. "But do not distress yourself unduly. Your wife and son were taken at Dhassa, but they are in no immediate danger that we can ascertain. Read for yourself."

Quickly Bran scanned down the dispatch, his lips compressing in a thin, tight line as he reached the end. "They are being brought here as hostages, yet you speak of no immediate danger?" His eyes lifted to Wencit's defiantly. "Suppose Kelson tries to use them against me. Do you think that I could stand by idly while my son's life was in danger? Could I watch him die?"

Rhydon raised an eyebrow, somewhat bemused by Bran's reaction. "Come now, Bran. Surely you know your king better than that. You or I might threaten a man's family to compel his obedience, but Kelson Haldane is not of that mettle. Besides," he glanced at his nails, a coy, bored look, "you can always make more sons, can you not?"

Bran's glare at Rhydon turned even more icy. "And just what is that supposed to mean?" he hissed.

Wencit chuckled and shook his head reprovingly. "Enough, Rhydon. You must not taunt our young friend. He does not understand our ways of banter. Bran, I have no intention of allowing your family to come to harm. Perhaps an exchange of hostages can be arranged. At any rate, Rhydon is correct in his assessment of Kelson. The young Haldane will not make war on innocent women and children."

"I suppose you can guarantee that?"

Wencit's smile faded and his eyes took on a steely glint. "I can guarantee to do my best," he said softly, dangerously. "Will you not concede that my best is far more than you could possibly hope to accomplish on your own?"

Bran lowered his eyes, sharply reminded of his position—becoming more precarious by the second—and reined himself back at once. "I do beg your pardon, Sire. I did not mean to question your judgment. My concern was for my family."

"If I thought otherwise, you would be dead," Wencit said calmly, holding out his hand for the dispatch Bran still held.

Bran handed over the document without a word, carefully

masking his discomfiture as Wencit returned the dispatch to its stack. After a pregnant silence, Wencit looked up again, his momentary anger apparently passed.

"Now, Rhydon. What word on our young Derry today? I trust that all is as it should be?"

"I am told that he is ready to see us," Rhydon allowed.

"Good, then." Wencit sipped at his cooling cup of darja, then drained it in a final swallow. "I think that you and I should go to see him."

IN the dungeons deep beneath Cardosa Keep, in the fortress known as Esgair Ddu, Derry lay supine on a pile of dry straw, his wrists dragged to one side by the weight of the chains fixed to the wall. Feverish from his wounds, he had lain there for nearly a day now without attention beyond a cupful of brackish water to drink and a few crusts of stale bread. His stomach was a hard knot of hunger, and his head ached, but he forced himself to open his eyes and focus on the damp ceiling, finally mustering the strength to roll to his side and lift his head.

Aches. Throbbing pain in shoulder and head. A sharp twinge in his thigh as he tried to bend a cramped knee.

Gritting his teeth, he struggled to a sitting position, pulling himself up by the chains that stretched from his wrists to a pair of iron rings set in the wall above head-height.

He knew why the rings were there. The jailers who had brought him here initially had chained him, spread-eagled against the wall, while they worked him over with fists and riding whips until he mercifully passed out. Hours later, he had come to, huddled on the dank, musty straw where he now sat.

He wiped his sweaty face against the shoulder that was not wounded and blinked his eyes in an attempt to clear his vision, then set about pulling himself to his feet. There was a window over to the left of where his chains were secured.

If he remembered the layout of Esgair Ddu correctly, he should be able to see part of the plain from here.

He steadied himself against the chains and caught his breath, then dragged himself to the window and peered out.

Far below on the plain, Wencit's armies had moved into position. Slightly to the north, atop a small rise, someone had ranged the bowmen to take advantage of the altitude. North and east were the cavalry and infantry, arranged to employ a pincer movement if the opportunity should arise.

More of Wencit's cavalry were moving down the pass to take up positions around the center of the encampment. Cavalry: the heart of Wencit's fighting force. He could see a steady stream of damp and bedraggled horsemen riding onto the plain from where he knew the last ford must be; could almost hear the shouts of the captains as they kept their men in order and put them through their paces.

To the southeast, directly opposite the pass, more Torenthi soldiers were swarming around what must be Wencit's own field camp, where the Torenthi sorcerer would probably go when Kelson's army approached, and from there direct the battle. Of Kelson's army he could see no sign as yet, but he knew that they must surely be on their way by now. Someone must have gotten through to warn him of what had happened to Jared's men. He only hoped that when Kelson's army came, it would be a united one, the internal factions resolved. He wondered if Morgan and Duncan had been able to make their peace with the archbishops.

With a sigh, Derry turned to regard his chains for at least the hundredth time and gave them a tentative rattle. There was no chance of gaining his freedom while he remained fettered here like an animal—and even if he somehow managed to escape the chains, he doubted he could go far with his wounds.

Even now, his leg was throbbing from standing upright, fresh twinges shooting up and down whenever he shifted his weight. His shoulder had stopped hurting a little with the enforced movement necessary to raise him to his present position, but he had a sinking feeling that it was this wound that was making him feel so lightheaded and feverish. He had tried to inspect the wound a few hours earlier, when the guards had brought his meager ration of water, but with little success. The bandage was wrapped tightly, and he had not been able to get at it. He wondered if the wound was beginning to fester.

The sound of a key in the lock broke his train of thought, and he turned painfully to peer at the door, bracing himself against his chains. The helmeted head of a guard was briefly thrust through the narrow opening; then the man stepped through the doorway and held the door for a tall, redheaded man in amber silks and furs: Wencit of Torenth, with Rhydon of Eastmarch close behind him.

Derry could not suppress a sharp intake of breath as the two Deryni entered the cell, and he stiffened warily. In the scant light from the single window, Wencit's pale eyes looked almost aquamarine as he studied the prisoner from the open doorway, gloved hands fiddling with a slender leather whip dangling from his left wrist by a thong.

Derry drew himself as straight as he could manage, trying to ignore the throbbing in his leg, the ringing in his ears, as Wencit moved a few steps closer. The guard stood impassively by the door, gazing straight ahead, and Rhydon leaned casually against the wall, one foot braced behind him, sinister-looking in deepest midnight blue.

"So," said Wencit, "our prisoner is awake—and on his feet, too. Well done, lad. Your master would be proud of you."

Derry did not reply, guessing that next Wencit would try to goad him to anger, and determined that the sorcerer should not succeed.

"Of course," Wencit continued languidly, "praise from such a master should not be valued too highly. After all, a man who is craven and a traitor is hardly likely to inspire too much loyalty, now is he?"

Affront blazed in Derry's eyes, but he forced himself to

hold his tongue. He did not know how long he would be able to endure Wencit's taunts; his temper, he knew, was sometimes a fault. His fever was affecting his ability to think clearly.

"Then, you agree?" Wencit asked, when Derry did not reply, arching an eyebrow and stepping closer still. "I had expected better of you, young Derry. But, then, that probably reflects on the man who trained you, does it not? For some say that you and Alaric Morgan are very close, my friend—far closer than your people deem proper; that you and he share . . . secrets. . . ."

Derry averted his gaze and turned his face away, trying not to listen, but Wencit flicked the end of his whip very near Derry's face, hateful blue eyes veiled by pale lashes.

"No reaction, Derry? Come now, let us not be coy. Is it true that you and Morgan are—how shall I put it?—intimate companions? That you share his bed as well as his powers?"

With a mindless cry, Derry flung himself at his tormentor, trying to swing the chains on his wrists to smash at the leering face. But Wencit had calculated to the fraction of an inch, and stood his ground without flinching, just beyond the reach of the chains. With a moan, Derry collapsed to the floor at the end of his bonds. Wencit regarded him disdainfully, then signaled the guard to haul him to his feet.

His chains were drawn taut through their rings and fastened, leaving Derry spread-eagled against the wall, half-dangling. Again Wencit studied his half-fainting captive, tapping his whip lightly against a gloved palm, then dismissed the guard with a curt nod. The door closed behind the jailer with a groan of un-oiled hinges, and a bored-looking Rhydon shot home the inside bolt and stationed himself against the heavy door, blocking the spy hole.

"So, there is pride left in you yet, eh, my young friend?" Wencit said, moving close to Derry and lifting his chin with the end of the whip. "What else has Morgan taught you that must be unlearned?"

Derry made himself focus on Wencit's right ear and tried

to pull himself together. He should never have lashed out like that. It had been exactly what Wencit wanted. It was this damned fever, clouding his judgment. If only he could think more clearly . . .

Wencit withdrew his whip, satisfied that he now had his captive's attention, and began playing with the thong that held the lash to his wrist.

"Tell me, Derry, what is it that you fear most? Is it death?" Derry gave no reaction. "No, I see by your eyes that it is not death alone. You have mastered that fear—unhappily for you. For this means that I must draw out yet more fearsome terrors from the dark recesses of your soul."

He turned away thoughtfully and paced a slow circle in the straw, musing aloud as he walked.

"So, it is not loss of life you fear, but it is loss. But loss of what, I wonder? Of station? Of wealth? Of honor?" He turned to face Derry again. "Is it that, Derry? Is it the loss of honor, of integrity, that you fear most? And if so, what kind of integrity? Of body? Of soul? Of mind?"

Derry allowed himself no answer, forcing himself instead to gaze serenely past Wencit's head and to focus on a thin crack in the wall behind him. There he spied a spider spinning a thin, fragile web to span the crack. He decided that he would concentrate on counting the strands in the spider's web so that he could ignore the words of the despicable—

Snap!

Pain burned across Derry's face like a saber cut as Wencit's whip lashed out.

"You are not paying attention, Derry!" the master barked. "I warn you, I don't tolerate dull pupils!"

Derry suppressed the instinct to cringe away and forced himself to face his tormentor. Wencit was standing not an arm's length away, the hated whip dangling from his wrist by that blasted thong. The sorcerer's eyes glowed like twin pools of quicksilver.

"Now," said Wencit softly, "you will listen to what I have to say, Sean Lord Derry. And you will not ignore me, or I *will* hurt you. I will hurt you again and again until you either pay attention or die. And the dying will not be easy, I promise you. Are you listening?"

Derry managed a stiff nod and forced himself to pay attention. His lips were dry, his tongue felt two sizes too big for his mouth, and he could feel something warm and wet trickling down his cheek where the whip had seared.

"Very good," Wencit murmured, trailing the lash of his whip along Derry's cheek and neck. "Now, your first lesson for today is to realize—and to realize fully—that I hold your life in my hands, quite literally. If I wished, I could make you beg for oblivion, whine for merciful death to end the torments I can bring."

Without warning, his free hand lanced out to twist Derry's wounded bicep. Derry cried out involuntarily, half-fainting with the pain, but it was gone almost before it could fully register.

"Look at me," Wencit said softly. And Derry, to his horror, found himself lifting his gaze obediently. Wencit's hand still rested lightly on the wounded shoulder, but Derry tried not to anticipate what the sorcerer might do next.

"Oh, did I hurt you?" Wencit purred, kneading Derry's shoulder with gentle fingers as he smiled a different sort of smile. "Ah, but that is not my ultimate intention. I have no need to torture you, for I already possess all the power over you that I could possibly want or need. You are already conditioned to obey me. And though your mind may shrink from what I require, and may balk, your body will perform whatever I command."

With a sly smile, Wencit ran a gloved hand lightly down Derry's body from shoulder to hip, then stood back to tap his whip thoughtfully against an elegantly booted leg. After a moment, he tossed the whip to Rhydon and pulled the cuffs of his gloves taut, first one and then the other, gazing disdainfully at Derry all the while.

"Tell me, have you ever been blessed?" he asked at last, interlocking his fingers to further smooth the fit of the gloves. "Has a holy man ever made the sacred signs above your head?"

Derry's brow furrowed as Wencit lifted his right hand in an attitude of benediction, for he could not fathom where Wencit was heading.

"Well, I fear that I am not a holy man; but then, this is not really a blessing, either," Wencit continued. "You will recall that we spoke earlier of loss of integrity—integrity of body, soul, mind. I think that we begin with the soul, Sean Lord Derry. And by this sign, I place you in my thrall."

The upraised hand descended slowly, the fingers curled in a perfect mimicry of priestly blessing, then passed smoothly to the right, then right to left. As the hand passed before Derry's eyes, he felt an eerie lethargy possess him, sending leaden coldness through his limbs. He gasped, unable to comprehend what was happening to his mind, then groaned as Wencit touched the shackles at his wrists and released him.

His legs would not support him. His limbs were nerveless, uncontrollable. As his knees started to give way, he felt strong arms beneath his, bearing him up. His head lolled helplessly against the stones of the cell wall, his hair catching painfully on the rough stone and mortar. Then the pale eyes were boring into his and looming closer, a cruel, ravening mouth pressing against his in a hard, obscene kiss.

When it ended, Derry slid from his captor's arms to slump helplessly against the wall, eyes tightly closed, jaws tensed in revulsion, his body trembling in unbidden response. As he buried his face against his aching arms, he could hear Wencit laughing through a thick, heavy fog, and Rhydon chuckling with him like a mocking echo.

Then Wencit's boot was prodding him insistently in the side, and he was lifting his head to gaze up queasily. Wencit smiled and glanced at Rhydon, who had watched all in amusement, then held out his hand for Rhydon's dagger. Rhydon flipped it through the air with an easy grace, and Wencit caught it. The hilt was gold, studded with pearls, and the blade gleamed cold and deadly in the gloom as Wencit stooped down to set the tip under Derry's chin.

"Ah, how you hate me," he said in a low voice. "You are thinking that if you could only get your hands on this weapon, you would stab me in the heart or slit my throat for what I have said and done to you. Well, you shall have your chance."

Without further ado, Wencit reversed the dagger to grasp the blade, then took Derry's right hand and wrapped it round the hilt of the weapon.

"Go ahead. Kill me, if you can."

Derry froze for just an instant, unable to believe that Wencit would actually give him such an opportunity, then launched himself hysterically at his tormentor.

He never made it, of course. Wencit sidestepped neatly, easily wrenching Derry's fingers from the dagger's hilt, then pushed him back against the wall again, weak as a kitten. Unable to summon any resistance whatsoever, Derry watched dully as Wencit laughed and bent to slip the blade into the neck of his shirt, ripping down the front of the garment with one deft stroke and then parting the two halves to bare his victim's chest.

He then crouched down and brought his right hand to rest lightly on Derry's chest above the heart, the dagger balanced neatly on the fingers of his left. His eyes were cool and distant in the dim cell, and Derry knew with a sinking certainty that he was about to die.

What, in the name of all things holy, had ever made him think he could kill Wencit with a blade? Why, the man was a demon!—no, the Devil himself!

"So, you see, my dear Lord Derry, how very futile it all is," Wencit said softly. "Your soul and will now are mine—and your body also, if I desire it. And you have lost even the power to kill. You cannot take *my* life . . . but I can order you to take your own, and you will obey me. Take the knife, Derry, and rest the point here by my hand, above your heart."

As though he were watching someone else's hand, Derry saw his fingers close around the hilt of the dagger Wencit offered, the blade angled downward, Wencit's gloved hand closing over his. He watched with disbelief and dread as Wencit guided it to press lightly on the skin above his heart. He felt no sense of panic this time, no sense of struggle against what was happening. He knew that the hand was his and that it would kill him if Wencit so ordered. And there was absolutely nothing he could do about it.

Smiling, Wencit removed his hand and rocked back on his heels, balancing easily in the rustling straw.

"Now, we shall begin with just a shallow cut, barely drawing blood," he said. "Do it."

The knife moved smoothly beneath Derry's fascinated gaze, his hand guiding it along a fine line, no longer than the breadth of three fingers. Blood welled from the cut in tiny beads like jewels against his white skin, until the tip of the blade poised just below the breastbone, awaiting its next command.

"So we have drawn blood together, you and I," Wencit whispered, his voice as soft as the silk he wore. "And now we may pause together on the brink of death, for just a little while. Make it so, my friend. Only a little pressure . . . and then we may converse with the angel of death in passing, here in this lonely cell of woe."

The point of the blade began to press into Derry's flesh, more blood welling up where steel met flesh, and Derry's face went gray. He could feel the blade piercing his skin, the cold sliver of death moving inexorably toward his heart— and there was nothing he could do to stop it. He closed his eyes against the sight and tried to calm his terror-stricken soul, calling on long-forgotten childhood saints and prayers in his despair.

Then Wencit's hand was on his wrist once more, drawing the blade away, and there was a square of white silk pressing lightly against the hurt. Wencit took his right hand and did something to it that felt cold. But then the sorcerer was rising, a satisfied smile on his face, and turning to signal Rhydon that it was time to go.

Derry struggled to his elbows as the door opened, the knife forgotten in his hand, and watched as the blue-cloaked Rhydon withdrew into the darkened corridor. A guard brought a torch to light the dimness as Wencit paused in the doorway and looked back, raising his riding whip in salute.

"Rest now, my young friend," he said, his eyes deep wells of pale sapphire in the torchlight. "I hope you have learned from our little diversion. For I *do* have a very important task in mind for you. It concerns you and Morgan, and how you shall work to betray him to me."

Derry's hand tightened around the dagger-hilt, and he suddenly remembered that he still had it. He tensed, hoping he could shield the weapon behind his body, but Wencit saw the movement and smiled.

"You may keep the toy. I doubt that Rhydon will miss it for a while. But I fear it will bring you no great amusement. You see, I cannot permit you to use it, my friend. But you will learn that soon enough."

As the door closed and the key turned in the lock once more, Derry sighed and lay back in the straw in exhaustion, the dagger slipping from his shaking fingers. For a few moments he only lay there and closed his eyes tightly, trying to slow his racing heart and calm the horror of the past hour.

But as his mind cleared and his pains receded, Wencit's words suddenly reverberated in his mind: *You will betray him to me.* With a hysterical sob, he rolled onto his side to bury his face against his good arm.

God! What had Wencit done to him? Had he heard aright? Oh, but he had! The sorcerer had said that Derry would betray his lord, that Derry would play Judas to his friend and liege lord, Morgan. No! It must not be!

Dragging himself to a sitting position, Derry felt around in the straw until he found the dagger again, snatched it up in feverish hands, and gazed at it in horror. He was distracted briefly by a strange ring glinting on his right forefinger, a ring he could not remember having seen before; but then the flash of the dagger blade caught his eye once more, and he was returned to his original purpose.

Wencit was responsible for all of this. A horrible cusp had been reached, and now Wencit controlled Derry's body just as certainly as he controlled his lowest underlings. He had said that he would make Derry betray his master, and Derry had no doubt that Wencit could do it, if he said he would. He had also forbidden Derry's escape through death—though that, perhaps, could be circumvented. Derry would not, could not, permit himself to be used as the instrument of Morgan's betrayal.

Digging down through the straw, Derry used the blade to clear away to the bare clay, hollowing out a narrow hole that was deep enough to hold the hilt. He glanced at the door, hoping that there was no one watching what he was about to do, then lay down on his stomach beside the hole he had prepared, propped on his elbows, and held the dagger in his two hands.

Suicide. It was an act forbidden even in thought for a man who believed, as Derry did, in the God of the Church Militant. For the believer, the taking of one's own life was a grave offense, damning one to an eternal torment in Hell.

But there were things worse than Hell, Derry argued with himself. The betrayal of self, the betrayal of friends . . . Himself he could not help. He had been tested against the master of Torenth and had been found wanting. There was no one to blame for that. But, Morgan—the powerful Deryni lord had saved Derry's life more than once, had more than once snatched him from the jaws of death against unthinkable odds. Could Derry, in conscience, now refuse to do the same for him?

Grasping the dagger by its blade, Derry gazed at the cross-hilt for a long moment, rehearsing half a dozen childhood prayers and discarding them. Then he touched the cross-hilt fervently to his lips before placing it pommel-first into the hole in the floor. A compassionate God would surely understand—and Derry's faith in that compassion would have to sustain him through that which he must now do . . . and whatever came after.

With the blade pointing upward like a silver flame, Derry raised himself from his elbows and shifted sideways, positioning himself with the blade angled up beneath his ribcage.

It should not take long in his depleted condition. His arms would give out in a few seconds, and he would no longer be able to hold his body off the shining steel. Even Wencit could not prevent the fall of an exhausted body.

He closed his eyes as his arms started to tremble with fatigue, thinking of a day long ago when he and Morgan had ridden laughing through the fields of Candor Rhea. He remembered the battles and the good horses, the girls he had tumbled in the hay of his father's stables, his first stag hunt . . .

And then he started to fall. . . .

CHAPTER TWENTY

*"The Lord hath delivered me into their hands,
from whom I am not able to rise up."*

LAMENTATIONS 1:14

PANIC! No! He could not do it!

As the blade began to press deeper against Derry's flesh, again drawing blood, his arms suddenly stiffened, bearing him up and to one side, away from the death he sought, to collapse into the straw. With an agonized moan, he wrenched the weapon from the floor and tried to slash it against his wrists, against his choking throat.

But it was no use. He could do nothing to injure himself. It was as though an unseen hand deflected every attempt, always guiding the blade to harmless destinations.

Wencit! Wencit had been right! Derry could not even kill himself!

Weeping uncontrollable tears of frustration, Derry flung himself onto his stomach and sobbed, his wounds burning with his exertion and his head ringing. The dagger was still in his hand, and he stabbed it hysterically into the straw-covered clay floor, again and again, until, after a while, the flailing ceased and the sobs subsided. Fading consciousness took with it some of the futility of his situation.

Once he thought he came to. Or perhaps he only dreamed it. He thought he had been asleep for only a few minutes when he became aware of a gentle touch on his shoulder— the tentative probe of a human hand.

He flinched and tensed, fearing that it was Wencit, come back to torment him, but the hand did not punish, and the pain did not come. When Derry finally gathered the courage to turn his head toward the intruder, he was astonished to see a gray-cowled stranger gazing down at him in concern. Somehow he was not afraid, though he knew he probably ought to be.

He started to open his mouth to speak, but the stranger shook his head and placed a cool, warning hand over his mouth. The stranger's eyes glowed with a silver, smoky hue, a frosty light in the shadow of the monkish hood; and Derry had the impression of silvered-gold hair, that he had seen the face somewhere before, though he could not remember where. But then his vision blurred, and he began to drift again.

He became vaguely aware of the man's hands gliding over his body, probing at his wounds, and of a lessening of the hurt from those wounds, but he could not seem to focus his eyes anymore. He felt the man's touch on his right hand and thought he heard a sigh of dismay as the man lifted the hand to inspect something cold and silvery on the right forefinger; but he could not seem to move a muscle to resist.

He started to drift again as the stranger rose. He wondered idly if he was truly seeing a nimbus of light around the man's head, or if he was only hallucinating. Somehow, even that did not seem to matter.

Then the man was backing toward the door, staring at him strangely. Derry had the distinct impression, as the door closed behind the gray-clad figure, that there was a touch of blue to the man's apparel, that a darker countenance flickered beneath the façade of fairness. The thought crossed his mind that something very odd had just occurred, that there was something he ought to be able to deduce regarding what had just happened.

But he could not make the connection. With that, his head fell back on the straw in merciful oblivion again, and he slept.

DERRY could not have known that Kelson's army even then was drawing near to the plain of Llyndruth. Since Kelson was eager to reach the proposed battle site before dark, the royal army had been on the march since before dawn. Reconnaissance patrols and single scouts had been sent ahead throughout the day, hoping to gain intelligence of the surrounding area before the entire army should come upon danger unprepared. But nothing out of the ordinary had been reported until late afternoon, when they were within three hours' march of the Cardosa plain. The news, when it did come, was most unsettling.

One of the patrols had been casting ahead and slightly to the west of the main line of march when they spotted what appeared to be a skirmish band of foot soldiers waiting silently in a brush-filled ravine: perhaps fifty men, with sunlight glinting off the polished steel of cuirass, helmet, and lance—an apparent ambush. Not wishing to reveal their own presence, the outriders had refrained from going close enough to make positive identification of the troop's battle pennons and returned immediately to inform the King.

Kelson frowned as he tried to fathom the enemy's intent. The planned ambush could only be a diversionary tactic of some sort, for so small a band could not hope to inflict serious damage on the entire combined forces of Gwynedd. But such a mission would be suicide for the ambushers—unless, of course, there was sorcery afoot to protect the men and change the seemingly impossible odds.

That thought sobered Kelson immediately, and after a moment's reflection he called General Gloddruth to his side. Gloddruth had been acting as Kelson's aide-de-camp since his return from the Rengarth treachery, and he listened carefully as the young commander-in-chief gave revised marching orders to be passed down the chain of command. Then, as Gloddruth turned to go, Kelson rode forward to locate Morgan and seek his opinion.

Kelson found the Deryni duke at the head of the main column astride a great white destrier, with Duncan, Nigel, and Bishop Cardiel gathered at his side. Morgan was questioning a frightened-looking scout on a bay rouncy, who seemed barely able to keep his skittish mount in check. Beyond, half a dozen more horsemen milled in a tight circle, churning up dust, their leather jerkins and badges identifying them as scouts of the same unit as the man with Morgan. The Deryni general looked annoyed as he talked to the scout, and Cardiel was fidgeting nervously with the ends of his reins.

Only Nigel nodded greeting as Kelson joined them. The king noted with a shock that Duncan was fingering the tattered remnants of a bloodstained battle pennon with the crimson roses and sleeping lion of Clan McLain. Wordlessly he kneed his mount closer to Morgan, his eyebrows lifting in question.

"I am not able to tell you what has happened, my prince," Morgan said, curbing his horse sharply as it reached out to nip at Kelson's black. "Apparently someone has left us a none-too-subtle warning on the other side of the rise. Dobbs brought back that banner," he gestured toward the silk in Duncan's hands, "but he seems reluctant to say much about it. I think we'd better investigate."

"Do you think it's a trap?" Kelson asked, shivering as he glanced again at the banner. "Dobbs, what did you see out there?"

Dobbs chanced a furtive look at his king, then gathered his reins more tightly in his fist and crossed himself with a shudder.

"God hae mercy on 'em, Sire, it—I cannae speak of it," he whispered, his voice rasping in his throat. "It was hideous, obscene. Sire, let us be away from this place now, while we still may! We cannae fight an enemy what would do this to its foes!"

"Let's go," Morgan said, shaking his head firmly to cut off further protests.

With an impatient yank at the bit, Morgan whirled his mount and urged it up the near side of the rise, followed closely by Kelson, Duncan, and the others. At the top, Warin and two of his lieutenants were already waiting. Bishop Arilan was with them, standing in his stirrups to stare out over the plain, and Warin nodded curtly as the others drew rein beside him.

"Something is very wrong, Sire," he said in a low voice, nodding toward the plain stretching before them. "Look at the kites and the hawks circling. There are some of them on the ground as well. I do not like it."

As Kelson followed Warin's gaze, a gasp escaped his lips. Out on the plain, perhaps half a mile away, he could see what appeared to be a band of armed men standing at attention amid a cluster of low brush. The men cast long, lean shadows in the late afternoon sun, and the sunlight turned their armor and helmets to a ruddy gold.

But he could see no movement save for the ceaseless wheeling of the carrion birds. As Kelson squinted against the sinking sun he could make out more of the birds, gorged and bloated, waddling drunkenly among the men standing there—and no man moved. Farther to the west, yet more of the carrion eaters darkened the sky above the small ravine where Kelson's scouts had first reported activity. It required little effort to imagine what was going on in the ravine, and Kelson ducked his head and swallowed visibly.

"Are—are all the banners ours?" he asked in a small voice.

One of Warin's lieutenants closed a spyglass and gave a curt nod. "Aye, Sire—an' they're all dead. Or at least I hope they are," he added in a lower voice, choking back an involuntary sob.

"Enough of this," Morgan said, momentarily taking command. "Wencit has left us a grisly message—that much is clear. The extent of that message remains to be read. Nigel, signal an escort to join us. The rest of you, come with me."

With that he touched spurs to his mount and began cantering down the slope, Duncan and the bishops falling in behind. Kelson glanced hesitantly at Nigel, who seemed to be waiting for some confirmation from his royal nephew, who nodded and then fell in behind Morgan and the others. Warin rode down the shallow slope at his side, as Nigel turned to summon the required escort. Though the beginning of their ride was brisk enough, the horses slowed as they drew near the gory scene, for the stench of death was heavy in the air. Several of the horses shied as the great, gorged carrion birds took wing and deserted their feast.

The fate of the men beneath the circling birds now became all too clear. The men wore the blue, silver, and crimson of Kierney and Cassan—Duncan's house—and each had been impaled upon a narrow wooden stake set firmly into the ground, driving the sharpened point of the stake upward into the body cavity. Several of the bodies—those originally protected by less armor than the others—had been almost completely devoured by the carrion eaters. The air reeked with the stench of sun-ripened flesh and bird droppings.

Kelson blanched whiter than the egret feather that trembled in the badge on his cap, and the others were pale and silent as they drew rein. Duncan shook his head and closed his eyes against the gory sight, and even Warin reeled in the saddle, as though he might faint away at any second.

Cardiel pulled a square of white linen from his sleeve and pressed it hard against his nose and mouth for a long moment, obviously fighting a rebellious stomach, then turned dull eyes on Kelson.

"Sire—" Cardiel's voice choked, and he had to begin again.

"Sire, what manner of man could do such a thing to fellow creatures? Has such a man no soul? Does he summon demons from the black reaches to serve him with magic?"

Kelson shook his head bitterly. "Not magic, Bishop," he whispered. "This is human horror, calculated to terrify far more than any mere magic Wencit could leave us at this distance."

"But, why *this*?"

Morgan curbed his skittish horse and swallowed with an effort. "Wencit knows human fears," he said in a low voice. "To see our own, maimed and mutilated unto death like this—what greater horror can there be for fighting men? The man who conceived this—"

"No mere man—a Deryni!" Warin spat, jerking his horse around to glare at Morgan. "One who is Deryni and deranged! Sire"—his eyes flashed a fanatic fire that Kelson had thought to see quenched forever—"you see now what the Deryni are capable of! No human lord would have visited such wrath upon an enemy. It was a Deryni who has done this thing! I told you that they were not to be trust—"

"Hold your tongue!" Kelson snapped, cutting him off. "I do not *condone* such an act, but there is ample historical precedent among humans for such atrocity—much to *all* our shame. You are not to bring up the Deryni matter for the duration. Is that clear?"

"Sire!" Warin began indignantly. "You wrong me. I never meant that you—"

"His Majesty knows what you meant," Arilan said wearily, shifting his weight in his saddle and scanning the scene before them. "What is more important at this point, however, is that . . ."

His voice trailed off thoughtfully as he glanced again at the impaled corpses, and he suddenly shifted his cloak to the horse's near side and swung down to the ground. As the others watched uncomprehendingly, the bishop approached the nearest corpse and pulled aside a fold of its cloak. After a reflective pause, he moved to another one and repeated the process. His head was cocked in consternation as he turned back to Kelson and the others, who still watched from their horses, mystified.

"Sire, would you come here a moment? This is very odd."

"Come and look at dead men? Arilan, I don't need to see them closer. They're dead, horribly murdered. Is that not enough?"

Arilan shook his head. "No, I do not think it is. Morgan, Duncan, come with him, if you please. I believe these men were dead before they were placed here—and likely not from impaling. Perhaps they even died in battle. All of them have massive wounds, but there is very little blood."

Exchanging puzzled glances, Morgan and Duncan dismounted and joined the Deryni bishop, Kelson scurrying after them. Nigel and an armed escort thundered down the slope from the army, drawing up in horror as they saw what lay before them. On the rise in the background, more of Kelson's officers were gathering on the crest, curious as to what was happening on the plain below. As Nigel swung down from his horse, Arilan beckoned him to join them and pointed to a third body.

"Look at this. Now I am certain they did not die here. Many of the wounds do not even match the blood and rents on the clothing. They may even have had their uniforms changed to make them look better at a distance. For that matter," he started to remove the helmet of the next man, "some of these men might not even be our—"

As he tugged at the helmet, he gave a sudden, horrified gasp as it came away empty in his hands. The corpse that had borne the helmet was headless, with a blackened stump of neck extending where the head should have been.

Arilan attempted to cover his consternation by moving on to the next corpse, but removal of this helmet produced the same result: another headless body. With a muffled curse, Arilan moved to another and another yet, each time knocking empty helmets from headless shoulders. In fury he turned away from the others and slammed a fist into an open palm.

"Damn them all to eternal perdition! I knew him ruthless, but I did not think even Wencit capable of this!"

"This—this is Wencit's work?" Nigel managed to stammer, swallowing down bile as he surveyed the carnage.

"So we must assume," Arilan murmured.

Nigel shook his head in disbelief. "My God, there must be half a hundred men here." He had to struggle to choke back a sob. "And I would be willing to wager that every one of them is headless. These men were our friends, our comrades in arms. Why, we don't even know *who* they are! We—"

He broke off and turned away abruptly to bury his face in one gloved hand, and Kelson dared a quick look at Morgan. Other than the nervous clenching and unclenching of gloved fists, the Deryni duke was standing impassively, showing no outward sign of emotion. Duncan, too, was controlling his anguish well—though at what cost, Kelson could not even begin to guess, for they had believed these to be Cassani and Kierney men, Duncan's own.

Morgan must have sensed Kelson's eyes upon him then, for at that moment he looked up, brushing Kelson's shoulder in reassurance as he moved past to confront the rest of the company.

"A burial detail will be required, gentlemen—no, a funeral pyre. There is no time to bury this many men. Someone must see to the ones across the plain, in the ravine, too. Sire," he turned slightly toward the king, "what is your feeling about informing the men what has happened?"

"They must be told."

"I agree," Morgan said with a nod. "And I think we must stress that these men were dead before they were brought here; that in all likelihood, they died in honorable battle—not spitted like so many wild animals."

"That should give *some* measure of comfort," Arilan agreed, "yet still remind them why we are fighting—and the measures a ruthless enemy may take to achieve his ends."

Kelson nodded, his composure returning. "Very well. Uncle Nigel, have your men take them down and prepare a funeral pyre."

Nigel nodded agreement.

"And Warin, if you and such of your men as you feel necessary would attend to the others in the ravine . . ."

Warin bowed stiffly in the saddle. "As you wish, Sire."

"Bishop Arilan, Bishop Cardiel—there will be no time for proper services just now, but perhaps you and your brethren can say a few words while the men prepare the pyres. And if any of you should find any indication of the identities of the victims, I—I should like to be informed. It is difficult, I know, without the heads, but—" He shuddered and averted his face slightly. "Please do what you can."

With his head lowered, Kelson walked briskly back to his horse, turning the animal's head as he mounted so that he would not have to look for even a second longer at the terrible sight he was leaving. As he cantered up the slope alone to rejoin his other generals and bishops, Arilan watched him go, watched Warin and his men start toward the ravine with Cardiel, watched the men of Nigel's escort dismount and begin the grisly task of laying the slaughtered men to rest. As the soldiers spread through the ranks of the dead to gently lift each man to the ground, Arilan moved slowly to where Morgan and Duncan stood watching dumbly, coming between them to lay a comforting arm across the shoulder of each.

"Our young king is sorely troubled, my friends, as am I," he said in a low voice, watching with morbid fascination as the soldiers slowly cleared a path in the terrible forest of stakes. "How do you think this will affect him in the days to come?"

Morgan snorted and crossed his arms across his chest. "You have a talent for asking questions I cannot answer,

Bishop. How will any of us react? Do you know what worries me more than this?"

Arilan shook his head, and Duncan looked at him in apprehension.

"Well," Morgan continued in a low voice, "for now these are just bodies—horribly defiled, I will grant you, but still only bodies. For all we know, they could be dead Torenthi soldiers dressed in captured Cassani livery—though I doubt it." He paused, and his eyes narrowed.

"But somewhere, someone knows who those men really are. The bodies may be here, but the heads are somewhere else—and I dread what may happen when we find those heads."

THEIR departure from that place was delayed yet another hour while the funeral pyres were lit, and then each column of soldiers must make its final salute as it passed the smoking pyres of the dead men. There had been rumblings among the ranks as the news of the slaughter spread, and the expected fears and speculations as to the identities of both victims and perpetrators. But in all, the army had taken the incident in stride. None could now question the evil of Wencit of Torenth, who could condone such atrocities upon a vanquished enemy—even if the mutilations had been done after the men were dead. Such a man deserved no mercy from the King of Gwynedd. When battle was joined in the morning, it was certain to be hard and bloody.

So the army had marched on, leaving in its wake two smoldering beacons whose greasy smoke spiraled upward in an ever-widening swath of black against the sky. They encountered no further harassment as they went, perhaps because the enemy had deemed the spectacle of the previous hour sufficient; or perhaps they were merely saving their strength for the battle in the morning.

Whatever their reason, Kelson was glad of it as they reached their final campsite, for darkness was falling. The day had been long and grueling, the past hours emotionally draining. The army would need all of the rest they could get.

It took nearly three hours to make camp, but finally Kelson was sufficiently satisfied with the camp's defenses to retire to his tent for a light supper. Morgan, Duncan, and Nigel joined him, but they kept the tone light all through the meal, none of them wishing to discuss the day in detail. After the last glasses of wine had been poured, Kelson stood and held his goblet aloft, the others rising as well.

"Gentlemen, I give you a final toast. To the loyal dead—and to victory: may it come tomorrow to the just!"

"And to the King!" Nigel added quickly, before Kelson could raise the cup to his lips. "Long may he reign!"

"To victory and the King!" the others repeated, and tossed off their drinks.

Kelson allowed himself a wan smile, then raised his own cup and drank, finally setting it on a small table and sinking back into his chair. He glanced at each of them wearily, then shook his head and sighed.

"If any of you are half as tired as I am . . ." He sighed again. "But, no matter. We all have further duties to attend to. Morgan, may I ask a favor of you?"

"Certainly, my prince."

Kelson nodded. "I should like you to see the Lady Richenda and inform her what has happened today—without elaborating on the graphic details, of course. She is a very refined lady. Tell her that I shall think no less of her if she chooses not to try appealing to her husband tomorrow."

"From what I have heard," Duncan said with a wry chuckle, "he will have his hands full convincing her of that. The Lady Richenda may be a very refined lady, but she seems to me a very stubborn one."

Kelson smiled. "So I have come to suspect. But I cannot fault her when that stubbornness is for the Crown. Morgan, try to make her understand what we are up against. I have no right to ask her assistance under the circumstances. I shouldn't even have allowed her to come."

"I shall do my best, my prince," Morgan agreed.

"Thank you. Now, Uncle Nigel, I wonder if you would come with me to look over the northernmost defenses. I am not convinced that they are adequate, and I should like your opinion."

As Kelson pulled out several maps to show to his uncle and went on with his briefing, Morgan took his leave and slipped out of the royal pavilion. Kelson's request both pleased and troubled him, for he had not been at all certain it was wise to seek out Richenda of Marley again—not after their all too brief but emotionally potent meeting at Dhassa.

A part of him, of course, positively yearned to see her again; but another, more cautious part of him—a part which, he strongly suspected, was closely bound up with his personal sense of honor—that part warned him to stay away, warned that no honor could come of permitting himself to become more emotionally involved with another man's wife—especially if he might have to kill that man on the morrow.

But now the matter had been taken out of his hands. He had been given an order by his king, and he must obey. Pushing aside a curious sense of elation at being thus forced to circumvent the proddings of his conscience, he made his way through the camp until he came to Bishop Cardiel's compound.

The bishop had not yet returned, was probably overseeing troop placement with Warin and Arilan somewhere, but the bishop's guards passed the King's Champion unchallenged. Very shortly Morgan was moving across the torch-lit common before the Countess of Marley's bright blue tent. Torches blazed to either side of the entry-way, but he could see through the open flap that the interior was lit by the softer glow of candles.

Swallowing nervously, Morgan stepped to the open flap of the tent and cleared his throat.

"My lady countess?" he called softly.

He heard a faint rustle of fabric, heralding the appearance of a tall, dark form in the opening to the tent. Morgan's heart missed a beat for just an instant, then resumed its normal pace, for the woman was a sister, not the Lady Richenda.

"Good evening, Your Grace," the sister murmured, inclining her wimpled head. "Her Ladyship is within, putting the young master to bed. Did you wish to speak with her?"

"If you please, Sister. I have a message for her from the king."

"I shall tell her, Your Grace. Wait here, please." As the sister withdrew, Morgan turned to gaze out into the darkness beyond the circle of torchlight. After what seemed like only a few seconds, another rustling heralded the appearance of a different form: Richenda of Marley, with a sky-blue mantle drawn over a flowing white under-robe, her flame-colored hair trailing loosely down her back. A single candle held in a silver holder shed a golden light across her face.

"My lady." Morgan inclined his head in salute, trying not to look too closely at her. Richenda dropped him the slightest of curtsies and also inclined her head.

"Good evening, Your Grace. Sister Luke mentioned something about a message from the king?"

"Yes, my lady. I suppose you have heard somewhat regarding the delay this afternoon, before we reached our campsite?"

"I have." The answer was quiet, direct, and the woman lowered her eyes, gesturing for him to enter. "Please come in, Your Grace. Your Deryni reputation will not be enhanced if you are seen loitering outside my tent. Nor will mine."

"Would you rather have me seen *entering* your tent, my lady?" Morgan quipped, ducking his head to step inside.

"I am certain that Sister Luke can attest to the propriety of our meeting," she replied with a slight smile. "Pray, excuse me a moment while I make certain my son is asleep."

"Of course."

The pavilion was divided within by a dense but faintly translucent curtain of royal blue. He could follow Richenda's movements behind the curtain by the glow of her candle, but he could not make out details. Presumably the sleeping accommodations for the countess, her son, and the sister were in the second chamber, since he could see no such preparations on the side where he was now standing.

The furnishings of his present location seemed to consist of two folding camp chairs, a few small trunks, and a rack of yellow candles set near the center pole. Carpets had been laid underfoot to keep the dampness out, but they were not of any special quality—doubtless borrowed from Cardiel's stores, with such short notice. He hoped that the lady and her boy were not enduring too much discomfort.

Richenda slipped back into the outer chamber and held a finger to her lips, a tender smile on her face.

"He is asleep now, Your Grace. Would you care to look in on him? He is only four, you know, but I'm afraid I am terribly proud of him."

Seeing that she wished it, Morgan nodded acquiescence and followed her into the inner chamber. As they entered, the sister looked up from a stack of bedclothes she was sorting and bowed slightly as though to leave, but Richenda shook her head and led Morgan to the small pallet where her son slept.

Brendan Coris had his mother's reddish-golden hair and, as far as Morgan could see, resembled his father Bran Coris very little. Certainly, there was a familial resemblance around the nose, but the rest was his mother's influence, delicate features almost too fragile for a man-child. The boy's long, thick lashes lay on his cheeks like cobwebs, and the rumpled, bright hair that Morgan had first seen in a coach by Saint Torin's was gold-rich in the candlelight. Morgan could not remember the color of the boy's eyes, but he suddenly knew that if the boy opened them, they would be the same cornflower hue as his mother's.

Richenda smiled and tucked the sleeping furs more

closely around her slumbering son, then signed for Morgan to withdraw with her to the outer chamber. As Morgan followed, he could not help noticing another sleeping-pallet in the inner chamber, this one canopied with blue and cream silk. Resolutely he put it from his mind as Richenda turned to face him again.

"I thank you for coming, Your Grace," Richenda said, sitting in one of the chairs and motioning him to the other. "I must confess, I have felt the lack of human company these past days since Dhassa. Sister Luke is a dear, but she says little beyond what is required. The others prefer not to associate with a traitor's wife."

"Even when the traitor's wife has offered to aid the Crown, and is a young and helpless woman?" Morgan asked softly.

"Even then."

Morgan lowered his head, wondering what he dared say to this exquisite creature to whom he was so strongly drawn.

"Your homeland—is it like Corwyn?" he asked abruptly, rising to begin pacing the confines of the outer chamber.

Richenda's eyes followed him as he paced, her face expressionless. "Somewhat. Not so hilly, though. It is said that Corwyn has a monopoly on the most beautiful mountains in this region. Bran says that—" Her voice faltered, and she began again.

"My husband says that our Marley has rich farmland, though—some of the richest in all the Eleven Kingdoms. Did you know that there has never been a serious famine in Marley, going back more than four hundred years? Even when there is drought and pestilence in other lands, Marley at least survives. I used to think it was a sign of divine favor."

"And now?"

Richenda studied her hands clasped in her lap and shrugged. "Oh, it changes nothing of the past, I suppose, but now that Bran—oh, what's the use? I keep coming back to the same subject, don't I? And I know that the last thing you wish to talk about on the eve of battle is a traitor earl. Why did the king send you, Your Grace?"

"Partly because of what we found today, my lady," he replied, after only the briefest of pauses. "You indicated that you had heard the reason for our delay. Are you aware of the extent—"

"Headless corpses impaled on wooden stakes," she interrupted in a clipped voice. "Cassani uniforms on hacked bodies whose wounds do not match their clothing." She looked him full in the eyes.

"Did the king send you to ask whether I thought my husband did these things? Do you wish me to say that, yes, Bran is at least capable of such acts? You must know that I have been in the king's custody for many days now, and hence cannot say whether my husband actually participated in the day's work!"

Morgan found himself momentarily speechless, taken aback both by her candor and by the tenor of her outburst.

"Forgive me, my lady, but you misjudge both the king and myself. No one ever meant to imply that you had knowledge of what your husband planned. Indeed, all signs point to his defection being strictly a matter of opportunity. A man who planned to betray his king would hardly leave his wife and heir in jeopardy. If you have received the impression that your loyalty is in question, I do apologize. It was not intended."

Richenda looked across at him for a long time, her blue eyes never wavering from his, then shifted her glance to her lap. Her betrothal ring gleamed dully in the candlelight.

"Pray, forgive me. I should not have taken out my frustration on you. Nor is the king to blame for my apprehensions." Her voice was rock-steady.

"As for Bran, I cannot say whether you are correct or not. I pray that his betrayal was not planned, yet I know that he was—is—ambitious. Even our marriage was largely brought about to consolidate vague claims he had for several manors adjoining Marley, that he knew would be part of my dowry.

"But he was a good father, if not a model husband. He loves Brendan dearly, even if our relationship is largely one of state." She paused, then shook her head. "No, that is hardly fair. I think that Bran did come to love me after a time, in his own fashion. After what has happened today, though, I hardly think that makes much difference."

"Then, you think he is beyond your reach?" Morgan said quietly, not wishing to touch further on her personal relationship with Bran.

Richenda shrugged. "I have no way of knowing, my lord. If he would agree to what happened today, then anything I might say will probably make little difference to him. Perhaps he would listen for Brendan's sake. I am still willing to make the effort, if the king will permit it."

"It is a needless risk, my lady."

"Perhaps. But we must, each of us, play out our parts as they have been written for us. Mine, it seems, is to play the traitor's wife and beg for my husband's life. And yet, I cannot expect the king to sacrifice whole armies for my sake. When all is said and done, Brendan and I can expect to be left with nothing but a traitor's name, regardless of the outcome of the battle. It is not a pleasant state to contemplate, is it?"

"No, it is not," Morgan agreed gently.

Sighing, Richenda rose to lean against the center pole of the tent, then turned to gaze across at Morgan.

"And you, Your Grace—what is it you hope to gain from all of this? You have great powers and much wealth, the king favors you, and yet you gamble everything on a single throw of the dice. If Gwynedd loses this war, you cannot possibly survive. It is well known that Wencit will not tolerate conquered Deryni in his dominions. Such men would always be a threat to his power."

Morgan lowered his eyes and studied the toes of his dusty boots.

"I am not certain I can answer that, my lady. As you doubtless know, I have been something of a rebel all my life. I have never made any secret of my Deryni heritage. I first used my powers openly to help King Brion keep his throne—more than fifteen years ago. Since then, I suppose my aim, in an indirect way, has been to continue using my powers openly, in the hope that one day all Deryni could be as free as I. Yet, even in that, there is irony—for when have I, as a Deryni, ever been entirely free?"

"But you *have* used your powers, have you not?"

"On occasion, and with great care." He waved a ringed hand depreciatingly. "But I must confess that such use has often brought about more ruin than reward. This present quarrel with the archbishops can be traced directly to my actions at Kelson's coronation, and then at Saint Torin's. If there had been no magic, we might all now be safely at home in our beds."

"We might," Richenda agreed. "Yet, if we were, Kelson would not now be king. And I doubt very much whether you and others of your kind would ever sleep well at night."

Morgan chuckled ironically, then sobered as Richenda remained silent.

"Forgive me, my lady, but I so seldom encounter a sympathetic stranger that I scarcely know how to behave. Most folk find it difficult to conceive how I can even admit to some of the things I have done. I sometimes wonder myself. It takes a bit of getting used to."

"Why should it? Are you ashamed of what you have done?"

Morgan cocked his head at her in faint surprise. "No, I am not. If I had to choose over again, I think I should make mostly the same choices. Of course, since that is not possible, the question is academic anyway, is it not?"

"Perhaps—though one must base future decisions on the past, do you not agree?"

"Your logic is flawless," Morgan admitted reluctantly. "But perhaps the problem goes deeper than you dream. We

Deryni are somewhat different from ordinary men, as you no doubt have gathered."

"*That* different?"

Richenda smiled at him rather oddly, then half-turned away from him. Against the light of the rack of candles behind her, Morgan could see her profile outlined in gold. After a moment she turned toward him again, her face unreadable against the brightness of the candlelight.

"My lord, may I make a confession to you?"

"I am not your priest, my lady," Morgan said lightly, leaning against the edge of a leather-bound trunk.

Richenda took a few steps toward him, her face still a gray blur against the candlelight, "Thank God and all the saints that you are *not* my priest, my lord! For if you were, I should never dare to say what is in my mind. I sense a bond between us that draws us close: fate, destiny, the will of God—call it what you will, though I think I—please don't look at me that way, my lord!"

Morgan had frozen with her first words and now sat in stunned silence, staring. That Richenda had spoken thus was at once too wondrous and too terrible to contemplate. He had thought his own emotions neatly tucked away and under control. But now, to have Richenda echoing those feelings . . .

He turned his face away and averted his eyes, trying to force himself to composure. "My lady, we must not. I—" He paused, then began again in words he hoped she would understand.

"My lady, long ago you took vows with a man. You bore his son. That man still lives. Regardless of the feelings, or their lack, that you and he shared, you still are—Richenda, I may have to kill your husband tomorrow. Does that mean nothing to you?"

Her voice was a whisper in the dim, flickering candlelight. "My husband is a traitor and must die, one way or another; I know that. I will mourn the goodness in him—for there was some of that. And I shall mourn that my son shall have no father, for Bran was that, too. But if fate guides your sword," her voice became softer still, "or your powers, to take his life tomorrow, I shall not hate you for it. How could I? You are my heart."

"Sweet *Jesu*, you must not say these things," he murmured, closing his eyes against the sight of her. "We *must* not, we *dare* not . . ."

"Oh, must I spell it out?" she whispered, taking one of his hands in hers and brushing her lips against its tanned back.

Morgan flinched at the contact of her flesh against his but forced himself to look down at her as she took his other hand in hers. As her hands closed over his, it was as though a great light glowed around them, and suddenly their minds were one.

Richenda was Deryni—Deryni in all the fullness born to those eldritch lords of old. Deryni—in all its splendor and pride and fulfilled power, with no guilt attached. In the first heady ecstasy of union with her mind, he was filled with a sense of wonder so profound that, in that instant, he knew with a certainty born at the root of all his powers that he had found that other part of himself, missing all his life. That whatever happened tomorrow, and for all the days of his life, he could endure it with this blessed woman at his side.

At length he saw her again through eyes instead of mind, and he staggered back a step and pulled his hands free in amazement. He stared at her for a long moment in awe, a part of him wondering idly if the sister in the next chamber was asleep—and praying that she was!—then lowered his eyes to stare blindly at the carpet beneath his feet. Reality had returned with a rush, and with it all the problems of the morrow.

"What has happened—this will make it that much more difficult for me tomorrow—you know that," he murmured reluctantly. "I have responsibilities which I assumed long before this burden was laid upon my heart. I have been the catalyst for much of what has happened."

"Then I have given you that much more to fight for," she said softly.

"Yes. And if I am forced to kill Bran tomorrow, or am instrumental in his death, then what?"

"We both will know that you do it for the right reasons, if it comes to that," she replied.

"Will we?"

Before she could answer, there was the slight clatter of guards coming to attention across the common outside, and then low voices in the darkness. Recalled to duty with a start, Morgan moved to the entryway and pulled back the flap farther to see who approached. At length a vague shadow dressed in black emerged from the ring of darkness beyond the torches and strode toward the tent: Duncan. And by the expression on his face, something was amiss.

"What is it?" Morgan asked, stepping into the entryway and blocking Duncan's view of the interior.

Duncan ducked his head apologetically. "Sorry to intrude, but I checked your tent and you weren't there. The king wishes you to see something."

With a clipped nod of agreement, Morgan turned back briefly to meet Richenda's eyes once more—there was no need for further words—then inclined his head in leave-taking and joined Duncan.

"Sorry. It took a bit longer than I expected. What have you got?"

Duncan's voice was carefully neutral, avoiding any reference to the place Morgan had just left. "I'm not sure. We are hoping you can tell us. It sounds like Wencit's men are building something."

"Building something?" They were passing a guard post, and Morgan almost missed the salute as he turned to stare at his cousin. Duncan shrugged.

"This way. We can hear it best from over here."

As they approached the northern limits of the camp, one of the guards from the last outpost detached himself from his comrades and headed into the darkness ahead, which was lightened only by starlight. Morgan and Duncan followed, dropping to a crouch at his gesture to snake along the last few yards on their bellies.

At the crest of the ridge, they found Kelson, Nigel, and a pair of scouts already there, lying on their stomachs and gazing out over the plain of the enemy encampment. The enemy watch fires stretched north as far as the eye could see, and high above at the summit of the pass, the torches on the rampart walls of captive Cardosa twinkled in the thin air.

Morgan scanned the array quickly, for he had inspected the plain earlier; then he squirmed into place beside Kelson and nudged the young king with his elbow.

"What's this about them building something?" he whispered.

Kelson shook his head slightly and nodded toward the enemy camp. "Listen. It's very faint, but sometimes the wind carries it better. What does it sound like to you?"

Morgan listened, slowly extending his Deryni senses to heighten his hearing. He was aware at first only of the normal sounds of military encampment, both from their camp and from the enemy below: the usual sounds of low voices, of horses blowing and stamping in the quiet, the call of the watch changing, the rattle of mess kits and weapons being cleaned.

But then he was able to filter out the ordinary sounds until he detected another which was far and strange. He cocked his head and closed his eyes to listen better, then glanced at Kelson with an odd expression on his face.

"You're right. It sounds like someone hammering on wood. And sometimes I hear what sounds like chopping."

"That's what it sounded like to us, too," Kelson replied, resting his chin on his hands and staring into the night once more.

"Now, the next question is, what is Wencit building? What is he doing with wood and hammers and axes in the middle of the night before battle? And why?"

CHAPTER TWENTY-ONE

*"He hath called an assembly against me to
crush my young men."*

LAMENTATIONS 1:15

THE next day looked to become unseasonably warm and hu-
mid once the sun fully rose, but at dawn it was still pleasant
enough as the army of Gwynedd took up its battle forma-
tions. Well before first light, the men had been roused, their
captains moving among them to supervise rationing and
arming before the priests came to perform their sacred functions. Often, final sacraments went hand in hand with final
briefings, for there was much to say and little time to say it.

By dawn the men were in position, column on column of
them, row on row—nearly two thousand mounted knights,
twice that many archers, and the rest foot soldiers. The men
were silent as they formed up, even the horses strangely
calm in the wan morning light. Of enemy activity there was
as yet little sign, though the men of Gwynedd knew that
they were there and preparing, less than a mile away. Whispered questions rippled through the ranks as the sun
climbed in the eastern sky behind the enemy and there still
came no sign whether or when battle would be joined.

On a small knoll to the right of the center lines, King

Kelson and his commanders had gathered to survey the site of the coming battle. The dawn had brought with it the not unexpected sight of severed heads stuck on pikes all along the leading edge of the enemy encampment. Warin and Nigel were taking turns scanning the faces of the slain with their glasses, hoping to make positive identifications.

The distance was too great, and decay too far progressed, for any real recognition, but the spectacle was having its desired effect on the waiting men. Though the troops of Gwynedd knew that Wencit was trying to undermine their morale, that the heads might not even belong to slain Cassani men, still they could not be sure. Eyes strained across the mile-wide space separating the two armies, and many lips framed speculations; but it was all futile. Frayed nerves grew yet more ragged as the hour wore on.

Kelson, meanwhile, was absorbed in his own concerns. He studied a map as he sat his horse, a hard biscuit clutched forgotten in one hand as he leaned to hear what Morgan was saying about the location of reserve cavalry units. The young king appeared rested and confident, but his gaze kept returning to the piked heads along the enemy's front lines. There was, as yet, no sign of Wencit or any of his ranking officers, and the enemy ranks stood at ease, row on row, as the sun rose higher still.

After a while, Bishops Arilan and Cardiel left their troops and rode up the knoll where Kelson sat, joining Duncan and a worried-looking General Gloddruth a few yards from the king's side. It was Arilan who first noticed the beginnings of movement behind the enemy lines, and kneed his horse closer to touch Kelson's sleeve and point as a gap opened and a small contingent of horsemen emerged. The lead rider bore a traditional white parley banner.

"Nigel, can you read the others' devices?" the king said, fumbling at his saddle to draw out his own spyglass.

"Not at this distance, Sire. Shall I send out a party to meet them?"

"Not yet. Let's be careful on this. Gloddruth, get one of your men ready to ride."

The horsemen drew to a halt perhaps four hundred yards from their own lines, only the rider with the parley banner continuing toward the center of the field. With a nod, Kelson signaled Gloddruth to send out his own man; and as the Gwynedd rider was dispatched, Kelson lifted his glass to scan the men waiting on the plain beyond.

Seven men sat blooded horses behind the banner rider. Four of them could be mostly dismissed as a military escort of mounted archers, liveried in the tawny orange of Torenth. The men were bearded, turbans swathed around their steel caps, with short recurve bows slung across their backs and short swords at their knees.

But the other three were not mere fighting men. One Kelson judged to be a priest or a monk, black robe kilted up around his knees, a dark cloak muffled and closely hooded around his shoulders. But the other two were High Lords of Torenth, bright as peacocks in their battle silks and steel. Arilan identified one of them as Duke Lionel of Arjenol, kinsman to Wencit himself. He was the one wearing white silk over his armor, the sun gleaming brightly from his gold-washed mail. An ebony braid hung down his back from beneath his mailed coif, and the helm itself was adorned with a ducal coronet set with jewels.

The other—and here, the Deryni bishop's face hardened— was Rhydon of Eastmarch: a full Deryni, and apparently one whom Arilan had no cause to love, though he did not say so. Rhydon wore a flowing caftan of blue and gold brocade over his armor. Kelson could not see the man's face at this distance, even through his glass.

Kelson lowered the glass. The two banner riders had met in the center of the plain half a mile away and held their mounts in tight, mincing circles as they conferred. Kelson glanced at Morgan for a reaction but saw that he was staring beyond the front lines of the enemy to where a small forest of bright silk banners was moving onto a small rise. Beneath the banners, Kelson could see a handful of well-born riders. Morgan grunted as he put a spyglass to his eye and brought it into focus.

"There's Wencit," he said in a low voice. "I thought it was about time for him to make an appearance. I believe that's Bran Coris to his left."

Kelson studied the group for a moment with his own glass, then glanced at Morgan once more.

"Morgan, I think we'd better abandon the idea of the Lady Richenda trying to sway her husband. I have never liked the idea—and this is no place for a woman. I never should have brought her here."

Morgan shrugged and slipped his glass into the case at his knee. "I think you would have been hard-pressed to dissuade her, my prince. I tried to talk her out of it last night, and she—well, she is a very determined woman."

"So I have gathered. " Kelson sighed, turning in his saddle as Duncan conferred briefly with a guard captain and then moved his roan near. The banner riders were now galloping toward the Gwynedd lines, their white pennants snapping in the breeze.

"Our spotters identify Wencit's man as Baron Torval of Netterhaven," Duncan said. "He is one of Wencit's elite officers. They'll be bringing him here under guard to deliver his message."

Kelson nodded and turned to Morgan. "You don't suppose Wencit wants to offer terms already, do you?"

"Unlikely, my prince. And if so, they will be terms you could not think of accepting. That's the way the game is played. My guess is that this will be yet another attempt to keep us off balance. Watch what you say to him."

"Don't worry."

As the two riders approached, the Gwynedd men parted, and a band of Kelson's crack cavalry fell in with the enemy messenger to escort him up the rise to the king. The man was bareheaded, his manner arrogant and assured as he reined his horse to a halt a few yards away. His jeweled satin surcoat glittered in the sunlight as he bowed slightly in the saddle. He could not have been more than twenty.

"Kelson of Gwynedd?"

"I am he. Speak your message."

The young man bowed again, an unctuous smile touching his lips. "Torval of Netterhaven, my lord. I bear greetings from my Lord Duke Lionel, kinsman to our king." He wagged his head toward the party still sitting their horses near the center of the plain. "His Grace comes at the behest of King Wencit to propose terms for the coming battle. He desires that you and a like number of your men ride out to discuss the matter."

"Indeed?" Kelson said evenly. "And why should I parley with a mere duke? Why should I risk my safety if your king will not do the same? I do not see Wencit there on the plain."

"Then name another in your stead," Torval said glibly. "I am to remain hostage until their safe return."

"I see." Kelson's tone was glacial, his eyes hard and cold, and he stared pointedly at Torval until the young Torenthi lord was finally obliged to lower his gaze. At that, Kelson glanced at Morgan, at his other commanders, then gathered up his reins.

"Very well, we will parley with your Duke Lionel. Uncle Nigel, you are in command until we return. Morgan, you and Arilan will accompany me to the actual meeting in mid-field. Father Duncan and Warin will ride with us partway with an escort." He gestured toward two of the riders who had accompanied Torval up the rise. "Sergeant, please relieve the baron of his weapons and then bring him along with us."

Torval chuckled as he handed over the short dagger at his belt and let himself be surrounded by the two burly cavalrymen, retaining an insolent smile as his guards guided him to follow Kelson and the others down the slope. Kelson's men cheered as he rode by, but the ranks closed and were silent as the party rode out onto the plain.

About four hundred yards out, the group drew rein momentarily, with only Kelson, Morgan, and Arilan continuing out toward the center of the plain. Duncan and Warin remained with the hostage and his guards. Almost immediately, Lionel and Rhydon broke away from their guardian archers and began riding out to meet them. The quiet drumming of the horses' hooves on the turf was the only sound in the still morning air.

Kelson kept his gaze on the pair as they galloped toward him, trying to keep his head erect and his hands steady on the reins. Even so, his hands must have telegraphed his tension to his mount, for the high-strung black warhorse began prancing sideways and curvetting against the bit as the two riders approached. Kelson chanced a look at Morgan to his right, but the Deryni duke's attention seemed riveted on the approaching riders. Arilan, to Kelson's other side, seemed serene and unruffled, his handsome features betraying no hint of emotion. He might almost have been riding to church, so calm was he—or so it appeared.

"Hail, Kelson of Gwynedd!" Rhydon called, giving a slight bow as the two groups met and drew rein. "I was not altogether certain that you would come to treat with us personally. But, no matter. My king sends cordial greetings."

Arilan stared across at him coldly, a muscle rippling in his clenched jaw. "Guard your tongue, Rhydon. If you are the bearer of greetings, we may be assured that they are not cordial. Your reputation is well-known, as is your master's."

Rhydon turned in the saddle to bow silkily to Arilan, then gestured gracefully to Lionel as he returned his attention to Kelson. "Allow me to present His Grace the Duke of Arjenol, kinsman to Wencit, as you may be aware—and I am Rhydon of Eastmarch. I know my lord Bishop Arilan from other days of which we dare not speak, so the other man who rides at your side can only be the infamous Alaric Morgan. My master of Torenth sends special greetings to you, Your Grace—and a gift."

He reached into the front of his tunic and withdrew

something which he closed in his leather-covered fist, then touched heels gently to his horse's flanks and moved knee to knee by Morgan's right. As Rhydon held out his hand, Morgan made a tentative probe to be certain no treachery was involved, then let his gaze come to rest on the slowly opening hand.

"I believe this is may be yours," Rhydon said softly as he revealed a shining mass of silver and chain. "Wencit thought you would like to have it back. He who wore it meant something to you at one time, I think. I fear that the chain is broken."

Without looking further, Morgan knew what it was that Rhydon held. Wordlessly he stretched out his gloved palm and let Rhydon pour the silver into his own hand, felt the fleeting edge of Derry's essence as his fist closed over the Camber medallion. He allowed himself no trace of emotion in face or voice as he raised his eyes to Rhydon's.

"Is Derry dead?"

"No. However, you may wish him so, if your king proves unreasonable."

"You threaten us with Derry's safety?" Kelson demanded.

Rhydon chuckled, low, dangerous. "Not precisely, my young friend. We have learned—never mind how—that you hold certain high-ranking prisoners who are of great interest to us. My Lord Wencit is willing to negotiate a trade: your Derry, alive and unharmed, in exchange for our people."

"I am not aware of any Torenthi prisoners in our midst, are you, Morgan?" Kelson frowned. "To whom are you referring, my lord?"

"Did I say that they were Torenthi? Pray, forgive my imprecision. The prisoners are the Countess of Marley and her young son, the Lord Brendan. The Earl Bran wishes the return of his family."

Morgan's eyes widened and his heart seemed to rise into his throat, but he dared not look at Kelson. He could sense

Kelson's astonishment at the demand, and knew the young king to be momentarily taken aback by it, but he also knew that this must be Kelson's decision, regardless of Morgan's personal involvement. The trade could not be made; Morgan knew that. But *he* could not be the one to seal Derry's death warrant. The young Marcher lord deserved better, even if Morgan could not give it to him.

Morgan's fist tightened around the medallion in his hand—he could feel Kelson's gaze upon him—but he would not permit his stony gaze to shift from Rhydon's face. Kelson shifted uneasily in his saddle, glancing both at Morgan and then Arilan, then returned his gaze to Rhydon once more. Arilan said nothing; he, too, aware that this must be Kelson's decision—and well aware what that decision must be.

"You offer a trade," Kelson said warily. "Even if we were to consider such an offer, how can we be certain that Derry is still alive and unharmed, as you claim?"

Rhydon made an unctuous bow, then turned to raise an arm to his waiting escort a few hundred yards behind. At once the black-clad figure Kelson had dismissed as a monk detached himself from their company and began riding slowly toward them, his hood falling back on his shoulders as he came. Derry's eyes met Morgan's briefly as he drew rein a few yards behind Lionel and Rhydon, but he said nothing. There could be no doubt who he was.

Kelson looked hard at Lionel and Rhydon, then deliberately kneed his horse between them to approach Derry. Derry's face was like whey as his gaze met the king's, and Kelson could see that his hands were grasping the high pommel of his saddle in a death grip, that he was well aware what was at stake and what the king's decision must be. All at once Kelson's heart went out to the young lord.

"Derry, is it truly you?" he asked softly.

"Alas, I fear it is, Sire. I—I was captured shortly after I learned of Bran's defection. There was no way I could warn you. I am truly sorry."

"I know," Kelson whispered. He reached across to touch Derry's wrist in sympathy, his eyes averted, then backed his horse from between Lionel and Rhydon to rejoin Morgan and Arilan. His face was pale against the crimson surcoat he wore, but his hands were steady on the reins now.

"Forgive me, Lord Derry, but I know you will understand what I must do," he said formally. "I cannot allow women and children under my protection to be used as pawns in this game." He turned his gaze squarely on Rhydon and Lionel.

"My lords, you may tell your master that a prisoner exchange is not acceptable. The Lady Richenda and her son are, indeed, in my care and will come to no harm, but I will not surrender them to you under any circumstances. They have naught to do with Lord Bran's treason, and I would neither ask nor permit them to give themselves into the control of my enemy—even to save the life of one of my most trusted and well-loved lords."

Derry flashed a brave and slightly defiant smile at that, then bowed his head in resignation. Rhydon nodded slowly.

"I expected your reply, young lord. I quite understand. It is, of course, quite futile to hope that my Lord Wencit will not be angry and seek retribution. He is not accustomed to breaking promises he has made to those who serve him well. I fear there will be a high price to pay for your decision."

"I did not expect otherwise."

"Very well, then."

Rhydon bowed again in his saddle, then gestured curtly for Derry to return to the waiting guards. Derry took a last look over his shoulder at Morgan and the king as he obeyed, but his head was high as he began his ride back toward the enemy lines, Rhydon and Lionel following half a dozen lengths behind. Morgan felt a pang of grief as the three moved away, for he knew that Derry was riding to his death. Unable to look anymore, he, too, turned his horse back toward his own lines, Kelson and Arilan falling in wordlessly beside him. Like Derry, they did not look back.

From midway back to the Gwynedd lines, Duncan McLain watched as the three riders started toward him and his hostage, knowing by their carriage that the meeting had not gone well. He knew that the third rider with the enemy party had been Derry—he had seen him through his glass—and he knew the decision which must have been taken by the king.

Beside Duncan, the haughty Lord Torval sat his horse unmoving, his satin surcoat still a-gleam in the morning sun. The young lord's face was serene and almost trancelike, his hands resting lightly on the pommel of his saddle; and just for an instant Duncan had the impression that the Torenthi lord was not really there in mind, so little concern did he seem to have for his own safety.

To Torval's right, Warin was fidgeting with the hilt of his sword, nervous as a cat in the aftermath of what had just been played out in the center of the field. The two guards sat their horses behind, grim eyes darting from their prisoner to the returning king and his companions. The tableau seemed strangely calm and peaceful, almost like a dream. Abruptly, Duncan knew that it could not last.

Nor did it. Before the retreating riders had ridden more than a dozen yards from their meeting place, a sudden flurry of activity boiled up behind the enemy lines. Dozens of sturdy poles were hoisted briskly upright and seated in holes dug to receive them, each pole bearing a stoutly nailed crossbar at the top. Over each arm of the crossbars trailed a rope ending in a noose. As the poles thudded into their sockets, Duncan stood in his stirrups and brought his spyglass to bear, unable to control a gasp as pairs of prisoners in the blue and silver livery of Cassan—scores of them!—were forced to stand up beneath the poles, hands lashed cruelly behind their backs.

Even as this occurred, a banner was unfurled toward the center of the line: the banner of the Duke of Cassan, Duncan's father. At the same time, a tall, graying man wearing Cassan's sleeping lion and roses on his surcoat was prodded up a short platform beneath one of the crossbars, hands bound behind him, and a rope halter was made fast around his neck, his feet also bound. Duncan let out a groan, for it was Duke Jared himself!

Frozen with horror, Duncan watched as more ropes were secured around the necks of the rest of the men with Jared, two men beneath each pole, and a great cheer erupted from the enemy lines as all the ropes were pulled taut, the prisoners briskly hoisted off their feet to dangle and die. At the same time Duncan saw Morgan, Kelson, and Arilan pausing in the field a few hundred yards away to turn and gape, Kelson's horse plunging and rearing as he tried to control it.

A roar of disbelieving rage went up from the massed army of Gwynedd, and the front ranks began to waver. And then three things happened simultaneously. Warin, with a strangled cry of outrage, drew his sword and plunged it into the side of the smirking Lord Torval, striking but an instant ahead of Duncan, whose face had gone savage with the horror of his father's brutal death.

Kelson, white-lipped as he tried to control his plunging mount, bolted with Arilan and Morgan for his own lines, frantically signaling Warin and Duncan to retreat.

But Morgan, after only an instant's hesitation, wrenched his mount on its haunches and began spurring straight for the retreating Rhydon and Lionel, his drawn sword like lightning in his hand.

"Derry!" he screamed as he rode, his face gray with helpless rage. Behind him, the front ranks of the royal army were heaving forward, ready to break and attack, but again and again Morgan screamed Derry's name.

Derry somehow heard him. At Morgan's shout, Derry glanced over his shoulder and pulled up to gape openmouthed, instantly assessing the situation: Rhydon and Lionel spurring toward him as they saw him wavering, the bodies jerking at the ends of ropes behind him, and Morgan thundering toward all of that disaster at a dead gallop, sword in fist and shouting defiance.

At once Derry spun his horse on its haunches and bolted toward Morgan and the Gwynedd lines, instinctively cutting a diagonal slightly away from Rhydon and Lionel. The enemy lords were close—they could not have been more than ten yards behind when Derry turned—and they were closing fast. He saw that Morgan was fast gaining on the heavier Torenthi warhorses, that he was now almost neck and neck with Lionel's big bay charger; but behind Derry, Rhydon's mounted archers were nocking arrows to their bowstrings.

Lionel tried to turn across Derry's path to block his escape, but Morgan was already abreast of him, yanking his horse's head to the left and throwing its weight against Lionel's. Lionel's horse missed a stride and stumbled, then went down as Morgan's spurred boot lashed out in a vicious kick.

Lionel was pitched head over heels as his mount hit the turf, and Morgan thundered on past to gain on Rhydon as Lionel picked himself up and snatched at the reins of his staggering horse. A hail of arrows began to rain down on them from the Torenthi escort. The arrows glanced off harmlessly against the steel helmets and mail hauberks of Morgan and Rhydon, but the horses were unprotected; a chance bolt transfixed Rhydon's mount through the throat and sent it screaming to its knees.

Rhydon landed on his feet as the horse collapsed under him, already running toward the now remounted Lionel and waving his arms frantically for the archers to cease fire. But another arrow caught Derry in the back even as Morgan was drawing abreast of him and the archers were lowering their bows. With an oath, Morgan yanked the faltering Derry across his saddle and wheeled to race back toward his own lines. At the same time, Rhydon scrambled up behind Lionel and the pair of them spurred back toward the east. Morgan, with a fearful glance back over his shoulder, could see Rhydon mouthing maledictions as he and Lionel rode for safety. Morgan steadied Derry's limp form across his saddle and crouched low as he rode for the Gwynedd army.

But the army was in turmoil, the men milling angrily behind the front lines, naked swords and axes brandished against the noonday sun. In a determined effort to restrain his officers, Kelson was galloping up and down the center of the line, but even he could not be everywhere at once. The troops' outrage was rising in a roaring crescendo as they angrily shook their weapons at what the treacherous enemy had just done to their comrades.

"Lower your weapons!" Kelson was shouting. "Hold, I say! Don't you see? He *wants* us to attack. Sheathe your weapons! I command you to hold!"

His words could scarcely be heard against the din. As the lines parted to admit Morgan and the limp Derry, the line to the left began to surge forward of its own accord, its officers no longer able to maintain control. Kelson saw their intention and made one last, futile attempt to order them back, then jerked his horse's head around and began galloping out ahead of the men. He pulled up short and whirled his black charger in a perfect levade, then dropped the reins as the animal stood stock-still. Standing slightly in the stirrups, he threw back his head and thrust his arms heavenward, pronouncing forbidden words that only the wind heard.

Light flashed from his fingertips like crimson fire as he thrust his arms upward again, flaring to sear a crimson line of warning in the spring turf. The riders who had broken from the line pulled up in fear and confusion, their crazed horses plunging wildly before the wall of flame that had sprung up where the red fire seared.

To Kelson's amazement and relief, the Torenthi lines held behind him. Rhydon, Lionel, and their archer escort had reached the safety of their own lines even as Kelson's army started to break.

But Kelson was not concerned with that just now. As he lowered his arms and glared at the men with his proud Haldane eyes, his soldiers managed to bring their terrified mounts under control and sped back to their places in the ranks, trying once more to bring some order out of chaos.

Quiet descended on both the armies as Kelson spread his arms again and passed his hands palm-down above the fire he had made. The flames died, the seared lines faded away. As he lowered his arms, the crimson aura that had surrounded him like a royal mantle fell away and disappeared, leaving the King of Gwynedd human once more.

Taut and stiff with repressed anger, Kelson gathered up his reins and turned his head to slowly survey the enemy. Not a sound disturbed the silence save the snorting and blowing of horses and the jingle and creak of harness. Kelson searched them long with his gray Haldane eyes, memorizing every banner, every detail of the awful fruit of the gallows trees.

Then, after a moment, he turned his face back toward his own army and began riding slowly back to them: regal, meticulous. The deadly silence persisted until he had nearly reached the lines; then a lone sword began beating against a shield in approval—an emphatic commentary that was quickly picked up and echoed by more and more men, until the entire army was vibrating to the music of steel on leather-covered wood and steel.

Kelson held his head high as he drew rein before them. After a moment he raised one hand for silence. Morgan, the limp form of Derry still held across his saddle, could only stare in amazement, watching in wonder as the royal eyes slowly became fully human once more.

"Is he dead?" Kelson asked quietly.

Morgan shook his head and motioned for two men-at-arms to lift Derry down from the saddle. "No, he's alive, but the wound is serious. Call Warin, will you, Captain?"

"See to it," Kelson said with a nod, returning his glance toward the distant Torenthi army. "Morgan, what think you of the little display that has just been staged for our benefit?"

Morgan quickly changed mental gears, a little surprised that Kelson could dismiss his own actions so quickly and get back to the heart of the matter.

"Wencit wished to goad us into battle before we were ready, my prince. And yet, I am not certain he is ready to fight, either. I confess that I do not understand why."

"Nor do I—and that was also my impression," Kelson agreed. He turned in his saddle to glance at Duncan. "Father Duncan, I very much regret what happened to your father—and all those other men of Cassan and Kierney. Are you all right?"

Duncan raised his head and stared dully at the king for a moment, then nodded slowly. He had sheathed his sword, but his hands were still red with the blood of the hostage he and Warin had slain. He glanced out at the enemy lines, at the dangling bodies, then down at his bloodstained hands.

"I—I killed that hostage in anger, Sire. It was not my place to do so. I should have stayed my sword."

"Not so." Kelson shook his head solemnly. "You and Warin have saved me the task of killing him myself. Torval knew, when he rode out here, that his life would be forfeit if there was treachery."

"Right deed, wrong reason." Duncan smiled cynically. "That does not make it right for me, my prince."

"Perhaps not, but it is forgivable. I would—"

"Sire! Wencit rides toward us!" a man suddenly gasped.

Kelson whirled in his saddle, half expecting to see the entire Torenthi horde advancing. Instead, there was only a handful of riders breaking away from the Torenthi lines now: a bannerman bearing Wencit's leaping hart standard, black on silver; Lionel and Rhydon; a slender, proud figure who could only be Bran Coris; and Wencit himself. The riders advanced at a brisk walk, drawing purposefully toward the center of the field once more. Kelson's eyes narrowed as he watched the advance.

"It's a trap," Duncan murmured, glaring at the riders through ice-blue eyes. "They wish no parley—only trickery. Do not trust them, Sire."

"Morgan, what say you?" Kelson asked, not taking his eyes from the advancing King of Torenth.

"I agree that they are not to be trusted, my prince. But I fear we must parley again—though I have no more cause than Duncan to love these treacherous foes."

"Very well." Kelson nodded. "Bishop Arilan, will you ride out with me again? I value your counsel."

"I will, Sire."

"Good. And Father Duncan—I value your counsel as well, and would desire your company, but I shall not command you, under the circumstances. Can you keep your righteous wrath in check for a while longer?"

"I'll not disgrace you, my prince."

"Then let us ride. Nigel, you are in command until I return."

"As you will, Sire."

Kelson wrapped his reins around his left hand, then glanced aside to where a young baron on foot held the royal lion banner. With a grim smile, Kelson sidestepped his horse toward the man, then reached out a gloved hand and closed his fist around the staff. The baron froze for just an instant, then broke into a wide grin and hefted the end of the standard up to rest in Kelson's stirrup. As Kelson steadied the standard at his right side, a cheer went up among his men, and the morning breeze picked up the crimson silk and spread it in the sun.

Then, with the lion banner snapping in the rising breeze, Kelson turned his horse toward the enemy and touched spurs to his mount. The great black warhorse minced and pranced as it led Morgan, Duncan, and the Bishop Arilan out to meet the Deryni enemy.

CHAPTER TWENTY-TWO

*"They shall hold the bow and the lance: they are cruel,
and will not shew mercy: their voice shall roar like the
sea, and they shall ride upon horses, every one put in
array, like a man to the battle, against thee."*

JEREMIAH 50:42

"SO, you are Kelson Haldane," Wencit said. His voice was
smooth, cultured, his manner supremely confident, and
Kelson instantly despised him.

"It pleases me that we can discuss the matter at hand in a
civilized fashion, like two grown men," Wencit continued,
eyeing Kelson up and down disdainfully. "Or, nearly grown."

Kelson would not permit himself the luxury of the
scathing retort he longed to unleash. Instead, he made himself return his enemy's scrutiny, gray eyes noting every aspect of the lean, red-haired Deryni known as Wencit of
Torenth.

Wencit sat his great golden steed as though born in the
saddle, gloved hands lightly holding wide velvet reins embellished with burnished golden bosses. A frothy purple
plume fastened in the headstall of the golden bridle trembled and floated on the breeze as the golden charger shook
its head and snorted at Kelson's black.

Wencit himself was attired all in gold and purple, every

part of his body save his head either encased in gilt-washed mail or adorned with cloth of gold or the rich purple and gold brocade of the mantle that swirled from his jeweled gold collar. Gem-studded wrist guards met supple kidskin gloves on his hands, and a heavy neck chain lay aglitter on the breast of his golden surcoat. His brow bore an ornate coronet of chased gold set with pearls and tawny-colored gems. On any other man, the cumulative effect might have seemed ludicrous, but on Wencit it but underlined his potency.

Almost, Kelson felt himself beginning to respond to the sheer visual *presence* of the man seated on the warhorse before him, and he forced himself to shake the feeling, drawing himself a little straighter and lifting his chin. Coolly he permitted his gaze to touch on Wencit's companions: the unctuous Lionel, the scowling Rhydon, traitor Bran, who would not meet his eyes just yet. Then he returned his full attention to Wencit. His eyes were flint-hard as he met the sorcerer's gaze, and he did not flinch at the contact.

"I assume, by your statement, that you consider yourself a civilized man," Kelson said carefully. "On the other hand, the brutal killing of scores of helpless prisoners hardly seems calculated to demonstrate any high degree of civilization."

"No, it was not," Wencit agreed amiably enough. "But it *was* calculated to demonstrate the extent to which I would go, if necessary, to ensure that you carefully consider the proposal I am about to make to you."

"Proposal?" Kelson snorted contemptuously. "Surely you don't think I'm of a mind to bargain, after the brutality I have just witnessed. What kind of a fool do you take me for?"

"Oh, not a fool," Wencit laughed. "Not the son of Brion Haldane. Nor am I so witless as to underestimate the threat you pose to me, even though you are contending outside your class. It is almost a pity that you shall have to die."

"Until that is an accomplished fact, I suggest that you

turn your words to other topics. Say what you have to say,
Wencit. The day grows later."

Wencit smiled and bowed slightly in the saddle. "Tell
me, how is my young friend, Lord Derry?"

"How *should* he be?"

Wencit clucked his tongue in disapproval and shook his
head. "Now, young Haldane, please give me credit for a little intelligence. Why would I have ordered Derry's death?
He was the token I had hoped to play for the recovery of my
Lord Bran's family. I assure you, the archers acted wholly
without my orders and have been punished. Is Derry alive?"

"That is not your concern," Kelson answered curtly.

"Then, he lives. That is well." Wencit nodded. He smiled
lightly, glancing down at his gloves, then looked up at Kelson again. "Very well, what I have come to say is this: So far
as I am concerned, there need be no great battle between our
respective armies. Men need not die in masses for us to settle our differences."

Kelson's eyes narrowed in suspicion. "Just what did you
have in mind as an alternative?"

"Personal combat," Wencit replied. "Or, to be more specific, personal combat on a group level: a duel to the death
by magic, Deryni against Deryni. Myself, Rhydon, Lionel,
and Bran against you and any other three whom you may
designate. I would assume that Morgan and McLain and
perhaps your royal uncle would be your logical choice—but
of course, you are free to choose whomever you wish. In ancient days, such combat was called the Duel Arcane."

Kelson scowled and glanced at Morgan, then at Arilan
and Duncan. He was suddenly uneasy at Wencit's proposal,
and the notion of another Duel Arcane filled him with
dread; the one with Charissa had been bad enough. There
was a trick involved, there had to be. He must discover what
it was.

"Your advantage in such a contest is obvious, my lord.
You and yours are trained Deryni; most of us are not. And
yet, even with these advantages, it does not strike me that

you are the sort of man to risk so much on one battle. What is it that you neglect to tell me?"

"Do you suspect me of subterfuge?" Wencit asked, raising an eyebrow in feigned surprise. "Well, perhaps you are well-advised. But I had thought the other advantages of such a resolution would be quite clear. If we join battle here, army against army, the flower of knighthood from both our sides will be destroyed. Of what use to me is a dead kingdom? A kingdom inhabited only by old men, young boys, women and children."

Kelson eyed the enemy king shrewdly. "I have no more wish than you to lose my finest fighting men in battle. If we fight here today, the impact will be felt for a generation to come. But I cannot trust you, Wencit of Torenth. Even if I defeat you here, who is to say what next spring will bring? Who is—"

Wencit threw back his head and laughed, the sound echoed lightly by his companions. Kelson shifted uncomfortably in his saddle, for he was not aware that he had said anything particularly amusing. But one glance at Morgan convinced him that the general knew. He was about to say something when Wencit suddenly stopped laughing and moved his horse a few steps closer.

"Forgive me, young prince, but your naïveté is touching. I offered a four-way battle to the death. Under those circumstances, the losers would hardly be in any position to threaten the victors—unless, of course, you believe that some men can return from the grave."

Kelson scowled at that, for far more bizarre things had been hinted about Wencit of Torenth over the years. But then he forced himself to dismiss the thought and return to what Wencit had actually proposed: a duel to the death by magic. His hesitation apparently did not set well with the Torenthi king, however, for Wencit abruptly frowned and kneed his horse still closer to reach out a gloved hand to Kelson's reins.

"If you have not already noticed, I am an impatient man,

Kelson Haldane. I do not brook interference with my plans. If you are considering rejecting my proposal, I suggest that you put it out of your mind immediately. I remind you that I still hold nearly a thousand of your men captive—and there are far worse ways to die than by simple hanging."

"And just what is that supposed to mean?" Kelson whispered icily.

"It means that if you do not accept my challenge, what you saw in the last hour will be as nothing. Unless your word prevents it, two hundred prisoners will be drawn and quartered before your army at dusk, and two hundred more impaled alive and left to die at the rising of the moon. If you hope to save them, I would not advise procrastination."

Kelson's face had blanched at Wencit's description of the intended fate of the prisoners, and his hands clenched tightly as he jerked his reins from Wencit's grasp. He glared across at the Deryni sorcerer as though to destroy him with a single thought as Wencit backed his mount a few casual steps, and would have moved after him, had not Morgan held out a restraining arm and kneed his own horse to block the king's. Kelson glanced at Morgan angrily, intending to order him back, but something in Morgan's expression made the young king hesitate. Morgan's eyes were cold as the midnight fog as he met Wencit's haughty gaze.

"You are trying to force us into a hasty decision," he said in a low voice. "I want to know why. Why is it so important that we accept the challenge on your terms?" He paused only slightly. "Or is there some new treachery afoot?"

Wencit turned his head deliberately to stare directly at Morgan, as though incensed that Morgan had dared to interrupt his negotiations with Kelson. Then he ran his glance disdainfully over the other's form. His voice was mocking when he finally spoke.

"You have much to learn of the Deryni, Alaric Morgan, for all that you claim that heritage for yourself. You will find, if you survive, that there are ancient codes of honor concerning our powers which even I would not willingly transgress." He returned his gaze to Kelson. "I have offered you formal duel under the laws set forth by the Camberian Council more than two centuries ago, Kelson Haldane. There are other laws, far older, which I am also bound to obey. I have sought and received permission from the Council to wage this duel with you on the terms that I have already specified, and to have Council arbitrators present. I assure you, there could be no treachery where the Council is concerned."

Kelson's brows furrowed in consternation. "The Camberian Coun—"

Arilan interrupted for the first time, cutting across Kelson's response. "My lord, you will forgive my intrusion, but His Majesty was not prepared to answer a challenge such as you have proposed to him today. You will understand that he must have time to consult with his advisors before giving you a final answer. If he accepts, the lives and fortunes of many thousands of his people will hang upon the talents of four men. You will appreciate that it is not a decision to be taken lightly."

Wencit turned to study Arilan as though he were some particularly noxious form of lower life. "If the King of Gwynedd feels that he cannot make a decision without consulting his inferiors, Bishop, that is his weakness, not mine. However, my original warning still stands. If I do not have the decision I require by nightfall, two hundred prisoners will be drawn and quartered where we now stand, and two hundred more impaled alive at the rising of the moon. Such measures will continue until all of the prisoners are dead, and then I shall take even sterner measures. See that you do not provoke me overmuch, Kelson of Gwynedd."

With that, Wencit backed his horse a few more deft paces, then whirled the animal on its haunches to begin cantering back toward his own lines. His companions wheeled with him in perfect formation and followed, leaving a stunned Kelson staring after their retreating forms.

Kelson was angry at Arilan for interrupting, at Morgan

for provoking Wencit, at himself for his indecision, but he did not trust himself to speak until they, too, had returned to their own lines and were dismounting outside the royal pavilion. He gave orders for the battle lines to be put at ease, since there was obviously to be no fighting until the morrow, at the earliest, then motioned the three who had ridden with him to follow him inside.

He decided to deal with the bishop first, since he was within reach, but as they entered the tent they found nearly a dozen men clustered around the unmoving form of Derry, stretched on a pallet to the left of the chamber. A blood-stained Warin was bending over him, and Nigel's son Conall was kneeling beside him with a reddened basin of water, a look of awe on his face as he watched the former rebel leader wipe his bloody hands on a piece of towelling. Derry's eyes were closed and his head was rolling back and forth as though still in some pain, but there were fragments of a half-shattered arrow shaft on the floor beside him.

As Kelson and the bishop entered, Morgan and Duncan right behind them, Warin looked up and nodded greeting. He was wan and obviously exhausted, but there was also satisfaction in his eyes.

"He should be all right, Sire. I withdrew the arrow and healed the wound. He is still feverish from whatever happened earlier, however. General Morgan, he keeps murmuring your name. Perhaps you should take a look at him."

Morgan moved quickly to Derry's side and dropped to one knee, laying a gentle hand on the young man's brow. Derry's eyes flickered open at the touch and looked up at the ceiling for just an instant; then he turned his head to gaze at Morgan, a frightened shadow flitting behind his eyes.

"Be easy, Sean," Morgan murmured. "You're safe now."

"My lord . . . You're all right." Then, "I didn't betr—"

He broke off and stiffened for just an instant, as though remembering something terrifying, then shuddered in revulsion and jerked his head away. Frowning, Morgan moved his fingertips to Derry's temples, intending to exert his powers and calm him, but met resistance there that he had never encountered in Derry before.

"Just relax," he whispered. "The worst is over. Rest now. You'll feel better after you've slept——"

"No! I mustn't sleep!"

The very thought seemed to terrify Derry, who began tossing his head from side to side so wildly that it was all Morgan could do to maintain contact. The younger man's eyes blazed with an animal fear, all reason gone, and Morgan realized that he was going to have to do something quickly or Derry would burn himself out in his exhausted state.

"Sean, relax. Don't fight me! It's all right, you're safe. Duncan, give me a hand here!"

"No! You mustn't make me sleep! You *mustn't*!" Derry caught a handful of Morgan's cloak and struggled to rise as Duncan scrambled in to grab his arms and Warin backed away.

"No! Let me go! You don't understand. Oh, God help me, what am I going to do?"

"It's all right——"

"No, it isn't all right! You don't understand! Wencit——"

Derry's expression became even more stricken, and he lifted his head to stare wildly into Morgan's eyes, his right hand still twined desperately in the edge of Morgan's cloak, despite Duncan's efforts to free it.

"Morgan, listen! They say there's no Devil, but they're wrong! I saw him! He has red hair and calls himself Wencit of Torenth, but he lies. He's the Devil himself! He made me—he made me——"

"Not now...." Morgan shook his head and forced Derry's shoulders back against the pallet. "No more for now. We'll talk about it later. Right now, you're weak from your wounds and captivity. You must rest. When you wake, you'll feel better. I promise nothing will happen to you. Trust me, Sean."

As Morgan spoke, imposing more and more control against Derry's weakening will, the younger man suddenly went limp, eyes closing and muscles going slack as he sank back against the pallet. Morgan disengaged his cloak from Derry's grasp, then laid the young lord's hands loosely across his chest and straightened the angle of his head. Conall, still watching from nearby, brought a sleeping-fur, which Morgan tucked loosely around the still form. Warin had retreated to stand against one of the walls of the tent. Morgan studied the sleeping Derry for several seconds, as though assuring himself that the sleep was deep enough, then exchanged a worried glance with Duncan before looking up at Kelson and the circle of anxious faces.

"I think he'll be all right when he's rested, Sire. But right now, I'd rather not think about what he must have gone through." His eyes darkened and took on a far-away look, and under his breath he murmured, "God help Wencit, when I find out, though."

He shuddered as the mood passed, then swept a strand of pale hair out of his eyes and got to his feet with a sigh. Duncan, after another look at the sleeping Derry, kept his eyes averted as he stood. Kelson, too, was much subdued and shifted uncomfortably from one foot to the other as his gaze wavered between the two of them.

"What do you think Wencit did do to him?" he finally asked in a small voice.

Morgan shook his head. "It's difficult to say at this point, my prince. Later I'll probe him more deeply, if it's indicated, but he's too weak now. He really fought me."

"I see."

Kelson studied the toes of his boots for several seconds, then looked up again. All eyes were now upon him, waiting for his next instructions, and he remembered abruptly what must be the next topic of discussion.

"Very well, gentlemen. There is nothing further we can do for Derry at this time, so I suggest that we get back to the business at hand." He glanced at Arilan and cocked his head. "Bishop Arilan, could you tell us about this Cam—"

Arilan cleared his throat and shook his head meaningfully,

glancing at Warin's retainers, at young Conall, at the few guards, and Kelson stopped in mid-word. Nodding slightly, the king moved to Conall's side and laid a hand on his shoulder, for he understood that Arilan did not wish to discuss the matter before comparative outsiders.

"Thanks for your aid, Cousin. Would you please send your father and Bishop Cardiel to me before returning to your duties? And gentlemen," he included Warin's men and the guards in his gesture, "I must ask that you likewise return to your posts. Thank you for your concern."

Conall and the others bowed and made their way out of the tent, and Warin watched them go, straightening and moving slightly as though to follow them.

"I sense that this is something not for the ears of outsiders, so I'll leave if you wish. I am not offended," Warin added hastily.

Kelson glanced at Arilan, but the bishop shook his head.

"No, you have a right to be present, just as we have called for Bishop Cardiel, who is perhaps less Deryni than any of us. Kelson, if you don't mind, I shall wait until Thomas and Nigel arrive before answering your questions. It will save me having to repeat myself."

"Of course."

The king made his way to his chair and sat, unclasping his cloak and letting it fall over the back of his chair. Then he sat back and stretched out his long legs on the fine Kheldish carpeting. Morgan and Duncan took seats on a pair of folding camp stools to Kelson's right, and Morgan unslung his sword from its hangers and laid it on the carpet between his feet. After a moment's thought, Duncan did the same, shifting his stool slightly to the left to accommodate Warin, who was propping a cushion so that he could lean against the tent's center pole. Arilan remained standing in the center of the carpet, pretending to be absorbed in the intricate design woven beneath his feet. He scarcely looked up as Cardiel and then Nigel entered the tent, and it was Kelson who had to direct the newcomers to take seats. When they were settled, the king looked up at Arilan expectantly. The bishop's blue-violet eyes were hooded as he met Kelson's gray gaze.

"Do you wish me to review what has happened, Sire, for the sake of Thomas and your uncle?"

"Please do."

"Very well." Arilan folded his hands and stared hard at his thumbnails for several seconds, then looked up.

"My lords, Wencit of Torenth has presented us with an ultimatum. His Majesty wished to consult with all of us before replying. If he does not respond by sunset, Wencit will begin slaying more hostages."

"Name of God, the man is a monster!" Nigel exclaimed, stiffening in anger.

"Agreed," Arilan replied. "But his ultimatum was quite specific and quite adamant. He has issued Kelson a challenge to the Duel Arcane: himself and his three henchmen, Rhydon, Lionel, and Bran Coris, against Kelson and any three Kelson chooses to name. I think I need not tell you that two of Kelson's three will be Morgan and Duncan; what may surprise some of you is that I am to be the third."

Warin looked up with a start

"That is correct, Warin. I am Deryni."

Warin swallowed hard, but Nigel only nodded his head slowly and raised an eyebrow.

"You speak as though my nephew's acceptance is an accomplished fact," he said.

"I believe that this can be his *only* decision," Arilan said quietly. "If he does not accept the challenge by nightfall, two hundred hostages will be drawn and quartered on the plain before our army. Any further delay, and two hundred more will be impaled and left to die at the rising of the moon. Tonight that occurs about four hours after sunset. This appears inescapable if Kelson refuses the challenge."

He scanned the chamber slowly, but no one made a move to speak. "If, on the other hand, Kelson accepts, the battle will be to the death, the survivor or survivors to take all.

Wencit obviously believes he will win, or he would not have proposed this sort of contest."

Warin had paled at the mention of drawing and quartering, but Nigel, better accustomed to the horrors of war, only repeated his knowing nod. After a few seconds' pause, he raised his hand slightly to speak.

"This Duel Arcane—would it be similar to the challenge issued to Kelson at his coronation?"

"Well, it would be governed by the same ancient laws of challenge," Arilan said with a nod, "except, of course, that it would be four against four instead of the single combat fought by Kelson and Charissa. There are fairly rigid rules governing the arbitration of a Duel Arcane, and Wencit has—ah—apparently received official sanction to hold the duel according to the ancient laws."

"Official sanction from whom?" Kelson interrupted eagerly. "This Camberian Council he mentioned? Why do you evade the issue when I . . ."

His voice trailed off as he saw Arilan had stiffened at the mention of the name, and he glanced at Morgan in surprise. Morgan was gazing at the bishop with rapt attention, apparently no more informed than Kelson, yet suddenly keenly interested in what the bishop would say. Duncan, too, had started at the sound of the name and now watched Arilan intently. Abruptly, Kelson wondered what he had stumbled onto.

"Arilan," he whispered softly, "what *is* the Camberian Council? Is it . . . Deryni?"

Arilan glanced at his feet, then raised his head to stare past Kelson as though in a daze. "Forgive me, my prince. It is difficult to break a lifetime of conditioning, but Wencit has left me no alternative. It was he who first mentioned the Council. It is only fair, since you must meet him in battle, that I tell you what I can." He glanced down at his hands, which were clasped tightly together, and forced himself to relax.

"There exists a secret organization of full Deryni called

the Camberian Council. Its origins lie in the times immediately after the Haldane Restoration, when those of high Deryni blood were called to somehow regulate and protect those who remained after the great persecutions. Only past and present members know the composition of the Council, and they are sworn by an oath of blood and power never to divulge the identity of their fellows.

"As you may be aware, very few Deryni have had the opportunity to fully develop their powers in recent times," he went on. "Many of our talents were lost in the persecutions— or at least our knowledge of how to use those powers was lost. Morgan's gift of healing may be a rediscovery of one of those lost talents.

"But there are some of us who are loosely organized and in regular communication with one another. The Council acts as a regulating body for those known Deryni, keeping the old laws and arbitrating in disputes of magic such as may arise from time to time. A Duel Arcane such as Wencit proposes would fall under the Council's jurisdiction."

"The Council determines the validity of duels?" Morgan asked suspiciously.

Arilan turned to look at Morgan rather strangely. "Yes. Why do you ask?"

"How about those not of full Deryni blood, like myself and Duncan?" Morgan persisted. "Are they also under the jurisdiction of the Council?"

Arilan's face blanched slightly. "Why do you ask?" he repeated in a strained voice.

Morgan glanced at Duncan and Duncan nodded.

"Tell him."

"Bishop Arilan, I think that Duncan and I may have had contact with one of your Camberian Council. In fact, I think it may have happened several times. At least the implication of our last encounter was similar to what you have just outlined."

"What happened?" Arilan whispered. His face was expressionless above his purple cassock.

"Well, we had a—a visitation is the best way to describe it, I suppose, when we were on our way to you at Dhassa. When we stopped at Saint Neot's to rest our horses, he appeared."

"*He?*"

Morgan nodded carefully. "We still don't know who he was. But each of us had seen him before in separate situations, which I haven't the time to enumerate just now. He looks like—well, let us simply say that he bears a striking resemblance to the portraits and written descriptions of Camber of Culdi."

"Saint Camber?" Arilan murmured, unable to believe what he was hearing.

Duncan shifted in his chair uneasily. "Please don't misunderstand, Excellency. We are not claiming that he *was* Saint Camber. He never said he was. In fact, this last time when Alaric and I finally saw him at the same time, he said that he *wasn't* Saint Camber—'only one of his faithful servants,' I believe he put it. From what you have just told us of the Camberian Council, perhaps it was one of them."

"That is impossible," Arilan murmured, shaking his head in disbelief. "What did he say to you?"

Morgan raised an eyebrow. "Well, he implied that we had Deryni enemies that we didn't know about. He said that 'those whose business it was to know such things' believed that Duncan and I might have more powers than we think, and that we might be challenged to a Duel Arcane to discover our strength. He seemed concerned that this not happen, though."

Arilan's face had gone white, and he had to reach out to the center pole to support himself. "It's impossible," he whispered, not listening anymore. "And yet, it almost has to be one of the Council." He groped his way to an empty stool and sat heavily.

"This puts an entirely different light on matters. Alaric, you and Duncan *were* made liable for challenge by any full Deryni—and for the reasons your visitant stated. I sit on the

Council; I was there when it happened, though I could not prevent it. But who could have come to you in that guise? Who would even have a motive? It simply does not make sense."

Arilan looked up at them, at all of them in the room, and realized he had been rambling on. Warin and Cardiel were staring at him with wide, faintly frightened eyes, unable in their humanness to comprehend; and even Nigel was regarding him in stunned confusion, only partially understanding the implications of the Deryni bishop's words. Morgan and Duncan measured him carefully, trying to reconcile what he was saying with all they could remember of their encounters with the stranger in Camber's guise. Kelson alone remained aloof, the sudden uncertainty of the situation seeming to isolate him, to infuse him with a cold sobriety, a logical detachment that enabled him to assess the growing crisis with a semblance of objectivity.

"Very well," Arilan said, shaking off his sense of foreboding and returning to the matter at hand. "Alaric, Duncan, I cannot explain the visitations you have had, but I intend, at least, to find out whether Wencit really has been in contact with the Council and coerced them into arbitrating a Duel Arcane. I know of no such ruling, and as a member of the Council directly involved in this matter, I should have been consulted. However, I have missed a few routine meetings lately because of our forced march, so it *is* possible. Morgan, do you possess a set of Ward cubes, and do you carry them with you?"

"Ward cubes? I—" Morgan hesitated and Arilan shook his head.

"Do not be coy with me; there isn't time. Do you or do you not?"

"Yes."

"Then, get them. Duncan, I shall need eight white candles, all about the same size. See what you can find."

"At once."

"Thank you. Thomas, help Warin and Nigel roll back

the carpet to expose bare earth. Kelson, I shall need something from the old times. May I borrow your Ring of Fire?"

"Certainly. What are you going to do?" Kelson asked, pulling off his ring and watching, mystified, as the carpet was pulled back to expose bare, matted grass.

Arilan slipped the Ring of Fire on his little finger and motioned for Morgan and Duncan to be off on their own errands. "I intend to construct a Transfer Portal, with your help. Happily, that is one of the old talents that has not been entirely lost. Nigel, I shall need a different sort of help from you and Warin and Thomas in a few moments. Can all of you obey me without question?"

The three exchanged apprehensive glances, but even Warin nodded. Arilan flashed them a fleeting smile of reassurance as he stepped onto the patch of grass and dropped to his knees. After raking through the grass with his fingertips and removing several small stones and bits of brush, he held out his hand for Nigel's dagger, which the prince handed over without a word. Then, with the four of them looking on, he began cutting a six-foot octagon in the turf.

"I can only imagine how strange this must seem to you," he said, cutting the second of the sides and moving on to the third. "Warin, I shall explain for your benefit and Nigel's that a Transfer Portal is a device whereby Deryni can travel from point to point without the passage of time. The process is instantaneous. Unfortunately, we cannot exercise this remarkable talent without a Portal—and that takes a great deal of power to construct.

"Which is where the three of you come in. What I should like to do is to place each of you in a deep trance and then draw on your strength to help us activate the Portal. I promise you'll be none the worse for it."

He had finished cutting the sixth side of the octagon and looked up to see Warin fidgeting in his place, obviously more than a little uncomfortable at the idea of being used in magic.

"You are uneasy at this thought, and I cannot say I blame

you, Warin. But there is nothing to be alarmed about, really. It will hardly be any different from when Morgan read you, except that you shan't remember anything."

"You swear it?"

Arilan nodded, and Warin shrugged nervously.

"Very well, I'll do what I can."

Arilan continued cutting his octagon, coming down the final facet as Morgan returned with a small, red leather box. Morgan halted at the edge of the octagon and watched as Arilan made his last cut and then straightened to dust his hands against his cassock. The dagger he returned to Nigel.

"The Wards?" Arilan asked, looking up.

Nodding, Morgan opened the box to spill eight tiny black and white cubes into his cupped hand, four each of black and white, each about the size of the end of his little finger. They glistened in the wan light as Morgan extended them on his open palm.

Arilan passed a hand over the cubes and cocked his head as though listening to something, then nodded and motioned for Morgan to proceed. As he moved clear of the octagon, Morgan stepped inside and dropped to his knees to begin laying out the cubes on the grass. Arilan watched him in silence for a moment, then cleared his throat.

"Can you set them up except for the last step, and then trigger the Ward from inside?"

Morgan looked up and nodded.

"Excellent. When Duncan comes back with the candles, you can have him set one at each angle of the octagon. Nigel, suppose you and Warin come over here now and make yourselves comfortable. Kelson, would you shift some of those sleeping-furs for them to lie on?"

As the two humans moved to their appointed places, Duncan returned with the required candles and knelt outside the octagon, trimming the candles to size with his dagger. Morgan watched him for a moment, indicating where the candles should be placed, then cast a last glance at the others and returned to setting out his cubes.

The black and white cubes were called Wards, the entire composite called a Ward Major, once activated; and each step must be performed correctly in order to make the Ward Major come alive. The four white cubes must first be arranged in a square, two sides of each cube touching its neighbors; and then the black cubes must be placed, one at each corner of the large square formed by the white ones, black and white not quite touching.

Morgan arranged the cubes in the requisite pattern, then reached out his right forefinger to rest lightly on the white cube at the upper left of the square, glancing up at Arilan as he whispered the nomen, *"Prime."* None of the others had been watching, and as Morgan glanced back down at his Wards, he was pleased to see that the first cube now glowed with a faint, milky light. He had not lost his touch.

"Seconde," Morgan whispered, touching the white cube in the upper right of the square. *"Tierce, Quarte,"* he repeated in rapid succession, touching the remaining white cubes.

The four white cubes now glowed in a single, larger square, which reflected coldly off the four black cubes remaining. Morgan moved his finger to the black cube in the upper left corner and drew a deep breath, then murmured, *"Quinte."* The process was quickly repeated for the three remaining black cubes as he hurried past their names, *"Sixte, Septime, Octave."* The black cubes now glowed from within with a deep, green-black flame. Where the light of the black cubes met the light of the white, there was a vague, shimmering area of darkness, as though the one cancelled out the effect of the other.

Morgan glanced up and was surprised to find that the others were well about their own tasks. Duncan had finished with his candles and set them in place without Morgan even being aware, and now knelt calmly beside the entranced Warin, the rebel leader's slack head resting against his knee, his own eyes closed. Arilan and Kelson were kneeling on either side of a sleeping Nigel, Arilan apparently assisting the young king with mastering a fine point of control.

But Cardiel was sitting apart from the others, one arm cradled around his upraised knee as he crouched on the rugs folded back at the edge of the octagon. He apparently had been watching Morgan closely for some time, and he looked down in embarrassment as Morgan caught his eye. The downward glance did not last for long, though, for Cardiel was clearly fascinated by what he had just seen.

"I'm sorry, I didn't mean to pry," he said in a low voice. "Do you mind if I watch?"

Morgan hesitated for just an instant, weighing the advisability of permitting the bishop to learn more than he already knew, then shrugged. "If you wish. Please don't interrupt me, though. The next part is a bit tedious, and I need to concentrate."

"Whatever you say," Cardiel murmured, sidling closer for a better view.

Suppressing a smile, Morgan wiped the palms of both hands against his thighs, then picked up *Prime*, the first white cube. Bringing it carefully to *Quinte*, its black counterpart, he let the two touch gently as he murmured, *"Primus!"*

With a muffled click, the two cubes merged into a silvery-gray oblong, which Morgan gently put aside before picking up *Seconde*. With a glance at the frozen Cardiel, he touched it to *Sixte* and whispered, *"Secundus!"* A second glowing oblong was formed, and Cardiel stifled a gasp as Morgan put the second one aside and picked up *Tierce*.

Morgan was beginning to feel the energy drain now, and he passed a hand lightly over his eyes as he fingered the third white cube. The weariness faded as he applied the Deryni technique for banishing fatigue, though he knew he would have to pay later. For now, though, the Wards must be set, whatever the cost in power. Quickly he steeled himself to touch *Tierce* to *Septime*.

"Tertius!"

The third oblong glowed. The Ward was now three-quarters complete.

"We're almost ready," Arilan said, moving quietly to

Cardiel's side as Morgan picked up *Quinte*. "Thomas, I need you now."

With an apprehensive swallow, Cardiel let himself be guided to a place on the rolled-up carpet, lying back as Arilan directed and letting the Deryni place a cool hand on his forehead. His eyelids fluttered briefly as he drifted into Arilan's trance. Morgan shook his head and took a deep breath, steeling his strength to meld the final pair of cubes.

"Quartus!"

Light flashed again as the two cubes became one; and then there were four silvery oblongs on the ground before him.

Morgan sat back on his haunches and glanced around him, then began moving the oblongs to the four compass points of the octagon. As he laid out the limits of the Ward's protection, Arilan moved within the circle and motioned Kelson and Duncan to do the same, each of them still retaining control of his charge at a distance. Morgan crouched in the center of the octagon and glanced around warily as the other three crowded close around him, then readjusted the position of a Ward that had gotten jostled in the process of moving into the circle.

"Go ahead and set the Wards," Arilan murmured, nodding toward their three entranced colleagues. "Include them in the protection, too. I'll light the candles as soon as you're done."

Morgan glanced at the circle, at the sleeping men just outside its confines, then raised his right hand to point in succession to the four wards.

"Primus, Secundus, Tertius, et Quartus, fiat lux!"

His words caused the light of the Wards to flare to a misty web of luminescence that bathed the seven men in faint milky-white light. As the net stabilized around them, Arilan reached out a tentative hand to probe the net, then passed his hands over the candles set at the points of the octagon, setting them alight. He then edged himself slightly closer to the center of the octagon and placed a hand on Morgan's shoulder.

"Very well. As soon as the four of us have linked minds, I shall guide all of us through the Portal-setting process. It will not be particularly pleasant—we must pull and focus a considerable amount of energy—but we can do it. I shall do what I can to shield you from the worst of any fluctuations. Any questions?"

There were none. With a short nod, Arilan reached out his free hand to grasp Duncan's and Kelson's, then bowed his head. A breath of wind stirred through the tent, making the candles gutter and flare, and then a pure white light began to grow around Arilan's head. The light brightened, becoming gradually diffused with swirls of crimson and green, and the three in thrall shuddered as power was drawn inexorably from minds and bodies.

Mists swirled and surged around the seven, beginning to spin in an ever-widening vortex as the light crackled and arced, until finally a blinding flash filled the entire tent for just an instant and then was gone.

Kelson cried out, and Morgan swayed near fainting as Duncan let out a moan. But even then the moment was past, the white light gone. As the four Deryni shakily opened their eyes, they felt the faint tingle of a viable Transfer Portal beneath their knees—a sensation familiar to all of them. With a satisfied sigh, Arilan got to his feet and began to pull Cardiel back and away from the circle, motioning for Duncan and Kelson to do the same for Nigel and Warin. Soon the circle was clear except for the hunched form of Morgan kneeling still in the center with bowed head. Biting at his lip, Arilan dropped to his knees beside Morgan and again put a hand on his shoulder.

"I know how tired you are, but I must ask one more favor before I go. The Wards must be extended to protect the whole tent. All of you are seriously depleted, and when I come back for you and Kelson and Duncan, we shall want to leave the others protected. They should sleep until midnight or so, but they might not rouse to defend themselves if someone were to come upon them unawares."

"I understand."

With a faint groan of fatigue, Morgan lurched to his feet and spread his hands to either side, palms up. He drew in his breath and exhaled heavily, marshalling new strength from somewhere deep within, then began the low words of the appropriate spell. As he spoke, he turned his hands to make a slight warding-off gesture, as though pushing back something with his palms. Then, when the net of light had extended to the tent walls, he turned his hands palms-up once again, lowering them slowly.

"Is that what you wanted?" he asked dully.

Arilan nodded carefully and motioned for Kelson and Duncan to help Morgan sit beside the circle.

"I shouldn't be gone for very long," he said, stepping into the center of the figure. "In the meantime, the two of you might try to help Alaric replenish his strength, insofar as that is possible at this time. Try to be ready to move as soon as I return, though. The Council is not going to like this at all, and I don't want to give them time to think about it."

"We'll be ready," Kelson replied.

Arilan nodded, then crossed his arms across his chest and bowed his head—and abruptly was gone.

CHAPTER TWENTY-THREE

"And I will bind up that which was broken, and I will strengthen that which was weak."

EZEKIEL 34:16

DARKNESS. Even before his eyes had adjusted to the dim light, Arilan knew that he was standing near the great doors to the Camberian Council chamber, in the slight alcove that defined the Transfer Portal. The area was deserted, as he had expected that it would be at this hour; nonetheless, he cast about carefully for several seconds before moving on toward the great golden doors. He did not relish the idea of any interruption just now.

The doors swung away as he approached the chamber, but the room beyond was as deserted as the antechamber, the fading afternoon sunlight glowing only dimly through the high violet skylight. Without missing a stride, Arilan raised his arms and made a sweeping gesture as he passed between the golden doors, and the torches and the violet glass glowed to life at his command. Settling into his chair, the sorcerer-bishop rested his hands on the ivory table and leaned his head back against the high headrest to compose himself for just a moment. Then he fixed his gaze on the great silvery crystal suspended above the octagonal table and began to Call the other members of the Council.

Incalculable minutes; the Call continued. Several times Arilan shifted restlessly in his chair, trying to conserve energy yet keep his Call at maximum intensity, impatient with the delay. After a time he ceased his efforts and sat back to wait. It was not long before the golden doors swung back once again and the members of the Council began to arrive.

First Kyri of the Flame, splendid and enchanting in deepest green hunting attire; then Laran ap Pardyce in flowing scholar's robes. Thorne Hagen, barefooted and swathed in an orange dressing gown, hastily donned; Stefan Coram looking ruffled in dark blue riding leathers. Finally came the blind Barrett de Laney on the arm of Vivienne, with Tiercel de Claron trailing behind them and looking vaguely dissolute, his burgundy tunic open at the throat.

As the last of them entered, Arilan lifted his gaze to scan them, blue-violet eyes aglow as he searched their questioning faces. Not a word was spoken as the seven took their places, though they eyed Arilan speculatively—there could be no doubt who had sent out the Call. The Deryni bishop studied them unrelentingly, making a bridge of his fingers as he drew breath to speak.

"Who volunteered the services of the Council to mediate a Duel Arcane for Wencit of Torenth?"

Shocked silence. Uneasiness. Astonishment. The seven looked among themselves aghast, as though wondering if their colleague had lost his sanity.

"I asked a question and I expect an answer," Arilan repeated, his hard eyes sweeping the seven. "Who authorized the mediation?"

All eyes turned to Stefan Coram, who slowly rose.

"No one has approached the Council about a mediation, Denis. You must be mistaken."

"Mistaken?"

Arilan stared at Coram in surprise, shock quickly yielding to suspicion as Coram's bland expression did not change.

"Oh, come now, don't act so innocent. Wencit of Torenth has many faults, but stupidity is not one of them. Not even he would dare to make a claim like that unless he could back it up. Do you dare to tell me that you know nothing about it?"

Tiercel sat back in his chair and sighed, a scowl creasing his handsome features. "Stefan speaks for us all, Denis. There has been no communication from Wencit regarding any matter, much less a Duel Arcane. You know that I side with you and the king. I would not lie to you."

Arilan forced himself to relax, willed his hands to be steady as he rested them on the edge of the table and sat back in his chair. If Wencit had not approached the Council, then . . . ?

"I begin to see," he murmured, his gaze softening as he continued to scan the Council. "My lords, ladies, you must forgive me. It appears that we—the king and I—have been the victims of an audacious hoax. Wencit tells us that there will be official Council arbitration of the duel, hoping to lull us into a feeling of false security. Then he appears at the duel with only his three—or, no. He and his chosen three appear at the duel with four additional men impersonating a Council arbitration team. He does not know that I am a member of the Council, or even that I am Deryni. And how could Kelson be expected to know the members of the Council by sight? Until a few hours ago, he didn't even know about us. Treachery, treachery!"

The Council was still in shock, ill-accustomed to dealing so quickly with matters so grave as this. It had been years since the authority of the Council had been openly defied. The older members still could not believe that such a thing was happening, though the younger ones were beginning to assess the implications. Tiercel, who had spoken before, glanced at his colleagues and then sat forward thoughtfully.

"Denis, who is named in Wencit's challenge?"

"Somewhat unusually, it is to be a four-way Duel Arcane," Arilan replied. "Wencit, his kinsman Lionel, Rhydon, and

Bran Coris, on Wencit's side. With Kelson would be Morgan and McLain and, presumably, myself. Wencit did not name us specifically, but there is no one else." He paused. "But I do not intend to fight Wencit where there is treachery involved—not under *his* terms, at least. I claim Council protection for myself and my colleagues. The protection of the *real* Council."

Barrett cleared his throat uneasily. "I fear that will be impossible, Denis, though I regret it for your sake. Not all of those whom you have named are Deryni."

"They are not all *full* Deryni," Arilan conceded. "However, all of them are being obliged to function as full Deryni. Do you object to Morgan and McLain still?"

"They are still half-breeds!" Vivienne snapped. "How could you expect that to change? We cannot alter our ways to suit your convenience."

"Lord, give me patience!" Arilan struck the table with the flat of his hand and lurched to his feet. "Are we so blind, so fettered by rules, that we must perish because of them?"

He slipped from his place at the table and strode vigorously toward the golden doors, pausing in the archway as the doors swung back from him.

"I shall return momentarily, my lords. Since I am challenged, I claim your duty for myself and I claim it for my new allies—my *Deryni* allies. I think it's high time you met them!"

With that he turned on his heel and stalked from the chamber, leaving a stunned Council in his wake. Seconds later he was striding back through the giant double doors, three others following closely behind him. Gasps accompanied Arilan's arrival, along with murmured words of indignation. Laran started to come to his feet in protest, but then thought better of it as Arilan's gaze touched his and scanned the rest of the Council. Arilan stopped behind his chair and waited until Kelson, Morgan, and Duncan had ranged themselves uneasily behind him. Only then did he address the Council.

"My lords and ladies, I hope you will indulge my seeming unorthodoxy in bringing these men here, but you have forced me to it. If I am to be drawn into public combat, forever jeopardizing the standing I once enjoyed in the human community, I must claim the ancient protections. The same holds true for my colleagues here, since a chain is only as strong as its weakest link. All of us must be equally assured of the benefits of your protection." He glanced behind him.

"My lords and ladies, I have the honor to present Kelson Cinhil Rhys Anthony Haldane, King of Gwynedd—your sovereign lord. Also the Duke of Corwyn, Sir Alaric Anthony Morgan, King's Champion. And lastly, Monsignor Duncan Howard McLain, His Majesty's Confessor and now, it appears, through the hideous treachery of Wencit of Torenth, Duke of Cassan and Earl of Kierney. His father, Duke Jared, was executed by Wencit today."

"What?" someone murmured.

"Each of these gentlemen is at least half-Deryni by our standards," Arilan went on, "to be counted full, since your declaration at our recent meeting." He turned to glance at the three. "Sire, my lords, I have the somewhat dubious honor to present the lords and ladies of the Camberian Council. Whether they continue to live up to its glorious heritage remains to be seen."

The three newcomers made cautious bows, and then Morgan inclined his head toward the bishop.

"Excellency, may I have leave to ask a few questions?"

"Surely—"

"*We* will ask the questions, sir," Vivienne interrupted imperiously. "Who gavest thou leave to approach this Council?"

"Why, my Lord Arilan did, my lady. Am I to understand that this Council speaks for all Deryni?"

"It is the bastion of the old ways," Vivienne replied coolly. "Dost thou, a half-breed, dispute our ancient customs?"

Morgan raised an eyebrow in surprise and turned wide,

guileless eyes on the venerable lady. "My lady, I certainly do not. If I am not mistaken, your ancient customs were at work last fall when our Lord King fought the Lady Charissa. Without the tempering force that I am led to believe that this Council wields, His Majesty might not have gained the time to discover his talents. There is good reason to be proud of him."

"Certainly there is," Vivienne said irritably. "Young Haldane is a worthy descendant of our race. On his mother's side is pure Deryni ancestry, though hidden for many years. On his father's side, he descends from the great Haldanes whom the Blessed Camber chose to restore to glory, inheritor of the fruits of the Great Discoveries. By combination of his birth, we count him as one of us. He has always had the benefit of challenge protection, even if he did not know it. He shall have it again, as shall Lord Arilan. The Council stands by these two."

"And myself? Duncan?"

Vivienne's reply was somewhat tempered by regret. "Thou art both born of Deryni mothers, of full sisters in the blood, and as such shouldst be dear to us. But thy fathers were human—which makes thee outcast."

"But what of their powers?" Tiercel asked eagerly, breaking in on Vivienne without hesitation. "Morgan, is it true that you and McLain can heal?"

The question elicited immediate silence as every face turned toward Morgan. He looked long into the eyes of Tiercel de Claron, then let his gaze slip across the others of the Council. There was anticipation there, some eager and some dread, and Morgan suddenly became uncertain just how much he wished to disclose about his newly discovered talent just yet. He glanced to Arilan for guidance, but the bishop gave no sign.

Very well. He would take the initiative on his own, try to put the Council on the defensive, let them know that, half-breed or not, Alaric Morgan was a man to be reckoned with.

"Can we heal?" he repeated softly. "Perhaps later I shall

tell you about that. For now, I would ask again of my and Duncan's status. If, as we have been led to believe, the two of us are subject to full challenge, by right of our maternal inheritance, may we not also claim the right to challenge protection? If I and my kinsman are liable only for the peril, and not the protection, of our blood heritage, where is the much-vaunted Deryni justice?"

"Do you presume to question our authority?" Coram asked carefully.

"I question your authority to place our lives in jeopardy because of circumstances which are outside our control, sir," Morgan replied. Coram sat back and nodded slowly as Morgan continued. "I do not pretend to understand all the ramifications of my inheritance, but His Majesty will assure you, I think, that I have a fair idea what justice is all about. If you bar us from the protection of our birthright and force us to stand against full Deryni who are formally trained in the use of their powers, it may be that you decree our deaths. Surely we have done nothing to warrant that."

Blind Barrett turned his head toward Arilan and nodded. "Please ask your friends to wait outside, Denis. This request bears discussion in plain language. I would not expose our inner bickerings to outsiders."

Arilan bowed and then glanced at the three behind him. "Wait beside the Portal until I call you," he said in a low voice. As soon as the doors had closed behind the three, Thorne Hagen was on his feet, pounding his plump hand against the inlaid table.

"This is preposterous! You cannot grant Council protection to a pair of half-breeds! You heard how belligerent Morgan was. Do you condone that?"

Barrett turned his head slowly toward Coram, ignoring Thorne's outburst.

"What think you, Stefan? I value your advice. Would it be worthwhile, do you think, to summon Wencit and Rhydon here and demand that they answer for what they allegedly have done?"

Coram's pale eyes darkened slightly, and his face took on a determined set. "I would be opposed to calling any outsider to this Council chamber, especially the two you have named. Three intruders are more than enough for one day."

"Oh, come now, Stefan," said the red-haired Kyri. "We all know how you feel about Rhydon, but that was years ago. This is an important matter. Surely you can set aside your petty quarrel with Rhydon for the sake of the safety of us all."

"It is not a matter of our safety. It is a matter of two half-breed Deryni who now are to be exposed to mortal danger because of their loyalty to their king. If the Council wishes to call Wencit and that other one into its presence, it has that right, of course. But it shall do so without my sanction and without my presence."

"You would withdraw from such deliberations?" Vivienne asked, amazement written across her seamed face.

"I would."

"I, too, should prefer not to have Rhydon come here," Arilan joined in. "He does not yet know me for Deryni, and I would as soon matters remained that way for as long as possible. It could give the king a much-needed edge in the Duel Arcane, since it appears certain we shall have to fight it."

Barrett nodded slowly. "That is a valid reason against. And the same argument applies to Wencit's presence. Does the Council agree? And regardless of your feelings on this matter, what is your will regarding Morgan and McLain? Are they or are they not to be afforded Council protection?"

"Certainly they are!" snapped Tiercel. "Not only has Wencit impugned the dignity of the Council by daring to present a false arbitration offer, but there are two full humans on Wencit's side, whose powers are only assumed. They haven't a drop of Deryni blood. Because of both factors, I say, why not agree to formally arbitrate this Duel Arcane in truth? Let a *real* Council arbitration team show up at the duel tomorrow and extend the protection to all eight parties concerned. It's a mere formality anyway, other than to guard against treachery from without. The outcome will depend on the strength and skill of the contestants. We all know that."

After a short silence Vivienne nodded her gray head. "Tiercel is correct, even in his brash youthfulness. We had neglected to consider Wencit's two non-Deryni combatants—and Wencit has affronted the Council by daring to misrepresent us. As for Morgan and McLain," she shrugged, "so be it. If their side should win, and they survive, it should be ample proof that they were worthy of our protection from the start. We stand on firm ground, regardless of the outcome."

"But—" Thorne began.

"Will you be quiet?" came the retort from Kyri, the other distaff member of the Council. "My lords, I concur with Vivienne, and I feel certain that Tiercel and Arilan will do the same. Laran, what say you? Will your curiosity and your pride permit what has been proposed?"

Laran nodded. "I will concede any point of order which might ordinarily be violated to permit this. And I hope that they do win. It would be criminal to lose the healing power, if Morgan does, indeed, have it."

"A practical rationalization if ever I heard one," Vivienne chuckled. "Well, my lords? Five of us support this measure. Is there any need for a formal vote?"

There was no word spoken, and Vivienne glanced toward Barrett with a slight smile. "Very well, my Lord Barrett. It appears that our august colleagues have agreed to take the half-breeds under our protection and to arbitrate the Duel Arcane tomorrow. Are you prepared to carry out your duties?"

Barrett nodded wearily. "I am. Arilan, recall your friends."

With a satisfied smile, Arilan strode to the golden doors, which opened silently as he approached. The three without turned to stare at him with anxious faces, but his expression told them all they needed to know. They entered the room behind Arilan with confidence in their stride, heads held high, no longer quite so intimidated by the Camberian Council.

"Stand with your colleagues, Arilan," Barrett said, as the four approached Arilan's chair. Arilan stopped, Kelson, Morgan, and Duncan gathering around him, and faced Barrett squarely.

"Kelson Haldane, Alaric Morgan, Duncan McLain, hear the decision of the Camberian Council. It has been decided that all of you have the right to Council protection in this matter, and hence it has been granted. The Duel Arcane shall be arbitrated by Laran ap Pardyce, the Lady Vivienne, Tiercel de Claron, and myself. Arilan, you are to have no further contact with the Council until the Duel Arcane is decided. Further, you will instruct these three in what will be required of them in order to fulfill the requirements of the duel. All shall be done according to the proper ritual, as it was in the beginning. None of you is to discuss what will happen tomorrow with any person now outside the confines of this chamber. Is that understood?"

Arilan bowed, a formal, stylized obeisance. "It will be done according to our ancient ways, my lord."

With that, he led the three out of the Council chamber, back onto the darkness of the Transfer Portal in the antechamber. Though he knew that they were bursting with questions, he would not permit them to speak while in the Council's precincts, but instead took them back through the Portal.

But in the first, confused seconds of their arrival, it was as though the preceding minutes had been but a dream. Only the sleeping forms of Nigel, Cardiel, and Warin, the rolled-back carpeting and knife-cut turf were immediate reminders that it had all been very real.

Kelson turned slowly to stare at Arilan. "It—it did happen, didn't it?"

"It certainly did." Arilan smiled. "And miracles do still occur, it seems. Kelson, if you will draft your acceptance of the challenge, we shall send it off to Wencit right away." He sighed as he kicked aside the candle stumps and slumped into a chair beside the patch of turf. "The Portal can be covered now, too. It still can be used, if necessary, but there is no further need for direct contact with the ground."

Kelson nodded and moved to a portable writing stand, taking out quill and parchment. "What tone do you wish me to set, Bishop? Confident? Belligerent?"

Arilan shook his head, "No, slightly apprehensive but resigned, I think—as though you have been forced into this against your better judgment. We do not want him to know we have contacted the real Council or seen through his little scheme." A diabolical gleam suddenly lit in the bishop's blue-violet eyes. "In fact, sound abject, frightened but trying to put a brave face on it. When the *real* Council shows up in the morning to arbitrate the Duel Arcane, we shall see how Wencit likes *that*!"

CHAPTER TWENTY-FOUR

"Thus saith the Lord, Behold, I will bring evil upon this place, and upon the inhabitants thereof."

II KINGS 22:16

THERE were many stars as Arilan stared up at the night sky from the shelter of Kelson's pavilion doorway later that night. Around him could be heard the sounds of the camp settling down to sleep—a sleep that could well be their last: the sounds of horses pulling at their tethers and snorting at the night-fears, of men calling the watch and pacing their assigned areas; conversation sounds, low voices, as the men prepared to sleep. Around Arilan, a ring of torches set in the ground lit the area before Kelson's pavilion with a hazy, orange glow, but mere fire could not compete with the stars tonight. Arilan thought he had never seen so bright a summer sky. Perhaps he never would again.

There was the sound of leather-shod feet behind him, and then Kelson was standing beside him, staring over his shoulder to gaze up at the stars also. Bareheaded, and with a simple soldier's cloak clasped around him, the young king stood silent for a long moment. He, too, felt the spell of the summer night.

"Are Alaric and Duncan on their way?" he finally asked.

"I've sent for them. They should be here shortly."

Kelson sighed and stretched his arms in front of him with fingers intertwined, glancing idly around at the circle of torches, at the guards just within range of the orange fire-light.

"This will be a short night. We probably ought to be ready well before dawn, just in case Wencit tries something else underhanded. The messenger who delivered our acceptance said he didn't look pleased at all."

"We shall be ready for him," Arilan said. "And as for surprises, I fear that Wencit is the one who will be getting that, once the sun rises."

He paused as a movement outside the ring of torchlight caught his eye, then nudged Kelson as Morgan and Duncan strode past the guards to make short bows.

"Is anything wrong?" Morgan asked the king.

Kelson shook his head. "No, I'm just restless, I suppose. I wanted to go up to the hilltop and look at Wencit's layout again. I don't trust him."

"And well you do not," Duncan murmured under his breath, as Morgan raised an eyebrow and glanced past Kelson into the tent.

"How is Derry?" Morgan asked, ignoring Duncan's comment.

Kelson followed Morgan's glance and moved out of the doorway. "He was sleeping peacefully, the last time I looked. Let him be. I want to go up to the hilltop."

"I'll join you in a moment. I want to check on him myself."

As the others moved into the darkness, Morgan turned away from them and entered the tent. One shielded candle burned in a wrought-iron holder near the great state bed, and by its light and the light of the brazier farther back in the pavilion, Morgan made his way to the form lying beneath sleeping-furs on the other side of the chamber. As he knelt down beside Derry, the sleeping-furs moved and Derry rolled face-up. His eyes were closed, but it was evident that he was either beginning or ending a nightmare.

He moaned softly and flung an arm across his eyes momentarily, then relaxed and passed into deeper sleep once again. Once Morgan thought he heard Derry murmur, "Bran," but he could not be sure.

Morgan frowned as he reached out to touch Derry's forehead lightly, but no impressions came through with his cursory scan of the troubled mind beneath his touch. Whatever the nightmare, it had passed. Perhaps now Derry would sleep peacefully.

Well it might have been, if Morgan had been able to dismiss what he had seen and continue about his business—but he could not. The fact that Derry still rested uneasily, when he should have been healed; that he had called out Bran Coris's name—that boded ill, no matter how one looked at it. Certainly, Derry had been through much—just how much, no one would know until Derry came out of his deep sleep and chose to share it with them.

But why was he not now recovered? Could his rantings when he was first brought back to the camp have held some darker meaning? Suppose the bonds imposed by Wencit on that tortured mind had not been entirely broken?

Morgan posted an extra guard just outside the doorway, then made his way into the night. He was not conscious of any particular destination—he was merely walking to burn off nervous energy, to calm his uneasiness. He never knew how he found himself beside Bishop Cardiel's compound—or what had made him seek out Richenda.

He pulled up short, gazing into the torchlight ahead as he pondered his motives, then moved past the bishop's guards toward her tent. He knew he should not be here, after what had passed between them last night—but perhaps she could shed some light on her husband's motives, he rationalized. Perhaps she could guess why Derry had called out the earl's name in his delirium. Besides, he could not deny that he ached to see her again, despite the fact that he knew he had no right to be here.

He moved into the circle of torchlight surrounding the entrance to her pavilion and took the salute of the perimeter guard, then strode softly to the pavilion entrance. There was no one in the front half of the structure, but beyond the divider curtain, he could hear a woman's voice singing a lullaby. He stood beside the center support pole and listened as she sang.

Hush, my angel, go to sleep.
Holy God thy slumber keeps.
'Gainst the terrors of the night,
He will be thy guiding light

Hush, thy mother lies nearby.
Hush, my angel, do not cry.
God and I will keep thee well,
And all fears from thee dispel.

Drawn by the song, Morgan drifted closer to the doorway and slightly widened a narrow gap in the curtain. Across the inner chamber, he could see Richenda bending over Brendan's bed, tucking the sleeping-furs tenderly around her little redheaded son. The boy was drifting into sleep, but as he reached chubby arms up to hug his mother's neck, he spied Morgan in the doorway and instantly roused, scrambling onto his knees with a pleased smile, his blue eyes wide with wonder.

"Papa? Have you come to tell me a story?"

Embarrassed, Morgan drew back from the entryway, but not before Richenda could turn and catch sight of him. Her start at the boy's words was quickly covered as she realized that it was Morgan and not her husband. Then she was picking up the boy in her arms and moving toward Morgan with a faintly nervous smile.

"No, dear, that isn't your father. It's Duke Alaric. Good

evening, Your Grace. Apparently in the dim light Brendan has mistaken you for his father."

As she made a slight curtsy, Brendan clung closer to her—he could see now that the man standing in the doorway was, indeed, not his father—but he was unsure just how to react. He looked to his mother for some cue and, seeing her smile, judged that the stranger was probably not an enemy, so he looked shyly across at Morgan again, then back at his mother.

"Duke Alaric?" he whispered. The name meant nothing to so small a boy; he was merely trying to sort out identities. But before the boy could have time to think about it further, Morgan took a few steps closer and made a short bow.

"Hello, Brendan. I've heard some very nice things about you."

Brendan eyed Morgan suspiciously, then turned back to his mother.

"Is my papa a duke?" he demanded.

"No, dear. He's an earl."

"Is that as big as a duke?"

"Well, almost. Do you think you can say hello to His Grace?"

"No."

"Certainly you can. Say, 'Good evening, Your Grace.'"

"Good ebening, Your Grathe," the boy lisped.

"Good evening, Brendan. How are you tonight?"

Brendan put two fingers in his mouth and looked down, suddenly shy again. "I'm fine," he drawled.

Morgan smiled and bent down closer to the boy's level.

"That was a very pretty song your mother sang to you. Do you think she might sing it again, if you asked her very nicely?"

Brendan grinned impishly, fingers still in his mouth, then shook his head. "Don't want songs. Songs are for babies. Want stories. Do you know any stories?"

Morgan straightened in surprise. A story? He had never thought himself particularly cunning with children, but

Brendan seemed to be responding quite remarkably. A story. God knew, he had heard some stories in his day, but few of them were at all suitable for a four-year-old boy. What in the name of—?

Richenda saw his indecision and started to take Brendan back to his bed. "Perhaps another time, dear. His Grace has had a very busy day, and I'm afraid he's too tired to tell stories to little boys tonight."

"No, not necessarily," Morgan said, following Richenda as she put the boy back in his bed. "Even dukes can make time to amuse clever little boys. What kind of story would you like to hear, Brendan?"

Brendan settled back on his pillows with a delighted grin and pulled the sleeping-furs up tightly around his chin.

"Tell me about my papa. He's the smartest and bravest man in the world. Tell me a story about him."

Morgan froze for just an instant and looked across at Richenda, who had also stiffened at the request. The boy did not know, could not know, of the traitorous deeds of his father, and they were certainly not his fault. But neither could Morgan bring himself to praise Bran Coris, even for the sake of his engaging son. He made himself smile one of his easy, casual grins, then sat down on the edge of the bed and smoothed the boy's hair across his forehead.

"No, I don't think so tonight, Brendan. Suppose I tell you instead about a time when the king was a little boy like you. It seems that the king, who was only a prince then, had a beautiful black pony named Nightwind. Well, one day, Nightwind got out of his paddock and . . ."

As Morgan spun his tale, Richenda withdrew slightly to watch the two of them, thankful that Brendan had been successfully sidetracked. Brendan was crowing delightedly at whatever Morgan was telling him, but she could only catch a word here and there. The Deryni duke was purposely keeping his voice low, enhancing his moment with the boy by making it an event that only the two of them shared. She watched the tall, blond lord bending over the spellbound child and was herself caught anew in the web of wonder that surrounded the man.

After a time, Morgan reached out his hand to touch the boy's forehead—Brendan's eyelids had drooped in sleep some minutes before—and bowed his head for a moment. When he straightened, it was to rise and turn once more to Richenda. He seemed strangely at peace, a relaxed feeling, which was at once alien and yet somehow right. He held out his hand to her and she came to him wordlessly. After a moment he glanced back at the sleeping boy.

"He is Deryni, my lady. You know that, do you not?"

She nodded solemnly. "I know."

Morgan shifted his weight from one foot to the other, suddenly uneasy. "He is much like I was at that age: innocent, vulnerable. I know the risks involved, but he should be trained. His secret cannot remain forever, and he must have the means to protect himself."

She nodded again, once more glancing at her sleeping son. "One day soon, he will discover it for himself, that he is not like other boys. He must be warned what to expect, and yet I dread being the one to destroy his innocence.

"And then, there is the matter of his father. He worships Bran, you know, as little boys should revere their sires. But now . . ."

Her voice trailed off and she did not finish her sentence, but Morgan guessed what she was thinking. Releasing her hand, he moved to the doorway and glanced into the outer chamber. Sister Luke had returned from whatever errand she had been about and was now bustling about efficiently, setting out goblets and a flask of red wine. Morgan flushed as he saw her, wondering how long she had been there, but the sister said nothing as she lit more candles and then bowed slightly to him. Morgan emerged into the outer chamber and nodded in return as Sister Luke disappeared into the inner chamber. After a short time Richenda joined him, and Morgan covered his uneasiness by pouring two glasses of the wine.

"Did she hear?" he murmured, as Richenda took her goblet and tasted.

Richenda shook her head and sat opposite him before a camp table. "No. But if she had, she would be discreet. Besides, I am sure the guards warned her I was not alone," she smiled, "and that you had not been here long enough for our honor to be in question."

Morgan smiled fleetingly, then looked down at the goblet between his hands once more.

"About tomorrow, my lady," he began in a low voice. "If Gwynedd is to endure, Bran must die. You know that."

"It was foretold," she murmured, "but I fear it nonetheless. What is to become of us, Alaric? What will become of all of us?"

IN Kelson's tent, another wrestled with that same gnawing question. Under his sleeping-furs near the dying fire, Derry stirred restlessly and then opened his eyes. He could no longer ignore the Call. He was awake, and the dread compulsion grew. He sat up unsteadily—the tent was deserted— then threw off the sleeping-furs and got shakily to his feet. He staggered once, as though struck by a heavy blow, but then he shook his head lightly, as if to shake off an unbidden thought, and he straightened. His eyes closed briefly as he caressed the ring on his finger. When he opened his eyes, a determination lit his glance that had not been there before. Without further hesitation, he turned on his heel and strode to the tent entrance, his eyes fever-bright.

"Guard?"

"Yes, my lord?"

The guard was attentive, eager to be of service, and saluted smartly as he entered the pavilion.

"Can you give me a hand here?" Derry found himself saying. "I seem to have lost the brooch from my cloak." He gestured toward the pile of furs where he had been sleeping and made a deprecating little smile. "I'd look for it myself, but my head still throbs when I bend down."

"No trouble, sir." The guard grinned, laying down his spear to bend over the furs. "Glad to see that you're up and feeling better. We were a bit anxious there for a while."

As the man talked, Derry closed his hand around the sheathed blade of a heavy hunting dagger and moved to the man's side. Without warning, he brought the weighted hilt down hard behind the guard's right ear; the man crumpled without a sound.

Derry lost no time. After dragging the unconscious guard to the Transfer Portal, he moved to the tent entrance and dropped the flap. Then he was back at the guard's side, kneeling with his hands on the man's temples, as a strange lethargy came over him. The guard's eyes fluttered and then opened, but the intelligence that gazed back at him was not that of the simple, honest guard. Derry's own involuntary shudder was overcome by the new power forcing him to do this, and he could only abide helplessly as he felt his eyes boring into those of the enthralled guard and making contact with the new intelligence.

"Well done, Derry," the guard murmured in a voice not precisely his own. "What have you learned? Where are the Deryni princeling and his friends?"

"Gone to the perimeter to observe your camp, Sire," Derry felt himself answering. And there was nothing he could do about it.

The guard blinked and gave a slight nod. "It is well. You were not observed overpowering the guard?"

Derry shook his head. "I think not, Sire. What is it you wish of me now?"

After a slight pause the guard turned his eyes on Derry with a new intensity. "The Lord Bran wishes the return of his son and his lady. Do you know where they are kept?"

"I can find them," Derry heard himself saying, though he despised himself for the words.

"Good. Then, find some ruse to bring them to the Portal here. Tell the Lady that—"

At the sound of voices outside the tent, Derry froze. He could not be certain, but it sounded like one of the guards was talking to—Warin?

Stealthily, he got to his feet and glided over to the doorway, staying to one side where he would be shielded by the flap as it opened. Footsteps approached on the other side of the canvas, and then a hand was pressing the flap aside. As the close-cropped head of Warin was thrust through the opening, he saw the guard lying in the center of the chamber. But before he could turn to give warning, Derry had tackled him and dragged him into the pavilion, stifling his attempted outcry with a savage hand across the mouth.

Within seconds, Warin, too, lay unconscious in the center of the pavilion. Soon he was trussed hand and foot and adequately gagged, his condition camouflaged in the folds of a heavy cloak. After dragging Warin to a place across the chamber, Derry made his way out of the pavilion, keeping to the shadows.

MORGAN lowered his eyes uncomfortably and looked down at his feet, forcing himself not to let his gaze wander toward Richenda standing a few feet away. The wine had been drunk and the words said—all the words that could be said for now. If he killed Bran tomorrow, it could destroy the love this incredible woman bore for him. And yet, if Bran did not die, there was no future whatever for any of them.

He raised his eyes to hers and realized abruptly that he had never held her in his arms, never really even touched her except for their earlier hand clasp and that brief moment the night before, when they had shared their Deryniness—and tomorrow it might be too late. Tomorrow the chance might be gone for all eternity. His eyes searched hers for a long moment, reading her indecision also. Then he was folding her into his embrace, his lips drinking deeply of her kiss as the candles dimmed in the chamber around them.

After what seemed like only an instant, they drew apart, and Morgan stood a long time gazing into her eyes, her fingertips resting lightly in his hands. But he had known, from the moment he came here tonight, that he could not stay. Honor would not permit it.

And so, after a time when the only sound in the tent was the music of their racing hearts, he took his leave of her, touching her silken fingertips lightly to his lips before gliding out into the night. As he disappeared into the darkness to join Kelson and the others, he could not know that another lurked nearby, under the thrall of an enemy spell, but awaiting the chance to make his move.

Richenda paused in the doorway of the tent and watched her visitor depart, then turned to gaze around the now so empty tent. The candles had flared to new life with his going, but somehow the tent still seemed dark. She wondered again how she had happened to fall in love with this tall, golden stranger not her husband, raised slightly trembling fingers to her lips and touched them gently. Then, still smiling, she moved into the inner chamber and knelt beside her sleeping son, her smile slowly fading to concern.

What would the future hold for them after tomorrow? Regardless of the outcome of the duel, there would always be Bran's spectre looming above their heads, in life or in death. For she was bound to Bran by this boy, by bonds more adamant than mere words or law. And if Alaric Morgan killed Bran Coris tomorrow . . . Where did loyalty lie?

She considered what she had always been taught, but she was no longer certain the answers lay there. A woman's loyalty lay with her husband, or so they said. But if one's husband were a traitor, then what? Was a woman bound to hate the man who brought that traitor to justice? Somehow she did not think so.

She sighed lightly and tucked Brendan's furs more closely around him, then froze as a sound outside her tent caught her attention. Standing up as quietly as possible, she moved to the doorway of the inner chamber and saw a man silhouetted in the outer doorway. He had not been challenged by the guards and made no move to step closer—did not, in fact, appear to be menacing—but who was he? She took a few steps into the outer chamber, squinting against the deeper darkness of the outside to discern his features.

"Who's there?" she said in a low voice, not wishing to rouse Brendan or Sister Luke. "Have you a message for me?"

The man in the doorway slipped just inside and dropped to one knee. "I am Sean Lord Derry, my lady—Morgan's aide. I—could you come to the king's tent with me right away? Lord Warin has taken quite ill, and Morgan is unable to attend him at this time. Father Duncan thought you might be able to help."

"Well, of course. I mean, I'll try," she said. She took a cloak from behind the inner doorway and began to fasten it around her shoulders. "What ails Lord Warin? Have you any idea?"

Derry shook his head and got to his feet. "No, my lady. I'm afraid I don't. He's feverish, delirious. . . ."

Richenda finished fastening the cloak and gestured toward the tent flap. "I'm ready, then. Lead the way."

Derry glanced at the floor in seeming embarrassment. "My lady, before we go, I—well, I don't know how to say this so that you won't think me foolish, but the king is—well, the king wishes you to bring young Lord Brendan with you."

"He wants me to bring Brendan? Why on earth—"

"Please, my lady, I—Bishop Arilan and Father Duncan fear that Wencit and your husband might try to kidnap the boy if he's left alone. It doesn't hurt to take precautions. Besides, Morgan has given me some measure of protection."

"Oh, my poor baby," Richenda murmured, crossing herself hastily and rushing to the doorway of the inner chamber. She stood there for several seconds without moving, staring at the sleeping child, then turned back to face Derry.

"They're right. It could be a plot. Bran loves Brendan dearly. He might very well be able to coerce Wencit into trying to steal him away. Please help me wrap him in this cloak, Derry," she whispered, handing Derry a fur-lined cloak and moving toward the boy's bed. "But be careful not to wake Sister Luke. We'll be all right."

Derry smiled to himself, but she could not see, since he was bent over the sleeping boy. "Of course you will, my lady," he said in a very low voice. "These priests must be humored sometimes, though. Come. Warin needs your aid."

MINUTES later, Richenda and Derry were entering the royal pavilion, Derry carrying the sleeping Brendan. It was bright inside, after the torch-touched blackness of the outer camp, and it took Richenda's eyes a moment to adjust to the new light level. Derry moved across the chamber and laid the boy atop a pile of furs in the center of the room, then gestured to the side where Warin lay. As Richenda crossed to Warin's side, Derry stepped back and folded his arms across his chest, a slight smile on his face; but Richenda did not notice.

"He's awfully still," Richenda said, kneeling down and reaching to touch Warin's brow. "Warin? Lord Warin, can you hear me?"

As she tried to turn his face toward the light, she suddenly recoiled as she found herself staring at a mouth that bulged with a gag hastily applied. Suddenly she knew the reason for the odd angle of Warin's shoulders beneath the cloak. The hands were bound.

Aghast, she raised her eyes to search for Derry and found him backing purposefully away from the sleeping Brendan, no longer aware of her presence. She stiffened as he stepped into shadow and a faint glow appeared around his head.

"Derry!"

Abruptly she knew his intent, sensed the Transfer Portal beginning to glow around her son. She sprang to her feet and brushed past Derry, reaching the Portal just as the energies began to shift. The Portal stabilized as she exerted her will to stop it, but only until Derry streaked onto the Portal behind her, pinning her against his chest and dragging her from the circle.

She tried to scream the boy's name to wake him, but Derry's hand was clapped tightly across her mouth. Even as the first guard stuck his head through the doorway in response to her cry, she saw there was a second shadowy figure silhouetted in the circle, and then a ghostly third who bent toward the sleeping child.

"No!" Richenda shrieked, wrenching halfway away from Derry as the man scooped up her son. "Bran, no!"

Power began to stream toward the man from her fingertips, but she could not control its direction with Derry pulling at her, and the guards seemed woefully slow. Helpless to stop it, she saw the circle flare with light and then dim. She cried out, "Brendan!" once more, as the guards pulled Derry away from her and tried to subdue him. But it was too late to save her son. The boy was gone.

CHAPTER TWENTY-FIVE

"Thou art a priest for ever . . ."

PSALMS 110:4

BY the time Kelson could be summoned, the royal pavilion was swarming with guardsmen. A hush descended as the king entered the chamber, accompanied by Morgan, Duncan, and Arilan. Then the only sounds were the forlorn sobs of Richenda, slumped in the center of the empty Portal, and Derry still struggling against his restraints. Several soldiers stood helplessly beside the lady, unable to offer any comfort, and others were attending to the unconscious Warin and untying the overpowered guard. Derry continued to make periodic shambles out of his side of the chamber, sometimes taxing the ability of five guards to hold him.

Kelson assessed the situation in a glance, and in the same motion waved the excess guards out of the tent. There were murmurs of consternation, but the men obeyed. When they had gone, Kelson and Morgan started to move toward Richenda. The lady looked up briefly, then turned her head away.

"Do not approach me, Sire. There is evil in this circle. They have taken away my son, and I cannot find him."

"Brendan is *taken?*" Morgan breathed, remembering how, so short a time ago, he had lulled the boy to sleep.

Without hesitation, Arilan moved into the circle and knelt beside Richenda, assisting her to her feet and giving her into Duncan's care. She wrung her hands as Duncan drew her away from the Portal, her red-gold hair tumbling around her shoulders and across her face in disarray. Morgan started to go to her, but Arilan shook his head, motioning Duncan to take her yet farther from the circle.

"Let her be, Alaric," he said in a low voice. "A priest's touch is better just now. Our more urgent task at present is to close this Portal before Wencit tries to use it again. I should never have left it open."

"Can we assist you?" Kelson asked, watching with concern as the bishop sat back on his haunches and rubbed his hand across his eyes.

"No, your strength is needed for Derry. Stand back while I do what must be done."

As they moved at his bidding, Arilan stared up at the ceiling for a moment and drew a deep breath, as though composing himself, then bowed his head and let his hands rest on the ground to either side of him. Light began to flare around his head, ebbing and flowing with his steady heartbeat.

Then, with a brilliant flash, it was over. Arilan reeled forward drunkenly on hands and knees, gulping for breath, but before Morgan could reach him, he shook his head.

"Leave me," he rasped. "See to Derry now. This is finished. I'll join you shortly."

With a glance at Kelson, at Richenda and Duncan across the chamber by Kelson's bed, Morgan focused himself and moved toward the guards holding Derry. The young earl's eyes touched him as he approached, and the bound limbs began thrashing again as the Deryni lord came nearer. Morgan looked down at Derry for several seconds without speaking, then knelt down and began removing his gloves.

"What did you actually see?" he asked one of the guards

who seemed to be more self-possessed than the others. "Someone told us that Derry carried the boy in here, wrapped up asleep in a cloak, and that the Lady Richenda came with him willingly."

"That's what it looked like, Your Grace. They'd been inside only a minute or two. I was on guard duty just at the perimeter when I heard the lady cry out. 'Derry!' she called.

"When we got inside, we could see her struggling with him over there, where the bishop was. And something happened to the boy, too. He was lying there on the furs, just where the bishop is sitting, and then there was a funny glow, and it looked like two more people were standing there."

Kelson, who had moved closer to listen as the guard spoke, dropped to his knees beside Morgan and searched the guard's face attentively.

"One of the guards who came to fetch us said that the men were Wencit of Torenth and the Earl of Marley. Does that agree with what you saw?"

"Well, I don't know about Wencit, Sire. But the other one could have been the Earl of Marley. I've only seen him a few times, but—"

"What happened then?" Morgan said impatiently.

"Well, Lord Derry here had dragged the lady out of the circle by the time we could reach her, and then the boy and the two men were suddenly gone. I can't explain it, sir."

"Don't even bother to try," Morgan muttered. He tucked his gloves under his belt as he gazed down at the still-struggling Derry. "Has he been this way ever since?"

"Yes, sir. He wanted to get back into that circle. He kept yelling something about not closing it—that he had to get back. We had to gag him so we could hear ourselves think."

"I can imagine," Morgan muttered.

He scanned Derry from head to toe, eyes downcast as he ran both hands close above Derry's body, then glanced up at the guards. "All right, remove the gag and the bonds, and hold him. This is not going to be easy."

"But, what's wrong with him?" Kelson murmured, as the guards obeyed. "Morgan, are you sure it's safe to untie him? He acts like a man possessed."

"Yes, and we have to find out exactly to what extent," Morgan agreed. "This is apparently what he was afraid of, when he first came around this afternoon. I should have gone after it then."

As he turned his attention back on Derry, the young man shuddered and closed his eyes tightly, inhaling sharply as Morgan touched his forehead. Then the eyes opened and gazed up at Morgan, sanity there now—and embarrassment, as his glance flicked out to touch the guards pinning his arms and legs spread-eagled. When he looked back at Morgan, the blue eyes were hurt and a little frightened. Of all the reactions, Morgan had not expected this.

"What—what did I do?" Derry asked in a small voice.

"You don't remember?"

Derry blinked and shook his head. "Was it terrible? Did I hurt someone?"

Morgan bit at his lip to hold back an angry retort, thinking of the grieving woman across the chamber. "I'm afraid you did, Derry. You helped Wencit and Bran Coris to steal a lady's child away. You also injured Warin and a guard. You really don't remember?"

A crestfallen Derry shook his head, his eyes mirroring Morgan's sorrow, and Morgan looked away, unable to bear Derry's gaze anymore. He started to lay a hand on Derry's arm in sympathy, but even as his hand touched the young man's sleeve, Derry arched upward, out of the grasp of his guards, to lock both hands around Morgan's throat.

"Get him!" shouted Kelson, throwing himself across Derry's legs as the guards moved into action.

For perhaps three seconds, Derry's grip held. But then Morgan was free, pressing him back against the floor, the guards sitting on his arms and legs. Even then, Derry continued to struggle and scream, "No! God help me, no! My lord, I can't help myself! Kill me! Oh, please kill me before I—"

Morgan's fist lashed out and connected with Derry's jaw in a sickening crack, and Derry went limp. Breathing heavily, Morgan hauled himself back to his knees, motioning the guards to hold Derry's limbs once more. Kelson straightened and peered at Morgan in concern, waving off several soldiers who had come bursting into the tent at Kelson's shout.

"God in heaven, what happened? Are you all right?" he breathed, straightening his tunic and looking at Morgan with new respect. "I think he really was trying to kill you."

Morgan nodded, rubbing his throat gingerly where marks were already beginning to show. "Quite probably. The only thing I can imagine is that Wencit must have placed a very powerful control over him, consisting of many layers. That would explain why I didn't discover it this afternoon. I did neutralize the outer spell, but there was a level—or levels—below it. That's what we must break now—either that, or kill him in the trying." He drew a ragged breath and forced himself to relax again. "When he comes around, will you stay with me, be ready to come in and help fight whatever it is that's holding him?"

Kelson nodded solemn agreement as Morgan turned his attention on the guards.

"And you men, hold him this time, dammit. I can do very little when he's thrashing around like a fish and trying to choke me to death."

The guards nodded sheepishly, tightening their grips as Derry moaned and began to stir. Before he could return to full consciousness, however, Morgan lifted his hands toward Derry's head, a faraway look coming into his eyes. "Sean, listen to me," he murmured.

His hands came lightly to rest on Derry's forehead, but the younger man's body contracted in a convulsive shudder, nearly throwing Morgan's hands free, even with the holding of the guards. Shaking his head slightly, Morgan firmed his touch and exerted his will.

"It's all right now, Sean. You're safe. We're going to release you. Now, relax and let me in, as you used to do. I'm going to free you from Wencit's binding."

Derry shuddered again, his body writhing under the restraints of his captors as Morgan concentrated. Then he went limp. Morgan remained motionless for a long time before raising his head slightly.

"Kelson, join me now. Follow me, and go where I go. And you men, don't relax for even a moment, until I tell you it's safe. He could go violent again without any warning."

"Aye, sir."

As Morgan bowed his head, his gaze unfocused, Kelson laid a hand on his arm and joined him in rapport. After a moment, there was no sound in the tent save the gentle sobbing of the Lady Richenda, still huddled in the refuge of Duncan's arms.

Across the chamber, Duncan gazed past his weeping charge and watched the tableau around the now-silent Derry. Arilan, exhausted from neutralizing the Portal, had summoned up enough strength to leave the circle and move closer to watch Morgan and Kelson; and the only guards now in the pavilion were occupied with Derry. Now, Duncan realized, was the time to attempt easing Richenda out of her despair, to urge her to talk about what had happened.

"My lady?" he said gently.

Richenda sniffled and swallowed noisily, lifting her head to wipe at her eyes with a handkerchief. Then she bowed her head miserably again, without looking up at him.

"I have done a terrible thing, Father," she whispered. "I have done a terrible thing, and I cannot even ask forgiveness, because I would do it again, if I had the chance."

Duncan's mind raced back over the events of the last little while and tried to think what she could be referring to, totally forgetting, for the moment, that he was still suspended from his priestly functions.

"What terrible thing is that, my lady?" he asked. "I don't see how you can blame yourself for anything that happened here tonight. Didn't Derry lure you here, to try to kidnap you and your son?"

Richenda shook her head. "You don't understand, Father. My—my husband was one of those in the circle, who stole my son away. And I—I tried to kill him."

"You tried to kill him?" Duncan repeated, wondering how this slip of a girl thought she was capable of such a thing.

"Yes, and I probably would have succeeded if Wencit hadn't been there and Derry hadn't hindered me. You are Deryni, Father. You know whereof I speak."

"*I* know?" Duncan broke off, suddenly realizing the implication of what she had said. "My lady," he whispered, drawing her nearer the pavilion wall, away from the others, "are *you* Deryni?"

She nodded but would not look up at him.

"Does Bran know?"

"He does now," she murmured, chancing a look at his face. "And I—oh, Father, what's the use? I cannot lie to you. I think there was another reason that I tried to kill Bran. He—I—oh, God help me, Father, but I've come to love another man. I've come to love your Alaric, and he loves me. I've not betrayed my marriage vows yet—at least not in deed. But if Alaric kills Bran tomorrow—and such is likely—the law . . . Oh, forgive me, Father. I am not even thinking about Bran. But he *is* a traitor. What am I to do?"

She began sobbing bitterly again, and Duncan gathered her against his shoulder, easing them both to sit on the edge of Kelson's great bed. Across the chamber, Morgan and Kelson still knelt motionless beside the enthralled Derry, Arilan and the restraining guards now watching impassively. Duncan could expect no help from that quarter. This was one cup that would not pass until he had drunk it in full measure. He bowed his head against the woman's hair and tried to sort out his jumbled emotions.

Richenda and Alaric. Of course. It all came together now. He had been blind not to see it sooner. Knowing Alaric's scrupulous conscience, nothing would have happened yet, so far as actual deeds were concerned. Richenda herself vowed that she had yet been faithful to her marriage bed.

But Duncan knew, too, the inward guilt the two must feel, the anguish over motives, and what tomorrow might bring. He wondered briefly why Alaric had not confided in him, then realized that there had really been no time—and even if there *had* been time, it was something that Alaric would have thought so shameful, so dishonorable, that he could not have mentioned it, even to his priest-kinsman. To lust after another man's wife would be totally unacceptable to Alaric Morgan.

That realization brought the mantle of his priesthood upon him once again—and the reminder that he had, for a time, actually forgotten his suspension. Further, his discovery of Richenda's Deryniness had brought back the other conflict that had warred within him for so many years. In appealing to him as priest, she had also struck the part of him that was Deryni. Could he reconcile the two at last? Who was he, really?

Very well, he was Deryni, first and foremost. He had been born that and had lived with that identity for nearly thirty years. The fact that it had been hidden from the outside world until recently had no real bearing on his present dilemma. He was Deryni.

But, what of his priesthood? He had been under technical suspension for several months now, and had obeyed that suspension since burying his brother at Culdi. Further, he had been cleared of the excommunication imposed upon him for his actions at Saint Torin's—in fact, had never really been excommunicated at all, so far as many of the bishops were concerned.

But where did he stand as a priest? Was it, perhaps, possible that he could reconcile the two identities and be both, despite the ancient bans to the contrary? Could he continue to function both as priest and as Deryni?

He glanced at Arilan and considered the possibility. From the time he had taken his first vows, there had never been any doubt in his mind that his calling to the priesthood was genuine, or that he had been a good priest. And Bishop Arilan—Arilan seemed to have none of the doubts that had always nagged at Duncan's conscience about the compatibility of the two identities, though the Deryni bishop had been careful to protect himself for many years, Duncan noted, so that the union of the two identities be not unduly endangered.

What was it that Arilan had said?—that he and Duncan were the only Deryni priests to be ordained since the Restoration, at least so far as Arilan knew. And there was certainly no doubt in Duncan's mind that Arilan believed in his calling, considered himself a true servant of God. Duncan had always sensed the aura of sanctity about the man, from their first meeting nearly six years ago. There was no doubt in his mind that Arilan was faithful to his priestly vows, that his ordination was valid. Why should Duncan's be any less valid, merely because he, too, was Deryni? Seeing Arilan's example, why should Duncan not function as a priest *and* Deryni?

He glanced down at Richenda again as she stirred against his shoulder and saw that she was drying her eyes, had finally composed herself. But before he could speak, she turned wide blue eyes on him and searched his face.

"I shall be all right now, Father. I know that I cannot expect forgiveness for what I have done, but will you hear my confession anyway? It may make it easier to live with myself."

Duncan lowered his eyes, remembering the one, last impediment, for Richenda's sake.

"Have you forgotten that I am suspended, my lady?"

"No. But my Uncle Cardiel says that continuing the

suspension is of your own doing, since Dhassa. He says that he and Arilan saw no reason at the time why you could not resume your priestly office."

Duncan raised an eyebrow at that, for it was true. Arilan had, indeed, mentioned something about lifting the suspension after the excommunication had been revoked—except that Duncan had wanted it to be done by Corrigan, who had suspended him in the first place. But now, with Corrigan out of power and exiled back to Rhemuth, the question was largely academic. He realized that, for the first time in his life, he was truly free to make the decision.

"Does the fact that I am Deryni mean nothing to you?" he asked, in a last effort to reassure himself of what he wished to do.

She looked at him strangely, impatiently. "It means a great deal to me, Father, for you will, perhaps, be better able to comprehend my anguish. But you ask as though your identity should be a detriment, simply because you are now known for what you are. Do you not intend to practice your priestly calling conscientiously, in the same fashion as you have done in the past?"

"Certainly."

"And you consider yourself to have been a good priest, in the years before your identity was known?"

He paused. "Yes."

Richenda smiled fleetingly, then sank slowly to her knees. "Then, shrive me, Father. As a soul in need, I call upon you to perform your sacred office. You have been idle far too long."

"But—"

"The suspension is lifted, so far as your superiors are concerned. Why do you resist? Is this not what you were born to do?"

Duncan smiled sheepishly, then bowed his head as Richenda crossed herself and clasped her hands. Abruptly he knew that he *was* doing what he was born to do, and that he would never doubt again. Serene and confident now, he listened as Richenda began her whispered confession.

ACROSS the tent, Morgan lifted his head and exhaled in a long sigh, signing for the guards to release their holds of Derry and withdraw. Derry lay quietly before him now, his eyes closed in natural sleep. As the guards drew back to the doorway, Morgan sat back on his haunches to contemplate a small circle of blackened metal in the palm of his hand. Kelson glanced at the ring, then looked up at Arilan. All of them avoided looking at Derry's right hand, at the forefinger, white and chill, where the ring had been. The ring and its spell had been removed, but at great cost to all concerned. Morgan tried to suppress a yawn, then gave it up and let himself stretch and luxuriate in it. When he had finished, he glanced lazily at the others, all of them relaxing a little, now that the ordeal was over.

"I think the danger is past now. The spell is shattered, and he's free."

Kelson glanced at Morgan's hand, which held the ring, and shuddered. "What he must have gone through, though. You shielded me from most of it, Morgan, but—*aiie*, what he'll have to live with!"

"He won't have to live with it." Morgan shook his head. "I took a few liberties and blurred his memory of what happened at Esgair Ddu. Some of the horror will be with him always, but I was able to ease the worst of it. In a few weeks, all this will be mostly a vague recollection. And he's going to be vexed he missed all the excitement tomorrow. He's likely to sleep for several days."

"He can have *my* share of the excitement tomorrow," Kelson murmured under his breath.

"Um?" Morgan grunted. He had been climbing to his feet, and had not caught the comment.

"Never mind, it wasn't kingly." Kelson grinned. "We'd best get some sleep. My lady?"

He held out his hand toward Richenda, who had finished with Duncan, and the lady crossed to curtsy meekly.

"My lady, I am truly sorry for what has transpired this night. Be assured that I shall do everything in my power to see that your son is restored to you tomorrow."

"Thank you, Sire."

"Then, let us away—all of us," Arilan said quietly. "The dawn will soon be upon us."

CHAPTER TWENTY-SIX

"It is he that sitteth upon the circle of the earth."

ISAIAH 40:22

THE day dawned unseasonably chill. There had been a heavy dew in the early morning hours, and the air still was heavy, oppressive, laden with the moisture of approaching weather. Sunrise was fiery, the east beyond the high Cardosa peaks slashed with crimson and gold and the gaunt gray of low-scudding clouds. In Kelson's camp, men looked up at the leaden sky and crossed themselves furtively, for the strange dawn seemed an evil portent. Sunlight would have made the day easier to bear.

Kelson frowned as he buckled a golden belt around his crimson lion tunic.

"This is ridiculous, Arilan. You say we can't go armed, we cannot wear steel or iron of any sort. I didn't have to go through all of this when I fought Charissa."

Arilan shook his head and smiled slightly, glancing at Morgan and Duncan. The four of them were the only ones in the royal pavilion; they had wished it that way, in light of what was to come. Earlier, Cardiel had celebrated Mass for them here, attended by Nigel, Warin, and a few of Kelson's most trusted and well-loved generals.

But now, by choice, they were alone, well aware that, once they left the solitude of this enclosure, there might never be the chance for solitude again. With a sigh of finality, Arilan tied the ribbons of his bishop's cloak under his chin, then crossed to set a reassuring hand on Kelson's shoulder.

"I know this all seems strange, Sire. But you must remember that, when you fought Charissa, you were not dueling under the formal protection and supervision of the Council. The rules are much more stringent for group challenges, because there are more chances for treachery."

"Treachery enough afoot," Morgan muttered under his breath, slinging a black cloak around his shoulders. "After seeing what Wencit did to Derry, I wouldn't put anything past him."

"Evil will be repaid," Arilan said mildly. "Come. Our escort awaits us."

Outside, Nigel and the generals waited with the horses, silent as the four emerged from the tent. Kelson was the last one out, and at his appearance his troops, to the man, dropped to one knee and bowed their heads in respect. Kelson tugged at the cuff of one red leather glove as he surveyed them, moved by their loyalty. With a curt nod to mask his true emotion, he signed for them to rise.

"I thank you, my lords," he said quietly. "I do not know when I shall see you again, if ever. This morning's battle is to the death, as you are well aware. If we prevail, we are assured that there will never again be invasion from the east. The power of Wencit of Torenth shall be crushed forever. If we lose—" He paused to wet his lips. "If we lose, it will fall to others to lead you after that. Part of the stipulation of this battle is that the winner shall spare the opposing army, since neither Wencit nor I have any wish to rule over a dead kingdom, despoiled of the flower of its knighthood. Beyond that, I cannot promise you anything except my best effort. I ask your prayers in return."

He lowered his gaze, as though finished, but Morgan leaned close and whispered something in his ear. Kelson listened, then nodded.

"I am reminded of one last duty before I take my leave from you, my lords: the naming of my successor. Know that it is our wish that our uncle, Prince Nigel Haldane, succeed us on the throne of Gwynedd, should we not return today. After him, the succession passes to his sons, and to their children after them. If we—" He paused and then began again. "If *I* do not return, you are to accord him the same respect and honor which you have graciously shown to me, and which was my father's due. Nigel will make you a noble king."

There was a heavy silence, and then Nigel himself moved to Kelson's side, dropped to both knees.

"You are our king, Sire—and so you shall remain! God save King Kelson!"

"God save King Kelson!" came the thunderous reply.

Kelson looked at his uncle, at the trusting and hopeful faces upturned toward him, then nodded briskly and turned to mount, accepted a leg up from Morgan. The big black charger pranced and curvetted as Kelson settled into the saddle and gathered up the red leather reins, snorted defiantly as the others mounted up around him.

Then Nigel took the animal's bridle and led them slowly through the camp to the edge of the battle lines, where a small group of mounted observers waited. Young Prince Conall was there, bearing the royal Gwynedd standard, along with Morgan's Hamilton, Bishop Wolfram, General Gloddruth, half a dozen others.

The Lady Richenda was also with them, muffled in a cloak of blue, her head bowed, sitting sidesaddle beside her kinsman Cardiel. She did not meet Morgan's eyes as he and the king passed, though she did glance at Duncan. Somehow Morgan knew that she would have to be there. Resolutely he put her out of his mind and turned to face the enemy.

Across the field, more than half a mile away, a similar group of horsemen was already drawing away from the enemy lines, riding out under a glowering, watery sun. Morgan glanced aside at Kelson, at Duncan, who seemed to have attained a new inner peace in the past twenty-four hours, at Arilan, calm and serene in his episcopal violet. Then he faced straight ahead, sensing Kelson's slow move forward from the corner of his eye and moving his horse to match pace. Duncan was at his right knee, Kelson to his left, with Arilan to Kelson's left. Behind them, at a respectful distance, followed Nigel and the others, the royal Gwynedd banner in their midst. Before them lay the enemy and his train.

They rode forward until the distance had closed to two hundred yards, then drew rein. For a handful of heartbeats Kelson sat his horse statue-like, staring at four similar riders across the stretch of damp grass. Then he and his three companions swung down from their horses as one, handing over the reins to a squire who rode forward and then retreated. His departure left the four of them standing alone, shivering slightly in the damp morning air despite their heavy cloaks, the wind ruffling Kelson's raven hair beneath his simple golden circlet.

"Where is the Council?" Morgan murmured, turning slightly toward Arilan as they began walking toward the enemy.

Arilan smiled slightly. "They are en route. They located those who were to impersonate them. The imposters have been dealt with, and the Council will appear on schedule. Except that they will not be those whom Wencit is expecting."

Kelson scowled. "I hope it does some good. I don't mind telling you—all of you!—that I am frightened."

"So are we all, my prince," Arilan murmured gently. "We can but do our best and trust to Divine Providence. The Lord will not suffer us to die the death if our faith is strong and our cause just."

"Pray God those are not empty words, Bishop," Kelson murmured. The four advancing enemy were within fifty yards now, and Kelson could begin to see their faces.

Wencit looked dour and almost worried this morning. He had appeared in something less than his usual splendor, choosing a simple tunic of violet velvet with his leaping hart on the chest, instead of more resplendent attire, and his kingly diadem was only slightly more ornate than Kelson's own plain circlet. Lionel, on the left, was garbed in his customary black and silver, though his flame-bladed dagger was conspicuously absent; Bran, to Wencit's immediate right, looked pale and nervous in royal blue. Rhydon, to the right of Bran, wore a plain tunic and cloak of midnight blue, his dark hair confined by a silver fillet across the brow. He and Wencit both kept glancing toward the hillocks to the north, as though expecting something—undoubtedly watching for the Council to arrive. Kelson wondered if they were getting suspicious.

He did not have long to speculate. Before the eight had come within thirty feet of each other, there came a rumble of hoofbeats from the north, and then the spectacle of four richly garbed riders cresting the rise. The white horses looked like ghosts beneath the sickly sun, and their riders wore the white and gold raiment of the ancient Deryni lords. As the eight watched the riders draw nearer, Kelson heard a whispered exchange between Wencit and Rhydon and glanced aside to see Wencit's face gray with fury, Rhydon's untouched by outward emotion.

But then the four newcomers were dismounting: blind Barrett, the physician Laran—and young Tiercel de Claron helping the Lady Vivienne from her mount. The white horses stood like statues as their riders gathered momentarily before them and adjusted their golden mantles. Blind Barrett's emerald eyes swept the waiting eight imperiously as he and his colleagues came within a few yards.

"Who has called the Camberian Council to this field of honor?"

Wencit, with a look of pure loathing at Kelson, stepped forward and dropped to one knee, his chin dipping stiffly in grudging salute. His voice was controlled but edged with suspicion as he spoke.

"Worthy Councilor, I, Wencit King of Torenth, a full Deryni of the blood, claim Council protection and arbitration for a Duel Arcane in challenge against that man." He pointed toward Kelson, his accusing finger like a lance. "I claim the Council's protection against treachery for myself and my colleagues: Duke Lionel"—the duke knelt, bowing his head—"the Earl of Marley, and Lord Rhydon of Eastmarch, who was once of your company." At the speaking of their names, Bran and Rhydon also knelt, and Wencit continued.

"We stipulate that this shall be a battle to the death, we four against the four others who stand before you—and that the circle be not broken until all of one side have perished. To this do we pledge our powers and our lives."

Barrett's emerald eyes turned slowly from Wencit to Kelson. "Is this likewise thy desire?"

Kelson, swallowing nervously, knelt also before the Deryni lords.

"My lord, I, Kelson Haldane King of Gwynedd, counted a full Deryni by thy reckoning, do affirm my acceptance of the challenge laid down by Wencit of Torenth, that no more blood be spilled between us in war. I also claim thy protection against treachery for myself, for my Lord Duke Alaric, for Bishop Arilan, and for Monsignor McLain." The three likewise knelt. "We do reluctantly agree that this shall be a battle to the death, the four of us against the other four who kneel before you—and that the circle be not broken until all of one side are dead. To this we pledge our powers and our lives."

Barrett nodded, then tapped the end of his tall ivory staff against the grass once. "So be it. Now, to the victors, what fruits are proposed? Have the lords of both thine armies agreed to abide by the outcome of this contest?"

"They have, my lord," Kelson spoke up, before Wencit could reply. "My men have been informed that, should we lose, their lives will be spared and that my heirs shall, in perpetuity, swear fealty to the Kings of Torenth, that there may be peace between our nations. Does the King of Torenth agree?"

Wencit glanced at his colleagues, then at Barrett. "I agree to the terms, my lord. If we should not prevail, I vow that my heirs shall, in perpetuity, swear fealty to the Crown of Gwynedd as their overlord."

Barrett nodded. "Who is thine heir, Wencit of Torenth?"

Wencit nodded toward Lionel. "Prince Alroy Furstán, eldest son of my sister Morag and my kinsman Lionel. After Alroy, his brothers Liam and Ronal."

"And Prince Alroy is prepared to swear fealty to Kelson of Gwynedd, if you and his father should perish today?"

Wencit nodded, tight-lipped. "He is."

Barrett turned to Kelson. "And you, Kelson of Gwynedd. Is your successor prepared to swear fealty to Wencit of Torenth, if you should perish?"

Kelson swallowed. "My heir is my father's brother, Prince Nigel Haldane, and after him, his sons, the Princes Conall, Rory, and Payne. Prince Nigel knows his duty, should I be killed."

"Very well," said Barrett. "And will these terms completely satisfy both sides?"

"Not entirely," Kelson found himself saying. "I have one further stipulation, my lord."

Wencit's eyes widened, but he checked himself from moving closer as Barrett's staff moved in his direction.

"State your stipulation, Kelson of Gwynedd," Barrett said.

"Last night, Wencit of Torenth and Bran Coris entered my camp and stole a lady's child. If I and mine prevail, I would require that the child be forfeit and given to me, that I may return him to his mother."

"No!" Bran cried, starting to get to his feet, "Brendan is my son! He belongs to *me*! She shall not have him!"

"Hold your peace, Bran Coris!" Vivienne snapped, speaking for the first time. "If Kelson wins, what matters it to you *who* gets the child? You will be dead."

"She speaks the truth, Bran," Wencit added, before Bran could object. "On the other hand, if *I* am victorious, I might stipulate that the boy's mother be returned to her husband, who stands here." He gestured toward Bran, and Bran nodded. "If Kelson will agree to that, I will agree to the return of the boy. I will also agree to return unharmed all the remaining prisoners I hold alive, if that will help to sweeten the terms."

"Kelson of Gwynedd?" Barrett said.

Kelson hesitated hardly an instant. "This is agreeable. I have no further terms."

"And you, Wencit of Torenth?"

"No further stipulations."

"Then, you may rise."

The eight got to their feet in a rustle of silks and velvets.

"You may now form the circle of combat," Barrett continued, walking between the two groups with Laran at his elbow. "We perceive that you have heeded our admonition against steel or weapons, so no further inspection will be necessary on that count. But if any man has question on how this duel is to be conducted, let him raise it now, before the Council closes the first circle."

Laran and Barrett had reached a point perhaps forty feet from their colleagues, and the four were now separating and going to the cardinal compass points, marking off a square perhaps forty feet on a side. When they had taken their positions, the eight combatants ranged themselves in two arcs of a smaller circle within the square. The two kings looked expectantly toward Barrett, but it was Tiercel who left his place and strode confidently into the center of the figure.

"Thus saith the Lord Camber of blessed memory, thus saith the Holy One, who taught us the Way. Thus it has been written, thus it shall be done. Blessed be the Name of the Most High," he said.

He knelt on one knee and, extending his right forefinger, began to trace a sign on the ground. Where his finger passed, the grass turned golden.

"Blessed be the Creator, yesterday and today, the Beginning and the End, the Alpha and the Omega." His finger had traced a cross, with the Greek letters inscribed at the top and bottom of the figure. "His are the seasons and the ages, to Him glory and dominion through all the ages of eternity. Blessed be the Lord, blessed be Holy Camber."

As he rose, more symbols could be seen inscribed in the four angles of the cross: the sigils of the four councilors, signifying their protection over this circle. As soon as Tiercel had returned to his place, Barrett picked up the chant, raising his hands beside his head.

"I am the Alpha and the Omega, the Beginning and the End, saith the Lord," Barrett intoned. "He that overcometh, the same shall be clothed in white raiment; and I will not blot out his name in the Book of Life, but I will confess his name before My Father, and before His angels."

"Blessing, and honor, and glory, and power, be unto Him that sitteth upon the throne, and unto the Lamb for ever and ever," Vivienne said, raising her arms heavenward. "Let the Lord lend His countenance to the virtuous and defend the cause of the just. Raise the light of Thy favor upon this circle, O Lord, that they who stand within shall know Thy majesty and shrink not from Thy judgement."

Laran formed the last link in the circle, raising his arms also. As he did so, light began to glow around the four Deryni nobles, amber and silver, crimson and blue. As Laran spoke, the light spread until the circle was complete. The colors merged and coalesced as his words rolled over the circle.

"Guard Thy servants, O Lord. Strengthen this circle, that nothing may enter from without, that none may aid the eight who stand embattled here. Protect those without the circle from the terrible powers soon to be unleashed within, and guard us from Thy wrath."

"As it was in the earliest days of our beginning," the four chanted, "and as it shall be for all time to come, O Lord, so let it be today. So let it be."

As they finished, there came a low rumble as of thunder, and the lights fused in a single hemisphere of pale, blue-violet brilliance around the twelve, councilors and combatants. The wall was transparent but veiled, obscuring slightly that which lay within. The next circle would be formed by the eight, and would seal them off not only from the outer world, but from the four who formed the outer ward. Not even the Camberian Council would be able to broach the inner circle.

"The Outerness is sealed," blind Barrett said. His voice echoed slightly in the glowing circle. "The Innerness must follow. Mark well: until all men of one defense shall perish, the Innerness remains. Only victors leave this arena."

There was silence as he let his words sink in, and then: "I charge you, then, to make your peace. Set forth the inner circle and do you what you will. On your honor, and in the Name of the Most High, proceed."

The eight gazed across at one another, each taking the measure of the opposition. Then Wencit took a step forward and made a formal bow.

"Will you begin, or shall I?"

Kelson shrugged. "It makes little difference, in the end. Proceed, if that is your will."

"Very well."

With a slight bow, Wencit stepped back into place, then spread his arms to either side. The setting of the inner circle was to be done by the leaders of the two groups, not jointly. Thus it was Wencit alone who spoke, his low voice echoing in the violet circle.

I am Wencit, Lord of Torenth.
I call forth fair Gwynedd's king
To answer to my mortal challenge,
With such aid as he may bring.

Once the circle's orb is fashioned,
Yours or mine must all embrace
Cold death, before the living victors
Pass from out this charmèd place.

Fire leaped from his fingertips to inscribe a semi-circle behind him and his three allies, a glittering arc of violet fire perhaps five feet from the outer ring. Kelson briefly pressed his lips tightly together, not looking at his companions, as he, too, spread his arms to either side.

Kelson, King of Royal Gwynedd,
Takes the gauntlet Wencit flings.
He accepts the mortal challenge
Which the King of Torenth brings.

None shall pass this holy circle
'Til the lives of four are done.
'Til the four of one side perish,
None may pass into the sun.

Crimson fire flared behind Kelson and joined with Wencit's, until they were all surrounded by a wine-dark hemisphere of purplish light. Kelson lowered his arms and glanced aside as his comrades moved closer to either side of him, now that the stage was set.

Across the circle, Wencit likewise gathered his men around him. The councilors could be seen dimly through the inner ring, watching what was about to unfold. But Kelson knew that they could not interfere now, come what may. From now on, he and his must rely on their own good wits.

"Will you cast the first strike, my doomed princeling?" Wencit mocked, his right hand already moving in a preliminary spell.

"No, hold!" said Rhydon. "We forget our manners, my lords. Even in war, the amenities must be observed."

As all eyes turned toward Rhydon, the Deryni lord pulled a small silver goblet from his belt, produced a leather flask. His comrades smiled as Rhydon worked the stopper from the neck of the flask, even Wencit folding his arms almost indulgently.

"It is the custom in our country," Rhydon began, as he filled the goblet from the flask, "to drink a toast to our opponents in any knightly contest." He raised the goblet in salute, then drained off half the contents.

"Of course," he continued, handing the goblet to Bran, "we realize that you may fear some treachery." He watched as Bran took a healthy swig, emptying the cup, then refilled the goblet and passed it to Lionel, "but we trust that we will allay your fears by drinking first ourselves." Lionel raised the cup and drank deeply, then passed the cup to Wencit, who held it patiently while Rhydon filled it yet another time.

"Rhydon speaks truly," Wencit said, holding the cup before him in both hands. "Our enemies, we drink to you."

With a sly smile, he raised the goblet to his lips and drank half its contents, then began crossing slowly toward Kelson, extending the cup.

"Willst dare to drink with me, doomed princeling?"

"No, he will not," Rhydon said quietly, his voice taking on a brittle, cutting edge.

Wencit stiffened, his face going very still, then turned slowly to Rhydon. Every eye had darted to the scarred Deryni, and Lionel and Bran moved uneasily together, edging closer to Wencit, away from this man who suddenly had become a stranger.

"What is the meaning of this?" Wencit said icily.

Rhydon returned Wencit's stare unwaveringly, a sardonic smile tugging at the corners of his mouth. "The meaning will become clear in a short while," he said easily. "For six years I have played my charade, worn another man's identity for nearly every hour of my life. I only regret that this day could not have come sooner."

An awful suspicion came across Wencit's face as his gaze dropped to the cup in his hand, and then he flung it to the ground with a choked cry of fury.

"What have you done?" The ice-eyes blazed across at Rhydon. *"Who are you?"*

Rhydon smiled, and his voice was low and deadly.

"I am *not* Rhydon."

CHAPTER TWENTY-SEVEN

"It is oft times a bitter lesson, to be a man."

SAINT CAMBER OF CULDI

"YOU are not Rhydon? What do you mean, you are *not Rhydon?*" Wencit demanded. "Have you gone mad? Do you realize what you've done?"

"I know exactly what I have done." Not-Rhydon smiled. "The real Rhydon of Eastmarch died of a heart seizure nearly six years ago. Fortunately, I was in a position to take his place, but you never suspected, did you, Wencit? No one did."

"You *are* mad!" Wencit said, glancing around him wildly. "This a trick, some monstrous plot." He pointed at Kelson and his stunned companions. "*They* put you up to it! You probably also arranged to have the real Council here. You never intended it to be a fair combat. Even the Council is biased!"

He turned to glare at the councilors peering into the circle, and could see their mouths working as they jabbered agitatedly to one another; but he could not hear them. Abruptly he realized that they were as stunned as he over what was happening—and in all candor, he could not deny that Kelson seemed just as mystified as anyone else. He turned to find Lionel and Bran looking very pale, whirled back in fury to face the man who was not Rhydon.

"Part of what you say is true," Not-Rhydon admitted. "I never did intend it to be fair—not for you. However, what I have done is not without its price. Though the way of my going will be a trifle different, we shall all meet the same end. Look behind you."

Wencit turned to see Bran Coris reel and stagger, reaching out a hand to steady himself against Lionel's shoulder. Alarmed and horrified, he watched Bran sink to the ground, a dizzy, muddled look upon his handsome face. Lionel had knelt to assist him, but then he, too, reeled and found himself abruptly sitting on the ground, unable to stand any longer.

Wencit plucked nervously at the collar of his tunic, his eyes going wide as he whirled back to face the man now proven to be a stranger, and his betrayer.

"What have you done to them?" he whispered. "You have poisoned them, haven't you?" He swallowed with difficulty. "And me—why am I not affected? Why have you done this?"

"It was poison of a sort," Rhydon conceded. "And do not delude yourself that you will be spared. It but takes a while longer to affect full Deryni . . . and you drank last.

"As for myself, I have even less time than you. The antidote I took delays the first reactions but speeds the final outcome. However, it will give me the time to reveal myself to you—and for you to know fear, perhaps for the first time in your life. Look at your hands, Wencit; they are shaking. That is one of the first signs of the drug taking effect."

"No!" Wencit whispered, clutching his hands together to still them and turning away.

Not-Rhydon watched Wencit impassively for several seconds, then turned toward Kelson for the first time since the tableau had begun, drew himself erect, then bowed slightly in his direction. "I am sorry to cheat you of the lawful victory you might have won, Kelson of Gwynedd, but I dared not risk the possibility that you might lose. Six years as Wencit's minion was high enough a price to pay. I could not afford to lose it all now."

As he spoke, Wencit suddenly reeled on his feet and, against his will, found himself sinking to his knees, barely able to hold up his head, much less speak. As Wencit struggled on hands and knees to rise again, Kelson watched aghast and then turned wide gray eyes on the man who claimed to not be Rhydon.

"What—what did you give them? And what of yourself?"

Not-Rhydon managed a wry smile. "The drug is similar to merasha in many respects. It, too, renders its victim unable to use any occult powers he might possess. But unlike merasha, it cannot immediately be detected as that; and also unlike merasha, it is a slow poison. I knew that when I drank; but I also knew that it was the price I must be willing to pay for deliverance from that man."

He pointed to Wencit, who now lay panting on the ground, glaring at all of them with undisguised hatred. Lionel and Bran were already motionless behind him, only their frightened eyes able to follow what was happening.

"But my death will be quick and relatively painless, even if certain," Not-Rhydon continued. "Theirs, because they have not drunk the antidote, will be slow and excruciating unless you intervene—a day at least. You cannot save them, Kelson of Gwynedd, but you can show them mercy and speed them on their way. Only four men may leave this circle alive. I have but ensured that you and yours shall be the four."

"But, this is treachery," Kelson murmured, unbelieving. "I had not thought to win by treachery."

"Believe me, their crimes more than justify the manner of their dying. There is no doubt of their guilt, despite the fact that they have had no trial. I know that—" He hesitated for just an instant, jaw clenching against apparent pain, then went on.

"Your pardon, the drugs' effects are beginning to make themselves felt. I have not much time. Will you take the victory I bring you, King of Gwynedd? Will you step into your place as a lawful king for Deryni as well as humans, and lead us back to our rightful place of honor and partnership in the Eleven Kingdoms?"

For the first time, Kelson turned to look at his companions. Duncan looked pale, silent, as did Morgan, but Arilan was staring at Rhydon as though he had seen a ghost. At Kelson's look, he started, then stepped to the young king's side. Carefully he stared at the man not Rhydon.

"I think I know you," he said uncertainly. "Oh, it is not by any fault in appearance or any nuance of voice. Your disguise is perfect. But what you have said—will you not reveal yourself now? What difference does it make?"

Not-Rhydon smiled, swaying slightly on his feet, then held out his arms to either side. His features blurred, a light seeming to glow around him faintly, and then Stefan Coram was standing before them, a strained expression on his face.

"Hello, Denis," he whispered, meeting the bishop's shocked gaze. "Please don't lecture me on the stupidity of what I've done. It is far too late for that now, and I happen to think it wasn't stupid at all. I am only sorry that I shan't be seeing any of you again." His glance flicked to the nearest councilor. "Believe me, this was the only way."

"Oh, Stefan, Stefan . . ." Arilan could only shake his head disbelievingly.

Coram smiled faintly, catching himself from swaying once again. "Yes. And I have appeared in another guise more familiar to your friends." His shape rippled again, and they could see a silver-haired man cowled in gray superimposed over the handsome features of Coram for just an instant.

"*You* were Saint Camber?" Morgan breathed.

"No, I told you I was not." Coram shook his head emphatically, going back to his Coram-shape. "I have only appeared to you a few times: at the king's coronation as a representative of the Council; to you, Duncan, on the Coroth road; at Saint Neot's—" He grimaced again and closed his eyes momentarily, and Arilan rushed to support him.

"Stefan?"

Coram shook his head in dismissal. "You cannot help me to live, my friend—only to die." He swallowed with difficulty and leaned even more heavily on Arilan's arm, dread shadowing his face. "Dear God . . .'Tis coming sooner than I thought."

As he sagged against Arilan's arm, the bishop eased him to the ground, Morgan and Duncan crowding to his other side. Kelson stood behind Arilan, watching them in dismay, but he did not join them. Now was a moment he could not really share with them. He hardly knew Stefan Coram, but the three now kneeling around the stricken man had been intimately involved with him in several ways, Morgan and Duncan in a way that Kelson could not begin to understand. He watched as Morgan pulled off his cloak and made a pillow of it under Coram's head. The man's eyes were closed, but he opened them at Morgan's touch and turned his attention to Arilan once more.

"I suppose that, in a way, I've taken my own life," he murmured, gazing up at Arilan. "But I—had no other choice. Do you—do you think He will understand?"

His eyes flicked to the pectoral cross on Arilan's chest, and the bishop bowed his head and nodded slowly. "I think He must, my friend. What you have done . . ." His voice caught, and he had to swallow before he could continue. "Is—is the pain bad?"

Coram shook his head. "Not really. Only once in a while. It will be over soon. Can—can the others see?—the members of the Council, I mean?"

Arilan glanced at the four standing at the circle's boundaries and nodded. "Yes, but the circle distorts their vision. Did you want to tell them something?"

"No." Coram shook his head. "But I do want you to have a say in choosing my successor on the Council. Despite the opposition I have seemed to show you in the past, I have valued your friendship and your courage in the Inner Circle. Promise that you will relay my wishes to them—when you tell them how I died."

His eyes closed, and he seemed to be fighting for breath. Morgan looked across at Arilan in concern.

"Isn't there anything we can do? Couldn't Duncan and I try to heal him?"

Arilan shook his head wearily. "I know what antidote he must have taken. Even a Deryni cannot cure that. The poison must have done dreadful damage already, for him to be feeling such pain. He tries to hide it, but the end is very near."

Morgan looked down at Coram again and shook his head, unconsciously moving closer to Duncan as he sat back on his haunches. Coram's eyes flicked open once again, but this time it was evident that he saw only Arilan.

"Denis," he whispered, "I just saw the strangest thing. There was a man's face, a blond man with a cowl—I think it was Ca-Cam—Oh, God, Denis, help me!"

As a vast shudder wracked his body, Coram seized Arilan's hand with both of his and grasped it hard, eyes squeezed shut. Arilan laid his other hand on Coram's forehead, trying to ease some of the pain, and gradually the older man calmed. When his eyes opened again, they were clearer, free of pain, but Arilan knew that it could not be much longer.

"Your cross, Denis," the dying man whispered. "May I hold it?"

Arilan looped the chain over his head and pressed the cross into his friend's hand. Coram gazed at it for several seconds, scarcely breathing, then pressed it briefly to his lips.

"In manuus tuas, Domini . . ." he whispered.

Then the eyes ceased to see, and the hands relaxed. With a sigh, Arilan bowed his head against his chest, lips moving in silent supplication for the soul now departed. Morgan and Duncan, after exchanging solemn glances, got slowly to their feet to back around toward Kelson.

"He's dead?" Kelson whispered, scarcely daring to break the awesome silence.

Duncan nodded, and Kelson bowed his head.

"There was nothing you could do?"

Morgan shook his head. "We asked if we might try to heal him, but Arilan said it was too late. One must assume that it's the same case with the others, except that it will take longer. What are you going to do?"

Kelson glanced at the three remaining opponents still lying on the ground but a few yards away and shook his head. "I don't know. I don't want to kill them in cold blood, helpless as they are, and yet Rhydon—uh, Coram—said that they would die slowly and painfully if I didn't."

"He said it would take at least a day," Duncan whispered.

"Aye, and if Coram's death was relatively quick and painless, I hate to think what may be in store for Wencit and the others," Kelson said softly.

Arilan rose abruptly and turned to face them, his eyes moist and shining. "We must end it, Sire. There is no other way. Coram was right—they are doomed. And I know what Coram felt as he died. There is no logic or mercy in putting even Wencit through that. It would be needless cruelty."

"But we have no weapons," Kelson said, practicality intruding. "We can't just—choke them to death, or smother them, or—or beat them in the heads with rocks while they're helpless. Besides, there aren't any rocks in this circle," he finished plaintively.

Arilan drew himself to his full height and looked at the three lying on the ground, then at the circle. "No, it must be done by magic, not by physical means. This was a Duel Arcane; magic must provide the means of their destruction."

"But how?" Kelson whispered. "Arilan, I've never killed a man before, even with steel. But at least I know how to do that."

There was silence for a long moment, Kelson looking at the ground, Arilan lost in his own world, the two other Deryni silent and uneasy. Then Morgan moved to Kelson's side and laid his hand on the young man's arm, bowing his head. But he would not look at the slightly writhing figures of Wencit and Lionel and Bran—especially not at Bran.

"The burden will be mine, then, my prince. Unlike you, I have killed. It is hardly more difficult than reaching out one's hand. Charissa used it to perfection on your father."

Duncan froze. "No. Not that way . . ."

Morgan shook his head, deliberately not looking at his kinsman. "There is no other way for us, here, in this place. Wencit and his allies are helpless, even as humans now. They must die as would humans. Wencit, especially, must die as Brion died. His was the ultimate responsibility for Brion's death. Vengeance comes upon him at last."

"Then, I should do it," Kelson breathed. "Brion was my father. I am his son. I should avenge his death."

"My prince, I had thought to spare you this," Morgan began.

"No! Vengeance is *mine*! I will repay. Tell me how to do it. Don't force me to command you."

"Kelson, I—" Morgan had intended to try to dissuade him, but the king's face was set, determined. Gray eyes clashed in a war of wills for several seconds, but then Morgan broke the contact, knowing he had lost. With a tired sigh, he bowed his head, extending his hand.

"Very well, my prince. Open your mind to me and I will show you what you seek."

Kelson complied. There was a moment of deep silence as his eyes assumed a far look. Then he was bringing into focus the rest of his surroundings once more, lifting both hands slightly in disbelief. His face was grave, incredulous, and more than a little awed.

"Even so?" he breathed, a little frightened at the power he now held in his hands.

"It is even so," Morgan confirmed.

As though he had not heard, Kelson turned away and scanned the circle around him, saw the four of the Council still turned inward to observe, their faces grave. His gaze

passed over the motionless form that had been Rhydon/
Camber/Coram, then moved on to the three on the ground a
little way across the circle. He walked toward them slowly,
as though in a trance, his fists clenching and unclenching
slightly as he came to a halt before Wencit of Torenth.
Though the sorcerer could not move, his pale eyes blazed up
at Kelson.

"Are you in pain?" Kelson murmured, his face impassive.

Wencit tried to move and could not, then tried to speak.
It cost him great effort, but the words managed to escape,
low and rasping.

"You could ask such a thing, knowing how Rhydon
died?"

Kelson turned his face away uncomfortably. "That was
not my doing. I had no wish to win by treachery. Better the
clean death of honest defeat than a tainted victory."

"If you think I believe that, you must take me for an even
greater fool than I have been," Wencit said bitterly. "At any
rate, you will not walk away from this victory and forget
what you have done, however much your precious pride de-
tests what you must do."

"What do you mean, what I *must* do?" Kelson said, his
gaze snapping back to Wencit.

"Well, I cannot think you truly mean to let us lie here
until we die." Wencit made a weak attempt at a chuckle.
"Your father was not one to let even a wounded hawk or stag
hound suffer needlessly. Would you do less for a man?"

"Are you saying that you *want* to die, that you don't care
if I must kill you?"

Wencit coughed weakly and tensed, as though the movement had cost him even more pain. When he looked up at
Kelson again, there was a pleading in his eyes, even though
he tried to bite back the words he now spoke.

"You little fool, of course I care," he whispered. "But I
cannot live; I know that. Rhydon—or rather, Coram—did
his work well. And I know what lies ahead of me before the
end, if I receive not the coup. Coram has already killed me.

My body is dead, though my mind does not know it yet. Spare me the awful agony of finding out for certain."

Kelson swallowed with difficulty, then knelt down beside Wencit. He did not yet know what he was going to do. A part of him was moved by the agony of this fellow being in pain, but another part rejoiced to see his father's murderer brought thus to his fate. He started to reach out his hand, then stopped and clenched his fist against his chest, bowed his head as Wencit's whisper repeated itself in his ear: "Release me . . . please. . . ."

Kelson heard the shift of feet behind him and knew that the others were standing now at his back, ready to support him—could almost feel their thoughts beating at the back of his head. Resolutely he closed them out, and his eyes went dark and hooded as he stretched forth his right hand over Wencit's chest. He started to move, then caught himself as another, final thought came to mind.

"Wencit of Torenth, do you claim the solace of Holy Church?"

Wencit blinked and would have smiled if the move had not cost him so much pain. "I claim only death, Kelson of Gwynedd, and welcome it. Spare me further torment. Do what you must do."

To the side, Kelson was aware of Lionel and Bran gazing silently at him, the pleading evident also in their pain-wracked eyes. Slowly, deliberately, Kelson turned his gaze back to Wencit, his right hand contracting slowly over Wencit's heart as he whispered low:

"Then, die, Wencit. Obtain release. Feel the cold hand of death at your heart, and the rustle of the death-angel's wings. Thus share you the death of my father Brion. Thus is the heart of Wencit *stopped*!"

At the last word, his fist clenched convulsively. Wencit stiffened, a faintly startled look in his eyes. Then the proud body of the one-time King of Torenth was but an empty shell, life and intelligence—and agony—now past.

Before the others could react, Kelson moved between Lionel and Bran and this time stretched forth both his hands, one above the heart of each man.

"Go with your master and the angel of death, Lionel of Arjenol and Bran Coris Earl of Marley. And may God, in His infinite wisdom, find you more mercy than *I* have been able to bestow upon you. Be *still*!"

Again, there was the convulsive clench of fists, the jerk of anguished bodies. Then all was still.

Slowly Kelson let his hands sink to his sides, to rest heavily against the grass beneath his knees. When he looked up, it was to search the three grave faces of his friends. But as he got to his feet, he drew away from the hand Arilan stretched out to assist him.

"Don't, Excellency. It is not fitting that a holy man should touch me. I have just killed, and my hands are bloody."

"You had no choice, my prince," Arilan said quietly, understanding, but lowering his hand just the same. "You rendered an act of mercy. And these men were your enemies. They deserved to die."

"Perhaps. But not like this. I would not have had it end this way."

Morgan looked down at the toes of his boots. "We are not always masters of our destinies, Sire. You know that. It is sometimes the awful duty of a king, that he must kill."

"But he is not obliged to like it," Kelson whispered. "It is not something of which he should be proud."

"And are you proud?" Duncan replied. "I think not. I have known you too long and too well to believe that of you."

"But I'm glad they are dead," Kelson said stiffly. "How do I reconcile that? And at the time, I wanted them to die. I willed it, and they died. No man should have that power, Father."

"But some men do," Morgan said. "Wencit had it once— and used it."

"Does that make it right?"

"No."

There was a long silence in which no one dared to speak; then Kelson moved slowly back to Wencit's side. He stared down at the body for a long moment, scarcely breathing, then bent slowly to take the crown from Wencit's head.

"This is our prize this day, my friends," he said bitterly. "The crown of a kingdom I never wished to rule, the death of a friend I had hardly come to know," he gestured toward Coram's body, "and a legacy of disappointment in myself, that there could be no other way."

Arilan started to speak, but Kelson held up an imperious hand. "No, I will not hear your comfort just now, Bishop. Allow me the luxury of feeling guilty for what I've had to do. In the realities of being who and what I am, I know that, all too soon, this will seem merely expedient. But not today.

"No, today I must go out of this circle, with you, my loyal friends, and face the cheers of my people, who will be overjoyed at the victory I have brought them. There I will receive the hollow homage of a child-prince whose father I have killed, give back another fatherless child to a woman whose husband I have slain—even though he deserved to die—and I will be expected to look as though I am pleased at the entire thing. You will pardon me, gentlemen, if I do not rejoice."

He hefted Wencit's crown in his hand and glanced at it dejectedly, then turned to look at them again.

"Come, gentlemen, the king plays out his role. The populace is waiting. If my smile of victory occasionally goes a little ragged around the edges, you will know the reason why."

He lifted his head, and the circle glowed and was dissolved; the magic fell away. And as the king emerged, bearing the crown of Torenth in his hands, there arose a great cheering from the army of Gwynedd, and a great battering of swords and spears against shields to show their approval, and a thundering of horses' hooves as the king's men came riding out to meet him.

The four Deryni who had overseen it all laid their white and golden mantles upon the shoulders of the victors, that the words of the scripture might be fulfilled. And the friends of the king placed him upon a white horse, that he might be better seen as he rode to the men of Torenth's lines to claim his victory.

But the crown lay heavily that day upon the Heir of Haldane.

INDEX OF CHARACTERS

(*Indicates a deceased character, or one only mentioned indirectly.)

ALAIN—Morgan's alias at Saint Torin's.

ALARIC Anthony Morgan, Duke—see MORGAN, Duke Alaric Anthony.

ALROY, Prince—eldest son of Duke Lionel, age twelve; heir to Wencit of Torenth.

ARILAN, Bishop Denis—see DENIS Arilan, Bishop.

BARRETT de Laney, Lord—blind coadjutor of the Camberian Council; full Deryni.

BENNETT—a sergeant in the service of Bran Coris.

BRADENE, Bishop—Bishop of Grecotha; a famed scholar; remained neutral in the Interdict schism at Dhassa.

BRAN Coris, Lord—traitor Earl of Marley; husband of Richenda and father of Brendan.

BRENDAN, Lord—four-year-old son of Bran Coris and Richenda.

*BRION Donal Cinhil Urien Haldane—late King of Gwynedd and father of Kelson; slain by Charissa's magic at Candor Rhea.

*BRONWYN de Morgan—deceased younger sister of Alaric Morgan; betrothed of Kevin McLain, with whom she was slain by illicit magic at Culdi.

BURCHARD, Lord—one of Jared's generals; escaped the slaughter at Rengarth with General Gloddruth.

*CAMBER of Culdi, Saint—full-Deryni patron of magic; responsible for the Haldane Restoration in 904.

CAMPBELL, Baron—a baron of Eastmarch and aide to Bran Coris.

CANLAVAY, Sieur de—a northern lord captured with Duke Jared at Rengarth.

*CARA—deceased daughter of Thorne Hagen; died at a young age.

CARDIEL, Bishop Thomas—see THOMAS Cardiel, Bishop.

CARSTEN of Meara, Bishop—one of the prelates who initially sided with Archbishops Loris and Corrigan in the Interdict schism; later took a neutral stance.

*CHARISSA of Tolan—Countess of Tolan, responsible for the death of King Brion; killed by Kelson at his coronation.

COLLIER, Lord—a lord captured with Duke Jared at Rengarth.

CONALL, Prince—eldest son of Prince Nigel, age fourteen.

CONLAN, Bishop—one of the twelve itinerant bishops of Gwynedd with no fixed see; initially sided with Loris in the Interdict schism; later went over to Cardiel and Arilan.

CORAM, Stefan—coadjutor of the Camberian Council; full Deryni.

CORDAN—chief surgeon to Bran Coris.

CORRIGAN, Archbishop Patrick—see PATRICK Corrigan, Archbishop.

CREODA, Bishop—Bishop of Carbury; initially sided with Archbishops Loris and Corrigan in the Interdict schism but later became neutral.

DANOC, Earl of—one of Kelson's lords present at the Dhassa war council.

*PETER Davency—an Eastmarch soldier killed by Derry.

*RALSON, Lord—deceased member of the Gwynedd Crown Council, replaced by Sean Lord Derry.

REMIE, General—one of Kelson's generals present at the Dhassa war council.

RHYDON of Eastmarch, Lord—a full Deryni ally of Wencit; former member of the Camberian Council.

*RHYS Thuryn—ancient Deryni physician associated with Saint Camber of Culdi.

RICHARD of Nyford, Bishop—one of the twelve itinerant bishops of Gwynedd with no fixed see; captured with Duke Jared at Rengarth.

RICHENDA, Lady—Countess of Marley and wife to Bran Coris, mother of Brendan.

*ROLF MacPherson—a Deryni lord of the tenth century who rebelled against the authority of the Camberian Council.

RONAL, Prince—youngest son of Duke Lionel, age three.

RORY, Prince—middle son of Prince Nigel, age eleven.

ROYSTON Richardson—a peasant boy, age ten; associated with healing of Malcolm Donalson.

SELDEN—one of Cardiel's soldiers who assisted in the capture of Morgan and Duncan at Dhassa.

SIWARD, Bishop—one of the twelve itinerant bishops of Gwynedd with no fixed see; sided with Bishops Cardiel and Arilan in the Interdict schism.

SMALF—a miller questioned by Morgan and Duncan on the Dhassa road.

STEPHEN de Longueville—a soldier of Bran Coris ordered to test Cordan's sleeping potion.

THIERRY, Master—a clerk to Lord Martin of Greystoke; detained and interrogated by Morgan and Duncan on the Dhassa road.

THOMAS Cardiel, Bishop—Bishop of Dhassa, age forty-one; leader of the Interdict schism with Arilan.

THORNE Hagen—a member of the Camberian Council; full Deryni.

TIERCEL de Claron—youngest member of the Camberian Council; full Deryni.

TOLLIVER, Bishop Ralf—Bishop of Coroth and Morgan's prelate, age fifty.

*TORIN, Saint—one of the patron saints of Dhassa, associated with forests.

TORVAL of Netterhaven, Baron—a messenger sent by Wencit to Kelson's camp as hostage; killed by Warin and Duncan.

VIVIENNE, Lady—a member of the Camberian Council; full Deryni.

VOLMER, Lord—an agent of Wencit.

WARIN de Grey—a self-appointed messiah who believes himself designated to destroy Deryni.

WENCIT of Torenth, King—sorcerer king of Torenth, at war with Gwynedd.

WOLFRAM de Blanet, Bishop—senior of the twelve itinerant bishops of Gwynedd; sided with Bishops Cardiel and Arilan in the Interdict schism.

INDEX OF PLACE NAMES

JASHAN, Lake—lake guarding the southern approach to Dhassa, at Saint Torin's, passable by ferry.

JENNAN Vale—village in Corwyn, near the northwest border; site of a skirmish between Prince Nigel's troops and rebel peasants.

KHARTHAT—site of the marketplace where Thorne Hagen first found Moira.

KHELDISH Riding—northern area, under direct Crown rule; famous for its weavers.

KIERNEY—former earldom of Lord Kevin McLain, bordering Cassan, the Meara Protectorate, and Gwynedd Crown lands.

LINDESTARK—honor of one of the ancient families of the Eleven Kingdoms.

LLYNDRUTH Meadows—grasslands at the foot of the Cardosa Defile; site of the final confrontation between Kelson and Wencit.

MARBURY—seat of the Bishop of Marbury, Ifor.

MARLEY—earldom held by Bran Coris.

MEARA—crown protectorate to the northwest of Gwynedd; the kings of Gwynedd are also princes of Meara.

NYFORD—city of origin of the itinerant Bishop Richard of Nyford.

PELAGOG—holding of one of the ancient families of the Eleven Kingdoms.

PURPLE March, the—vast meadowlands north of Rhemuth under Crown rule; one of the titles of the kings of Gwynedd is Lord of the Purple March.

RAMOS—site of the infamous Council of 917; promulgated stringent anti-Deryni measures that set limits on the ability of Deryni to own property and forbade them to hold office, enter the priesthood, etc.

RENGARTH—site of the betrayal of Duke Jared's army by Bran Coris Earl of Eastmarch.

RHELJAN Range—mountains separating Torenth from Eastmarch; site of the walled city of Cardosa.

RHEMUTH—capital city of Gwynedd.

RHENDALL—area famed for its blue lakes.

RHORAU—holding of one of the ancient families of the Eleven Kingdoms.

R'KASSI—desert kingdom south and east of the Hort of Orsal; famed for its blooded horses.

SAINT Ethelburga's Shrine—shrine of the patroness of Dhassa, guarding the northern approach to Dhassa.

SAINT Neot's—former Deryni monastic school, now in ruins; located in the Lendour Mountains between Corwyn and Dhassa.

SAINT Senan's Cathedral—seat of the Bishop of Dhassa, Denis Arilan.

SAINT Torin's—shrine of the patron saint of Dhassa, south of the city of Dhassa and Lake Jashan.

STAVENHAM—seat of the Bishop of Stavenham, de Lacey.

TOPHEL Peak—mountain visible from Thorne Hagen's castle.

TORENTH—vast kingdom to the east of Gwynedd, ruled by the Deryni King Wencit of Torenth.

VALORET—interim capital of Gwynedd during the Festillic Interregnum; seat of the Archbishop of Valoret, Edmund Loris, and site of the Abbey of Saint Mark; located between Eastmarch and the Haldane Honor.

VARIAN—holding of one of the ancient families of the Eleven Kingdoms.

PARTIAL TIME LINE FOR THE HISTORY OF THE ELEVEN KINGDOMS

822   The Festillic Coup. Ifor Haldane is deposed and executed. Festil I is crowned in Valoret, which becomes the new Festillic capital. Interregnum begins, lasting eighty-two years.

THE FESTILLIC KINGS OF GWYNEDD

Festil I	822–839	(17 years)
Festil II	839–851	(12 years)
Festil III	851–885	(34 years)
Blaine	885–900	(15 years)
Imre	900–904	(4 years)

846   Camber of Culdi born at Cor Culdi.

900   King Blaine dies; Prince Imre succeeds to the throne.

904   The Restoration. King Imre is deposed and executed; Cinhil Haldane, great-grandson of Ifor Haldane, is crowned in Rhemuth.

905   Unsuccessful attempt by Imre's supporters to overthrow the Restoration; Camber dies.

906   Camber of Culdi canonized by the Council of Bishops.

917   First of the great Deryni persecutions; Council of Ramos repudiates Camber's sainthood, forbids all use of magic on pain of anathema, bars Deryni from holding high office, inheriting lands without direct Crown approval, from entering priesthood.

THE POST-INTERREGNUM KINGS OF GWYNEDD

Cinhil	904–917	(13 years)
Alroy	917–921	(4 years)
Javan	921–922	(1 year)
Rhys	922–928	(6 years)
Owain	928–948	(20 years)
Uthyr	948–980	(32 years)
Nygel	980–983	(3 years)
Jasher	983–985	(2 years)
Cluim	985–994	(9 years)
Urien	994–1025	(31 years)
Malcolm	1025–1074	(49 years)
Donal	1074–1095	(21 years)
Brion	1095–1120	(25 years)
Kelson	1120–	

1081   Prince Brion born.

1087   Prince Nigel born.

1091   Alaric Morgan born.

1092   Duncan McLain born.

1095   King Donal dies; King Brion succeeds to the throne; Lady Alyce de Corwyn de Morgan dies following the birth of her daughter Bronwyn.

1100   Lord Kenneth Morgan dies; Alaric Morgan goes to court as a royal page.

1104   King Brion marries Jehana.

1105 Brion and Morgan slay the Marluk.

1106 Prince Kelson born.

1120 King Brion assassinated; King Kelson succeeds to the throne; Kelson slays Charissa, daughter of the Marluk, at his coronation.

1121 The Cardosa Campaign; King Kelson overcomes Wencit of Torenth at Llyndruth Meadows.

THE GENETIC BASIS FOR
DERYNI INHERITANCE: 1974

The primary genetic factor governing standard Deryni inheritance seems to be a simple sex-linked dominant carried on the X chromosome (designated X'). Thus, Deryniness per se is determined by the maternal line—not the paternal—and a male child displaying the Deryni capabilities must have had at least a heterozygous (X'X) Deryni mother.

$$X'X\text{-}XY$$
$$X'Y$$

Only one X' factor is necessary for the individual to display the full spectrum of Deryni capabilities; nor is there any appreciable difference between the power potentials of male and female, X'Y and X'X. One may readily see, however, that because of the double X configuration of the female, there is the possibility of an X'X' combination. This so-called "double-Deryni," a homozygous Deryni female, is no more powerful than her heterozygous sisters, however, for the X' factor is not cumulative. The only advantage that a homozygous Deryni female would have over a heterozygous Deryni female is that all of her offspring would be Deryni—and even this is not a significant difference, since the prime factor appears to strengthen the X chromosome carrying it, so that a heterozygous Deryni female is likely to pass on the X′ to her offspring rather than the X. (X′ eggs are more hardy than X eggs, and more likely to be fertile.) This propensity of the X′ chromosome to be passed on in preference to the X accounts, in part, for the survival of the Deryni through the great persecutions. Following are the probable outcomes of any Deryni mating, with non-Deryni offspring shown in brackets:

X′X-XY	X′X-X′Y	XX-X′Y	X′X′-X′Y	X′X′-XY
X′Y	X′Y	XX′	X′X′	X′Y
X′X	X′X′	XX′	X′X′	X′Y
[XX]	XX′	[XY]	X′Y	X′X
[XY]	[XY]	[XY]	X′Y	X′X

A second Deryni factor, carried only on the Y chromosome, is the basis for the human assumption of Deryni powers. (The potential for this phenomenon was discovered by Camber of Culdi and Rhys Thuryn in the mid-890s, though they would not have been aware of any genetic basis for it.) This factor, when activated, is fully equal to the X′ factor in power capacity, but is, of course, passed on only through the male line. Hence, a male showing the potential for assumption of Deryni power certainly had a father with the same capability—though this factor may be held and passed without the carrier's knowledge for generations, as may the X′ factor. By itself, the Y′ factor will not confer Deryni powers on a male child, for the assumption of power is a difficult and tedious process and may be hampered or enhanced by numerous psychological and physiological factors.

As for those rare individuals who seem to display this potential for power assumption without the requisite Deryni parentage to account for it (Sean Lord Derry, for example), we may find that this is due to a long-dormant Y′ factor that has been passed on unwittingly for several generations. Unless the carrier of a Y′ factor (or the X′) is discovered by a true Deryni, and is informed and guided in realizing this potential, he or she will likely never become aware of this capability.

Nor is the potential to assume Deryni power limited to one bearer at a time in any given family, though the Haldanes have always encouraged this belief, probably to lessen the likelihood of arcane dueling among potential heirs when the succession was in question. Nigel Haldane may be somewhat aware of the truth of the matter; he carries the Y' factor, as do his three sons, and both he and Conall had the Haldane potential activated while Kelson was still alive. In earlier generations, however, it is easy to see how, in a collateral branch of a family carrying the power assumption potential, as Nigel's is destined to become, that the very awareness of this heritage could be lost—and who is to say how many Haldanes might have spread their seed and sired a line of potential Deryni? Derry, descendant of a long and noble line, may well have gotten his potential this way— perhaps as far back as seven or eight generations. And in an individual of peasant origin, like Warin de Grey? The *droit du seigneur* may account for many anomalies of birth.

The two Deryni factors, X' and Y', are independent, however—which means that both may be present in a given individual—by definition, male, because of the Y' factor. Again, the Deryni factors are not cumulative, so an $X'Y'$ male would have no appreciable advantage over an $X'Y$ male or an XY' male; however, an $X'Y'$ Deryni might be able to use his powers with greater efficiency, since the powers assumed through the Y' factor come upon him fully functional, with no practice necessary. (An $X'Y$ Deryni must learn to use his powers and hence may be at a disadvantage if he has not had the benefit of formal training.) Thus Kelson, who carries the double-prime configuration $X'Y'$, was able to function as a fully trained Deryni from the start, as soon as he had fully assumed his father's powers— even though he had had no formal schooling in the use of those powers and had not suspected his X' inheritance. His father Brion likewise came to power at full potential, without training, from the power ritual of *his* father. Jehana, on the other hand, whether an $X'X$ or an $X'X'$ Deryni, had never permitted herself to use her inheritance and hence could be easily defeated by the puissant and practiced Charissa, descendant of a long line of proficient Deryni sorcerers.

This examination of the genetic nature of Deryniness points up another important point: that the myth of being only "half-Deryni" (having only one parent who is Deryni) is exactly that—a myth. Since the X' is the only factor governing full Deryni inheritance, Deryni like Morgan and Duncan, with Deryni mothers only, are just as much Deryni as Kelson, Charissa, or any other "full Deryni." Since Deryniness is inherited in its entirety from either parent, there is no half-way measure. One is either Deryni or not. The prime factors make all the difference.

A GENETIC RETROSPECTIVE, THIRTY YEARS LATER

Over the past three decades, many readers of the Deryni Saga have spent many hours puzzling over the genetic aspects of what makes a person Deryni. Like them, I have become aware that the matter is far more complicated than I posited as a fledgling author, pretty much fresh out of medical school (and with the genetic understanding of the early 1970s), and while the Deryni universe was still taking shape—and it is still evolving. As the back history has gradually unfolded, I have developed further and perhaps more plausible explanations for the Deryni's extraordinary powers.

But the key concept, around which nearly all of the key conflicts in Deryni history seem to revolve, always seems to come back to some aspect of a single question: Just what is it that makes a Deryni? Today, well into the first decade of the twenty-first century, it has become increasingly obvious that the question is far more complicated than a simple sex-linked gene marker.

We know, for example, that people with Deryni powers—or at least with powers *like* Deryni—do crop up from time to

time, both male and female—and not just from plot necessity! We also know that there are talents within the broad
spectrum of Deryni powers that are not accessible to all
Deryni. The Healing talent would appear to be the most
notable of these, surfacing only rarely—and the bearers of
this gift usually are male. (We know that one of Evaine's
daughters was a Healer—and that this was remarked upon,
even before her birth. The legendary Jodotha was also a female Healer.) A possible explanation for this apparent im-
balance is that the emergence of this particular talent in
females renders the carrier more fragile than her male coun-
terparts, less apt to survive to adulthood.

The Healing talent would appear to be further differenti-
ated, in that some Healers can block the powers of other
Deryni, even other Healers—but not all Healers can do this.
Indeed, we have met only three, thus far: Rhys Thuryn,
Tavis O'Neill, and Sylvan O'Sullivan. Were these men
anomalies, even among their own kind, or is it simply that
no Healer had ever thought to use his powers in this manner
before Rhys discovered it quite by accident? We know that
Dom Queron tried and failed to emulate what Rhys had
accomplished—and he was a highly trained and skilled
Healer as well as a powerful Deryni. (For that matter, we
must consider whether the blocking ability is even unique
to Healers. What if certain non-Healer Deryni can also
block powers, but we simply have not encountered any of
them?)

From here we progress to the very intriguing matter of
human assumption of Deryni powers, apparently first ex-
ploited by Camber, Evaine, and Rhys when they discovered
this propensity in Cinhil Haldane and made it part of his
preparation to reclaim the crown of Gwynedd. Whether the
so-called Haldane potential is unique to this particular genetic line or is only a specific instance of a more generally
occurring phenomenon, we do not know.

We do know, however, that some individuals of no previously known Deryni lineage are able to assume at least some

Deryni-like powers. Whether this simply taps into a pre-existing reservoir of unrecognized or forgotten Deryni lineage or else somehow activates a purely human factor, enabling hitherto absent abilities, we do not know. Some such individuals may descend from Deryni originally blocked by Tavis O'Neill or Sylvan O'Sullivan during the brief heyday of Revan's baptizer cult, 917–922; and some supposed humans will descend from Deryni by-blows, as noted previously.

It is possible, too, that the right circumstances do enable some humans of no Deryni background to assume some powers like those of the Deryni. Close association with functioning Deryni sometimes seems to awaken some of the most rudimentary psychic characteristics commonly present in Deryni, such as mind shields and some slight ability to resist psychic probes and attempts to control. Most recently, in *In the King's Service* and *Childe Morgan*, we have seen aspects of such psychic awakening in Zoë Morgan and her father, Kenneth, through close association with Alyce de Corwyn. Derry's early propensity for magic could also stem from such association, at least in part, though after his rough treatment at the hands of Wencit of Torenth—and later, by Wencit's sister Morag—he may be too scarred ever to regain his previous openness to Deryni magic, even after the healing ministrations of Morgan and other benign Deryni.

Bran Coris is another example of a supposed human taking on Deryni-like powers, though it may be that he had unwittingly experienced initial stirrings of psychic potential through close association with his Deryni wife, Richenda—which, in turn, might have facilitated Wencit's efforts to subvert him with the promise of power. In a possibly related occurrence, Duke Lionel is described in the first trilogy only as a kinsman of Wencit—the husband of Wencit's sister Morag—and also allegedly has assumed powers. However, in keeping with later expansion of the Torenthi bloodlines, which reveals that Lionel is the scion of another powerful Torenthi family, the dukes of Arjenol—and half-brother to Mahael and Teymuraz, destined to cause so much trouble for Kelson a decade later—we must surmise that Lionel, the king's brother-in-law and the father of Wencit's presumed heirs, actually must be a very powerful Deryni in his own right, and that Wencit only *claimed* that Lionel's powers were assumed, to strengthen his rough wooing of Bran Coris.

Such is the nature of making things up as one goes along, and trying to remain true to established canon while still keeping the world-building moving forward. After thirty-five years, with fifteen novels in the Deryni cycle (not to mention numerous short stories set in that universe), I still find it somewhat amazing that I have managed to remain as consistent as I have. In the end, however—and for the purposes of telling a good story—I suppose that Deryni are what I say they are. However, I do promise that I will do my best, if at all possible, to avoid summoning too many *dei* out of the *machina*!